THE DEVIL'S PARTY

Who Killed the Sixties?

Bob Rodgers

 FriesenPress

Suite 300 – 990 Fort Street
Victoria, BC, Canada V8V 3K2
www.friesenpress.com

Copyright © 2015 by Bob Rodgers
First Edition — 2015

Cover Image: *Sculptor* W Jerry Pethick
Le Semeur/Sunlight and Flies, 1984/2002
Glass bottles, silicone, rubber corks, aluminum, surveillance mirror
Compliments of Margaret Pethick
94 ½ x 48 x 43 ¼ inches (240 x 122 x 110 cm)
Courtesy Catriona Jeffries Gallery, Vancouver
Collection of Seattle Art Museum, Washington

Photography: Scott Massey

Edited by Gail Singer.

ISBN
978-1-4602-5347-2 (Hardcover)
978-1-4602-5348-9 (Paperback)
978-1-4602-5349-6 (eBook)

1. Fiction, Literary

Distributed to the trade by The Ingram Book Company

Acknowledgements

I am indebted to Gail Singer for guiding me through much-needed pruning and foreshortening of the narrative; to Maureen Lukie for devising a format to accommodate the multiple narrative voices, and for matters of grammatical style; and to Bruce Valpy, Michael Rodgers, Eliana Chan, and Mike Nader for their labors in proofing. For valued critical comments on earlier versions of the manuscript, I owe thanks to Eric Wright, Graeme Gibson, Sean Kane, Vladimir Ganev, and once again Mike Nader. And much appreciation for those who have shared memories of the times with me, some living but not all: Jackie and Vic Cowey, Art Adamson, Reg Gibson, Bill Lobchuck, Jimmy and Mesh Silden, Janet and Kelly Clark, and Elsie and Lennie Anderson. I am much obliged to Jon Sturgis for supplying me with a portrait for the back cover, and especially to my great friend, the late Jerry Pethick, for his wonderful bottle man who graces my front cover, and to his wonderful wife, Margaret, for letting me put it there.

The fiery limbs, the flaming hair,
shot like the sinking sun into the western sea.

from
A Song of Liberty
William Blake

Part I
The Echoing Green

Chapter One

On my first day back to the University of Manitoba in September, 1958, I stood off to one side in the hallway of the old Arts Building preparing to leap into the void, which is to say, into a fourth year Honours English seminar on the Seventeenth Century with the formidable professor John Peter. Honours English! It was an idea that would never have crossed my mind a year ago. I had been, as they say, 'good at English' at high school, and I did well in my literature courses in my second and third year university. But the invitation to go for an Honours Degree in a fourth year came as a complete surprise that left me teetering on a decision up to the last moment.

Suddenly breaking my concentration on the intricate patterns on the marble floor outside the seminar room, a voice made me jump. "Hey, aren't you Big Faraday? You were the guard in that play-off game against Fargo when you stole the ball mid-court in the last seconds and went in for the winning lay-up. Jesus that was a beautiful thing!"

"Long time ago," was all I could think to say. The last thing I wanted right then was to be identified as a jock pretending to be an intellectual. Also, no one since my basketball days called me 'Big' anymore. At five-foot-seven and three-quarters with my runners on, I was named 'Big' for being the shortest player in the western league. So here I am, trying to distance myself from basketball, tentatively aiming at literary things, and along comes this stranger and blows the whistle on me.

"That moment when you stole the ball. The crowd went berserk." The man beamed at me with that slightly sycophantic look sport fans tend to wear in the presence of their idols. It always made me uneasy. I had on my new Harris Tweed jacket with elbow patches. Why was I being identified as a jock?

But I must have given off a whiff of unpurged vanity from the glory days. His response was to focus on the ceiling, with a grin that squeezed his eyes shut. Then suddenly he looked at me straight on. "Etched in memory though, right, a great moment like that? I can hardly imagine." He wore a skewered smile. Just as I began to think he was having me on, the smile broke into a look of such openness and generosity of interest that I felt mean-spirited for my suspicion.

"To tell you the truth," I said, "it *was* a great moment, stealing that ball and making that basket—a bird in flight I was, an angel. Unforgettable!" I let this out with a breath of relief. I had tried to hide. He had recognized my deception and made me come clean.

"Great! That was a great move," he said. I couldn't be sure whether he meant my moment of triumph on the court or my coming clean about my basketball memory. He reached out his hand: "Name's Lennie Boyce."

"Jason Faraday," I said. "Skip the 'Big' part. Guard or forward, Lennie?" He was about five-foot-eleven, with dense, red-pepper hair that looked as if it would go curly when wet, high cheek bones, arched nose, jagged jaw, and green eyes with black centres hidden away under steep eyebrows and a built-in squint that made them disappear almost entirely when he laughed. He looked in good shape. I took him for more than likely a forward.

"No, Nooo," he said. "Don't play. Not me. Never did. Can't even dribble the ball. Just a fan. Love the ballet of the game. Athletic ballet—that's what basketball is." Then, without preamble: "I hear this John Peter is top of the heap despite having to teach Milton. Well, here I am to gather the pearls."

The sudden switch of subject caught me off guard. I had been in John Peter's hugely attended Milton lectures in second year and the class had been collectively dazzled. He spoke without notes in perfect periodic sentences. His accent and intonation (Cape town via Cambridge and F. R. Leaves) were like music. As far as I could tell, he knew as much as there is to know about Milton, and possibly most other things. Much as I admired him in the anonymity of the lecture hall, I was nervous at the prospect of sitting across the table from him in the fearsome intimacy of a seminar.

"So where do you come from, Mr. Lennie?" I said. If there was condescension in my voice, it was unintended but I was floored by the guy's response. He paused, his brows came down, and he eyed me up and down. "Vat? You immigration ovisser?" There was no fun in his voice at all. It was so unexpected, I thought at first he was joking. But something at the black centres of those green eyes of his left me guessing. "I vrom Vinnipej," he said, and he turned and picked up his briefcase as, just then, John Peter came down the hall and we trooped into the seminar room.

People jockeyed for places around the table, generally as far away from the great man as possible until choice ran out ... except for Lennie, who went directly to the empty chair next to John Peter and sat down. This was an in-depth course on Jacobean Drama and the Metaphysical Poets. I knew nothing much about them, but I had enough awe for John Peter to do a little boning up so as not to have to face a question from him in abject ignorance.

"Tell me then," John Peter began, having seated himself at the end of the table, loosened his tie, and set in front of himself a single sheet of blank paper and an old Parker fountain pen: "What are some distinguishing features of Metaphysical Poetry?"

A wave of panic rolled through the room. My spade-work on Donne had turned up things like argumentative structure, personal address, colloquial diction, hyperbole, arcane allusions. Others in the group, I was certain, had answers they could have given, too, but no one spoke up. I was ready to blurt out that John Donne was Renaissance in manner but Medieval in sensibility (a notion I had picked up from some critic or other), but I wasn't sure I could elaborate on what that meant if asked to, and I lost my nerve. I felt sweat start down behind my ears. I longed for someone to speak up so as not to disgrace us in front of the great man.

"Outlandish metaphor," broke the silence. Lennie's voice crackled with a nasal sharpness, almost a boy's voice, giving way to un-programmed bursts of treble. "That's what they meant by a conceit, right sir? Dr. Johnson talked about Donne's heterogeneous ideas yoked by violence together. It seems to me more like the violence is not in the ideas but in the metaphor itself, an apparent inconsistency between the tenor and the vehicle. So, when Donne sees two lovers bitten by the same flea, it represents the commingling of their bodies during sexual intercourse. When he compares lovers to the two legs of a compass, well, that's pretty far out too, isn't't it? At first glimpse, a compass, the one you use in geometry to make a circle, isn't your ordinary kind of metaphor for love. Then you see it. The legs are the lovers. One leg travels. The other stays fixed and guides the roamer's movement until it comes full circle. That's true love that never alters with spatial separation, right? But get this. As the lover returns, the legs come together like the legs of copulating lovers. And in Donne's words, the lovers become *erect*. I'd say that's poetry moving at quite a few levels, don't you think?"

John Peter's bearing was distant, world-weary, disappointed-looking, as if he knew nothing would ever be as good as it once was in South Africa, certainly never as good as it should be. As Lennie's words tumbled out, Peter's hunched body uncoiled slowly until he managed a fully upright posture.

Lennie continued. "Or, okay, take Donne's holy sonnet where the woman says: 'Batter my heart, three-personned God/ For you as yet but knock, breathe, shine, and seek to mend.' Her heart may be a pot needing mending by a tinker, but it is also a walled town. God can't conquer the town by diplomacy, so he is being importuned, in the form of the Trinity, to break down the gates with a battering ram. Is that a penis? The tenors of the sonnets' metaphors, different kinds of love, are matched by a set of startling vehicles, especially at the end where the speaker says that she, 'Except you enthral me never shall be free/ Nor ever chaste, except you ravish me'. I mean, wow! She is talking about what amounts to God raping her to save her soul. Wild stuff for sure to describe a religious experience, but it works, right? The spark strikes."

By now, John Peter's back was fully vertical in his chair. The two of them carried on for ten minutes as if the rest of us weren't there. Then before I knew it, everyone was piping up, leaning forward, trying to get a word in. I couldn't take my eyes off Lennie. After his ice breaker, he sat quietly and viewed the action like the sports fan he let on he was when he reminded me of my basketball days, his head turning this way and that, following, as it were, the action on the court. Two hours flew by. The talk carried on down the corridor afterwards. John Peter looked nearly happy as he ambled off across the quadrangle, the blank piece of paper he had brought into the seminar fluttering in his hand like a captured bird.

As the fall term got going, Lennie and I became cafeteria friends. Lennie had clearly read half a library more than I had, but he never rubbed it in. He sent me off to books unrelated to course work, until then an alien idea for me. I had been conditioned to stick to the curriculum, absorb it, and spill it out at exam time. Lennie had his own set of subjects. Aquinas was big with him, and Nietzsche, Camus, and Spengler, all of them outside course prescriptions. Spengler was especially big. *Decline of the West* was Lennie's arsenal against western civilization. He said Spengler read history the way literary critics read poetry. A cluster of images define a poem as a cluster of symbols define a culture, and that was how I should learn to read Spengler.

Wanting to keep up, I spent time in the library leafing through the fat, two-volume version of *Decline of the West*. I was fascinated, then baffled, then guilt-ridden.

One afternoon after John Peter's seminar, half a dozen of us wound up at the Pembina Beer Parlour. I got talking about wasting my time reading about Spengler's depressing fatalism instead of reading stuff I would be asked for on exams and that led Lennie straight into his patented topic: "Spengler's sense of destiny, all that obscure transcendentalism he picked up from Kant and Hegel, and that dour German Calvinism about predestination and unredeemable man–don't fall for it. What Spengler saw that counts is that Michelangelo or Napoleon or Cecil Rhodes or the light bulb and the telephone are not just random happenings of history. They are enormous symbols of the soul of a period, god-like powers that rule over us, or at least try to, just like any tribal god in primitive times. That's where Spengler shines. Not in his botanical fantasies about cultures that mature like plants into civilizations and then decay. Bad analogy that, as Toynbee said. It's the way Spengler reads the signs that's so fantastic. It's like history is some gigantic epic poem and he's the exegete unravelling its meaning, a master of cultural hermeneutics."

Two older men in the beer parlour at the next table wearing Canadian Legion pins gravitated over to ours. Where I came from, it was a bad sign. We were smart-alec students talking a lot of airy-fairy ideas, and they were working men out for a nice cold beer. To my surprise one of the men suddenly chimed in: "This Spengler guy, what's he on about saying we're all going down the drain?"

I couldn't believe it. Lennie didn't skip a beat or alter his delivery. If anything, his energy went up a notch as he launched into an explanation of how Freud's *Civilization And Its Discontents* was even better than Spengler's *Decline of the West* at explaining the roots of World War II, how sexual repression festers in the psyche and erupts into wholesale destruction, not just in a maniac like Hitler, but in a whole repressed society. Within minutes, he had the two legionnaires hanging on his words.

As I listened, I realized I had to keep on my toes with Lennie, try to preserve some distance so as not to get gobbled up. But I was also drawn to a notion I had never thought of before–the idea that maybe he was right about there being a way of reading events that went beneath the surface so that everything was potentially a symbol of something deeper. It was an attractive idea in my quest to make sense of things. It bothered me though that if you went too deep and everything meant something other than what was stated, maybe nothing meant anything at all.

I played bridge in the Student Union with Lennie and two rich girls in Honours English. They were quite different looking from each other, one the blonde Daisy of F. Scott Fitzgerald, the other the dark lady of Shakespeare's sonnets, each so alluring in her own way that men were forever speculating which one they would prefer to bed ... as if they had a chance with either. At first, the girls seemed intimidated by Lennie as he dealt the cards, but I sensed the feeling was mutual. Lennie was subdued, even awkward, and he didn't play his cards well. I thought it was because their good looks disarmed him. But Lennie was never shy with women. When I questioned him, he gave me that not entirely friendly look of his, and then smiled sweetly in deference to my ingenuousness. "They are River Heights girls," he said. "I'm North End."

If you hadn't grown up in Winnipeg, there were a lot of things like this you had to learn. I was pretty sure that in my last two years living downtown at River and Osborne I'd learned how to tell a River Heights girl when I saw one. But a North Ender? I had met none, other than Lennie. The North End was a blank on my map of the city. Lennie found such insouciance hard to believe when I told him. Then he laughed.

"Remember", he said, "when we first met and you asked me where I was from? I said 'Vinnipej', remember. That's how Anglo kids from River Heights or French kids from St. Boniface used to pronounce Winnipeg when they were making fun of the old Hunkies from the North End ghetto. How could you know that? And how could I know you didn't know? I thought you were trying to take the Mickey out of me, so I shot back at you."

I still didn't get it. "But you're not Ukrainian. Boyce?"

"Mr. Faraday, Mr. Faraday. Thousands of Jews and Ukrainians in the North End anglicised their names for reasons I should not have to explain to you. I'm sure it's nice for you to come from a small northern town where such indignities were never perpetrated upon you. Don't tell me. You drank fountain cokes and ate cinnamon buns at the soda bar after school. It wasn't like that here." He paused and looked me over as if trying to make up his mind, then said: "Come with me and see, come get pissed in authentic Ukrainian Fashion."

The evening began off Selkirk Avenue at a blind pig, my introduction to both the word and the reality. It was early evening. A big man called Zoltan gave us a bottle of soda water and alcohol distilled from Manitoba potatoes. Then we went to Nordic Billiards, crowded with rough-talking characters playing pea pool for a quarter per cash-in, big money, a dollar or two every five minutes for the winner. They weren't particularly friendly to Lennie, but they all seemed to know him. One guy came over and borrowed money from him. As we played, Lennie never let up about books he was reading. Only once, when he was still sinking reds and angling for position on the black, did he break in with a down-to-earth question. "What did you think of Zoltan's Potion?"

"It wasn't exactly a beaker full of the warm South", I said, "but it gets the job done, doesn't it?" Thanks to my one good high school teacher I had learned by heart a small store of poetry, one or two-liners like Keats' 'O for a beaker full of the warm South/With beaded bubbles winking at the brim'. When I could, I used lines I remembered from high school to put Lennie off-balance. I knew he hadn't met many basketball players who quoted Keats. Partly, it was a way of showing off, and partly a way of defending myself from being trampled by him.

"That poor kid," Lennie said. (Were we the only patrons in the Nordic Billiards discussing Keats?) "You know John Locke was still a big deal in Keats' time. He had asserted that a flower has primary qualities like figure and extension and mass, but colour is a mere secondary quality, not inherent in the flower at all. Then along comes Bishop Berkeley and says there aren't even any secondary qualities and no colour in nature at all. It's all in the beholder's eye."

I listened but I didn't really follow. Lennie never let up his talk until the moment just before he cued up and took a shot. The moment after, whatever the result, he carried on as if we were in a seminar. "What a knockout blow for Keats who was so sensitized he could practically smell colour. Was he making it all up, deluding himself? There he sat on Hampstead Heath, coughing blood and struggling with metaphor. That poem, *La Belle Dame Sans Merci* isn't about his girl Fanny at all. It's about the chilling possibility that nature's colour is an illusion, that in reality, the earth is a pallid lady, a monochrome polyp careening through space, not a belle dame at all. All because of old Locke's and Berkeley's downplaying imagination in favour of ratiocination, and of course, Newton who also did his bit to empty the haunted air."

I had read Keats' odes in high school–the big five–and loved them. And I knew Berkeley was the bishop who asked whether a tree in the bush fell or not if there was no one there to hear it. Still, I strained to understand what Lennie was getting at, connecting Locke and Berkeley to Keats. The whole business of modes of perception, the poet's way of seeing, the deadening effect of abstract systems, the correspondences between mind and the material world, the mystery of metaphor–these were all getting a lot of attention in our table talk outside the classroom, which is what made me suspect their currency was Lennie's doing. I knew all about the need to concentrate if you want to win at pool. I'd been playing snooker since I was fifteen, and I got good enough to make meaningful pocket money if I chose my opponents selectively. Unquestionably the better shot, I lost three games in a row, distracted by Lennie's ardent and suspect declamations.

I went visiting North End homes with him where some people were friendly, others less so–Lennie's trap line. Whether he was talking to educated or uneducated people, young or old, he never made allowances. It didn't matter whether they had the faintest idea what he was talking about, he treated them as if they did. What astonished me was that they responded as if they did. An elderly woman who clearly spoke little English sat at her kitchen table beaming at him as if his words were music while he launched into a spate against cross-breeding vegetables. He explained how the poet, Andrew Marvell, had warned about it three hundred years ago. Kids listened attentively. He spoke straight to them and it never seemed to cross his mind that the things he was saying were wildly over their heads. It made no difference to them either. Whatever the kids were listening to seemed more like what Chaucer called *solace* than *sentence*.

Winding up our rambling after a stint at Kelekis' Cafe on North Main for hot dogs and chips, then the Moon Café to watch the late-night mating scene, we landed at Higgins Avenue in a coffee shop across from the CPR

Station and the then Royal Alexandra Hotel. The train tracks were what separated Winnipeg proper from the North End. The so-called coffee shop had a back room accessible through beaded curtains where a few men sat playing cards. They waved hello to Lennie, gave me the eye without really looking, and resumed their play. The proprietor brought over a can of apple juice and a bottle of potato vodka. We sat with him, listening partly to Lennie talk and partly to the radio reporting on the winner of the Snow Queen Contest. I remember hearing Lennie say, "Know what? I think I raddled that chick once."

Except for the radio, all went quiet. Talk stopped at the card table as heads turned toward us. The proprietor, a big man to start with, puffed up like some poisonous tropical fish. I was delivered outside undamaged. Lennie hit the sidewalk with an awful crunch, nothing broken, but with blood on his face and running down his front. It was the kind of scene I had witnessed often enough as a kid when disputes among miners broke out in the alley behind the beer parlours of the Corona or the Richmond hotel on Saturday night, but I was astounded. This was another side of Winnipeg for me and another side of Lennie. "What the hell happened?' I asked.

"I realized only after I had spoken: the Snow Queen is the old moujik's daughter. There's no end to traps in the North End, Mister JJ." He had never called me JJ before. Maybe it was a diminutive in the Slavic mode, I thought, a sign of trust and endearment. I was christened. I wondered, not without misgivings, what responsibilities that might bring along with it as time went on.

I began seeing less of Lennie. Did he have a separate life in that strange world I caught a glimpse of the night of our North End revelry? At the same time, I noticed a general cooling of camaraderie, the village square thing that had been getting started among the Honours English bunch. Then it dawned on me. With exams pending, combat had begun. People were secreting themselves in library carrels and other dark corners or disappearing altogether. Our little communal fish bowl started feeling like a shark tank. It was time to win. I had experienced it before in basketball when the time came to see who would make the first line.

One pre-exam evening, on the bus on the long haul downtown from Fort Garry, I sat next to Lennie, contemplating the cold gloom of the sunset filtering through the smoke from the sugar beet factory off Pembina Highway to the West. Without preamble, he burst into a harangue:

"We're freaks, you know, JJ. All this stuff about the past we're into, all this ... history. Take T. S. Eliot's *Tradition and the Individual Talent*–the primacy of the historical sense, of being in command of the entire western canon down through the ages, etcetera. So what's it doing for us, this possession of the great tradition, for guys like you and me out here? Is it making us part of the grand family of Western Culture? That's a lot of hooey! It's dislodging us from our friends and families, orphaning us, severing us from our beginnings, sacrificing us on the altar of art and ideas. I'm going to my mom's for supper tonight. She and the rest will be talking pirogues and borscht and the stocking sale at Eaton's. What am I doing? I'm trying to figure out what the miracle plays meant in England in the Middle Ages. We're becoming aliens and weirdoes, I tell you. We're being deracinated. Listen to William Blake: 'A man's worst enemies are those of his own house and family'. He's saying we have to leave wives and families and all that domestic stuff that stands in the way of the art. We are to become rootless in the name of intellect."

What was he talking about? This was another Lennie. Disparaging learning? Turning against art and ideas? I snapped out of my sugar beet reverie to give battle. "Come on, Lennie, all Blake meant was domestic stuff can interfere. All kinds of things can interfere. That does't mean if you are an artist or an intellectual you have to cut yourself off from your parents, or never get married and have kids. Look at all the great thinkers who did both."

"Name one," Lennie said.

"Karl Marx," I said.

"Sure," Lennie said, "freezing in the British Museum, sitting in his hovel on Deane Street surrounded by moribund children. He left an orange on his desk one day, a rare treat then, and he came back to find it stabbed with a pencil by one of the kids. Jesus! No wonder *Das Kapital* is unreadable."

"William Blake," I said. "Didn't he live for fifty years with Catherine? Domesticity didn't exactly destroy his creative juices or even slow him down the way I heard it. In fact, it probably helped make him. She helped him paint his frescoes."

"Blake doesn't count. They didn't have kids. Sure, Catherine helped colour his images, but that's not the point. Blake hardly ever lived in the world as we know it. He was a visionary. He consorted with angels. Blake's's marriage doesn't count."

He was slipping sideways on me. But I was getting to know that logic rarely won arguments with Lennie. I remembered a piece of gossip that might explain what this strange outburst of his might be about. "I hear you're getting married", I said.

"If I do, I'll invite you to the wedding, JJ," was all he said back.

"So what's eating you?"

He sat silent, took a long breath, and then blurted it out: "I can't write exams, OK?"

I didn't understand. The idea of his having some special handicap made no sense. No one I knew could match him in debate. I assured him he knew it all and then some. I played Sancho Panza to his Don Quixote. Humouring him did nothing but put him on edge and he responded with a crushing reply: "It's OK for you, JJ. No one expects anything of you."

I felt like he had smacked me in the face. Yet I detected no awareness of a slur on his part. By the time we reached downtown, I had worked the matter through and calmed down. It was something I hadn't thought about and it was useful for me to know. What he said of me was true. My mother, a schoolteacher, had she lived long enough, would certainly have expected great things of me. My father, a railroad man living in the North, was encouraging but bemused by my studies. During one of his visits to my flat the year before, he picked up Dostoevsky's *The Idiot* from the bookshelf and said, albeit with a grin: "So this is what they've got you doing down here." On one occasion when I visited him in the caboose at Hudson's Bay Junction, he introduced me to his train crew with: "This is my son, the preacher." Afterwards, he said to me: "Sorry about that, Jason, but by God, it's hard to explain to the boys what the hell you're up to."

Little as I knew about Lennie's family, I knew enough to suspect the whole North End could be waiting to see if he would crash or fly. I decided that was what he meant about the difference between us as regards expectations. He was just telling me the truth.

In our Anglo-Saxon/Middle English exam, Lennie sat two rows in front of me on the opposite aisle. I tried not to let it distract me, but every time I looked up, I saw him scribbling furiously. I kept looking back at the questions. What was I missing? I could drum up enough to fill only half a booklet.

At the end of the exam, Lennie was working on his third booklet, in volume at least, an achievement rivalling the entire canon handed down from *The Voyages of Ohthere and Wulfstan* and *Piers Plowman* put together. I gathered by this that he'd overcome his phobia. But when I saw him, he looked like a tortured prisoner, his face colourless, except for a rash on his forehead.

"You doing Bennies?" I said.

"Yah. You?" he said. I had tried them a year ago. They were an early version of Dexedrine, sold at drug stores as 'No Nod' for truckers who have to drive all night. I told Lennie no, I wasn't using anything. "I don't like the come-downs."

"No joy without sorrow, eh, JJ? The old Methodist creed."

"Right, Lennie, it's the inveterate Puritan in me. I'm just not interested in boiling my brains with speed right now."

Except in the coming and going outside the gym where we wrote our exams, I didn't see Lennie again until the exams were over. I was passing through the engineering cafeteria and there he was, no mistake, laying into a couple of engineering students. "So you know Pythagoras' Theory and Archimedes Principle?", he was saying. "Do you know Pythagoras was a vegetarian and thought numbers were symbols of a higher reality? Do you know that Archimedes invented the spiral conveyer, used mechanical advantage to lever ships out of the water at Samos during the Second Punic War, and was finally killed there by the Romans—or that the two men lived three centuries apart? This is what I don't understand. They don't teach you any of this in Engineering. How in hell do they expect you to understand the conclusions of science and physics and astronomy if you have no idea of their origins?" I lured him away before the engineers got ugly. "Hypocrite", I said, and reminded him of the diatribe he had levelled at me on the bus against T. S. Eliot and the deracinating consequences of tradition on the individual talent.

"Ever read Keats' letters?" he said.

"Can't say I have."

"Negative capability. Keats laid it out brilliantly: 'the ability to hold two or more conflicting notions in your mind at the same time without any irritable reaching after fact and reason'. It's the mark of the poet. Try it, JJ, negative capability. It could be the making of you." End of argument. Lennie was back in full flight.

How could someone as down and despondent as he had been a week before be so suddenly back in form? Was it just because exams were over? "No, no," he said. "I'm in love, JJ, I'm going to get married."

Chapter Two

As it does every year in Manitoba, the spring of 1959 arrived overnight. My regular guiding job waited for me north of Lake of the Woods on the English River. My new love, Delia, hailing from my home town, would stay on in Winnipeg to do her home visits with the Victorian Order of Nurses. We would squirrel away our money over the summer to get married and get me to graduate school in Toronto in the fall.

The chill that had descended on our little group at exam time receded with the snows. Word circulated of a get-together. We had never become a cohesive bunch in the way of grander centres of learning, but we had shared an intellectual journey and it prompted a touch of ritual. There was still no public place where women could drink in 1959, so Lennie set things up at The Edgewater Inn where you kept your bottle in a paper bag under the table and ordered 7-Up and a hot turkey sandwich with peas, or a cheese tray. A local singer called Jake Clark was performing, a folk singer with a literary, ironic kind of patter. Lennie knew him, as he seemed to know people wherever he went. At one point, as the bottles under the table were going dry, Jake broke into a Pete Seeger ditty I hadn't heard before. I guessed Lennie put him up to it. The song went: "Little boxes, little boxes, they're all made out of ticky-tacky, and they all go to university, and they all live in little boxes, little boxes all the same". We loved it as tourists love to hear other tourists ridiculed, while somehow excluding themselves from the category. At closing time, we swore deathless friendship sealed with an agreement to re-congregate at the end of summer for a weekend bash at a cabin up on the Winnipeg River to watch the leaves fall and say goodbye to one more year of our golden youth.

Lennie was not having us on about the marriage. I learned only a bit about the courtship. Angela Stockton was Church of England, her father the pastor of one of the oldest parishes in River Heights. I loved the 'Heights' part. On terrain as flat as Winnipeg's, you couldn't help knowing the word meant something other than geographical elevation above the flood plain. Even I knew you shouldn't muck around with River Heights.

"We announced our intention at the drawing room table in the rectory," Lennie told me. As he described it, the Reverend Stockton, a towering six-foot-two, lunged at him and they went into a chase around the table that ended with Lennie taking off down the street and Angela being placed in solitary confinement. Recounting the scene, Lennie howled with laughter. "I never heard a preacher curse so fluently," he said. "That son of a bitch gave me a lesson. But do you know what kind of creep the preacher is? One of his parishioners leaves a fur coat for the poor, see, as if there were such people in the Reverend's cosy parish. Momma Stockton, small, quiet, not a bad sort, asks if she can keep it because she's never had a fur coat. The Reverend decides not. Too ostentatious. What happens? The Reverend has the fur sewn into the lining of his overcoat, to keep him warm on his rounds. No problem, see? It won't show. God almighty, JJ, the English. What a cold bed of hypocrisy and pleasure denial the pious make for themselves!"

I was getting to know Lennie. But his affection for English literature and his contempt for so many aspects of the culture that created it seemed a strange contradiction, though certainly not the only one I was becoming acquainted with in him. Possibly what I was dealing with here, I thought, was another one of those mysterious cases of negative capability.

The courtship with Angela didn't strike me as a particularly auspicious one. Their backgrounds were less than a perfect match. But for Lennie, it may have been only *because* of the obstacles that the whole thing went ahead. The wedding was held in a Ukrainian Orthodox church not far from the Red River off North Main, quite a leap from Angela's Episcopalian roots at River Heights over on the Assiniboine.

Angela was lovely, milky-skinned, only an inch under Lennie's height, robust yet delicately featured in the Grace Kelly mould, and–as Lennie confided to me, telling me more than I wanted to know or knew what to do with about his sex life–she was, except for him, a virgin. The best man was an undefined relative of Lennie's who was in his final year of law school. I hadn't known of his existence before then, but that wasn't unusual. Lennie told me next to nothing about his family. The relative didn't resemble him at all. Girls found Lennie attractive. The best man, taller, leaner, wearing a scowl, could have been an undertaker by the look of him.

Sophie, Lennie's mother, was another story. Decked out in billowing bright silks ornamented with embroidered Balkan motifs, sporting a flowered headpiece in her flaming red hair, multi-layered necklaces, bracelets, charms, and rings, she smiled on all round, gestured often and grandly, a lady who, like Mae West in her prime, looked intriguingly exaggerated.

A hundred wedding guests trailed out at the end of the ceremony, all but a tiny contingent of them from the groom's side of the aisle. From the bride's side, there were a half-dozen friends from United College where Angela had just graduated with a BA in Fine Art. As the procession moved outdoors under the stained glass windows and copper spires and cupolas into the Manitoba sunlight, I caught a glimpse of the Reverend Stockton, as you might notice an approaching assassin, when it was too late. He came forward out of the crowd, in black suit and white collar. Just after the bridal couple passed, as Lennie's mother and best man came by, the Reverend stepped forward and spit on them, not once but twice, before turning on his heel and walking off. Not a word was spoken. Angela and Lennie were too far ahead to see. Sophie and the best man never so much as raised a hand in defence or acknowledgment that anything had happened. The guests continued to their cars and onward in horn-honking procession to the Ukrainian Labour Temple off Salter Street for the reception.

As I stood watching Angela being whirled around in a polka by a great burly man with a beaming face, Lennie's best man introduced himself to me as Lennie's cousin, and asked me:

"Friend of the bride?"

"No, the groom."

"From the university?"

"Yes."

"Winnipeg your home?"

"Nope, up north." I was deliberately non-specific. I was tired of saying I was from Flin Flon and then having to explain what it was like up there in the far North to people who were uninterested, but for some reason, perhaps because of its silly name, felt obliged to ask about what life was like 'up' there.

"Not a friend of the bride's then?" I detected a chill. Had I been a friend of the bride, I wouldn't have admitted it, suspecting this man, by his looks, capable of committing some horrendous act of revenge for the spitting episode. Probably, I thought, he was relieved that I came from afar and so might not spread the story locally.

"Only just met her," I said. As it was clear this best man was a person who disapproved of things in general, I took it for granted this marriage would be a new addition to a long list of bad occurrences in his life. I raised my glass and said: "Here's to the beautiful bride."

"Yes, to the bride," he said, and managed to get his glass about elbow high without drinking, then sidled off. I remember thinking rather woozily that he was just pretending to be a law student, that probably he had been interrupted from his real job and was in a hurry to return and get on with the embalming. What struck me most was the contrast between him and Sophie. He was Charon poling the barge across Styx on the way to Hell. She was Demeter coming up from the underworld with the beautiful Persephone in a cascade of flowers.

Angela wore a glow. She stood straight-backed, slender-waisted, broad-shouldered, voluptuously filled out beneath folds of satin and taffeta and lace, reminding me suddenly of the description of the maiden in Milton's L'Allegro in the passage so highly praised by Lennie–'the daughter fair/so buxom, blithe and debonair'. She must have been feeling anxiety about the family situation but she didn't show it. Men, young and old, made a great fuss over her. She was not treated as you might expect, as a foreigner in their midst, an ice princess from the distant glaciers of River Heights. She was an object of wonder, perhaps a trophy. What that meant was more than passive admiration. It meant money. The more she danced, the more the beer and vodka flowed, the more the money accumulated--pinned to her dress as she was whirled by, one and two dollar bills at first, rising to fives and tens as competition began, not only to win a few dance steps with her, but to display the generosity and good will of the giver. I was stationed at the outside end of the head table, at the tip of a crescent with both dance floor and wedding party in full view. At the centre of everyone's attention was, of course, Angela. But I was drawn to the end of the table where Sophie sat with her sisters Stella and Yelena on either side. All three stood out from the crowd in colours of purple and gold, their feisty ornamentation sparkling in the light reflected from shards of mirror pasted on the sphere that revolved high in the middle of the ballroom. I thought of *The Three Sisters,* though they had little in common with Chekhov's expended gentry. These were tough, garrulous women, larger than life, Sophie clearly the dominant one. People fluttered around her like fireflies, whispering in her ear as they passed, or just tapping her arm and giving a look. She acknowledged them with a hand up, a shrug, the bat of an eye, uproarious laughter. She got up and danced, a gypsy polka at a furious pace, a waltz, an astonishing if not classically pure rendition of the tango. I studied her for signs of her attitude to this new beauty Lennie had reined in, but I caught her only once or twice paying attention to Angela, and I could detect no acrimony, no jealousy in her aspect, not the slightest sign of resentment at her treatment by the Reverend Stockton. What I think I saw was something like motherly pride that her son could attract such a comely bride. There was no mistaking that Sophie had been a great beauty herself in her day, with a capacious appetite for life, and also that underneath her regal self-possession, she probably knew a thing or two about heartbreak.

Whether it was official protocol or not, someone cut the music and Sophie waved off a microphone and stood up to speak: "You all heard me before and you know I don't whisper. Also, I don't make speeches unless someone does something wrong. Well, nothing wrong tonight, so no speech. Just a toast to this beautiful bride we have here before us." All hooted and raised their glasses. "And to this not bad-looking kid who found this beautiful bride. I hope he will bring her a good life. Well, he goddamn well better or I tell you there'll be hell to pay". The roar was tumultuous.

The mic was handed to Angela. When she could no longer refuse it, the noise died down. "You have all been so nice to me, I want you to know that I am sorry my parents are not here tonight." The hush was absolute. She had just acknowledged that there *was* an elephant in the room and they didn't have to ignore it. Relief was tangible. She must have picked something up from the tone of Sophie's non-speech when she added: "If you were my mother and father and caught me marrying this man, Lennie, what would you have done?" The crowd was in the palm of her hand.

She handed Lennie the mic. He pretended reluctance and then mock-bashfully whispered into it: "Well, okay then". The gesture and the whisper got the laugh it was after. Then he stood up and began: "Those who know me know I'm no speechifier either." (More laughter). "But what the hell … here goes." His bearing and facial expression went through a metamorphosis. His brow fell like a storm cloud.

"Like many of you, I originated in a far-away place. All of us here tonight come from a far-away place. This is a garden we've come to. A virtual paradise. A garden that has winters but also has springs. All we have to do to make not a virtual but a real paradise is to husband this garden, look after it, love it. And that is something we can't do alone – only together.

"Yet look at us in Winnipeg here tonight. In the North End, we have the Poles, the Ukrainians, the Jews, and the flotsam of a screwed-up century from Europe. Out along the Assiniboine, we have the first-comers and their children, the Scots and English. In between, we have all the varieties of people on the planet. Instead of making the garden together, what do we do? We distrust each other, discount each other, stay away from each other.

"This has to end. We are not this human being or that human being. We are humans. You are just as I am. This wedding of Angela and me is not just a love affair. It's an affirmation of our humanity, however our ancestries may differ." The broad grin he had begun with suddenly burst out once more. "If I'm not careful here, I'm going to begin sounding like a preacher. Maybe one preacher in a family is enough. All I really want to do, folks, is thank you all for being here. And thank you especially for your potatoes and the spirit in which they are given."

Chapter Three

At Wilderness Lodge I read as many books as I could between bouts of beer in the evenings and days on the water. I cooked enough beautiful pickerel shore lunches to last a lifetime, and absorbed enough sun to look well-done myself. A guest-angler asked me: "You an Indian?" I said, "Yep", and passed muster. By the end of summer, I got anaesthetized by hot days staring at shimmering water and listening to the hypnotic banalities of sports fishermen on holiday as they flailed the back bays and weed beds for big jackfish and bass. Then a letter came from Lennie, so unexpected it shocked me into remembering there was still a world out there beyond the anodyne of the guiding life on the English River.

August 5, 1959
American Express
Port of Ibiza, Spain

Dear JJ:

I can't believe it's coming to an end. It's gone so fast. Yet in another sense it seems time has stood still here. Yes, that's it. That's the sense I have, that time has stopped at the still point of the turning world. Better still (I've been reading Northrop Frye on Blake), here is the image Frye borrows from Blake (originally I think from St. Augustine), no image at all really when you try to imagine it. I've come to a circle whose centre is everywhere and whose circumference is nowhere. How to explain this place? I've been reading the first pirated copies of Kerouac's *On The Road* and Ginsberg's

Howl and I've got to tell you something strange is coming down the road from San Francisco and New York and all along the highway in between.

OK, it's an artists' colony here. There is even a bunch of Canadians who come and go–Graham Coughtry, Gordon Raynor, writers like Mordecai Richler, film makers Ted Kotcheff and Richard Leiterman. There's a guy called Clifford Irving working on a scheme with another guy called Richard Suskind to write a biography of Howard Hughes. There's the great Canadian film animator, whatsisname Williams, working with the musician Tristram Cary, Joyce Cary's son. They did that fantastically scary animated film called *The Little Island* about how the world ends in nuclear war. And so on. I haven't bothered looking the Canadians up. What for? The place is a rainbow of mad people from all over. Gaggles of Swedes and Germans and French. Murmurations of Londoners. And mucho Americanos, the best kind, the anti-American kind, bums and aging beatniks and hucksters and tricksters and mountebanks and poets and shills. Aside from the local farmers and fishermen, hardly anyone speaks Spanish, which means I learn nothing of the language except 'dos kilos des platanos por favor', and 'quanta est?'

Meanwhile how do we spend our days besides eating bananas? We get up, go to the patio at the Hotel Figueretos, have coffee and Fundador, put on flippers and snorkels, then fan off into the bay, never more than fifteen feet deep, filled with fish and coral and diorama-like undersea forests. Thence to lunch and siesta and then up and out to the crowds on the Ramblas where anything can happen, and once almost did. It's still bugging me.

There are two people we became friends with very quickly (well, I more than Angela truth be told). The woman's name is Faye, a Dutch lady of much elegance and sophistication, a little over thirty, whose husband was formerly a factory owner in Indonesia, until Sukarno confiscated everything and ousted the Dutch. Faye escaped by swimming across the harbour in Jakarta with her daughter. Her husband didn't. Her boyfriend is a New Yorker called Gig, a twenty-three-year old Adonis with golden locks and an angelic face but no dummy, a sweet and dreamy guy. The nickname 'Gig' draws no comment here. On the beach at Figueretos, there are plenty of older women, European and American, with boys of summer. Gig has an Isetta and I've had a great time touring the island with him and having him explain its past back to the Vikings, Romans and Phoenicians. Maybe Odysseus was here. The Sirens may have been too, and left their progeny. Gig's been a year-rounder in Ibiza since he was nineteen. He knows all the drills.

A couple of days ago, I went back to Faye's and Gig's with them as the sun was going down. Angela stayed at the hotel for a doze. Four of us sat in Faye's villa overlooking the beach. Faye and Gig were on the sofa. I sat on a cushion on the floor. Faye's daughter, Giselle, the one she swam the bay with in Jakarta, just turned fifteen, sat beside me. We were all in our bathing suits. *The Bossa Nova* was playing, the Stan Getz/Charlie Bird version. We had a few tokes. The heat of the day was still heavy in the air, and something else, an almost palpable vibration of sexuality. It was transfixing. Not a word was spoken. Faye came over and put my hand on Giselle's stomach, and I watched the girl's eyelids flutter and close. I looked up at Gig. He was glass-eyed. Then Faye stood Giselle up, slowly pulled her bathing suit down, and took me in her hand. She pushed me onto my back and brought Giselle to stand over me. Her breasts were bigger than they seemed under her bathing suit, standing high up with rosebuds that came to tiny points. Her mound was just beginning to show curvature under a garland of blonde fluff. The effect was hallucinatory. One second, she seemed to be a grown woman, the next, just a little girl. I snapped. I jumped up and ran from the house.

So what do you think, JJ? Am I a saint or a fool? You don't suppose your Methodist conscience has rubbed off on me do you? And one other thing while I'm at it. Which is the real world? Those moments of rapture suspended in time, or that other world where the clocks keep on ticking even without hands or a face? Lemme know will you?

Your co-agitator,
Lennie

The letter renewed the conundrum of Lennie's verbal stigmatism. How could he write to me so fluently and not be able to ace his exams? Was it because exams weren't personal?

August 17, 1959

Dear Lennie:

I'm sending this to Winnipeg as it's not likely to reach you in Ibiza and you'll no doubt be back before I am. I can't answer your goddamn question about the girl. I'd have to have been there, wouldn't I? I think they call it an existential quandary. But yes, maybe a little Methodism has rubbed off on you. And a good thing, too. Keep you out of trouble, it might ... if you pay attention.

As for your other question about the still point, the answer's the same. I'd have to be there to know, and I'm not, you lucky bastard. I've been reading Andrew Marvell under cover of my go-deeper hat while my anglers angle, and at shore lunch when I'm frying pickerel I try to annihilate all that's made 'to a green thought in a green shade'. That's as close as I can come to Eliot's still point of the turning world. The trouble is, at shore lunch, if I'm not cooking, I'm either filleting fish or washing up the clutter so we can get back to thrashing the water. There's no time for still points around here. No time for timelessness, get it? Too busy marauding the great Canadian fish tank with my Yankee captains of industry and other buccaneers.

See you at the shindig on the Winnipeg River.

J.F.

Ten of the graduating class, with Lennie's spouse Angela and my girlfriend Delia bringing the total to a dozen, made it to the diaspora at the cabin on the Winnipeg River on Labour Day Weekend. Our host, Peter Coultry, a good friend of Lennie and me, was the only one among us not intending to go to graduate school. He declared himself off to England to write a novel about Canada Geese and the folly of shooting them, an activity his nature-loving, forest ranger father insisted was healthy for the goose population but which Peter could not accept. This was to be the crux of the father/son conflict in the novel. Purely as a formality, however, to satisfy his parents, he applied to U of T graduate school and to his family's delight and his dismay he was admitted. The novel would have to wait.

No such detour was necessary for another member of our group. Five years older than the rest of us, a fugitive from East End London, Mark Woodward and I had become friends because he felt foreign and saw me as typically Canadian, and I found him, despite his having the tail end of a Cockney accent, the most cosmopolitan person I had ever met.

Mark's first job upon immigrating to Canada from London's East End had been in a radium mine in the Northwest Territories. "I feel a bit of an outsider," he told me. "Most of the students here seem to live at home with their parents."

"I bet we have something else in common too," I said. "We both know what it's like to freeze our balls off." It wasn't the first time for me that a mutual connection with life in the cold had established a bond. Within a week in our third year, we were sharing a flat at River and Osbourne, Winnipeg's first effort to create a "village", and commuting to the Fort Garry Campus from downtown. In our French class, we were reading Voltaire. I couldn't help comparing Mark and me to Pangloss and Candide. Mark cooked things like kippers and cabbage and clam chowder, but also on occasion things like Boeuf Bourguignon and Beef Strogaonoff (what? meat and sour cream?). We ate artichokes and mangoes and egg plant, things I had never heard of before, let alone tasted. Sometimes, for dessert he made his favourite–Poire Belle Helene. I was good at bacon and eggs and meat and potatoes, and Mark adapted when my turn came.

I probably had my rituals, like working at night and making up for it by sleeping during the day when I could. Not an easy thing to accommodate in a bachelor apartment with two cots separated by a brick and plank bookcase. Mark never complained. He had some rituals too. He liked the Metropolitan Opera on Sunday radio. I tried but couldn't get into it. Was it because I grew up too far away from a seat in the God's at Covent Garden and, like Lennie, had never been exposed to the zeitgeist of high art as a child? Instead of the opera, I would go out to see a movie or a high school basketball game to bathe in nostalgia.

Mark's main ritual was Sunday morning when, without fail, he dashed off to Portage News to pick up his *New Yorker*. After the opera, he was not to be disturbed. He had been reading the magazine religiously since he was fifteen, he told me. It partly explained his astonishing achievement the year we all graduated in Honours. He had a sheaf of short stories, one of which I found exceptional although I failed to recognize how exceptional. He sold it (of all places) to the *New Yorker*. "Blitzkrieg Days" it is called, about the bizarre side of the London bombings in 1941. As far as any of us knew, no Canadian had ever sold a story to the *New Yorker* before Mark. Stephen Leacock maybe, Morley Callahan maybe. For sure, no freshly graduated university student from Winnipeg. Mark's triumph elevated us all. It was the focus of our celebration when we gathered in the fall of 1959 to say goodbye.

We congregated at the Coultry cabin at the end of a logging road on the Winnipeg River up-stream from Lac du Bonnet. It was a warmly rustic place, with open rafters and trusses, stone fireplace, giant wood stove in the kitchen, back shed hung with old goose hunting jackets and fishing gear, and a screened porch on two sides with wicker chairs and couches. Back from the river, there were two sleeping cabins, and a male and female outhouse with stained glass windows rescued from a demolished country church, which let you contemplate the passing river in technicolor as you sat.

Labour Day Weekend in Manitoba has a way of bringing on fall like the slamming of a door, but as we drove into the forest of yellow and red blazing leaves, Friday was lovely. Once everyone got their billets straightened out, we had snacks and hot toddies around the fire, and listened to records of Sonny Terry and Brownie McGhee, Muddy Waters, Pete Seeger singing the ancient dirge about *"Mary Seaton and Mary Beaton and Mary Carmichael and Me"*, and Woody Guthrie doing *"Railroad Bill"*. Plans were made. Lennie was determined that I take him fishing, something that he had never done before. It was like someone from Detroit saying he's never driven a car.

Lennie had prepared himself for this outdoor foray with hours in the library and was full of questions. Do pickerel spawn in fast water or in reedy bays? Do lake trout come into the shallows in the spring just when the birch buds break out? Why do shiner minnows school on beaches when the moon is full? Do fish ever go to sleep? He had built our tiny outdoor sally into a grand wilderness adventure, his first ever, and he was as excited as a kid about it. Well all right, I thought to myself, it wouldn't hurt for a change for me to know more about something than he did. After all, I *was* a licensed fishing guide.

There was a problem. We had to go up river and the only outfit Peter had was a seven horse kicker and a freighter canoe with a hole in it. But the canoe was fixable. There were leftover cedar shingles in the shed, bendable ash from old snowshoes that could be persuaded to replace the broken oak ribs, some old tent canvas, everything but paint and glue. I got up while it was still dark, or supposed to be dark. The moon was so bright it was like blue sunlight, highlighting anything that reflected it and making patches of eerie shadow. I took a flashlight to a stand of spruce and scraped off a can of gum. Crisp birch and poplar leaves swept by in the wind and the blotched leaves of Manitoba maples. A touch of frost, a little more wind, and they'd be gone in a flash. With the moon so bright, I had no trouble working. I pried out the broken sections of rib and planking, tacked in the bent ash, cut the shingles and canvas to size and made a small fire of chips to melt the spruce gum. I loved working with wood.

I was lost to the world when the sound of a chair scraping came from the screened porch fifty feet away. It gave me a start. I could just make out a figure sitting there. As I squinted, Lennie waved and came out across the frosty grass to where I was working.

"So you weren't bullshitting me about being a boy scout," he said.

"How long have you been sitting there?"

"Hour maybe."

"That's creepy, Lennie. Spying, I think they call it."

Suddenly he hunched up his shoulders, stretched his arms forward at me and stammered. "What the ... what ... I mean how the hell did you do that? How did you know the goddamn pieces would fit?"

I was about to laugh when I realized he was serious. A bit of manual dexterity, a skill I shared with anyone who'd had to fix things as a kid, something I'd taken for granted without a second thought was, to Lennie, a deep mystery. I guessed he'd never in his life put back together anything that was broken, never taken a bicycle apart or built a crystal set or a model aeroplane, never played basketball with volley balls and hoops with no nets, or shot frozen horse turds through goalposts of snow, never done leather crafts, or made a toothbrush holder in shop, or darned his own socks, or smoked the inner layer of red willow rolled in birch bark. Once, he told me, he'd never cooked himself a meal.

At eight in the morning we set off upriver to where Peter said the best swirls were, between current and backwater, good for pickerel this late in the year. He told me to gas up at a place called Loon Lodge. When we got there, I took the tank over to the pump and Lennie wandered off down the dock to stretch his legs. The next thing I knew, as I was plugging the gas hose back into the outboard, Lennie came barging up, white-faced. "Come here," he said and ran back up the dock. I followed him around behind the storage tanks to where the diesel generators were housed, and then a bit beyond to where the bush started. There was a cross-piece between two trees and, hanging from it, an immense thing of blood. I didn't recognize it at first and then I saw what it was. It was the stripped torso of a bear. There were no paws or head left. The carcass hung upside down, cuts made to the body by the skinning knife wept trails of blood, and the neck cavity oozed blood and innards. The ground underneath was sodden. The whole operation couldn't have taken place more than an hour earlier.

It was a sight I'd seen before on the English River when hunting season opened in the fall, during my last summer days as fishing guide. But I had never seen it so unexpectedly. I couldn't imagine what it was like for Lennie to come upon it without warning, not to know what it was at first, except that it was something unspeakably obscene, then to have me try to explain, as the giant, denuded hulk trickled blood and slime and twisted in the trees.

The camp had looked empty except for the boy mixing the oil and gas. He was about twelve and seemed excited. When I questioned him, he blurted it out:

"Dinja hear? We got the bugger," he said. "Black bear. Big one."

"It's out of season," I said.

"Not if they're scavengin', it ain't," the boy said. "Threat to life and property. Dad got him the s'mornin'. Right outside the cookhouse. Mouth full of pancakes and steak bones. Real big son of a bitch, maybe two-fifty pounds. Couple of American fishermen took him for the rug. Paid cash."

"That's not legal either," I said. Suddenly the boy looked scared, as if I might be the law in plainclothes. We barely got started up river when Lennie waved me to stop. "Go back," he said. I tried to talk him into carrying on, into not letting a bunch of trophy morons spoil his fishing trip, but it was no use.

That night we didn't have a pickerel feed, but a great feast anyway and lots to drink. Around the fireplace, we gabbed and told stories and when everyone got mellow, we sang silly old songs from the *Manitoba School Songbook* that we had learned as kids–*Men of Harlech, Down by the Ash Grove, Early One Morning,* and *Old King Cole* in fractured three-part harmony, even *Old Black Joe,* a song which had about as much relevance to our lives as fashions in China. Peter was an attentive host, discreetly keeping everyone's glass full. Angela stayed close to the fire but Lennie sat off behind in the semi-dark. Like a couple of the others, he wasn't singing and you could tell he was getting sloshed.

Peter's date, a professor's daughter, specialized in Irish folk songs and was good enough to sing on CBC Radio. We shut up and listened to her sweet soprano. Suddenly there was another voice, a raspy, falsetto lament: "O where hae ye been, Lord Randal, my son?/O where hae ye been, my handsome young man?" It was Lennie from the shadows, not a sweet voice but in perfect pitch and with great feeling to it. There was a moment of unease and then a hush fell as Lennie went on with the assurance of a seasoned performer. Everyone was silent as he sang all five verses, ending with:

> What gat ye to your dinner, my handsome young man?
> I gat eels boiled in broo; mother, make my bed soon ...
> For I'm sick at the heart, and I fain wald lie down.

Shortly afterward, no one more surprised than I that Lennie could carry a tune, let alone sing with such emotion, we drifted off to our camp beds.

On Sunday morning, I took Delia for an outing upriver. We built a campfire and ate shore lunch and made love on the leaves as we hadn't done since high school. When we came back, mid-afternoon, Angela was sitting on the bank and came down to meet us. "How's things?" I asked. I sensed there was more amiss than the trauma of the slaughtered bear.

She gave us a circus shrug, palms up. "Oh, he's a live wire," she said, "sitting there reading old National Geographics and sloshing down the vodka and tonic." Within the hour, the temperature plunged ten degrees, a great leaden cloud from the northwest fell on us like a lid, and we packed it in early and headed home.

Part II
Burning Bright

Chapter Four

Only three days in town and Delia managed to set up house in Toronto–a bachelor apartment in the spanking new Yorkville Towers just off Yorkville and Yonge Street. Her nursing experience gave her a no-nonsense approach to getting things done. We promptly acquired a table, chairs, mattress, brick and board bookcase, drapes made from bed sheets rigged to cover the futuristic feature of a floor-to-ceiling glass wall, and a rubber-bottomed doormat to keep us from upending when we stepped onto our glistening new parquet floor. Establishing a base seemed the sensible first step before facing the mysteries of graduate school.

Lennie took a different approach. He and Angela were at the Park Plaza Hotel while he worked out his program. The idea stunned me. Delia's and my bachelor apartment, hardly a slum with its eight shimmering glass storeys and its upper floor still to be completed, was a hundred and fifteen dollars a month. The Park Plaza was sixty dollars a night.

Money never seemed a problem for Lennie by the way he dressed, not to mention that he didn't take a summer job and had honeymooned in Europe. During the busy year in which we had become friends, pecuniary concerns were irrelevant in the face of the perversion of Marxism under Stalin, Spengler's *Decline Of The West* as applied to the capitalist takeover of the American republic, the arms race, the Cold War, and not to be discounted, the battle in literature between the New Critics and the old guard of biographical and impressionist critics. In this battle, armed with I.A. Richards and F.R. Leavis of the Cambridge School, as filtered down to us through their secret agent in Manitoba, John Peter, our allegiance to close reading and textual analysis became absolute. These things counted. Not money.

What I couldn't understand was why someone with Lennie's brains wasn't better at getting his affairs together. I remembered him watching me patch the old freighter canoe at Peter Coultry's as if I were making a Stradivarius. Maybe that's what it was. What other people found simple, like taking an apartment and setting up house, looked dauntingly complicated to him. Or was it just that mundane concerns were for him irrelevant to the real business of life which, right now, was choosing courses of study.

"So who've you seen?" Lennie asked, as I joined him with my coffee under the Gothic ogee arches and leaded glass windows of the hallowed Arbour Room at Hart House.

"You're the first," I said. I thought he was talking about fellow travellers from Winnipeg. He looked puzzled for a moment, then closed the book he was reading and exhaled at me.

"No, JJ. I mean which professors have you seen? You know, the people we came here for?" I offered I was just getting round to it. But the truth was I hadn't been thinking about any such thing. My intention was to sign up for modern poetry and drama and maybe a course on the modern novel. (Would it help me write one?) What I should have known was that subjects and historical periods as such were of no interest to him. He was shopping for professors, the smartest ones, not the course offerings. He researched their reputation, then paid them a visit, as if he were conducting job interviews. Those who met with his approval would get the job of teaching him. The sensible idea of specializing in a field when you start graduate school in order to lay the groundwork for a job and a career did not seem to have crossed Lennie's mind.

"I had a problem yesterday with A.S.P." Lennie said. This was A.S.P. Woodhouse he was talking about, internationally renowned Milton scholar, Chairman of The Graduate School, plenipotentiary of the university's governing Senate, and from what I had heard, power broker of literary studies with tentacles extending into all major English departments in the land and as far afield as Harvard and Oxford, a man of classical erudition and imperious bearing, Canada's unchallenged grandee of Christian Humanism.

"He's against the New Criticism, the old fraud," Lennie said. "The guy's a holy terror for biography, history of ideas, historical context. It gets worse. He goes on forever about nature and grace. The Greeks and Romans are confined *in nature*. Christians get divine revelation from *above* nature through grace. That way, get it, Christians don't have to kick the classics out of school. They can redeem the pagans. Ergo, *Christian* Humanism. Double talk! Of course, the greatest Christian Humanist of them all for him is Milton. I ask you, can you get an image from Milton's description of the divine presence: 'bright effluence of bright essence uncreate'? I mean what the hell does *that* look like when you wake up even without a hangover?"

"I've always had a soft spot for Milton," I said.

"As in 'soft spot' in the head?"

"I used to do a lot of speaking *Paradise Lost* out loud to help me memorize for exams. It drove Delia nuts. But I began to like it, the great thundering voice of the bard. I wasn't much into the theology of the thing."

"You surprise me, JJ. And you took your Milton from John Peter."

"It doesn't mean I agreed with Peter on everything." We all knew that John Peter disliked Milton, and the book he was writing was designed to expose Milton as a doctrinaire versifier suffering from what T. S. Eliot called 'dissociated sensibility', meaning, as I understood it, an unhealthy loss of integration of thought and feeling, or to put it simply, a problem with sex. Or who knows, maybe John Peter faulted Milton simply because his grand Latinate style was so different from the 'Englishness' of Chaucer, Shakespeare, and Donne. I didn't care. I loved John Donne. Who could help it? But loving him wasn't reason to reject Milton, one of the great wordsmiths of the language, at least not for my money.

"All I can say, JJ, is you're nothing if not a generous and fair-minded toiler in the fields of the Muses."

I didn't like being so lightly dismissed. "Try reading Milton out loud," I said. "There are all kinds of poets, aren't there? It seems pretty silly for someone like you or me, or John Peter for that matter, to call a man a bad poet who could put together something as big as *Paradise Lost*."

I paused while Lennie held his hands up like shields, as if to protect himself. "Besides," I said, "we've all heard A.S.P. Woodhouse runs the show around here, right? And that he's recognized all over the goddamn world as a prize-fighting Milton scholar, right? So it won't kill you to be nice to the guy, just for a little while. If it's absolutely necessary for you to stamp out Christian Humanism at the University of Toronto, give it a couple of weeks until you get your feet on the ground, will you?"

"You're right, JJ, you're absolutely right. Either that or you're the tempter in disguise, leading me down the path of conformity and compromise. Here, read this while I stock us up on coffee."

He pushed the book he'd been reading toward me. It was *The Collected Works of William Blake*, the Keynes edition of 1956. He left a page open where I read: "The reason Milton wrote in fetters when he wrote of Angels & God, and at liberty when of Devils & Hell, is because he was a true Poet and of the Devil's party without knowing it." I read the lines several times, trying to grasp what they were getting at.

Lennie returned with coffee and sat watching as I skipped through the pages he had flagged, most of them in the *Marriage of Heaven and Hell* section. My acquaintance with Blake had been restricted to reading a few chapters about his life and the standard anthologised poems: *London, Ah Sunflower, The Tyger,* and of course the *Jerusalem* lyric, which we sang in public school as children on occasions of patriotic celebration of the British Empire. I knew about Northrop Frye, not through *Fearful Symmetry*, his book on Blake, but through his *Anatomy of Criticism*, which I had staggered through up to the middle of the *First Essay* and then decided to set aside until I felt I was old enough. I pushed on with Lennie's yellow-flagged gleanings in the Keynes edition of Blake.

> Energy is the only life, and is from the Body; Reason
> is the bound or outward circumference of Energy.

> How do you know but evr'y Bird that cuts the airy way is
> an immense world of delight, clos'd by your senses five?

> Prudence is a rich, ugly old maid courted by Incapacity.

> Pity could be no more if we did not make someone poor.

> He who desires and acts not breeds pestilence.

> Prisons are built with stones of law, broth-
> els with bricks of religion.

> The cistern contains. The fountain overflows.

> The head sublime, the heart pathos, the genitals beauty,

> The hands and feet proportion, the human form divine.

Where man is not Nature is barren.

Exuberance is beauty.

I picked my way through these startling lines as if tackling a dish of walnuts with my teeth at Christmas time. Some cracked open right away, others not at all. When I looked up, Lennie was watching me as if I were an egg he expected to see hatch.

"You been hiding this stuff?" I said. How had I not stumbled on these Blake things before?

"No, I've been trying to figure out how this place works," he said. "The Truth is, it was a bad start for me today, JJ. You know the cloisters at University College? They look Neo Gothic, with gables and parapets and cornices and pilasters and corbels and archways and what-not. I took hold of this medieval-looking ring on a huge oak door and gave it a tug. It was like there was a spring on it and it yanked back. So I let go and bang, there was someone on the other side and the door hit him on the forehead. The guy standing there, white shirt sleeves rolled up, pot belly, black suspenders, looked like the janitor. He pulled out his hanky and daubed his forehead where the door had caught him.

'Can I help you?' he said.

'I'm looking for Woodhouse,' I said.

'Professor Woodhouse?'

'Professor A.S.P. Woodhouse.'

'Well now, I am professor A.S.P. Woodhouse,' he said.

"Holy shit! How could anything go well after that? He sat me down and quizzed me about what he called Nineteenth Century Thought, as if I'd never heard of it before. He was able to make me out to be almost illiterate by asking me about the likes of DeQuincey, Macaulay, Hazlitt, Ruskin, Carlyle, Morris, Pater, all those miscellaneous Victorians. Everyone knows that except for John Stuart Mill, Darwin, Lyell, maybe Sir James Fraser, a few Frenchmen like Bergson, and that crazy Dane, Kierkegaard, original thought in the Nineteenth Century was done by Germans. He just didn't like me, JJ, and I could see where it was leading."

"Don't tell me. Bottomless perdition," I said.

"I made a last ditch effort at redemption. Behind his desk, there's a two-by-four portrait, putridly framed. I was pretty sure it was a copy of the portrait of Dr. Johnson by Joshua Reynolds. I gave it a shot. "That portrait of you, sir," I said, "is a nice piece of work, worthy of a Joshua Reynolds." He gave me a double-take in slow motion, looking pleased for a moment, then he just didn't buy me.

"That portrait, young man," he said, "is a facsimile of a famous portrait by Sir Joshua Reynolds to be sure, not a portrait of me, for although I know a mighty lot about the Eighteenth Century, I'm obliged to inform you I did not live in it. The subject is Dr. Johnson, as I'm sure you are well aware, or you would not be a candidate for the PhD at this university."

"The old faker. He knew damned well he looked like Dr. Johnson. He probably spent half a lifetime cultivating the likeness. I made the worst kind of blunder. I let him see that I wasn't taking him seriously. As punishment, I have now been forcibly signed up for a make-up course in Nineteenth Century Thought, taught by A. S. P. Woodhouse, which is, no question, the last course I would have chosen on my own. Maybe you're doing it right, JJ. Maybe it's safer to stay home, read the syllabus, and keep your trap shut."

"Speaking of which, where is home going to be, Lennie?" I said.

He waved me off, so I suggested, as it was a nice autumn afternoon, that we take a scout of the neighbourhood to get a feel for the city. If he saw anything he liked, he could get Angela to look into it later on. My assumption was that, however impractical Angela might be, she could be no worse than Lennie when it came to nest-building.

We made our way north up Philosopher's Walk between Hallam and Bloor, a dirt path overhung by greenery that followed the ancient channel of Taddle Creek, which you can see in old pictures of the campus. There's no creek today, it having long since been diverted into the sewerage system of the city. We talked about how different the season was from what we'd left behind in Winnipeg. Back home, there would be snow by now. Here, the leaves were just turning and the air was balmy. "Know what, JJ?" Lennie said, taking a deep breath and stretching his arms to the sky, "This is our Deep South."

As we tramped through the Annex district, he kept pointing to old coach houses in the St. George area behind one-time one-family mansions. I told him you had to be a millionaire to afford a coach house. I knew because I had naively inquired before settling for our affordable high-rise. I told Lennie I guessed you needed old family connections even to be invited in to take a look at one of the coach houses. Lennie smiled, squinted, and nodded his head. "Enemy territory."

Yorkville was different. On the streets running off Hazelton, there were still tiny wooden houses, lived in not so long ago by working families and servants of Rosedale's rich, now being taken over by students and musicians and painters and poets, giving the place the aura of a budding Bohemia. I thought it would be a perfect place for Lennie and Angela, an arty place, a tree-lined, intellectually stimulating neighbourhood, a potential Greenwich Village. Lennie hated it.

"This is phonyville, JJ," he said. "Ersatz Montparnasse. La Vie de Bohème is dead and gone. All they had to fight was the bourgeoisie. That's not our battle. We're facing the giant corporations, the Bay Street money-grubbers, the power elite, worst of all, the mob of indoctrinated consumer sheep. We are facing engineered homogenization on a titanic scale, a concerted suppression of critical thought, a melting down of individuals into a polyglot of consumers brainwashed by advertising to buy gewgaws. Orwell called advertising stirring a stick in a pail of slops."

I still wasn't used to the way Lennie could suddenly erupt like this without apparent cause. "Is it something you ate that didn't agree with you, Lennie?" I said. "It's just a place to live we're talking about, for crying out loud!" It was no use. There was something about Yorkville's servant class roots and the first whiff of gentrification the neighbourhood gave off that triggered his aversion. And no doubt much, too, from his North Winnipeg past.

But there were things about Toronto Lennie took to as enthusiastically as I did. In 1959 the city's streetlights no longer flickered on alternating current, but it was still a sufficiently dingy place by night to conjure up foggy London town, the old world backdrop of British B-movies that inhabited our imagination as kids. Bloor Street, from Yonge to St. George, was lined with renovated old mansions housing Holt Renfrew, Birks Jewellers, Creeds and The Gold Shoppe. There were sepia-walled beer parlours–the King Cole Room, The Embassy, The Bay Bloor. There was the Royal Ontario Museum and the teetering Victorian grand dame of The Royal Conservatory of Music. And of course there were Palmer's Drug Store, Diana Sweets, Murray's Restaurant, and the lordly Park Plaza Hotel at the corner of Bloor and Avenue Road.

At the Park Plaza, we discovered the Roof Lounge where, on Friday afternoons when we could afford it, with the immortal Harold there to

serve us, we were able to look down on Queen's Park, the legislative buildings and the weathered stone edifices of the university, and feel connected
with an immensely more lived-in world than the spacious but sparse one
we had grown up in out West. Maybe it was the absence of neon (compared
to Winnipeg where the Neon revolution was transforming the once bucolic
Pembina Highway into a garish strip mall). Maybe it was the clanking and
grinding of the street cars with their squeaks and trolley sparks, the ferries
still going to a rural Ward's Island from where you could look back at the
skyline and (despite its irrelevance to anything we were doing) feel a twinge
of identity with the British Commonwealth's grandest hotel, the Royal
York, and its tallest building, the Canadian Imperial Bank of Commerce,
just before the coming of the skyscrapers. There were almost exclusively
Orientals on the streets of old China Town, soon to be churned up by the
architectural wonder of the new City Hall. Kensington market and Spadina
were thoroughly Jewish. To the North and West was Italian. Greeks were
congregating along the Danforth. Cabbage Town by the Don River was a
hybrid of unskilled workers and down-and-outs, heavily weighted with job
hunters from the Maritimes. In other neighbourhoods, new waves were
trickling in from India, Korea, Hong Kong, Jamaica, South America, and
voluminously from the Azores. At night, you could still hear foghorns on
the Seaway joining Port Arthur, a thousand miles inland, to the Atlantic.
Although there wasn't much left standing older than a hundred and fifty
years (the first wooden structures at Fort York began in the 1790s), to us
children of the West, Toronto felt like an old town, with a venerable past, by
Manitoba standards as good as medieval, and we loved the feel of it, just as
Americans, for similar reasons, have been known to love Paris.

I saw my coming to Toronto as a huge leap into new experience, like Nick
Carraway's moving from the mid-west to New York in *The Great Gatsby*,
except that I was not heading for the stock exchange in pursuit of riches
but for intellectual excitement in a city on the verge of cultural bloom. The
promise and challenge of it invigorated all of us who came from Winnipeg
that year, none more so than Lennie. Yet, at unexpected moments, a mood
would come over him that was off-kilter and I would sense in him something
smouldering, unsettled, possibly even dangerous. It troubled me, but at the
same time it intrigued me. I tried to write something using him as the basis
for a fictional character. I couldn't deny he was the most interesting man

I had ever met but I couldn't get a handle on him. I made a decision. I would record talks with him and what friends said about him. I would keep a Lennie file. Maybe someday a story would take shape.

Chapter Five

It was getting on five by the time Lennie and I finished our tour of the neighbourhood and reached Yonge and Bloor. We were about to turn home when we found ourselves standing in front of The Pilot Tavern. The sign had wings on it and the head of a pilot wearing a 1920's leather flyer's helmet. It seemed a handy place to stop for a beer. After an hour, I called Delia and said I'd be late and I tried to get Lennie to call Angela at the Park Plaza. He never got around to it.

"What got you into all this?" he said. "You being a basketball jock and all?" I knew he would ask me sometime. He wore a trace of the smile he had greeted me with when first we met in the hall of the old Arts Building in Manitoba.

"It started in grade eleven." A couple of beers had loosened my tongue. "Teachers in Flin Flon were paid well. They got a northern bonus from the Hudson's Bay Mining & Smelting Company to keep the miners believing their kids had a chance for a better life. We got quality teachers. The guy who taught English, Carlyle Mayes, was a blonde beanpole who knew not only Latin but even some Greek. I thought he was a fairy at first. He had effeminate gestures and he pronounced all his consonants. He assigned me to write a critique of *Word Magic*, an essay in *High Roads To Reading*. It was a very thinky-feely article about how lovely poetry sounded. Some lines stick in my memory to this day: 'Sat grey haired Saturn quiet as a nun', 'Yet still the blood is strong, the heart is highland/And we in dreams behold the Hebrides', 'Break, break, break, on thy cold grey stones Oh sea'. I could go on. Very gilded stuff. Very sonorous. It infected me. I had never thought about words themselves before. Then all of a sudden the sound of words and the pictures they made got me going."

"I remember that. I swear to God, I do remember that," said Lennie. "It was a strange thing wasn't it, suddenly getting bitten like that by words?"

"After Christmas Carlyle Mayes said *High Roads To Reading* wasn't good enough for us. He handed us copies of *Understanding Poetry*, the anthology by Brookes and Warren. It was like catnip. Even *The Wasteland* was there and Carlyle did his best to crack it open for us. This was North of '54, as our hockey jackets proclaimed, a dog-sled ride from the tundra. We were seventeen, and he got us reading:

> April is the cruellest month, breeding
> Lilacs out of the dead land, mixing
> Memory and desire, stirring
> Dull roots with spring rain
> Winter kept us warm

"Winter in Flin Flon being forty below," broke in Lennie.

"Only on mild days. It didn't keep anybody warm that's for sure. This was a foreign world old Carlyle took us into. He would roll his eyes and gaze despondently out the window when we responded stupidly to his questions. But when someone clicked on an image, he could barely hide his joy. 'Yes', he would say. 'Yes, yes,' and do a gangling sort of dance across the front of the room, waving his book in the air, like Ichabod Crane on horseback. Had our parents seen him, most would have sent him flouncing back south with the tail of a beaver hat blowing in the wind and a pair of mukluks to remember them by.

"That's the real deal," said Lennie. "Getting a teacher like that. Just *one* who can really do it."

"I told old Carlyle one day I especially liked a line of Eliot's: 'The worlds revolve like ancient women/Gathering fuel in vacant lots'. He looked at me a long moment. 'Why'? he asked. I said I had seen old women like that when I was a kid, old Indian women lurching around picking up stuff. They wore black. Everything was black. It must have been after a forest fire because there was nothing around but black stumps and smouldering muskeg. Eliot's ancient women in the vacant lot were like that, I said.

"It's a great metaphor, Jason. You're quite right," he said. "It's a marvellous metaphor. And good for you."

"This makes him sound patronizing, but I didn't take it that way, and I don't think that's how he meant it. It was around then that I started reading poetry for fun, not great volumes of it, but a grab bag of ancient and modern stuff in paperback anthologies from the drug store rack, paying no attention to who wrote what or when. I kept the dirty secret to myself."

"Naturally," said Lennie. "I mean what kind of weirdo goes around reading poetry, for Christ's sake? Life in a small town, eh? I was pretty sure you didn't versify to each other on the basketball team at U of M. It had to come from somewhere else."

After my third beer, I went to the can. When I came back, I was ready to wrap it up and go home but Lennie had ordered four more draughts. It was a Winnipeg thing we brought with us to Toronto. No one ever ordered a single glass. If there were two of you, you ordered four glasses. If there were six of you, you ordered twelve. Maybe it was because the old blue laws of Manitoba made us feel as if it were always closing time, which it was between 6:00 and 8:00 to get the workers home for supper. When the spirit of revolt was upon us, an evening wasn't complete unless before closing we quaffed enough beer at the last minute to ensure we fell down once or twice on the way home.

"Come on, I want to show you something," Lennie said. The Pilot had a back door opening into the alley and I followed him out. "Ever done one of these?" He pulled out what looked to me like an Ogden's Fine Cut roll-your-own in a Zig Zag paper, and he lit it up.

"Is it ...?" I wasn't sure what to call it. The strongest drug I ever tried was over-proof Hudson's Bay Rum. I knew zero about dope. My vocabulary on the subject was purely literary. "Is it a reefer?"

"Don't blow the smoke out. Hold it in," Lennie said.

When we went back and sat down I said it had no effect on me. I said I didn't understand what all the fuss was about with the jazz musicians and the beats in San Francisco. I felt guilty about not getting home to Delia and I looked at my watch. "Do you realize how stupid we are?" I said. "I mean, look at us. This ridiculous watch hand goes round and round in a circle and we jump up and down to it as if we were actually getting some place, going ahead to something. Every day it starts over and away we go again. And that's just the big hand. If you keep your eye on the little hand, it's like film speeded up, so we get nowhere faster."

Lennie burst out with a breathy, phissing sound and began to laugh. Before I knew it, we were both whooping it up, I had no idea at what. Then we went silent and I drifted into a trough between waves of colourful patterns.

"It happened to me that way too, JJ," he said. "In Ibiza, time stopped. The sun shone every day. Café con leche with Fundador in the morning. A walk to the platform of the Figueretos Hotel perched over the sea, a plate of pinchitas, or a toasted bacon and egg sandwich if you felt like a taste of home. Yesterday and tomorrow were illusions. Yesterday never was and tomorrow never would be. It was now that counted. On with the mask and flippers and off into the Technicolor bay to set you dreaming. Later, back to land, as the mood came on for a snack of squid or a paella that had been simmering since morning and, if you liked, a toke. There was nothing furtive about it. Wherever you visited, there was Fundador and wine on the table, and a mortar and pestle filled with green or brown Moroccan for you to take or leave as you pleased.

"For me, it wasn't the hands of my wristwatch as it was for you just now. It was the clock tower of the cathedral at the high point of the old Port of Ibiza. I was sitting at Clive's Bar on the embankment, inundated by the latest trippers like myself off-loading from the ship that had just docked from Barcelona, and I was gazing up at the cathedral, a thousand years old, with its foundations begun in pre-Christian times, back to the Phoenicians, probably even before that. How can I say? I smoked a joint sitting there. A resounding gong went off from the cathedral tower that broke through the noise of the street. New arrivals swirled around me. I had, all right, a quasi-epiphany. All this fevered rush was charging through time without end. The clock tower wasn't summoning these hordes to prayer as once it had done. It was mocking them. It was saying: 'You innocents are lost. Your past has gone. You have no future. There is no time coming. Only now, only the gong you hear now. This moment. Outside that ... de nada. Nowhere to go.'"

I broke in: "So you had a downer and went morbid."

He pinned me with his dark eyes and said nothing for a moment. Then: "Don't you sometimes want to end it all?"

"No, I bloody well don't."

"That's what I like about you, JJ. Sunny side up. But it's funny, isn't it? We both got hit by the freakiness of time. Maybe that's what pot does. Maybe it gives people a glimpse into the sham of time, forces them to look at events from way beyond. *Sub specie aeternitatis.* If that's what it does, it explains why the control freaks who run the engines of industry and the big machines of politics and religion are so shit-scared of the green, no?"

The bright colours returned. The glass I was drinking from shimmered. The draught tasted not like cigarettes and sour malt at all, but like honey. "I think you're right for once, Lennie," I said. "I think a little of this stuff could change the world." Then I broke out giggling. When I quietened down, lusting for a peanut butter sandwich, Lennie took a sharp turn.

"Are you having a good sex life?" Except for fraternity boys swaggering in beer parlours, nobody I knew talked about their sex life in those days, certainly not superannuated basketball players. I thought of sex as a private matter. I don't recall even Delia and I talking to each other about it, not explicitly, not in an analytical way, not at that time. All that came later.

I shrugged my shoulders in confusion. He spread his hands out as if he were pressing them to a window:

"Look, a person has to bring these things into the light. Otherwise the birds quit singing. See, that's Angela's problem. She just clams up. I tell her to remember what it was like when we travelled Europe. She was a panther let out of a cage. One morning in Rome, in the tiny roof garden of a hotel called The Three Nuns just up from the Spanish Steps (it was a stone's throw from where Keats died), we had just made love and come out for food. Shafts of sunlight came poking through foliage and left leafy patterns on the tablecloth. There were hot rolls and cold butter and fresh strawberries and cream and café latte. We spoke hardly a word. We sat looking about, waiting for the sap to rise, touching hands. The old waiter never took his eyes off us. He stood quietly by, smiling to himself, like an aging lover pleased to be reminded.

"When we hit Ibiza, it got even better, I think now because of the pot. It's true what you hear. Pot's an aphrodisiac. It takes you right out of yourself, up and beyond into what feels like the rhythm of the cosmos. It was so good, it was scary. It made me wonder: Is this it? The high point? Will life ever be this astonishing again?"

Why was he telling me all this? Was he boasting? Was he confessing? About what?

"Then something changed for us," he said. "Maybe it was the freedom, the sensual extravagance, that became too much for Angela. A shadow fell, not just the shadow of that evil old goblin of a father of hers, but of the whole imprint of her past. Maybe it was the pot. Maybe we went too far. If I try to bring the subject up she leaves the room. She doesn't want me near her. You know how I distrust shrinks. I'm starting to wonder if a shrink might be a good idea for her, that's how bad it is. I suggested it to her and she looked at me as if I were crazy. That look she gave me! It got me to write a poem I called 'Ghost Town'.

> Such bright flashes
> Of passion
> Dazzle the vision
> With Klondikes of love
> Then the boarding up of windows
> The nailing shut of doors
> The thistledown
> Blowing down
> Ghost town streets
> The incendiary memory
> Of the last fresh start
> At the first bright flash in the pan
> Of your fool's gold heart

I wasn't surprised Lennie wrote poetry. Most of us did whether we confessed to it or not. It didn't always seem so great after the job was done but it felt necessary at the time, like masturbation. We just didn't talk about it much.

"This is good, Lennie," I said. "This is a fine poem." I felt silly. I should have come up with higher praise because it was a damn good poem, and there I was sounding like Earnest Hemingway in a fit of understatement. It didn't matter. Lennie suddenly pointed to the wall of the Pilot that faced him over my shoulder.

"Sonovabitch, see what it is?" he said. I turned round to where he pointed. It was a four-foot by twenty-foot long mural that I hadn't paid particular attention to when we came in. I studied the wall, seeing only what looked like chaos in Technicolor.

"Vomit?" I said.

"No, you dumb cluck, it's a naked woman. See, the guy has covered the girl in acrylic and rolled her like a rolling pin across the canvas."

I pretended admiration: "Now there's a lovin' woman for you, not to mention an artistic breakthrough of astonishing power."

It was a mural by one of the lesser Pilot Tavern artists, and it marked the moment, for me, of psychedelia bursting through the orderly decor of the '50s. Looking there on the tavern wall, for a blazing moment I was sure I saw the future. We drank up and went home. It was the prelude to many a night at the Pilot Tavern.

Next afternoon we headed for our first graduate seminar with Norhrop Frye. What I knew about him was that people were calling *The Anatomy of Criticism* the modern equivalent of Aristotle's *Poetics*, and that Lennie had read *Fearful Symmetry* when he was in Ibiza and had raved about it ever since as one of the best critical studies ever done.

All this made me imagine Frye as a tall, Abraham Lincoln type, like that other famous Canadian nonconformist, John Kenneth Galbraith. But Frye was a foot shy of Galbraith and didn't look like Abraham Lincoln at all. His body was slight, topped with a plume of wavy, butter-coloured hair. He was maybe in his late forties, looking younger, and yet older too in the way his face was composed of semicircles–the chin, the cheeks, the eyebrows, the lines in the forehead, the swirl of the hair. It was a face that if you squinted at produced a Picasso. The eyes were what held you. I imagined the right one a blue searchlight, expectantly scanning the crowd for signs of life; the left one, half hooded by a drooping eyelid, the critical eye ... analytic, ironic, lethal to hypocrites and fools.

Frye stood behind a chair, holding it by the back, its seat facing forward, rocking it gently. He had no lecture notes, just a copy of Blake he set on the podium and never returned to. He surveyed the room for a good half-minute without a word. I had heard he was shy, but that wasn't it. The impression he gave was of a superlative musician who had committed himself to perform at a municipal social function and was going to do his level best not to condescend. The lecture was being taped by the Robarts library archives so I was able to access it later on. Tilting dangerously forward over his chair back, he began.

"Those of you wanting to become acquainted with Blake will, I warn you, have to know something about at least two other things, not about the mystic or occult traditions as you may have been led to believe, but about Milton and the Bible. I expect that most of you know Milton well, or you would certainly not have been admitted to this graduate school by our formidably Miltonic chairman, Professor Woodhouse.

"And I suspect that a lot of you, Christians or crypto–Christians, will be passingly familiar with Biblical stories from Sunday school, and the parables of Jesus. Or if you got your Biblical knowledge in Jewish schools, you will no doubt know a lot more about the Old Testament stories, and probably, because of the rigorous standards of Jewish schools, in considerably more depth. All this will help. The poetry of Blake is grounded in the poetry of the Bible, Old and New Testaments, and you can no more understand Blake without the Bible than you could have made sense as an aboriginal a thousand years ago in Tahiti of Picasso's Guenerica while listening to Stravinsky's Firebird."

I felt a thrill go through me. The precision, the clarity, the challenge! I had never heard words put together with such easy grace, not by Carlyle Mayes in high school, not even by John Peter at U of M. And something more–his eyes never looked down. They swept the room from side to side as he spoke, giving the impression that he was attending to each one of us personally; at the same time, that there was nowhere to hide. As he continued, I became aware something brand new was happening, something exhilarating and not a little frightening. Was I smart enough for this? Pay attention Jason!

"Some years ago, as a junior instructor, I found a good deal of difficulty in getting my students to understand what was going on in Blake's most accessible poems, like *Songs of Innocence* and *Songs of Experience*, which I was trying to teach. It was pretty clear to everybody that the difficulty was a lack of knowledge of the Bible. I asked my chairman about this and he said: 'Well, how do you expect to teach Blake to people who don't know a Philistine from a Pharisee?' I was tempted to answer that, given the generally middle class status of my students, that particular distinction would perhaps not be too important for them. What seemed to me missing, whether the student was Catholic, Protestant, Hebrew, Hindu, Buddhist, or Zoroastrian, even whether the student's main interest was literary or not, was an appreciation for some knowledge of the cultural traditions that we've all been brought up in and which we are all conditioned by, every time we draw a breath, whether we realise it or not."

He stopped and waited. "Is everyone with me up to this point?" I felt stunned. The pause that followed seemed endless. I hunkered down while he surveyed the room, clearing his throat. Then, swaying dangerously on the back of his tilted chair with one hand, with the other he formed a hemisphere, as if he were holding an invisible globe and if only you concentrated on it hard enough, you would see a crystal ball, possibly a microcosm of the universe.

"Like it or not, if you are in what we call western civilisation, especially if you were brought up speaking English, then Chaucer and Shakespeare and Milton and Blake are not just your reading materials. They are the expression of what you are, and even more important, what you can be."

I was sitting close to the front. Lennie was near the back. I turned to catch his eye. He saw me, but acknowledged my look with no more than a raised eyebrow, as if afraid to break a spell. Frye moved to the blackboard where he drew boxes and vortices and peaks and graphs and pies and arrows and circles within circles. They were not works of art. To follow him, you had to see the diagrams and labels and charts and squiggles as they proliferated across the blackboard in the context of what he was saying. The words that went with the scrawls were electric. Eventually he set his chalk down, dusted off his hands, resumed his off-balance stance at the back of his chair, and said: "All right then?"

The silence was absolute. What was he waiting for, as he stood poised over his chair back, rocking on his heels? I stole a glance around the room and the looks on peoples' faces covered the spectrum from veneration to dismay. At the back of the room, Lennie was looking at the floor, wearing a smile so broad, his eyes had almost completely disappeared under his eyebrows. It took me back to our first seminar with John Peter at Manitoba, except this time it wasn't fear of being exposed as unworthy that gripped me. It was the feeling that I had just entered a new country and had better get hold of a map before I got lost. On my way home, I stopped at Britnell's bookstore at Yonge and Bloor to buy *Fearful Symmetry* and made my way back to my new home in the Yorkville Towers without stopping at the Pilot Tavern.

Chapter Six

M r. and Mrs. Lennie Boyce found a home. What a coincidence that it
was identical to ours except that ours was a bachelor and theirs was
a one bedroom, one floor above us. "Not that I mind," said Delia. "I like
Angela. And I like a little female company when you guys get yakking. But
do you have a feeling we're being followed?"

"I do," I said. "And I don't think we've heard the last of it. Now they're in
the same building, we may have to cook for them and do their laundry too."

"Great!" said Delia. "Bring me your lame and your halt. I'm a nurse. It's
what I'm trained for."

As it turned out, it wasn't Lennie's collision with A.S.P. Woodhouse
that obliged him to take Nineteenth Century Thought. No one was spared
taking it who had not taken it as an undergraduate at U of T. The course
gave no credit. Woodhouse called it 'make-up'. He was determined to keep
Nineteenth Century British civilization front and centre, no matter what was
going on in the Twentieth Century in the rest of the world, and for the time
being, he had the clout to do it.

I signed up for the Victorian Novel with John Robson, Modern Poetry
with James Endicott, and for Northrop Frye's course on Blake. Lennie congratulated me on the fact that, aside from being in the English language, my
choices had no connection with each other. He joined me for Blake and the
compulsory Woodhouse course, chose Miller McLure's course on Spenser,
and rounded off his dance card with Father Shook's course on Chaucer.
Lennie insisted these were hitching posts only. We must also sit in on Milton
Wilson's Romantic Poetry, Kenneth McLean's course on Eighteenth Century
oddballs like Cowper, Grey, Chesterton and Walpole, J. B. Priestly's course
on Literature and Science, and a lecture series at the Pontifical Institute by

the great Thomist, Etiènne Gilson. Being allowed to audit lectures by just going in and sitting down seemed like a free ticket to a smorgasbord. Lennie and I ran around like kids at a circus, looking for interesting stuff in philosophy and history, not just what we signed up for. We were all over the campus. It gave me something like the adrenalin rush I used to get at the start of a basketball game. Only later did I realize that I was at a place, at that particular time, that was on a level with the best centres for the study of the humanities in the world.

One Saturday after snooker, at which I beat him mercilessly, as I normally did ever since he beat me in Winnipeg by hexing me with the tragedy of Keats, Lennie asked me to help carry a chair home he had bought at Scandia House on Bay Street south of Bloor. It was an elegant thing, a mahogany frame slung with soft black leather. We wrestled it down the street up to his apartment, and he threw himself into it. It was a very expensive chair. I didn't say a word. "Sure, sure, I know," he said. "I'm a hypocrite ... a limousine socialist. But look at it this way. I have no deep urge to surround myself in material splendour. But I do like to have a *few* nice things, just to remind me that there's more than shit in the world, OK? Look around. Am I indulging myself in the spoils of consumerism?"

As there was nothing else in the room but an arborite table, two chrome and plastic chairs, and a dozen cardboard boxes of books, all I could say was: "So how's Angela?"

"Would you believe? I give her a hundred bucks to go buy a really nice pair of shoes on Bloor Street. What happens?" He got up, went into the bedroom, came out with three pairs of cheap shoes from Woolworth's. "Is she doing this to screw up my head, or is she just an innocent?" Before I could answer, a low growl erupted, followed by sounds of someone being tortured.

"Christ, there she goes again," Lennie said.

I tried to make out where the sound was coming from. Lennie zipped his lips shut, hunched up his shoulders, and pointed to the wall. I joined him by the window. By some design flaw I had not noticed in my nearly identical apartment, the cylindrical pillars supporting the building, at the juncture where pillar meets glass wall, left a divider no more than an inch thick. By pressing an ear against the glass next to the pillar, you could hear your neighbour breathing. No need to press at all in this instance. The wails and huffings were primordial, peppered with words in a throaty female growl: "Pliss, yah yah, pliss. Vok me. Oh mine got, vok me more. Vok me. Vok me. Goddam vok me crassy." I could hear a man wheezing and once in a while a groan, but otherwise the man remained a spectre, like radio, his sounds inducing unfettered imaginings. When the sounds stopped, there came the 'click, click, click' of high heels on the parquet floor. The sound was so vivid I imagined a woman wearing nothing but shoes as her footsteps receded and a door closed. What I heard had nothing to do with any lovemaking I knew. It was hilarious and intimidating, and enormously erotic.

"This is what I need right now, right?" Lennie paced back and forth punching his hand. "It goes on without warning. Sometimes it wakes us up at six in the morning. It drives Angela batty. She turns the music up full volume or else gets up and goes out. You know what I'm saying? She's off it right now, anything to do with sex, and we get this stuff through the goddamn wall!"

He stopped pacing and flopped heavily into his new Danish modern chair. With a resounding crack, it collapsed beneath him and sent him crashing to the floor. "God dammit," he roared. "Doesn't anybody have any pride? Doesn't anybody care about making anything that will hold up until tomorrow? Not even the fucking Danes?"

We carried the chair back to Scandia House, where they pointed out it was just a faulty wooden dowel and they would fix it. It was mid-afternoon by the time we got back to the Towers. Going up in the elevator, we were joined by a gorgeous woman. She looked to be in her early thirties, dressed by Bloor Street's Creeds or Holt Renfrew. Her manner smacked of the haughty narcissism of a pampered mannequin. She was all fantasy. Her face, her hands, her legs were finely cast. Yet she was unquestionably flesh. In the elevator, I looked upward so as not to be seen gawking at her. Lennie did the same. We couldn't hazard a glance at each other for fear of letting go with some dumb gesture like rolling our eyes. All three of us stood motionless, heads tilted back, eyes skyward, as if ascending to some longed for objective. No one punched a button.

"Vat vloor pliss?" the lady asked, in a voice so gutturally rich it made me jump.

"Seven!" I blurted. When I got off, leaving Lennie to rise to the eighth floor with his newly identified neighbour, my last impression was of a woman fussing with unwieldy shopping bags and a man wearing a frozen grimace as the elevator door clamped shut.

Chapter Seven

Several days later, I joined Lennie at the King Cole Room in the basement of the Park Plaza, a respectably grungy pub in the otherwise up-scale hotel. He came in with a new acquaintance and introduced him as Mike Nader, a graduate student at the Pontifical Institute where Etiènne Gilson lectured. Because of the Institute's connection with the Catholic population at St. Michael's College, a sizeable complement of American Catholics came there to pursue its offerings in philosophy and theology (aka Augustine and Aquinas). Mike spoke with a slightly non-Canadian accent, so I asked: "American?"

"Lebanese/Croatian/American to be exact."

"New Yorker then?"

"Nope, Detroit."

"So medieval studies, right?"

"Nope again. Ezra Pound."

"Jesus, I've got to get *something* right. Who knows Pound at St. Mike's?"

"Marshall McLuhan."

"McLuhan's a Catholic?"

"A convert. Worst kind."

"Let me guess, Mike. You drink Budweiser."

"No. Molson Canadian."

It was as if simultaneously we realised that I sounded like an inept inquisitor and he an evasive apostate in the dock. His eyes, suspicious at first, turned merry, and we laughed at each other. As we placed our orders, Lennie leaned in and said to Mike, "Tell him." With a sigh (Mike seemed embarrassed by the attention), he explained that he had been writing to Ezra Pound and it was Pound who advised him to study with McLuhan if he wanted to do a thesis on the *Cantos*.

"You mean you actually correspond with Ezra Pound?" I said. "And he actually writes back?"

"Off and on. I was beginning to feel my letters to him were pretty lame stuff. I told him I was sorry for wasting his time. This is what he wrote back." Mike handed me the letter:

> Dear Nader:
>
> Please refrain from apologetics. I live on the contents of my post bag.
>
> Yours faithfully,
>
> E P
> St. Elizabeth's Hospital
> Washington, DC

"Holy shit!" I was awe-struck. I didn't even know Pound was still alive. Would I ever have thought of writing T.S. Eliot or W.H. Auden or Robert Lowell to ask where I should go to study their work? This Mike was a new kind of character. As I handed the letter back to him, Lennie gave me a saucy sideways glance, which I read to mean: "Look what I found!"

"Mike's joining the Frye course," Lennie said.

"How does Blake fit in with Pound?" I asked.

"That's what I'm asking myself," Mike said. "What Frye says about archetypes is what grabbed me. Pound started as an imagist and became something else. I think Frye's stuff can open up things Pound was trying to do."

"Also," Lennie broke in, "you know how Pound is seen these days as a traitor for his pro-fascist broadcasts for Mussolini, as a screwball economist, a haywire eccentric, and now a tourist attraction at St. Elizabeth's loony bin in Washington. In fact, Mike here may shortly be charged for un-American activities for daring to consort with Pound." Lennie was enjoying himself. Mike let it pass with a grin and a shrug.

"The thing is," Mike said, "Pound thought an upstart like Mussolini might transform the degenerate economy of Italy that began with usury and the Medicis in the Fifteenth Century–the embryo of capitalism–and flowered with the Mafia. Redistributing property and restoring workers to the land and so forth might be the cure. That's how Pound's *Cantos* were supposed to culminate–in a rebuilding of the earthly paradise. *The Cantos* aren't finished. They never will be. Pound wrote the *Pisan Cantos* while incarcerated by the American Army in a gorilla cage after the war. Frye's got a lot to say about that, too, about the gulf between the poet as only too human and the poet as visionary. Maybe it's a mistake to work for paradise in a fallen world, unless you can take the whole world with you."

Lennie was enjoying what I suppose was a wide-eyed look on my face. I liked Mike. Raising his glass, Lennie said: "Oh, what a world of profit and delight is promised to the studious artisan, right JJ?" I knew the line. It was Marlowe's Dr. Faust speaking, the prototype of Renaissance ambition, the man for whom even the favours of Cleopatra ("the face that sank a thousand ships") were insufficient, the man who wanted it all, and sold his soul to the devil to get it. Mike didn't strike me as the kind of man who would do that. Whether Lennie would or not was another matter.

Rolling home from the King Cole Room some time after sensible people had left, Lennie and I stopped at the Pilot Tavern for a nightcap. Until we sat down, he didn't say much. He hurried down a draught, let out a great puff of air, and pulled one of his surprises.

"How long have I known you, JJ?"

"Two years?"

"Mike believes in God. Do you?"

"Jesus, Lennie, grown-ups don't talk about these things," I said. Who would ask such a question point blank and so late at night?

"Don't give me that prissy shit," Lennie said. "Maybe we die tomorrow. Maybe Kruschev's big bomb goes boom. What are you going to do with all your 'what grownups talk about and what they don't' stuff then?" He looked offended. Then he smiled. He was good at that–giving you a jab, then suddenly looking like the world's most fascinated listener.

"I grew up in the United Church," I said. "In case you don't know, it's a Canadian variety of Protestantism long after Protestants ceased to protest. But no one ever told me what my theology was supposed to be when I was a kid, so I had a very scanty notion of God."

"Did you pray and things like that?"

"I remember sitting for a long time in a church in Saskatchewan at my grandfather's funeral. I prayed as fast as I could because I knew the ladies had made fried chicken in the church basement. I could smell them cooking, real chickens from the farm, fried in real farm butter. By the time I was ten, I realized that my dad didn't go to church. He and my mother may have had words about it, but they never reached my ears. It seemed a natural thing. Women went to church. A few men went along to sing in the choir. Dad didn't sing.

"On Sundays kids were siphoned off downstairs for Sunday School. They might have come up with a better name. Since we hated school Monday to Friday, why should we be expected to like another school on Sunday? But I did like it because of my Sunday school teacher, Mrs. Marsh. She gave us each a card with five star beams radiating from the bottom. Each had a name—*The Lord's Prayer, The Ten Commandments, The Books of the Bible: New Testament, The Books of the Bible: Old Testament* and *The 23rd Psalm.*"

"Ah, the love of poetry," said Lennie.

"When we could perform one of these for her by rote, she gave us a star to stick in the blank above the appropriate star beam, and she had us over to her home Sunday afternoon for cinnamon buns and hot chocolate. If I close my eyes and concentrate, I can not only taste the buns, I can still do the Ten Commandments (long form as they were called then, not the measly abridged version) and for some reason I can rattle off all the crazy sounding books of the Old Testament, though oddly not the far easier New Testament books beyond Mathew, Mark, Luke, and John who went to bed with their britches on. Nothing I remember motivated me religiously more than Mrs. Marsh's stars and cinnamon buns. According to Mrs. Marsh, Jesus loved me because the Bible told me so, and God was his father who saw the little sparrows fall."

"So everything made sense to you, you pampered little sparrow," said Lennie.

"Not for long. When I turned thirteen, after my mother had *battled* cancer (as they cloyingly put it) for three years, she died a hard death. Living close to her over that period, day in and day out, I lost whatever belief I had in any kind of god. That was at the same time newsreels came out, even in our distant northern outpost, showing stacks of human carcasses and furnaces of skeletons. I was less stunned by these images than my friends were.

Atrocity wasn't as incomprehensible to me as it seemed to them. I figured if God let the pain happen that happened to my mother, he couldn't be all that concerned about suffering in the rest of the world either."

"You sound like Raskolnikov," said Lennie. "He killed the old money lender just to see if God would punish him."

"What wasn't possible was for me to believe any longer in a god that they told me saw little sparrows fall. That was the first of a hundred lies. As I grew older, and read a bit, I began to see what a delusion the idea of a god is, maybe not a god in the form of a prime mover, but certainly a god that had anything to do with the events we call human history. Stuck with history's unbroken panorama of war and carnage, I couldn't understand how people could be so dumb as to swallow the notion of what they called a 'loving' god. I knew people want one. No question about that. So maybe it's not unforgivable gullibility that's to blame. Maybe, I thought, it's something forgivable, people's longing to be loved and protected from above, and their consequent acceptance of a fantasy, but of course that doesn't change anything. However universal the longing, delusion remains delusion.

"By the time I got to university I didn't particularly blame God for the Slaughter of the Innocents or the Holocaust or Hiroshima or for my mother's suffering and death. But I decided I had no use for a god who was incapable of intervening in such things. I can't say my view of the matter has changed much since then."

"So you worked it all out. No fairness, no God."

"The idea that there is something like fairness governing things seems pretty puerile to me. Look at history. Anyway, I never asked anyone else to think the way I do."

Lennie sat hunched for a moment, then straightened up, pulled his hands away from his face and grinned. "You know what, JJ?" he said. "I can't say I entirely disagree with you. I side with the Enlightenment when Voltaire and the boys did away with cockeyed superstitions and taboos and oracles. They had no use for manna from heaven, or feeding the multitude with a few loaves and fishes, or raising Lazarus from the dead, let alone walking on water. But I never liked the engineer Deity they replaced God with either. He showed no sign of caring about humanity one way or the other, just as you say. But what I hold onto is the *possibility* of a god of concern. What I mean is a god in the making who, as some philosophers and Blake say, is imminent, a latency, a divine embryo. Nietzsche said God is dead, by which I think he meant traditional ideas of God are dead. He also said 'man is the unfinished animal who finishes himself'. So maybe god isn't 'out there' anymore, but 'in here', a potentiality, the way a pine tree is in an acorn. Cripes, that's Aristotle! But in a different way. It's what the existentialists mean when they say existence precedes essence, not the other way around in the old Platonic sense, not essence precedes existence. God did not create man. Man, against heavy odds, may be in the process of trying to create God. Yes, I think I'm at least tentatively that kind of existentialist, not fully fledged, but not a forlorn atheist like you either, JJ."

I thought I saw what was going on. Lennie led me into saying something private about myself that would give him an excuse to say something private. I felt no resentment. How could I? To the extent that I understood what he was saying about man and God, I had no disagreement. Also, I suspected that Lennie's ideas didn't become fully real to him until he could speak them out loud and it was no great hardship for me to sit and listen to them.

Chapter Eight

The note on Marshall McLuhan's office door on St Joseph's Street read: "Dr. McLuhan is on Sabbatical but will continue to hold his informal Monday night seminars as he is available. Those wishing to join please deposit one sentence giving their reason."

Mike Nader thought McLuhan might need reminding and wrote: "I wish to attend because you are my thesis advisor for Ezra Pound." I wrote: "I've just read *The Mechanical Bride*. Have I missed the wedding?" Lennie told us he wrote: "I'm looking for a teacher who can unravel the mystery of metaphor". A few days later I received a phone call from a secretary instructing me to go to the home of Professor McLuhan at 29 Wells Hill Avenue, near Casa Loma, Monday at 7:30 PM.

Lennie, Mike Nader and I splurged on a taxi, and joined two dozen others crammed into the front room of McLuhan's far from capacious two-story family home. The numbers swelled by four or five as McLuhan's kids, ranging from thirteen on down, kept popping up and disappearing like a colony of gophers. We didn't look like a graduate seminar. McLuhan, a stringy and handsome six-foot-two, with a literary moustache, could also have passed for a cowboy in the Gary Cooper mould. He invited us to introduce ourselves. Anthropologist Ted Carpenter, well-known as an advocate of de-institutionalized education and a cohort of McLuhan, muttered his name and gave a folksy wave. A boy and a girl of uncertain adolescence said they were beatniks, and proved it with sockless ankles and matching hair-styles. A sallow young man who wore a guitar and looked like Bob Dylan gave a drowsy nod. A man in long short pants with knee socks, who looked like an Eagle Scout, gave a perky salute and announced he was seeking a fresh outlook. Sheila Watson was there, whom I recognised as the author of a highly regarded poetic novel of the West called *The Double Hook*. A dapper little man with a three-day shadow and a slur reported that he had just handed in his executive washroom key at the advertising firm of Caulfield/Brown and that he had come because he was looking for reality. Stanley Burke, an announcer who read the national TV news on CBC, was there, also a professional magician wearing a cape, a dark-haired, bespangled fortune-teller, an Inuit carver from Igloolik, and a popular wrestler called Whipper Billy Watson. The rest of us looked more or less like graduate students.

McLuhan led off talking about movies. "Film is high definition. You don't have to fill in the blanks, so you're detached and can think critically. Radio, telephone–they give you less to go on, and you have to enhance the message at least partly with your own story. But they're still relatively hot. At the far end of the spectrum is TV. It's cool, low definition, so you're completely absorbed by it. I'm not talking about pictures here, which is what we are taught to think movies and TV have in common. I'm talking about the kind of patterns in which information is organized. Visual information is lineal and sequential, the way we see this way or that. Auditory information is simultaneous and resonating, the way we hear. We can see only one field at a time, but we can hear many things at once, and even around corners. That's why film is an eye medium and TV an ear medium."

Looking around, I noticed eyes widening, others gazing into the mid-distance, and a few faces with hugely satisfied grins. But I felt most of the people in the room shared the question I wanted to ask: "What the hell are you talking about?" Before anyone could butt in too much, McLuhan went on to talk about the dots shot out at us from the electron tube from inside the TV screen. "The mosaic this bombardment produces, at 30 frames per second, each frame with 520 dots, tricks our perceptual apparatus into thinking we are seeing pictures. This makes huge demands on our attention to decipher the input, and if we are not alert to its cajolery, it can virtually suck us in." From that point on, as with the all-enveloping character of sound McLuhan associated with ear culture, he gushed fragments of percepts in a downpour.

> The phonetic alphabet fell like a bombshell on tribal man.
> The printing press hit him like a hydrogen bomb. Now
> we've been blitzkrieged by TV.

Why should the sending or receiving of a telegram seem more dramatic than even the ringing of a telephone?

The horseless buggy was the only way people could describe the automobile. Families whose wealth was based on carriages and buggy whips soon went bankrupt. Horsepower moved from animals into cars.

The wheel extends the foot in an automobile. In this way the wheel amplifies the power and speed of the foot, but at the same time it amputates. In the act of pressing the gas pedal, the foot becomes so specialized it no longer performs its original function, which is to walk.

If the wheel is an extension of the foot, then money is an extension of muscle, radio an amplification of the human voice, and the hydrogen bomb an outgrowth of fingernails.

What do you think Hitler meant when he said: "I go my way with the assurance of a sleepwalker?

Lennie stirred on his cushion. "That's a tribal witch-doctor speaking," he piped up. "Spirit possession. Like an Indian shaman transmitting from the unconscious reservoir of folk memory. The medium is the spoken word, but for Hitler the spoken word magnified through radio and loud speakers. It fits, doesn't it, with the Nazi notion of the 'herrenvolk', where the crowd is concentrated into a single animal. Hitler the spellbinder, a banal but not a stupid man, and the anaesthetised mob before him glued into a single mass, like the screaming, mind-stunned fans at a rock concert. I would say it means something like that, if what you say about the nature of acoustic space is correct."

McLuhan said nothing for a moment, looking Lennie over. Then he broke into a laugh and said: "Oh, I don't know about correct, Mr. . . . ?

"Boyce, sir."

"Ah, the Boyce in quest of the workings of metaphor. Well, you needn't think me correct or incorrect, Mr. Boyce. I'm distrustful of secular certainties. At any rate, look here, if it turns out you don't like my acoustic percept, well I've plenty more available for you to try on."

The evening went like that. We walked home. It was only a half-mile from Casa Loma down Well's Hill and Spadina to St. George Street for Mike, and a few blocks farther on to Yonge and Bloor for Lennie and me. It was a balmy October evening, damp, a mist hovering, with frog-like ships' horns croaking from the seaway. Nobody said anything for a while as we walked. Finally Lennie said: "I don't trust the bugger. I think he's having us on."

"I think he's trying to tell us to take pop culture seriously," Mike said. "I've seen it coming. Because of how fast everything is moving, artists are saying we don't have to wait a hundred years to look back for understanding. If we pay attention, we can see who we are right now, while our lives are unfolding. It's what Pound meant about the poet being the antennae of the race. Hey, I'm a Jesuit, right? Well, Basilican, now I'm here at U of T. I'm steeped in Augustine and Aquinas, aren't I? Logic and discursive reason are my stock in trade. But they're no damned use in trying to understand Ezra Pound or Mondrian, or the Twentieth Century, when you come right down to it. That's what I like about McLuhan. His mind works like Pound's, jumping from one idea cluster to another, challenging you to find your own connections, and sometimes driving you nuts because maybe there are no connections at all, like the stories in a newspaper."

"I don't like it," I said. "I don't like it at all. It's incoherent. There's no informing structure. No organization or line of grace. So I'm a dinosaur cub. Calf? What the hell's the word for a baby dinosaur, a theropod? I don't like Dadaism or surrealism or abstract expressionism or stream of consciousness ... the easy way out. Give me good old sense over nonsense any day."

Lennie and Mike exchanged glances. For a moment, I felt like the kid in the group who said "no thanks" when everyone else was smoking. Then I let it go and so did they.

"What I *do* like about McLuhan," Lennie said, "is how he keeps shifting the ground. You follow him, think you've landed, and whoosh, you're off again. It gets your noggin churning. It's not structured, but it's not chaotic either. How about his idea that one sense extended can change the world? When Galileo saw the solar system through the telescope, the Ptolemaic universe became defunct. Fifteen hundred years of neat and serviceable metaphor for the cosmos–good enough for Dante and Donne and even Shakespeare–was shattered by a glass lens that amplified the eye. If that's possible, maybe there are other technologies that can completely redo our way of seeing, make us all poets and visionaries. Drugs for instance."

We were nearly home. I could feel it coming on, Lennie's fixation on the dynamics of metaphor had suddenly made a connection with McLuhan's world of the percept. I didn't feel up to an all-night session so I tried a diversion that would let me peel off home without dishonour. I said. "When I played basketball in Manitoba I drove a 1932 Model B Ford I picked up from a farmer for $75. It ran like a top. With a big battery for four small cylinders, it started without a crank at 30 below zero. Whatever McLuhan says, I personally have nothing against Henry Ford and the assembly line."

Kidding now, Mike said: "It's all right for you guys. *You've* never had to *work* on an assembly line. We Detroit kids are expected to spend our lives there."

"Yah, right," I said. "And who dug the filthy iron out of the ground in Algoma to feed Ford's assembly line?"

"Boys, boys," said Lennie. "If you're going to carry on about how hard up you were as depression babies, I have no choice but to enlighten you about true deprivation. When I was a boy, to keep up appearances, my mother made me go sit in the outhouse twice a day to make our neighbours think we'd had something to eat."

On that uplifting note we parted without further probing of the McLuhan perplex for the time being.

Chapter Nine

Lennie got tickets and he and Angela and Delia and I went to *Waiting For Godot*. It was a modest production mounted by the Crest Theatre group in the old CBC radio studio on Parliament Street. At intermission, the audience of about eighty avant-gardes milled about, smoking in the dark in the back lane behind the studio. A motorcycle cop pulled up and gave us the eye. His radio crackled as he reported in, and the faint voice of his dispatcher responded. The cop called out to us: "What are you folks doing out here?" Without a pause, Lennie shot back: "We're waiting for Godot". The crowd let go with its first real belly laugh of the night, finally something that made sense. As we got ready to return to the performance, butting cigarettes, I heard the cop talking into his radio:

"They say they're waiting for someone called Godot. Should I stick around and see if he shows up?"

When the play was over, we walked to Murray's Restaurant on Bloor and Avenue Road and ordered coffee and flapper pie. Delia was first to speak: "That character shouting gibberish-what the hell was that all about?" I was baffled by the play too but didn't want them to know.

"I think it's about advertising," Lennie said, "about the way a might-have-been poet has his imagination corrupted by the propaganda system of merchandising and ends up spouting bafflegab."

"I wish I knew where you got that crap from," Angela said. It was all she said. Everyone got tense. It was pretty clear there was more bothering her than *Waiting for Godot*.

"He made it up," I said. "Pay no attention to him. He's just practising to become a drama critic. Lennie will make a great drama critic. Drama critics say whatever comes to mind that will make them sound clever." I didn't want to see a domestic squabble in Murray's Restaurant.

When we got home, Delia asked what was going on with Angela. Aside from the wedding and the say-goodbye party at Peter Coultry's on the Winnipeg River, I had seen little of her. I told Delia she knew as much as I did. Which wasn't true. But I couldn't go blurting out what Lennie told me about his and Angela's torrid summer in Europe, and for sure nothing about the temptation scene in Ibiza. That's the trouble with confidences. I never wanted to know about Lennie's private life in the first place. Because when he talked about it, it embarrassed me? Yes. Because I envied his orgiastic junket through Europe? Absolutely. Because hearing of his romps had a certain pornographic appeal? I'll admit to that too. But now I wished he had kept all this stuff to himself, because now here I was in a situation where I had no choice but to tell on him or lie to Delia.

"Why don't you ask Angela?" I said.

"Maybe I will," Delia said. "I like her. I sympathize with her. But there's a lot boiling in there. I'll be honest. I'm not infatuated with Lennie. He's your friend. I can take him. But if you don't mind my saying, he's a bit bent somewhere. As for that play with that Didi and Gogo and the rest flouncing around and squawking like chickens, I mean, for goodness sake, Jason, what the hell, spare me that kind of shit will you please?" This was one of the things I liked about Delia. She hardly ever said things I felt a great need to argue about.

Lennie asked me to help carry his prized Danish chair home now that it was repaired. The door at Scandia House was locked. After we did some rattling, a large man, wearing what looked like motorcycle goggles, opened the door a crack to report that Scandia House was in receivership. Lennie said he was sorry to hear that, but he had come to pick up a chair he had bought and brought back for repairs.

"Don't matter," the man said. "Nothin' goes out."

"It's paid for," Lennie said, and held up his receipt. "It's my chair. I just brought it back for them to fix it."

"Tough bananas, bud," the man said. "Nothin' goes out." He closed the door, and disappeared into the back of the shop. Lennie hammered on the window. I half-pulled, half-talked him away before he did something crazy.

For the time being, that chair became a Spenglerian symbol for the decline of the West.

A week later, after Northrop Frye's seminar, the so-called 'Winnipeg Mafia' convened in the Arbour Room in Hart House. Lennie didn't like the term because, he said, it smacked of exclusivity and he went out of his way to have others join us. Women still weren't allowed in Hart House, so it was an all-male table. Joining the four of us from Manitoba were Mike Nader, a Japanese grad student called Ken Takasuki, and an Oxford and a Harvard man.

As on every Thursday afternoon, I was still a bit distracted by trying to absorb Frye's lecture, which made complete sense to me in his presence, but the details of which faded away shortly afterwards the way dreams do as you wake up. It took me a moment to register the fact that someone was not only unimpressed with the class we had just left, but was actually putting it down. It was the Harvard man.

"What about it?" he was saying. "You've all tried to read Blake's so-called prophesies–*America, The Four Zoas, Milton, Jerusalem.* Can you seriously swallow all that solipsistic mythology–Orc and Urizen and Enitharmon and Los and god knows what? All that weeping and wailing that goes on, the numbing repetitions of 'desolate mountains rifted furious', and 'black winds of perturbation', and 'vast clouds of blood that rolled round the dim rocks'. Jesus Murphy, spare me the gobbledygook!"

Unexpectedly, Peter Coultry spoke up. I knew that he, like me, was going through something dangerously close to a religious experience in Frye's classes. But he had always been self-effacing, a placid listener. When he expressed himself back in our seminars in Manitoba, he would go red in the face and stammer, as he did now. "I think I know who Orc and Urizen are for Blake", he said. "Orc is youth and energy filled with hope, and Urizen is ... is all the ... tyrants, parents, and advisors ... the people who think they know everything and want to run everyone else's life."

Harvard seemed barely to hear Peter and turned to our Mark Woodward who commanded more respect, not just because he was older than Peter, but because his English accent, even if fraying at the edges by now, retained vestiges of transatlantic prestige. "What about it, Woodward?" Harvard said. "We've all read *Fearful Symmetry*, and of course, that's the book, ain't it? That's the open sesame to Blake, and purportedly to everything else, not so?"

There was a long silence. I knew Mark, my one-time flat mate back in Winnipeg, well enough to suspect he was preparing his riposte carefully. That was his way. He loved short, pithy sayings and worked hard to create his own. Chaucer's 'The life so short/The craft so long to learn', Pope's 'Brevity is the soul of wit', Flaubert's 'le *mot juste*', Pater's 'to burn with a hard gemlike flame', Wilde's 'how do I know what I mean until I hear what I say'. Felicitous expressions like these were close to Mark's heart and he regularly tried for them. Spontaneous effusion was not his way. His carefully crafted verbal pronouncements may have been what made him a stylish enough prose writer to have sold "Blitzkrieg Days" to the New Yorker.

"When I first started to read *Fearful Symmetry*," Mark finally said, "I did what I've always done with important works of non-fiction that I felt I might have reason to remember sometime in the future. I underlined cogent passages with a pencil. After ten pages of *Fearful Symmetry* I realized that I had underlined every line. At that point I put my pencil down and have not marked a line since. I now simply consider the whole book underlined."

Everyone laughed. Harvard, for a moment, seemed unsure where to go. He may not have wanted the job, but it was clear that for now the table was his. "Well, Frye's a real problem," he said, "all those archetypes–heroes from across the sea, grail questers, hanged gods, mothers seeking their daughters in the underworld, girls wanting a dick like their dad's, and boys yearning to return to their mother's womb. Half a century ago, we got all that stuff from Fraser and Freud, didn't we, and from Jung and his collective unconscious?

"Trouble is it leaves no room for individual creativity, does it? All this schematisation of myths and symbols corrals inspiration, boxes it in, smothers it. Where's distinctiveness? Where's poetic invention? If all you're doing is juggling archetypes, Humpty Dumpty falling off a wall–the egg that once broken can't be reconstituted even by all the kings' men–well, that's on a par with King Lear divvying up his kingdom, isn't it? *Mary Had a Little Lamb* is just another version of the Virgin Mary and Jesus. The whole archetypal pigeon-holing is like farting Annie Laurie through a key hole, damn clever, but what's the point?"

"I can't credit your simile," broke in our Oxford man." We all continued to pay homage to Oxford and Harvard, and of course Cambridge and Princeton and Yale, as the great standard bearers of humanist studies, but we tried not to grovel in their presence. We could even stand back and be amused when they got too puffed up. So here was an event to behold. It was like watching Oxford row against Harvard and secretly hoping both sculls would capsize.

"What bothers me about what you say," said Oxford, "is your reference to farting Annie Laurie through a keyhole. That's from Joyce Cary's *The Horse's Mouth*, in which the hero, Gully Jimson, lives by what he and Joyce Cary, however misguidedly, imagine to be the revolutionary artistic credo of William Blake. So you see, you can't possibly use Gully's line to disparage Blake who is Gully's spiritual mentor. In doing so, you completely undermine your rejection of archetypal criticism."

"Well puh–lease," said Harvard. "Do you guys from Oxford need footnotes for everything said in informal discourse?"

"Authenticity," said Oxford. "Just evidence that you're speaking from what can be verified, not from make-believe."

Harvard handled it well. I didn't like his cocksureness, or his Ivy League airs, but he had guts. "Let's get down to it, my friends," he said. "Frye has this notion that there is a universal language of metaphor most fully articulated in the Bible and dominant or recessive in all literature, the magic at the heart of words as it were, and that the dynamics of this cryptic core of meaning went unrecognized until its discovery at the end of the Eighteenth Century by an obscure and eccentric London engraver called William Blake.

"Not only that. Blake's 'apocalyptic' world view, to stick with his own vocabulary, went unrecognized in his own time, and was ploughed under for another hundred years, until resurrected by a literary critic in Toronto named Northrop Frye who was a speed typist and once worked as a Methodist preacher on the Canadian prairies. Now I ask you! Is this credible? Come on, Nader, help me out here!"

"Well if you're asking me to defend the American flag, I can't do that," Mike said. He had been twirling his thumbs until then, a Detroit boy clearly uncomfortable with his countryman's New England bravado. "But I say we should tread with care here. Personally, I don't mind saying Frye is the most astonishing teacher I've so far come across, but there's always a problem with apostles, the Frydalogues, the Frygians, the Small Frye, the Frye-Babies, and so on. I ran into a few of them before I came here. They bothered me with their archetypal certainties, like reborn Christians out to convert the unenlightened. I'm with Nietzsche when he says be wary of disciples because what originates in the light has a way of proceeding in the dark. I want to give Frye some time before becoming a proselyte or a debunker. But maybe you shouldn't listen to me. I'm an American Roman Catholic, remember, and Northrop Frye's a Canadian anti-clerical Protestant."

I kept my eye on Lennie. He didn't say a word as he watched the table, his eyes dancing back and forth from speaker to listener, just as once they had back in my first John Peter seminar when Lennie played catalyst. He was sitting across from Harvard and, all at once, he got up and went around to sit beside him, putting his arm around his shoulder. "Let me tell you something, my good fellow," he said. "You're not a bad guy. But the thing is, you're full of shit."

Harvard made to get up out of his grasp, but Lennie held him down. "Don't take offence now, old man," he said. "This is very big stuff we're into here. We've all got to expand our horizons on this one. Not be too know-it-all just because we're smart as hell, know what I mean?"

The table went silent. I thought of the stillness that falls just before a prairie storm when the birds stop singing and (as some people believe) the cows lie down. "Really!" Harvard said. "I mean *really!* I thought we were having a little rational chat here." He was handsome, well turned out, without question well-read, and it was a good bet that anyone who thought they might have a go at him in verbal warfare would end up licking his wounds. But Lennie didn't play by the rules. Maybe it was the same thing that let him maintain his ranking in Nordic Billiards in North End Winnipeg.

"Okay, so you don't dig the nutty names Blake gives his demiurges, and you don't like all their weeping and wailing and moaning about. But look here." Lennie reached for his copy of Blake and thumbed the pages as if looking for a random passage. If I knew Lennie, he would come up with anything *but* a random passage, more like one he had singled out and memorized in anticipation of just such a moment as this. "Here, for example. I'm reading from Book Two of *The Four Zoas*: 'Enion sees not the terrors of the uncertain/And thus she wails from the dark deep; the golden heavens tremble.' All right, I'll grant you that's a bit murky and you might think who the hell is Enion? But look what follows. Do you really have to know where a figure called Enion fits in Blake's pantheon of mental powers to know who's doing the talking here, or the kind of person who's talking?

To hear sounds of love in the thunder storm that destroy our enemy's house;

To rejoice in the blight that covers his field, & the sickness that cuts off his children,

While our olive & vine sing & laugh round our door and our children bring fruits and flowers.

....

Then the groan & the dolour are quite forgotten, & the slave grinding at the mill

And the captive in chains, & the poor in the prison, and the soldier in the field

When the shatter'd bone hath laid him groaning among the happier dead.

It is an easy thing to rejoice in the tents of prosperity:

"I don't find a passage like that at all vague," Lennie went on. "Blake's eyes were so wide open and his shaping powers, what Coleridge called 'esemplastic powers', were so stoked up, he could actually see his visionary world, not just in bursts of insight into a super sensory, numinous beyond as Plato or Plotinus or Shelley did, or Wordsworth when he was young and plucky, but daily and even hourly throughout his life. Imagine! Blake could actually *see* 'infinity in a grain of sand/eternity in an hour'. Now we shouldn't be making fun of someone like that, should we? Remember what the man said: 'You throw the sand into the wind, and the wind blows it back again'. Do you comprehend what I'm telling you here?"

"Okay, okay", Harvard said. "But you're still not answering my opposition to Frye's rage for classification. Why his obsessive schematics, his weird chalk diagrams where he shows the sevenfold story of the tribes of Israel in the Old Testament to be parallel to the sevenfold career of Jesus in the New Testament? And all his numerology about threes and sevens and twenty-eights and the rest? Twelve disciples and Jesus the thirteenth, twelve tribes and the lost thirteenth, twelve months in the year and the apocalypse, twelve hours on the clock and then the end of time, twelve steps to the gallows and the big thirteenth?"

From one of the quieter members of the table, Ken Takasuki, who in those early days was as deeply intrigued and perplexed by Frye's Blake as I was, came a voice just loud enough for everyone to hear: "Thirteen in a baker's dozen."

Harvard waved to Ken's perceived support without missing a beat. "On the subject of pastry, what about Frye's big pie? Cut it four ways, you get comedy, tragedy, romance, and irony. And that about covers it. Right?"

"I think you're getting sucked in," said Lennie. "You're falling for Blake's 'mathematic form' as opposed to his 'living form divine'. Mathematic form is rigid and abstract like the letter of the law. Living form is produced by the human imagination, not by the letter but by the spirit of the law. Categorization is bad only when it diminishes. When it gives a road map through the forests of the night, it's a beacon to follow."

Harvard hesitated. It was all between him and Lennie now. The rest of us had moved into the grandstand. Suddenly, Lennie broke into a huge grin. "You devious bastard," he said, putting his arm around Derek again. "You haven't read the *Anatomy of Criticism*, have you?"

"I haven't," said Harvard. "But I'm familiar with articles in *The Kenyon Review* and *The Hudson Review*, where Frye explains his grounds."

What I had learned from my earliest exposure to the intellectual scrums in Winnipeg was that you must master your evidence or die. Graduate school could be a warm and friendly place. It could also be a shark tank. It was now just a matter of watching Lennie close in for the kill.

"Oh tut, tut," said Lennie. "You should be ashamed of yourself. Pontificating to us without having read the book? You bad boy."

"Look here," said Harvard. "You know as well as I do that archetypal criticism is based on Jung's allegedly primordial storehouse of universal myths and symbols that have endured in the mind since our evolution into consciousness and govern us still in ways we don't understand. Well, I just don't think there *is* a universal language like that. Take that Japanese film, *Hari Kari*, where the hero, played by Toshima Mifune, commits seppuku. The concept of honour through suicide, and the value system and rituals that went with it, worked for the Greeks and Romans, and apparently still work for the Japanese. But there's nothing archetypically human about it. In fact, in the West, we find it atypical and absurd."

He surveyed the table, then turned to Ken Takasuki. "Come on, Ken," he said, "I could use a little support here. What can you tell us about the significance of ritual suicide in Japanese culture, like in the movie when Toshimo Mifune cuts off his top knot before sticking the bamboo sword into his guts?"

"Fucked if I know," said Ken. "I was born in Moose Jaw." Even Harvard burst out laughing, thereby making it possible for all parties to retire without having to lose face and commit suicide.

Walking back to Yorkville Towers, I asked Lennie where he had found time to read *Anatomy of Criticism*, which he had used so effectively to make his case. "I haven't read it," he said. "I saw it sitting in Mike Nader's carrel and I got him to fill me in on the essentials."

"So now we know who the *real* devious bastard is," I said.

"Well shit, JJ. Whoever said a nice bringing-up should guarantee an easy go of it? Somebody had to slow that slick son of a bitch down. He did okay though. He's one tough to-the-manor-born specimen that one is."

"And you're just an innocent little slum bunny from North End Winnipeg totally lacking in breeding."

"You got it, daddy-o." Lennie was laughing as he spoke. Without changing stride, we ducked into the Pilot Tavern and ordered a beer. It was suddenly as if we had walked out of the sunshine into a morgue. Lennie's deep-set eyes all but disappeared in the pub's half-light as he sipped his beer. "Seriously, JJ," he said. "Sometimes I think we are in Paradise right now but lack the creative imagination to know it. Isn't that what Blake is saying?"

"Do you mind explaining, Lennie?"

"It's just what I feel when I listen to Frye opening our eyes about Blake. He makes it sound literally true: "Man has closed himself up, till he sees all things thro' narrow chinks of his cavern.""

Chapter Ten

The *Here and Now Gallery* on Yorkville, run by Dorothy Cameron, and the *Greenwich Gallery* at Bay and Hayter, run by Av Isaacs, were the epicentre of what Lennie saw as the rebirth of Canadian painting. Both galleries soon moved to Yonge Street just up from the Pilot Tavern, with their stables–William Ronald, Harold Town, Jack Bush, Kazuo Nakamura, Tom Hodgson, Michael Snow, Joyce Wieland, Robert Markle, Dennis Burton, Gordon Raynor, Graham Coughtry, and more. On my way home to Yorkville Towers, through the window at the *Here and Now*, I saw some eye-catching canvasses, so I went in to take a look. To my surprise, there stood Angela.

Dorothy Cameron had hired her on the basis of Angela's Fine Arts degree and (as Dorothy admitted) because Angela was an exceptionally attractive woman, which didn't hurt when selling art. It was one of the few times I talked to Angela one-on-one. Wearing a skimpy outfit that showed a lot of elegant neck, milky cleavage, a perfect bum, and silky legs, she stood before me like an emanation of the paintings on the wall. As we chatted, I became aware of a not very abstract canvas just behind her. I distinguished a frilly triangle of lace less than fully concealing a plump and luscious mound of Venus just over Angela's shoulder. It was a Dennis Burton. It was like peeking at Angela in diaphanous underclothes, leaving me in a fit of guilty fantasy, unable to do more than mumble my admiration for the painting. That done, I made my way onward to Britnell's Book store in pursuit of a quite different kind of body, fulfilling a long-time promise to purchase my own copy of Frye's *Anatomy of Criticism*.

Lennie hadn't brought up the subject of Angela recently. His vacillation between secretiveness and unwanted confidences was nothing unusual. The secretiveness tended to have to do with the past; the confidences, with day-to-day things, such as sex. Anyone could see Angela was unhappy. I asked Delia about it: "I saw Angela in Dorothy Cameron's Gallery. She said you two go for coffee?"

There was a pause. Then Delia said: "That Lennie really is a creep, you know. I didn't intend to tell you. I hate all this story-telling about people. But he's your friend and you should know. Before they left Ibiza, there was an incident. They befriended a Dutch woman and her American boyfriend, and they used to go to their place and smoke marijuana. On this day, Angela awoke from her siesta and wandered over to the friend's place. Coming down a ramp from the back, she saw the others inside through the kitchen window and stopped in her tracks. It took a minute for her to register what she was seeing. The boyfriend sat in a chair watching. Lennie lay on his back on the floor and on top of him was the woman's fifteen-year-old daughter, with the mother sitting on the floor beside her, holding the child's hand, for god's sake. I mean, Jesus Christ, what a bunch of perverts. Angela told me she went back to their hotel and was sick. She's still sick about it and I don't blame her. I'll never see your friend Lennie in the same light again. I wish Angela had never told me this, but who else has she got to talk to?"

I considered telling Delia about the letter in which Lennie had told me he had backed off and fled the scene, but then I thought better of it. It would make him look even worse. Not only a sexual predator in Delia's eyes, but a liar to boot.

Why did he lie to me? He must have assumed that, with what he saw as my congenital pudeur, I would automatically condemn him if he told me the truth. So then why bother telling me at all? I could think of only one reason. Having committed the dire act, however differently he would have viewed it from the way Delia or Angela did, he must have felt ambivalent about his complicity. So lying to me let him get my honest opinion, unclouded by what he would have assumed would be my Methodist disapproval had he told me outright what really happened.

Or else he may have thought, if I believed his story about his noble self-denial, I would have abandoned my putative Puritanism and called him a fool for walking away from such an exceptional sexual experience. But then why, after his return to Canada, had he never brought up the letter in which he had falsely reported the episode to me? I could only guess. Does a person feel differently about such things over here than over there? Or maybe he sensed Angela had twigged to something, without realizing she had actually witnessed the act, and he was trying to blot the whole thing out.

"That explains it," I said.

"What do you mean *explains* it?" said Delia. "What explains what?"

"Angela's distress. No wonder ... well, no wonder she's been keeping away from him. Especially if she's never told him she knows what he did."

"No, but she's going to. I told her she has to face him with it."

"You think that's a good idea, I mean, right now? Or any of our business?" I wondered if Delia might be overplaying her calling as care-giver.

"She can't just sit around and let this thing eat her up." Delia paused and gave it some thought. "Jason, if you were put in that situation, what would you have done?"

"Whoa now. I didn't even hear that."

Immediately, of course, I saw myself at the scene of what I was now thinking of as *Lennie's Temptation*. There was all the stuff we saw coming, a new age of sexual liberation, Nietzsche's transvaluation of values and so on. That would have given Lennie a pretext for yielding to mother Faye and her fifteen-year-old daughter. Even in my less than worldly exposure, I'd seen enough European movies to accept the idea that sexual mores were different elsewhere, and I guessed they might be even more so in Indonesia at the end of Dutch rule. But the real point for me was that there was no indication that anything was forced on the girl. The way I heard it, it seemed more like an initiation ceremony. These things went on in other cultures all over the world with even younger girls, didn't they? Who was I to judge? These were all considerations that would get me exactly nowhere with Delia, so I kept them to myself. Anyway, it was all theory. If I'd been there instead of Lennie, what *would* I have done? I expect I would have run away. But maybe I wouldn't have. As I had put it to Lennie in my letter to him in Ibiza, it was all very existential.

Existence, that was my problem. I was reading Kierkegaard and came across a phrase that hit home: "It is perfectly true, as philosophers say, that life must be understood backwards, but they forget the other proposition, that it must be lived forwards." So simple, but not a heartening idea. Lennie's problem when it came to going forward seemed huge compared to Delia's and mine, but we were not entirely exempt. If you're not careful, domesticity can eat you up; so Blake had warned.

Delia worked to pay the rent. Who did the dishes and the laundry? Who got the groceries? Did the cleaning? There were no models, no people I knew of who had lived this way before, the male grown up and still going to school, the female out foraging for sustenance. Our differences were never about who paid for what. We'd known each other as kids, long enough not to grouse about such things as money. I still had a little grubstake from summer guiding, and Delia was bringing in reasonable money from nursing. We were short at times but we barely noticed. We stayed home when we had to and ate Kraft Dinner and read books and made love. There was no battle about who did the cooking. She hated to cook and I enjoyed it.

The real problem had to do with time. Did I work all day while she was working? Taking into account what went on around the coffee table at Hart House, I considered myself as much a worker as she was. So then, why was I always working at night, too, is what she wanted to know. Time *together*, that was the issue. Even when we were home together, where was my head? Was I really there with her or off in some distant world in a book? All of which made for a kind of gnawing uneasiness, although as I realized, Little League compared to Lennie's and Angela's tribulations.

Although I lived on the seventh floor and Lennie a floor above, it had always been *noblesse oblige* that we phone each other before visiting. One afternoon, I broke protocol. On my way up in the elevator, my head dangerously overloaded with Blakean conundrums, I drifted past my floor and found myself on the eighth. When the elevator opened, I was standing in front of Lennie's apartment instead of my own. I went ahead and knocked. He shouted at me to wait, then appeared at the door in his dressing gown.

"Pool?" I said.

"Can't at the moment. I'll give you a call."

"I'll be home."

I wondered at the glazed look on his face and a sound I heard in the background. Then it dawned. The sound was the click of high heels on the parquet floor. So Angela had finally bought the posh shoes Lennie had been so determined she wear, and there she was parading them in front of him, otherwise wearing only the diaphanous veil of the lady in Dennis Burton's painting in the *Here and Now* gallery. Lennie's troubles were over. I was still grinning when I went back to my apartment on the floor below. Delia greeted me at the door.

"Angela's gone back to Winnipeg."

"When?"

"Two days ago. She phoned to ask me to send her things."

Lennie called me. He was at the Pilot Tavern and told me to meet him there. We'd go for pool. "I suppose you're off to get the lowdown," Delia said.

"That, my dear," I said, "is probably a very accurate way of putting it."

We never got to the poolroom. We sat upstairs at the back of the Pilot under the well-length mural of the naked girl dipped in paint and rolled across the canvas, harbinger of the New Age.

"I guess you know," Lennie said. "It was a mistake."

"Angela?"

"The whole thing."

"That's not the way you described last summer in Europe."

"Honeymoons!" he sat silent. "Even then, I knew I didn't rate her."

"You're a tall order, Lennie. It looks like it hasn't taken you too long to fill in the blanks."

"I knew you picked up on that. What can I say? It was the day after Angela left. The woman nailed me in the elevator, like that day you and I saw her. I spoke a few words to her in my bad Ukrainian. She's Ukrainian. I can't help it, JJ. I'm a carnal man, a hormonal slave. It's my destiny. The woman puts out like Molly Bloom. She even talks like Molly Bloom during the process, only with a Russian accent."

"I've heard her. Remember? Don't tell me anymore."

"He who desires and acts not, breeds pestilence."

"Sure, Lennie, and 'the cut worm forgives the plough'. I'm not so sure about all that stuff." I was thinking of the scene of the little girl in Ibiza and his lying to me about it, but I didn't say so. I could see he was more disturbed than he pretended to be. He spluttered and finally got out the line he was looking for. "Prudence is a rich, ugly old maid courted by incapacity."

He glared at me and then, without warning, his face opened into wide-eyed innocence and he said: "By the way, do you know of any rich ugly old maids you could line me up with?" We laughed.

It had happened before. Lennie read my thoughts. "Do you remember that letter I wrote from Ibiza about the lady Faye and her daughter? Well, I lied."

"Egads, so you *are* a bounder after all."

"Lust, JJ. Lust pure and simple. And yes, I knew you'd come down on the side of the angels."

"Hold on! I thought you'd accept 'bounder'. I didn't call you a sex fiend. And look here, I've a confession to make. I knew the truth anyway ... from Delia."

"Jesus! Angela told her?"

"Last week sometime."

"Christ, I didn't know Angela had watched. Not until she laid it on me."

"That was Delia's doing. She told Angela she had to face you with it."

"Delia must think I'm an all-time lowlife."

"Worse. A complete degenerate."

"You think so too, right? Even more so now you know about Molly Bloom. Go ahead, tell me you haven't thought it."

"I haven't."

"Not even a little bit, not even a tweak of disapproval?"

"OK, a tweak".

"So what would you have done in my place? I mean it's not as if I started anything. I happened to be in that particular hacienda in Ibiza on that particular sultry afternoon is all, just as I happened to be in the elevator at the wrong, or maybe it was the right, time."

I had thought over the Ibiza letter many times. So what I said was the best I could come up with. If he was looking for me to condone or condemn him, I told him, I couldn't do either. "I just don't know, Lennie," I said. "If someone told me he would never have screwed your little fifteen-year-old under the circumstances, I would call him a hypocrite. If someone told me he wouldn't have hesitated for a second to screw her, I would consider him a feckless bastard, even morally retarded. From what I know about you, my guess is that you fall somewhere in between. I expect I would land there too. I like to think I would be sorely tempted and I would resist because of the girl's age, but I just don't know."

"When Delia told you about Angela watching," Lennie said, "did she say how long she watched?" I shook my head. "Because that's the trouble, see. If Angela just looked in and left, well, that must have been hard for her. But if she stayed and saw it all ... I can't imagine. Jesus H Christ, why are we all so afraid to admit that a fifteen-year-old is a woman? Every culture in history has acknowledged it. The girl was fine. Everybody was fine. It was Ibiza. But

Christ, if Angela was watching all along, what must it have been like for her with her insulated, Winnipeg, Episcopalian absence of exposure to what goes on in the world?"

On the way home from the Pilot, I suggested that maybe he could patch things up with Angela. Let her cool down in Winnipeg for a while and try again. Meanwhile, I told him, it wasn't a good idea to carry on with Molly Bloom. Not only would it rule out reconciliation, it could get him into serious trouble with the guy whose name was on her mailbox and who obviously paid her rent and kept her in high fashion.

Lennie had a way of dismissing what he considered petty concerns. For a change, he promised to take my advice. I passed him most days in his library carrel behind a stack of books. "Too bad it's not the Middle Ages, JJ," he said one day with his squinty smile. "I'd be safe and sound reading out loud to myself in a cloister."

It turned out Molly's keeper was a travelling man, coming and going irregularly, and Lennie had at least enough sense to meet her only in his own apartment. Of course, I didn't tell Delia about Molly. Her opinion of Lennie was low enough without that. I found myself caught in an absurd rift, as if I had to make a choice between Delia and Lennie. Was there some deep homoerotic bond lurking here that put him into competition with her? If so, I decided, it was too deep for me to fathom. I just liked the guy, yet sometimes I couldn't help feeling a bit like a suitor having to choose between two lovers.

I met Lennie for a parting drink at the Roof of the Park Plaza before Christmas break. From our perch on the 18th floor, we looked out over a postcard scene, a feathery snowfall making the legislative building and the university, dotted with fuzzy Christmas lights, look fanciful and otherworldly. Lennie was on a first-name basis with Harold who gave us a wink as he poured double scotches for the price of singles, a Christmas bonus.

"I've been having a dream that's really bugging me," Lennie said. I settled back and waited for whatever was coming.

"It opens with three voluptuous beauties taking my arms and ushering me into a huge space. It's sometimes a forum, or a circus tent, or an underground cavern. The women are wildly sexy, scantily dressed with luscious hips and pointed breasts, and lips like candy. I try not to walk with them but I am partly paralysed. I can move only in the direction they take me. There's a table at the centre of a theatre. My ushers escort me there and a dozen figures, male and female, in white lab coats, strap me down on the table. All around in a gallery, eager young faces are watching.

"The white coats cut me open. The expression on their faces is commiserative. The faces in the gallery have the intense concentration of serious students. They strip my intestines out, then my liver and kidneys and stomach sac. They go on for my lungs and my gizzard and my heart, and then for my testicles. I am screaming now, but my voice is tiny.

"The white coats go way. Black-robed priests replace them, with censors and offertories filled with smouldering sawdust. They have huge needles and thread. They fill me with sawdust and sew everything up. They hook up my limbs with wires and unstrap me from the table.

"As I stagger to my feet, the lights come up. I am in the centre of a vast stadium and the music begins. It's a Doumi played in the old Ukrainian way on a thirty-string lyre/harp/guitar type thing called a Kobza. Then the cymbals and fifes join in, then the violins and drums. I give the faces looking on from the gallery the sign of the Dulia, putting my thumb between my forefingers, a salute of contempt. Against my will, my body starts to move to the music. Midgets come somersaulting in, swaggering gymnasts, preening gypsies, tumbling bears. I begin to dance. I look up and high at the top circle of the stadium, far above the frenzied crowd, I see a ring of white gowns and black robes. They have in their hands the ends of the strings that make me dance.

"I curse them. I'm the hit of the show. I feel a slither of sawdust leaking from an old scar. I'm lifted off my feet and hauled up by puppet strings. I unhook myself from the strings, first one, then another and another. I go hurtling down from up high like a dead bird. All that's left is a heap of sawdust and rags."

Lennie looked to me as he had looked before exams back in Winnipeg, his face gone pale and damp, with red blotches breaking out on his forehead.

"Jesus," I said. "Where in hell did that come from?"

"What do you make of it?" Lennie said.

"I'm not touching it," I said. "I'm only trained for minor cuts and bruises."

Harold returned from the bar with fresh Scotches and Lennie took a couple of giant slugs. We sat quietly for a moment. "Ever wanted someone dead?" he said.

"I don't think so. Hitler, I suppose, but no, not anyone I know."

"I have. His name is Yuri. He hung around our place from the time I was a kid. Everybody knew him as 'Red Yuri' because he had a mane of red hair. It must have come from those Vikings who made their way up the Vistula and the Dnieper into Eastern Europe in the Ninth Century. 'Rus' is a Viking word, you know, it's where 'Russian' came from. Also they said Yuri was called 'Red' because he was a Communist. Ridiculous! Yuri was too stupid to be a Communist. I never understood why Sophie put up with him. From the time I was a kid, he kept turning up. He never stayed long, a few months, and then he'd disappear. But he always came back. When he did, I'd go into hiding sometimes, stay away for days at a time. I had a place I would sneak off to under the stage at the Ukrainian Labour Temple. It was next to the heating pipes. Red Yuri never hit me, but he was always sucking up to Sophie, taking money from her and acting like a lap dog. Then, when he was drinking hard, he would smack her around. I used to think up ways of killing him. He still comes and goes and I would still like to kill that hunky honcho."

When Lennie talked about his early years, which was hardly ever, he talked about the North End in general, almost never about his family; never, that I could remember, about his father. I was curious and (with the whiskey taking effect) my question seemed permissible. "Where was your dad through all this?"

"I never knew my dad. I rode on his shoulders once, or at least I seem to remember I did when I was about three years old. His name was Vladi Feschuck. He died when I was four."

"He must have been a young man," I said.

"There was a phenomenal liquor trade in the North End even after 1933 for a while when Prohibition ended in the States. It was when the Bronfmans made their first fortune supplying the Chicago mobs, and drivers were needed to run booze over the border from Moose Jaw. People said Vladi was a runner. Nothing was clear about his death. He was found up on the CPR tracks across from Higgens Avenue on the overpass, next to the old Royal Alex Hotel, with a bullet in his head. There was a gun in his hand. No one could say whether it was a mob killing or a suicide."

"Jesus, Lennie! That's awful."

"Life in the big city."

We were getting drunk. Harold, deft and smiling as always, suggested we go for a stroll to enjoy the night air. We got as far as the Pilot Tavern and sat for a nightcap. Thinking about Lennie's dream and what sounded like a homicidal fixation on Red Yuri, I wondered if I could risk trying to get Lennie to a shrink again. After a scrape with a therapist over his split with Angela, I knew how deeply he distrusted psychotherapy in all its forms. I brought up the subject indirectly and he went into orbit.

"What I can't stand is the look the guy gets on his face. You know that purse-lipped smirk, and that sizzling sound as you feel yourself turning into cooked marshmallow. The shrink can be a nice enough fellow. He is probably exceptionally intelligent. But he has been conditioned by a system that, despite its claims and universal popularity, has barely scratched the surface of the human psyche. Yet it presumes to have the keys to the kingdom.

"The trouble is too many obviously well-balanced people are heading for the couch. They're turning psychotherapy into just another diversion for the elite, as if all it takes to become hip is to go to a shrink and talk to your friends about your hang-ups afterwards. The irony is that cost doesn't matter. Not in Canada. Whether you are a desperate psychotic urgently needing help not to kill your father or yourself, or an affluent and comfy professional in search of a hit of cosmetic therapy, it makes no difference. A headache can be diagnosed as manic depression and the government foots the bill."

"Are you sure, Lennie," I broke in, "that you're not indulging in a flight of hubris?"

"What the hell does that mean?"

"Well, refusing to admit that a shrink, or anyone else for that matter, might know something about you that you don't know about yourself."

"Like Milton's Satan believing he knows more about himself than God does, you mean."

"Something like that. "

"How many people do you know who have been going to a shrink half their lives and who are likely to keep on going for the rest of their lives but who don't change, don't as we used to say about surviving an illness, 'get better'? Do you know any who do get better? Or do they just keep going to the shrink? Doesn't this mean their life is just one long sickness with a government subsidy? Unhappiness and dejection, states of depression and gloom are part of the human condition from time to time–must they now be treated as sickness requiring medical intervention?

"Even ordinary people who don't know their id from their ego can't take their friends or lovers to mean what they say any more. To truly dig a person nowadays, you have to understand that what that person says might actually mean something else, often the opposite of what is expressed. The latent meaning is always more important than the manifest meaning, the unsaid always more significant than the said. Conversation isn't about notions and opinions or dialogue aimed at establishing something that makes sense any more. It's about extracting hidden significance and semiotic undercurrents sometimes even the speaker is unaware of, to the point where everything uttered becomes susceptible to veiled subtexts, and conversation becomes a series of Freudian slips.

"It's the same for literature. All kinds of so-called experimental novels use what was once called stream-of-consciousness as a disguise for random drivel. But look here, a stream flows in some direction, from collecting ponds, down through rivulets, into rivers and then into the sea, as earlier stream-of-consciousness writers like Joyce and Woolf knew very well. They were making intelligible forms, not letting loose from Rorschach blots of free association and half-crazed daydreams in an effort to disguise the harsh sociology of no talent.

"We've got all these categories–transference, libido, hysteria, complex, neurosis, psychosis, paranoia, schizophrenia, manic depression, dementia, shadow, anima, animus, individuation, extroversion, introversion, archetypes, attention deficiency–the lot. Do these name tags ever quite fit? In 1916, American psychiatrist Stanley Hall identified 132 phobias. Why not 133? Why not 500? My money's on a contemporary of Freud, the famous Austrian critic and satirist, Karl Kraus: 'Freudian therapy is the disease of which it professes to be the cure.'"

As we made our way home to the Yorkville Towers, Lennie began to laugh. "What's so funny?" I asked.

"It's not what you think, JJ."

"What then?"

"I just started going to a shrink again."

Chapter Eleven

I went to the Pilot with Lennie to meet his old friend (new to me) by the name of Yossel Shublik, a former Winnipeg North Ender passing through Toronto on his way home from France where he was completing his PhD in philosophy at the Sorbonne. Yossel, Lennie informed me, had never been known by his first name. As far back in their childhood as either of them could remember, he was plain 'Shabby'.

"Look at me," Yossel said. "Which do I look like, a Yossel or a Shabby?" He was a miracle of dishevelment. He wore a pair of World War II flight boots with broken zippers and tongues hanging out, no doubt gasping for air. His pants were a foot wide, draped like shrouds over his knees. The crotch came so far down, the pants looked like they had been handed down from a giant and cut off at the knees. His overcoat, presumably belonging to the same giant, came to his ankles. The act of opening it required no unbut-toning, rather the unclasping of two of the largest safety pins I had ever seen, to reveal a mammoth wool sweater mottled with burn holes and streaked with cigarette ash. Apparently, when in the grip of metaphysical speculation, Shabby left his cigarette in his mouth and just blew his ashes. His hair stood up in hay stooks at all angles. His head was large, with a disproportionately big nose ('hamulous' he called it) and wide, darting, onion eyes. You couldn't help but like him. He and Lennie wore cats' grins as they waited for my reply to his question. I took the plunge.

"Offhand," I said, "I prefer Shabby to Yossel." They laughed. I had learned back in Winnipeg how to make quick friends from the North End. All you had to do was add insult to injury. As I listened, Shabby and Lennie spoke of school days at St. John's High School and how the two of them were under continuous pressure. For Lennie, it came from the Canadian Ukrainian

Orthodox Church trying to get him to study for the priesthood. The church in Western Canada had gone though decades of turmoil to separate itself from the Russian Orthodox Church in both Russia and America, part of the general struggle of Ukrainian nationalism. After the war, the Canadian Ukrainian church was consolidating throughout Manitoba, Saskatchewan and Alberta, and it was urgently enlisting bright young men of Ukrainian extraction for ordination.

Meanwhile, Shabby, who dominated his classes at both school and schul, was being prevailed upon by family and rabbi to attend rabbinical college in Chicago.

"You know," Shabby said, "I think they would have snared us if it weren't for old G. J. Reeve."

"Explain," Lennie said, pointing to me. "Explain how a wayward Hunkie and a socially dysfunctional Hebe were saved by a Wasp."

Shabby called G. J. Reeve, principal of St John's, the Thomas Arnold of the North End. The school population was predominantly Jewish and Slavic. Shabby claimed that more graduates of St. John's went on to collect PhD's than students from any other high school in North America, and G. J. Reeve was the reason. Reeve kept an eye on students and took the promising ones aside for special advice and encouragement. His unconcern about their ethnic background, so uncharacteristic of Winnipeg in those days, cemented the influence he had on them.

"What emerged," said Shabby, "was an intellectual revolution on the street, a yearning to learn, a respect for being smart, an explosive curiosity about everything in life. What we talked about was often extravagantly philosophical for a bunch of kids. I remember one discussion about where life came from that went on and on and then there was silence, and then someone said: 'Life is the breath of the universe'. Not bad for a teenager from the ghetto. That wasn't you, was it, Lennie?"

"I think it was you, Shabby," said Lennie.

They talked about Paris, about cheap bistros in Montmartre and the Hotel California on Rue des École where Lennie lived, the tiny elevator that always got stuck, the sleazy concierge, the sound of women's sandals on the cobblestones at six in the morning as they padded by to get their morning croissants.

"You never told me you were in Paris," I said to Lennie.

"It wasn't a good year," said Lennie. I was flabbergasted. If I had done a year in Paris, it would probably be the first thing a new friend would learn about me. Yet never had Lennie mentioned that he had been a student in Paris.

"How did you get there?" I asked.

Lennie glanced up quickly at Shabby who was looking the other way and then, drawing a stick figure in a slick of beer on the table, he said: "At the end of high school Sophie asked me what the best university in the world was and, just for the hell of it, I said 'the Sorbonne.' 'Then that's where you're going,' she said. And that's where I went."

"Let's just say he went to Paris," said Shabby smiling. "Did I ever see you at the Sorbonne, Lennie?"

"Technically no," said Lennie with a shrug. "My French was the shits. What could I do?"

When Lennie left the beer parlour, I stayed on with Shabby. They weren't exactly buddy-buddy as kids, he said, but they got along together without combat and, by co-incidence, they both sailed on the *Homeric* on their way to Europe in 1952. During the eight-day trip, said Shabby, Lennie kept his distance.

"I understood. He was a posh dresser, I didn't exactly come across as a boulevardier, and there was a plethora of co-eds on their way to discover Europe. Maybe there were other factors peculiar to Winnipeg. In the North End, a Jewish family's Ukrainian neighbour might have a grandfather who had engaged in a pogrom in Bukovina. That tension underlay a lot of friendships from kindergarten onward. But for Lennie, I think it was my looks. What were the girls on board going to make of a slickster who hung out with a guy who looked like a Sephardic Jew?

"In Paris, I had nothing to live on. Lennie loaned me one of his jackets. He's smaller than me right? I wore it for a year without ever being able to button it up, walking around like a drill sergeant with my shoulders pulled back till the jacket fell to pieces. My shoulders sort of stuck there. Lennie's mom sent money. He offered to lend me some but I couldn't take it. Then, a curious routine began. About twice a week, we would run into each other along St. Germaine. There were always a few other students around. Lennie would order food and, after he'd eaten half of it, he'd push his plate over my way, as if he didn't feel well. We never spoke of it and no one else paid any attention. It went on all winter. But I'll tell you what I remember best. It was Lennie peeing in the pissoirs. You know, the kiosks along the boulevard where you stand with your head and feet sticking out and piss in a trough. He couldn't pass one by without stopping for a dribble, like a dog marking his territory. And then 'goddamn', he'd shout, 'now this is what I call civilization. In Winnipeg, you'd be fined and locked up for pissing in the street.'

"In the early days back in Winnipeg, it wasn't all sweetness and light as administered by the good Samaritan G. J. Reeves. When we were eleven, Lennie and I worked for a guy called Blomberg who made chocolates in his garage. His business wasn't registered. He sold his chocolates under the table to confectionaries in the North End. Blomberg was no good at inventory control and Lennie and I did a lucrative trade in the schoolyard for a while. But Blomberg was a regular supplier for Sophie's confectionary and when she found out we were skimming chocolates for our own black market, she hit the roof. I was with Lennie in her restaurant when she confronted him. "You stole from the man who trusted you," she shouted. What seemed to anger her, I remember thinking, had something to do with honor among thieves, since, as we all knew, Sophie was not exactly the driven snow herself. All of a sudden, she hauled off and whacked him across the head so hard it made his nose bleed. He stood there for a minute sort of stunned and then did what I couldn't imagine doing to my mother. He punched her in the stomach. She fell back gasping and the last I remember is her pointing at me shouting: 'And you, you little shit. You get the hell out of here.' What shocked me most was that Lennie, who hated Red Yuri so much for mistreating his mother, would do the same thing himself.

From what I knew of of Sophie, I'm surprised she didn't punch him back.

"When Lennie and I were fourteen, I got involved in another Sophie squabble. There was a seventeen-year-old Ukrainian girl down from a farm up by Dauphin. Her name was Anna something. She was from a family Lennie's mother knew back in Bukovina. Anna had won a scholarship to St. Mary's College and Sophie had promised her family she would look after her in Winnipeg. She placed Anna in the YWCA and had her over frequently for visits. Lennie came to know her, not entirely in the way Sophia thought. Lennie called her 'Anna of Green Gobbles'. 'That's the way it is with farm girls,' he said. 'They're used to coupling among farm animals and they don't think twice about it.'

"For someone as imposed upon by celibacy as I was, listening to him talk that way was pure torment. I asked if he could do something to help me out. Anna from Dauphin promised to be an angel of mercy. We wound up in Lennie's room, all three of us, naked, preparing to do I didn't know what next, when Sophie came bursting through the door howling with rage. I fled down the stairs without my shoes. Poor Anna was sent packing and I never saw her again. Whatever went on between Sophie and Lennie, the next thing I heard, Lennie was off to some kind of reform school in Alberta."

Meeting Shabby made me realize again how little I knew of Lennie's past. The trust he had extended to me on our first trip to the North End and by inviting me to his wedding, gave me glimpses only of his home in one of those old-fashioned diners on North Main with living quarters above, of Sophie as a reasonably prosperous steaks-and-chops restaurateur and confectioner, and beyond that, something of a mover and shaker on Main Street. I never spoke of these things to our university friends. Lennie's reticence about his early life was a clear signal I was trusted not to.

Chapter Twelve

Having moved in to Mrs. Blanchard's boarding house with Peter Coultry and Mike Nader at 99 St. George Street, Lennie looked to be settling into the monastic life he had often declared to be his true calling. Mike and Peter had rooms on the second floor, Mrs. Blanchard her quarters and the dining room at the back on the ground floor. Lennie had the apartment on the ground floor at the front of the house, a bedroom and a good-sized study cum sitting room. His habit was to leave his louvered door ajar when he wanted company. Coming in, Mike and Peter had to pass by, and if the door was open, they often stuck their head in to say hello. It led to a lot of late night gab sessions. Lennie told me what with Mrs. Blanchard and her tea trays and Mike and Peter popping in and out, it made him feel like Sherlock Holmes with two Dr. Watsons. Mike told me about his first meeting Lennie back in the fall of 1959.

"We were standing in line for registration at graduate school and this guy comes up and asks what did I know about Marshall McLuhan's class on modern criticism. I tell him McLuhan is my thesis advisor but the course isn't being offered this year because he's on Sabbatical doing a big education project for the U.S. government. He'll be around during the year for me to consult, but he won't be teaching.

'So you'll get to see him?' Lennie says.

'See him, yes. But only about my thesis'. I was trying to scare him off.

'Maybe I could come see McLuhan with you', he says.

"I was at a loss for words that a complete stranger would make such a proposition. Then I noticed a sly smile come over his face that made me think he might be having me on. He dropped McLuhan and asked if I was taking Miller McLure's course on Spenser, or Northrop Frye's course on

Blake. I told him I was taking both. He reached out his hand and took mine in his.

'I'm Lennie Boyce,' he said. 'We can compete.'

'For what?' I said.

'For A's,' he said.

"I could hardly believe my ears. 'I'm not the competitive type,' I said.

'Well in truth, neither am I,' he said, breaking into a sweet smile. 'But that seems to be the way things work around here.'

"I found myself warming to this strange fellow. His face was friendly. He was clean-cut, well-dressed, like all of us in those days wearing a tie and sport jacket, with polished shoes. Yet there was something appealingly unsmooth about the overall effect. He spoke in a voice that reminded me of Eddie Albert, high-pitched, scratchy with enthusiasm, nothing pompous about it, not at all patronizing. Innocent?

"Soon, I got to know all you guys–Peter the Prairie Keats, Mark Woodward the New Yorker writer, and you. It was a grand old time for an alien from Detroit–lunches in the basement of the Windsor Arms, beer at the Bay/Bloor and the Pilot Tavern, concerts, plays, foreign movies, a lot of talk in the Arbour Room or the Great Hall at Hart House, folk songs and pizza and wine at yours and Delia's and Lennie's and Angela's. That's where I met Angela, Lennie's wife. So elegant she seemed to me, so sexy and yet goddess-like. Is that because I'm Catholic?

"One evening, Lennie and I were reading Spenser out loud to each other. It seemed the only way to make sense of *The Faerie Queene*. The poetry was archaic, with unfamiliar idioms and diction. But I remember a shiver passing through me at the lines of the knight, Sir Artegal, as Lennie read them:

> His study was true justice how to deal
> And day and night employed his busy pain
> How to reform that ragged commonweal

"Lennie's voice had a strange effect on me that night. There was such conviction in it, I imagined I was hearing Spenser's gentle knight himself. It wasn't an actor's voice. Intense rather, honest. I felt a tear coming. Then, out of the blue, he said, "Do you think Spenser was a fairy queen?"

"You mean queer?"

"Yeah, you know, a ponce."

"Why would you say that?"

"Just a thought," said Lennie, and carried on reading.

"I invited him to hear Pete Seeger when he performed at Convocation Hall. Because he had never seen Seeger live, I was excited about introducing him to one of his old favourites. But after the concert, he suddenly turned sour, as if compelled to stick a pin in a pretty balloon once he'd inflated it. He put on a nasty face and said, 'I hear Seeger's a pouf.' I thought, holy hell, not this again. Then he laughed and said, 'Just kidding.' But was he?

"Mark Woodward stopped by one afternoon not long after Lennie had moved into the digs at 99 St. George St. where Peter Coultry and I lived. We had a cup of tea in Mrs. Blanchard's dining room. Mark told me about Peter Coultry's parents in Winnipeg, what decent folks they were and how he promised Mrs. Coultry, as an older man and good friend of Peter, that he would keep an eye out for Peter's welfare. It all seemed pleasant enough. I thought Mark was simply providing me with background on Peter. Suddenly I realized something was eating him and then it dawned on me that he thought I was a homosexual with designs on Peter. I was stunned. When I assured Mark his suspicions were wrong, he made an embarrassed apology. He was greatly relieved to find me (I think it was his phrase) 'above suspicion'.

"How had this silly rumour got started? It had to come from Lennie. He must have suspected me of homosexuality and sought confirmation. That was why he cast a shadow on Spenser and Pete Seeger. He wanted to see my reaction. There was a streak of mischief in Lennie and I don't think he realized how far beyond playfulness it could go. If Mark Woodward was led to suspect me of devious designs, I wondered if you and Delia did, too. I walked on eggshells with Peter. When I think back, Peter must have known what was in the air, because he seemed to be walking on eggshells, too.

"Lennie asked me to take him to Mass one day. We went to my church, the rather imposing St. Joseph's Cathedral at Trinity College. 'Know what?' he told me afterwards. 'You're a Catholic by nurture from first awareness. It has nothing to do with your brains. Deep inside, you have stained glass windows, magnificent robes, the colours and candles of the altar, the litany, the chants and spells and smells, all the child's imprints of the numinous in the folderol of the Mass, a whole environment of god-feeling. For me, it's just an idea, an attractive and consoling hierarchical structure rising above the chaos of history. If I became a Catholic, it would be like a white wannabe joining a drum dance and a sweat lodge so he can cohort with the Great Spirit.'

"Would you want to be a Catholic?" I asked him.

"Not intellectually possible. Our guys are just an unusually successful branch of the trunk of the original church of the Patriarchs of Alexandria and Antioch and Jerusalem and Constantinople and Rome. Rome caught hold only because the Roman Empire finally routed the others in the West. Backed by the canon of St. Paul and St. Ignatius (who coined the word 'Catholic'), St. Augustine laid down the new order for Rome, not an order of this world but of the next. His orthodoxy prevailed against the warring schismatics, the Manicheans and Donatists and Arians, and the Nestorians, and Gnostics and their lot, and paved the way for the transformation of the patriarch of Rome to be elevated to Pope–a figure mysteriously anointed as sole spokesman of the one God, thence succession of holy bureaucrats, many of whom believed themselves infallible. Me, you see, my heart is in the east, back with the original monks and mystics and patriarchs of Asia Minor who beat Augustine to the punch by a few centuries."

I had heard all this before from better theologians than Lennie. And of course I couldn't be sure if Lennie really believed what he said, if he was scoring debating points, or if he was just having me on to see how I would react. "I guess then," I said, "you are some kind of exotic Eastern Catholic at heart."

"I wouldn't go so far as to confess to that," is all I got for a reply.

"When I was there in Toronto with all of you, despite his dark side, Lennie's inner lustre never faded. Was he angel or demon? Or was he just a random comet flashing across the sky?"

Chapter Thirteen

Lennie had been summoned to Winnipeg to give Angela the divorce her father demanded. All the powers of River Heights had come down on his head and he knew better than to contest them. He never saw Angela. The Reverend Stockton and his operatives made the necessary arrangements. In Manitoba, at that time, if you wanted a divorce, proof of adultery was required. All Lennie had to do was appear at the Edgewater Inn on the Pembina Highway on the appointed afternoon and there would be waiting a young lady in brassiere and panties and a photographer cued to burst in, snap compromising photos, and deliver the evidence to the plaintiff.

"I find it hard to explain," Lennie told me, "what profound respect for the law this whole episode has given me. The first screw-up was that I arrived early, or else the photographer arrived late. The girl was a knockout, sitting there on the edge of the bed in her skimpies. I asked her what was I supposed to do and she said take my clothes off except for my shorts and wait for the photographer. She told me she had never done anything like this before. Know what? I believed her.

"Understand, we're sitting quietly, two strangers, nearly naked. Within five minutes she has captured my heart. She's nineteen, from Beausejour, a farming community. She's going to get married in a year to her childhood sweetheart who fixes heavy equipment. I ask her if she likes him and she says 'oh yes, I love him', and then she breaks into tears and falls on my shoulder. I'm feeling very horny and she is exquisite. I get to thinking about her life as she tells me about it, maybe the first time she's ever spoken out this way to anyone, and suddenly my lust evaporates. I'm overwhelmed with sadness, with an immense wave of helplessness at her predicament, This vulnerable, voluptuous creature contains all the potential the world has to offer, the joys of the body, the delights of new experience. But she is doomed to no more than meagre scraps from the great banquet of life. I tear up. Then surprise, surprise. The heavy equipment man comes bursting through the door with bright red eyes, delivers a crusher to my solar plexus, and smacks me in the eye. The girl screams. The guy with the camera appears and shouts louder. He persuades the heavy equipment guy to quit beating me, and the girl to quit screaming. It's just an arrangement, he explains. It's necessary to make everything legal.

"By now the girl is huddled in her lover's arms. She's assuring him that nothing happened, that this was just a way for her to make a bit of extra cash for her trousseau. Under no circumstances would she let a no good like me anywhere near her. "I'm coming round, patting away blood from my nose with a paper towel, though still dazed and defensive. I'm thinking that even the remorseless Reverend Stockton, with all his resources, couldn't have master-minded a more effective retribution for what I did by marrying his daughter. Only the gods themselves have that kind of power. They can start you off on a bad day and go on to make things worse and worse.

The next thing I know, the heavy equipment guy is helping me to my feet while I'm still ducking his potential blows. He tells me how sorry he is. He gets a damp towel from the bathroom to put on my eye and daubs away at my face. The photographer points out that he still has no pictures and could we please get on with the show, which instantly turns our heavy equipment man into a movie director. 'We've got to see more of your face', he says. 'Sit this way so your eye don't show.' They have a creative consultation, then they re-block the shot–a model of collaboration between director and cameraman.

"The girl and I sit like mannequins, she patting a shiny forehead with powder, I pressing a swath of toilet paper to my nose. Now that there's art involved, the director-mechanic has a burst of inspiration. He instructs his star to take off her brassiere, 'for realism' he says, and he places her in tight against me with one of her stupendous breasts plunging into my chest. I see the girl is sympathetic toward my injuries, and even in my semi-delirious state I detect it's not entirely a maternal thing. As the director and DOP work out the final details of the shot, she gives me a sidelong look, one of those looks that amount to a wink without blinking.

"The shoot session over, we dress and make ready to leave. 'My name's Jack," says the mechanic-director. "And this here's Virginia you been workin' with. Listen, I'm real sorry about pounding you that way. I mean, shit, no one told me what the deal was. Here, you take my phone number and give me a call. We'll go have a beer ... on me. Least I can do to make it up to you.'

"I called the number the next mid-afternoon, and was of course surprised to find that old Jack was at work. 'Why don't we meet for coffee anyways,' says Virginia.' I suggest a place in St. Vital near a motel of my acquaintance. Did we go wild? We barely made it through the motel door before we were entangled. She told me what a piss poor lover old Jack was. She said she'd heard about orgasms from girlfriends but she had no idea they could be so nice. By the end of the afternoon she was churning and bucking like a beached dolphin. Peach tits, panther bum, boa-constrictor legs. It was a safari. That's what it was. A genuine wild safari. And worth every punch old Jack landed.

Virginia dropped me off afterwards and I told her I'd call in a day or two. I didn't. I caught the train back to Toronto. But I sent a note: "Dear Jack and Virginia. It was a real pleasure making your acquaintance despite the initial misunderstanding. Jack, don't feel guilty. Almost all the black has gone from my eye and my shoulder's working fine again. Virginia, have a great future. You can, you know. Don't do what other people want. Do what you want. Give it some thought. I really mean that. Your friend, Freddy.'

"All right, so you think I'm a vengeful bastard. I seriously can't agree. I feel more like a missionary. I think there's a chance I changed that girl for the better, gave her a glimpse of a world beyond the one old Jack was preparing for her. Maybe she will even go on and get a few kicks out of life instead of the joyless hum-drum the gods have laid out for her in Beausejeur.

Chapter Fourteen

"There's something I've been meaning to tell you," said Lennie. We were sitting in the Arbor room at Hart House drinking awful coffee when he blurted it out: "Yuri is dead."

"The ... the friend of your mother?"

"The same."

"What happened?"

"He got drunk and fell off Sophie's third floor fire escape."

"How did you hear?"

"It happened when I was in the 'Peg settling the divorce."

"You're a funny man, Lennie. You never said a word."

"Yah, I'm a funny man. And, thanks to the gods, that baboon Yuri bought the biscuit."

A week later, word arrived from Winnipeg that Sophie was being charged with manslaughter for the death of Red Yuri. "They have a witness," Lennie told me, "a lady who said she heard a noise in the alley and when she looked out the window, she saw a woman standing on the fire escape, silhouetted against the light coming from the opened door. She said the woman stood there for a good minute before going back into the building. She said she hadn't realized there was a body on the pavement below until she heard people talking about it the next day, and put two and two together. The cops say it was Sophie on the fire escape when Yuri went over."

"Christ, Lennie, what does she say?"

"You have to understand, JJ. Sophie's a shrewd customer when it comes to the law. Remember the best man at my wedding, the dark, rangy guy? That's my cousin Boris, now a lawyer. Well, he's managed to get Sophie out on bail and to have the case remanded on the basis of a doctor's report on Sophie's poor state of health."

"That won't get her off. I mean, eventually, she'll have to face the charges, won't she?"

"You don't know Sophie. She always has an angle. The doctor's report happens to be true. She hasn't told the prosecution but she's filled with cancer. She'll be gone before the case comes up for trial. When she's on her last breath, she'll plead guilty. That'll be the day, I can tell you, when Sophie loses to the law."

What he had predicted came to pass. At her trial Sophie pleaded guilty to Yuri's murder and before she was sentenced she died. Without saying goodbye to any of us, Lennie was off to Winnipeg and there was no word from him until late summer, when he turned up back at 99 St. George. At the end of spring term, with graduate school papers due all round, his professors had been sympathetic. They granted him compassionate extensions that allowed him to postpone unfinished assignments until the fall of 1960.

I looked him up as soon as I got back from my guiding job. He had lost weight and looked sallow. I didn't ask him how things had gone and he volunteered nothing. Then one evening he called me to come for a beer to the Pilot Tavern. We sat in the semi-dark upstairs at the back and talked small talk. Finally, "I have a confession to make," he said. "At the funeral, I was more upset than I expected to be. You know from what I've told you I never quite felt close to my mother in the way sons are expected to feel. But all of a sudden, standing by the coffin, I began to cry. I'm not afraid of crying, but you know what, JJ? I realized later they were crocodile tears. I may have been in mourning, but I was also feeling a sense of relief, as if a huge burden had been lifted from my back.

"Had I, deep down, resented Sophie because of her profession when I was a kid? I don't think so. Our neighbourhood along Main didn't make a big deal about such things. It was generally understood that survival didn't often go hand in hand with rectitude. No, it was something about the personality she presented to the world that embarrassed me–her flamboyance, her fits of blustering in broken English with a thick stage accent, her posturing with her feather and fox-fur shawls, costume jewellery, and long cigarette holder. That embarrassment kept me arms length from her even when I knew she craved my affection. I had a vague recollection of my father, so I was pretty sure I wasn't a bastard, but I acted like one for sure."

By this time, Lennie was settled back in at 99 St. George and the rest of the Mafia were heading off in different directions. Mark Woodward and Vanessa, a lass from the Park Plaza Book Store, moved into a flat on Cumberland Street. Delia and I landed a one-bedroom on Kendal Avenue in the Annex, near the university, with a fireplace and a tiny back porch that the landlord allowed me to winterize so as to accommodate our brand new baby boy. Peter Coultry went to England to write his novel about geese and his father. Mike Nader was back at 99 St. George for his final PhD year.

Mark Woodward called me in late summer to say there were jobs going at Ryerson Institute at Yonge and Gould, and I'd better get right down there. We were both trying to finish our MA theses, but we were also married and broke. A blessing for us, English teachers were abnormally scarce. Mark and I both got jobs. We were classified as civil servants. We had to swear allegiance to the Queen, teach eighteen hours a week of whatever we were assigned, including the business letter, and be at our desks the rest of the time, whether there was anything for us to do there or not. Academic friends thought it a come-down from a teaching fellowship at the university. For Mark and me, it was not only a lifesaver, it paid three times as much. We tried to persuade Lennie to join us. He said he wasn't interested in swearing allegiance to the Queen, and besides, he didn't need the money.

Years later, Mike Nader spoke to me about Lennie's return to Toronto that fall after Sophie's death: "I was glad he came back to 99 St. George. At his best, Lennie was a fully alive person it was a joy to be around. And he had a capacity, not all the time, mind you, for great generosity of feeling. He could play the fool. He could play the gadfly, repudiating every orthodoxy he could lay his hands on. He could get high and drunk and crazy, sometimes to the point where you wanted to put him in a straight jacket and shut him away. But my goodness, sometimes he could feel a person's pain as if it were his own. It was as if an electric current was passing through you and he could reach into you and the charge went through him too. If you were speaking the truth about yourself, it was a good thing. If you were lying to yourself, he wouldn't let you get away with it.

"In my case, the truth was young love confounded. The lie was suicide in proper romantic fashion. Everything had gone wrong for me, and that fall when I came back, Lennie was the only one I could confide in. His concern got me back on track, even when he mocked me. Quit looking from below to above, he said. Look from above to below, sub-specie aeternitatis. In the big picture, he said, what did my despair really amount to? It was only personal. He would say this with a wink and then say that suicide was okay for Protestants, because all it did was kill them, but for Catholics, it meant serious punishment for eternity.

"Lennie had left Toronto in the spring, owing term papers once postponed because of his mother's illness. He also left with half an idea of doing a PhD thesis on W.B. Yeats which he was working up to asking McLuhan to supervise. He wasn't the least concerned about what was known as 'the McLuhan Taint', an infection in the English Department that spread in direct proportion to Marshall's rising celebrity as international media oracle.

"Remember, Jason, after you gave up on McLuhan's Monday night sessions, Lennie and I continued going. For 1960-61, Lennie signed up for McLuhan's course on Modern Criticism and he often came with me to his office on St. Joseph Street where we had wild bull sessions. I was getting good help on Ezra Pound and modernism. Lennie seemed to want something more from McLuhan. Was it the meaning of life? The sparring between them sounded sometimes like an Italian domestic dispute, not without mutual relish.

"McLuhan had powerful adversaries in academe, never mind U of T. Listen to this, from a hugely influential classicist from Yale whom I won't name: 'There is afoot a mindless orgy of trend-catching anti-literacy, best typified by the appalling popularity of the jargon-laden, hyped-up, and profoundly ahistorical works of Marshall McLuhan, designed to flatter just about all the prejudices of a TV generation in which functional illiteracy is already well- advanced.' This kind of thing made Lennie love McLuhan all the more, of course. He knew these establishment ostriches had no comprehension of McLuhan's real stance, which was anything but a defence of television and illiteracy. Lennie delighted in the idea that he could line himself up with McLuhan against what he regarded as the stagnant forces of sclerotic scholarship and cowardly specialization.

"But Lennie was no star-struck McLuhan zealot either. Every time he and Marshall came together, he had a new attack ready.'What do you mean,' Lennie asked, 'when you say the content of one medium is another medium instead of saying the content is the narrative or the idea the medium puts across?'

"'Well consider,' McLuhan said. 'The telegraph contains the printed word, the printed word contains what before Gutenburg was hand-writing. Script and print contain, or at least pretend to contain, speech. And speech contains thought.'

"'So then what does thought contain?' Lennie asked. 'Aha,' McLuhan said, 'nothing, only itself. Thought is a pure medium, like electric light, or faith, irreducible.' It would drive Lennie up the wall.

"For a while, as you know, Lennie was enthralled by the idea that, as a product of the historically illiterate, oral culture of the Russian outback, he was genetically pre-ordained to be a talker, not a writer. But he was eventually honest enough to admit that designating himself McLuhan's oral/auditory man wasn't going to save him from having to turn in written essays.

"By Christmas break, the pressure for him to turn in work, including holdovers from the year before owing to 'family tragedy', was reaching emergency pitch. The onus was not only on Lennie, but (I might as well come out and say it) on me. Somehow it had become established that I was his editor. More accurately, between you and me, Jason, I had become his stenographer and rewrite man. I'm not saying I did his work for him. The papers we did were all his ideas, and bright, sometimes explosively bright ones they were. But a lot of the phrasing and the structure was my doing. It felt a bit like a musical comedy act with Lennie tap dancing around cane in hand singing, 'I'm content', and me tipping my top hat and singing, 'I'm form'. Gradually I saw what his problem was. He just couldn't write. Lennie's prose moved from A to C where C would be something suggested by A, and then on to F, which was suggested by C, and thence to R, which was suggested by F, and onward in great broken helixes of ideas. By the time you got two pages in, they lost all connective tissue. 'When I'm on my feet,' he told me one day, 'I can build word castles. As soon as I sit down to write, I get lost in cold rooms and windy corridors.'

"It didn't make sense. Something about the words he put down on the page, just the sight of them, seemed to bewitch him, as if each word had a trajectory of its own outside his control and he had to follow it. It may be there was a deep strain of irrationality in Lennie's Slavic soul as he was always proud to admit, but it had nothing to do with the way his mind worked when his instrument was the spoken word.

"Sometimes I thought of him as a spiritual descendent of one of those legendary Celtic gleemen who, before there were written records, carried the whole tradition of their race memorized in their shaggy heads. It was like musical memory, or like the memory of those medieval monks sitting alone in their vaults, reading out loud, the sound getting imprinted on the muscles of their voice box, allowing them to play back the original sounds pretty much intact.

"Once when I was re-jigging a paragraph in one of Lennie's essays, he skimmed it off my desk, read it aloud, and looked at me in dismay. 'How in the name of Jesus did you do that?' he said, as if I'd just conducted a successful alchemical transformation. I'm not sure whether he loved me or hated me for it.

"When it came to sitting down at a desk and writing, if another truth be told, Lennie could be just plain lazy. No matter how brilliantly he shone in the free-for-all of our seminars, he was obliged to turn in written work to get credit for his courses. By the end of his second year of residence (and he was first to admit that he was much bolstered by my editorial ministrations), he had caught up with written work in most of his courses, but I had a concern. There was still another year for him, a PhD thesis to come, and I would be long gone.

Chapter Fifteen

Younger than the rest of us, Peter Coultry was the quiet one. He spoke in a near whisper, yet with such intensity you could always hear him clearly. He loved Bruckner and Sibelius and prairie storms. In Manitoba, his enthusiasm for flora and fauna led us to brand him our Keats of the Wilderness. He spent a lot of time in the outdoors with his forest ranger father, the gentlest of men, and their two Labrador retrievers, especially in goose hunting season. It was the source of Peter's deep conflict. Hunting was in his blood and upbringing, but it was contrary to his constitution. At least, the stories he wrote for *Creative Campus* and *The Manitoban* back in Winnipeg came out that way. If you were lost in the bush, Peter was the person you would want to be with, and yet, you had the feeling that even if you were both starving he might scare a deer away instead of shooting it for food.

One night back in 1960 Delia and I had Peter over for dinner. He was awkward. Delia's being eight months pregnant might have had something to do with it. She looked beautiful, disconcertingly ripe. He blushed when she attempted a hug at the door and he didn't quite know where to look. I could see, as I had seen before, that if I ever ran off, Peter would not be far away. When Delia left for bed she gave his cheek a touch, and Peter and I got into the bottle of Glenmorangie he had brought, which lead inevitably to Lennie.

Peter began: "Remember the weird situation after Lennie took the digs at 99 St. George with Mike Nader and me? Poor Mark Woodward, who had been my mother's favorite Sunday dinner Englishman. Imagine his discomfort, fastidious Mark, the last person to pry into other people's business, and yet the most responsible of men, feeling indebted to my mother and assuring her he would watch over me. When he finally got the nerve to speak out:

'Is there something going on between you and Mike?' I was astounded, and then I just laughed. So did Mark. 'Then I won't have to report you to your mother after all,' he said. I never thought at the time to ask him where he had picked up the homosexual rumour. Who else could it have come from but Lennie? And why?

"Don't get me wrong. I think the world of Lennie, though he used to scare the daylights out of me. One afternoon in the Pilot Tavern, just the two of us there, he cornered me as if I were the wedding guest and he the Ancient Mariner.

'You want to be a writer, right?'

'I want to write, yes.'

'Then you've got to get away from here.'

'You mean Toronto?'

'Academe! Listen to me, Peter, I met an old professor the other day. His name's Downy. He's retired but he's got a carrel near mine at the library and he hangs around the reading room. He used to teach Romantic Poetry. We get talking and he tells me about this poem he's been writing for the last forty-two years. It's a long poem called '*A Civil Vision*'. I mean a long poem, 700 pages at last count, he tells me. He says it's almost finished. He gives me a dozen pages to read and do you know what? It's not bad stuff. It's in blank verse, iambic pentameter, and for all I know it has more literary allusions per gallon than *Paradise Lost*. It reads smooth. But Jesus, Peter, it scared the shit out of me. I mean, why didn't the old bugger try a few novels or something with a remote chance someone might read?

'No sooner do I leave old Downy in the library and strike off across Queen's Park, than I run into this wild-eyed beatnik with long greasy locks who sells me a handful of poems for a dollar. One is called: '*I Write and I Paint*.'

> In my carrel
> At the library
> I write a poem
> About desire
> Then I return
> To my model
> At the morgue
> To work on
> My still-life

'That's when it hit me. Are we fooling ourselves? Why did we take up this thing called Eng Lit? To become English professors? A hundred years ago, there was no such thing. I think we did it because we wanted to be writers, real artists, and something told us this was the easiest way to go about it. Wrong. It's the deadliest thing a would-be writer can do. Not the reading. You have to do all that if you're not going to be another half-wit inventing the sonnet. But once university has given you the lay of the land, you have to set out making your own tracks, digesting what you read for your own purposes, not to meet assignments or to fill your cud so that later on you can regurgitate on demand to calves in a classroom. Or, god save us, so you can specialize in unreadable, deeply researched trivia.

'Okay, the good poets of academe are exceptions–John Crowe Ransom, Allan Tate, John Berryman, Randall Jarrell, Theodore Roethke, Robert Penn Warren, Brits like George Barker, William Empson, Howard Sergent, Phillip Larkin, Ted Hughes. These are genuine poets, exceptions that prove the rule. Why, among the throngs of poetasters in the English faculties across the western world, is there such a paucity of imaginative output, just solipsistic meanderings and obscurantist baloney?

'And what happens to the would-be scholars, not to the genuine origi-nals–the Fryes and McLuhans and Milton Wilsons and Miller McLures and Father Shooks and, gaddamnit, the A.S.P. Woodhouses, too? What happens to the multitudes who swarm the Modern Language Association conferences who've never had an original thought since high school, currying advancement in warm climates that offer big salaries? Their creative juices just dwindle away into note cards for the next obligatory article, on what? Hamlet? Huckleberry Finn? Henry James? Jesus Christ, there are already enough shelves of studies on them to last humanity for the next millennium. I'm not against scholarship, Peter, real breakthrough literary criticism like Frye's. It's essential. I just question the industrial mills of Eng Lit that grind out inconsequential studies, forests of paper that would be more use in lava-tories, and all the youthful vigour gone to waste there. Tell me true, Peter! Do you think of yourself as someone who wants to do this?'

"Lennie knew how to leave you pinned and wriggling, didn't he? He could get right into your head, put you face-to-face with yourself. My answer was the only thing it could have been: 'No, I'm no scholar.'

"Lennie said: 'Peter, if I didn't love you like a brother, I'd keep my mouth shut. Don't hold up your hands. You're smart. You're nice. You worry about animals. You have creative fuel ready to ignite. You're even a good-looking sonofabitch. You're like the West, open to hope, innocent of old iniquities, full of possibility. Jesus, don't fritter it all away in the stacks of some smothering library writing a book about the twenty-one novels of Joyce Cary.'

"I felt like I was under attack. I tried to fight back. 'Where do you fit into all this, Lennie? When are you planning your escape from academe?'

'We're not the same sort, Peter.'

'You mean you're not vulnerable to the blandishments of a career at the University of Florida where you can get a sun tan and regular seduction?'

'That might do for me, Peter. I'm no poet, and I like the sunshine.'

'If you aren't a poet, what are you? I'll tell you what I think. I'm Blake's Palamabron, the tamed, house-broken literary man, and you're Blake's fiery Rintrah, revolutionary scourge of the power elite. I run Blake's harrow, planting the seeds of pity. You drive a plough, churning up the furrows of wrath. I write engaging stories to amuse people and you ... what do you do, Lennie? Rage in the wilderness like the prophet Jeremiah?'

'That's pretty much it, Peter. I rage in the wilderness of moral virtue as practiced in church and state by spiritual eunuchs, worshipers of vicious ideologies and repressive regimes that rule in the hope that life will bring no surprises. These are the elect of the world, the complacent ones, who observe the letter of the law from their youth onwards, and their days are long and peaceful in the lands they possess.'

"You couldn't beat the guy, Jason. Not just his words but the way he looked into you. That afternoon tipped the balance for me. Come spring, I quit graduate school and went to England to write."

Chapter Sixteen

I invited Lennie to talk to one of my Ryerson classes before he left to go
back to Winnipeg for the summer of 1961. The class was Business 201,
a tough bunch when it came to their compulsory course in English. The
students were all males, certainly no dummies, half of them older than me
and hard to break through to. *Death of a Salesman* was the subject that week,
a work chosen, I was told, for its vocational relevance to students of business. So much for curriculum planners. The business students hated the play.
I could get no sympathy for Willy Loman. The class's attitude was simple:
Willy couldn't hack it. He's a loser. Tough bananas!

Lennie began his talk by saying that, when he was last in New York, he
had gone to an Art Cinema to see *Citizen Kane* and, going for a pee afterward, he had recognized the tall man peeing next to him was Arthur Miller,
author of *Death of a Salesman*. "The man," Lennie said, "has the biggest dick
I've ever seen. As you may have heard, he married Marilyn Monroe." For the
first time in weeks, Business 201 sat up to listen, and Lennie set off.

"I also want to tell you guys about Shelley. He was a poet. I don't know
how big his dick was. I never saw it. Shelley died when he was thirty after
having written a half-dozen of the best poems in the English language, you
know, the language we more or less speak. He also practised free love and a
lot of bad things I'm not going into.

"Well, never mind what he wrote. It won't be on your exam. Think of the
kind of images he used that we can all recognize–autumn leaves and clouds
blown by the wind–but we never see the wind. Melting glaciers and rivers
and oceans and rain that manifest but never reveal the system that contains
them, the precipitation cycle. The song of the skylark can be heard, but the
bird soars so high it can't be seen. Life itself, said Shelley, is 'like a dome of

many-coloured glass that stains the white radiance of Eternity'. That would be a shaft of pure white light before it passes through the colour spectrum. These are all images that suggest, but never let you see, the force that infuses them. Do writers have trademarks like that, a type of imagery that individuates them?

"You must have read in high school about the boy swinging from the birch tree who lets himself leap out at precisely the right distance up the tree to carry him gracefully to the ground, not so far up that the branch breaks, nor so far down that the tree has no spring? That's what happens in Robert Frost's poem, *Birches*. There's the same balance between love and hate in a poem of his called *Fire and Ice*. There's the dividing wall in *Good Fences Make Good Neighbors*. There are a lot of borderline-type situations in his poems, like the point at the brim of a full cup where one more drop will break surface tension and make the contents overflow. Frost's poems, never mind their simple surface, often balance like this on a kind of tightrope. Is Frost the tightrope walker, the poet of equipoise?

"So what about old Arthur Miller? Can you find anything in the play, not image clusters (Miller isn't a poet) but trademark scenes—the two boys polishing the family car, Willy's suitcase full of samples? We're dealing with a family here who believes in all the values of the American dream, just like us, but for some reason can't make it work. What are we to do with these unfortunates? Sweep them into the trash? Throw them away like an orange peel? At one point Willie says: 'Attention must be paid!' What happens when a person gets to the point where, like Willy, he says: 'You've got to take me off the road, Howard'? Let's hope it never gets like that for any of us guys."

Over beer afterward at the Brown Derby on Yonge and Gould, I said to Lennie: "What in the name of Jesus were you talking about to that bunch?"

"Look, I wasn't there to suck up to your boys. If they don't have any interest in a little mental fermentation, I can't help them. So some of them didn't know Shelley from Norman Vincent Peel or Robert Frost from Ayn Rand. But you must have seen it. A couple of the boys were getting turned on. Ain't that what teaching is all about? Why don't you get them to write an essay on "The Stereotype and the Reality of the American Salesman"? See what they come up with?"

"I know what they'll come up with. They'll begin with something like: 'Marilyn Monroe married Arthur Miller because he has a big dick'."

"Well, it's a start."

"Anyway, does he?"

"I had to get their attention, JJ. I never pissed in a urinal with Arthur Miller. I have no more idea how big his dick is than you do."

Lennie's parting triumph that spring, with Mike Nader's editorial repairs, was to submit, finally, a term paper for McLuhan as a kind of prologue for his PhD thesis. It was about conceptions of poetic inspiration since the Renaissance. Lennie told me the story. When he took his idea to McLuhan, McLuhan said, "Boyce, I'm going to let you mark this paper yourself." Lennie couldn't believe it. "Who's ever heard of such a thing? What if I cheat?" he asked McLuhan. "What if I give myself too high a grade?" McLuhan said, "The exercise will be worth it. It will teach you to hone your skills as a critic and be self-critical at the same time."

"I knew his way of marking. He restricted his marginalia to either 'Three good ideas', or 'Two good ideas', or 'One good idea' or 'No ideas here'. He graded papers A, B, C, or P accordingly. Marshall never gave an F as far as I know. P was understood to mean not just 'Pass' but 'Pass On By'. I wasn't worried. I knew I had at least three good ideas. Maybe more. So I gave myself an A."

When Lennie's mark for the course came back in the summer, he got a B. On the phone to me from Winnipeg, he was spluttering mad. "I called McLuhan. Do you know what he told me? 'Boyce, yours was an excellent paper. But you must understand. With my reputation at U of T, any student who gets an A from me stands a very good chance of being washed up for good in graduate school. Remember who runs things here. What a B from me represents is positive. It means you weren't a sucker for everything I said, and so you might deserve advancement within the system which is, after all, the objective of every graduate student, is it not? Remember this advice. I give it you with my blessing. Get your union card before you speak too loudly. Get your legitimacy. Then you can say whatever the hell you like.'

"So I didn't get a mark from Northrop Frye because I left owing him a term paper on Blake. From McLuhan, my certain hope, I got a dismal B. There I was, student of two of the great luminaries of my time, and I walked away with half a loaf in one hand and nothing in the other. I ask you, JJ, am I jinxed or am I jinxed? Of all the screwball situations!"

When Lennie came back to Toronto for his third year in the fall of 1961, the world had changed again. Delia and I had a second baby. Mark Woodward and Vanessa were saving for a house. Mike Nader was back in Detroit. Peter Coultry was writing his novel in England. Maybe the graduate courses didn't look as enticing as once they did. Maybe it was lonely at 99 St. George without Mike Nader and Peter around. Lennie stayed on for a month and then went back to Winnipeg without warning. He told me he'd had it with the university and was working on the idea of starting a school of his own.

We spoke regularly on the phone. Lennie said he was living at Sophie's old restaurant on Main Street, trying to sell it for a good price, but not doing much else. He said he had an evening with Peter Coultry who had returned from England to spend Christmas with his mother and father. He said he had done his best to encourage Peter to work on his novel and not think about coming back to academe.

"London's done wonders for him, JJ. 'I met a girl,' he told me. Remember he had always been on the shy side with women. 'She read some of my stuff about geese and so on. She said that what I was doing was vague, fine writing, too purple. Even by her body language, I could tell what I wrote was no good.'

'You fell in love,' I said to Peter.

'I don't know,' he said. 'In lust, yes. She's a Holly Golightly, but without symptoms of tragic excess. She doesn't believe in marriage and she has no use whatsoever for children unless they belong to someone else and she's in a mood to play with them. A fresh brand of woman in my experience. And she's terrifically smart. She looked me straight in the eye and gave me the best assessment of my writing I've ever had. Not like you guys when you were cushioning me from the awful truth. She said I sounded like I was still trying to write *Look Homeward Angel*—too many adjectives, too many subordinate clauses, not enough verbs. I don't know what felt better, throwing my pages in the sea at Suffolk, or falling into bed with her afterwards at Pinmill Inn.'

'No more Canada geese then?' I said.

'No more Canada geese.'

'Then what?'

'Naive lad from the Midwest journeys to the flesh pots of Europe. No more Henry James with sentences that need an enema. Billy Bud corrupted.

The wild colonial boy reinvents himself on the soiled mattress of the old world.'

"I tell you, Jason, he's much changed by his continental adventure, though he can't disguise the fact that under the skin he's as sweet and straight and untainted a laddie as ever was."

Two days after Christmas, 1961, Lennie called me again. "Jesus Christ, Jason. Peter's dead." Peter loved curling. During his stay with his family in Winnipeg, he had gone with some friends to a bonspiel in Brandon and they had a head-on collision with a tractor-trailer on the way back. "Remember I did my damnedist to get Peter the hell out of academe and out into the world so he had chance to become the writer he wanted to be? Why didn't I leave him alone to rest peacefully among the groves? What the hell, did I put some kind of hex on him?"

Chapter Seventeen

A long with his old Paris pal, Shabby Shublik, and some prairie painters, post-beatniks, pre-hippies, jaded academics, and an assortment of like-minded malcontents, Lennie founded *Umbilicus*, a school for drop-outs and vagrants fed up with the education system. *Umbilicus*, he told me, the belly button, represented contemplation, the receiving of sustenance, the need to break from mothers, also the geometrical centre of the body, as Winnipeg was the geometrical centre of North America.

"Fine," I said to him, "but what the hell do you know about running a school?"

"JJ, let me put it to you this way—whatever kind of school I put together, Immaculate Conception is not the model I have in mind. I know a good deal about how not to run a school. When I was 13, there was family trouble and I got sent off to Immaculate Conception College in Alberta. It was a Catholic boarding school with a reputation for converting wayward boys to the straight and narrow and teaching timid and under-performing adolescents the arts of manhood. Everybody praised the place because, year after year, it fielded an unbeatable hockey team. Its ideals were Spartan and, well, its methods were classical in more ways than one.

"One of the reverend fathers prided himself on his garden. Surrounded by a high fence, it featured rollicking Grecian statues, not sculpted but moulded in concrete, and polished smooth with much labour. I know, because I was one of the three boys during my stay at Immaculate Conception chosen to perform this labour. As in all such schools, everything that went on was known to everyone, if only by innuendo. After a polishing session, accompanied by numerous glasses of sacramental wine and such delicate titbits as canned cocktail sausages and salted anchovies on slices of hard boiled eggs,

I was regularly invited to the reverend father's knee where I was given the privilege of servicing him, after which, overflowing with fellow-feeling, the good father would insist on reciprocating. You see, I do know a thing or two about how <u>not</u> to run a school."

"You were buggered by a priest?" I broke in.

"I didn't say 'buggered'."

"Jesus, Lennie. All the same...."

"Irish you are, but not Catholic, eh, JJ?"

"What the hell does that mean?"

"Nothing really, because it doesn't matter what persuasion it was–High Church, Low Church, Anywhere-in-between-Church it went on throughout the residential schools. When you were playing basketball at your community hall and stopping for a piece of flapper pie and a fountain coke at the soda bar on your way home, other things were happening in less happy schools elsewhere."

"I'd have blown the whistle on the bastard."

"Not so fast, Captain Marvel. Whose ear would you have blown it in? Besides, the reverend father served great food compared to what they fed us in the cafeteria. The wine was too sweet for my liking, though I have to admit I enjoyed the high. But that wasn't it. It's the essence of all scams–once you're in, you're part of the game.

"One of the 'chosen three' was a boy called Hezzie, an unrepentant house breaker with an impressive portfolio of reform schools before his parents sent him to Immaculate Conception as a last resort. One night, there was an official dinner with important guests at the head table–local politicians and rich benefactors of the school. We had seen fresh fruit being delivered by the dray wagon from the railway station, plums and grapes out of ice-cooled boxcars from British Columbia. They never showed up at our meals, so Hezzie and I broke into the larder to steal some. After sampling the plums, I had an idea. We took a few plums and grape bunches and rubbed them in our assholes. They sat the next night in baskets at the head table. After dinner and speeches, they were enthusiastically consumed by the high muck-a-mucks."

Chapter Eighteen

Over the next two years I kept busy trying to establish myself as a TV reporter on the North. That meant making Winnipeg my operations base for the Arctic. During my stopovers, I watched Lennie's renegade renaissance take shape. It wasn't the only thing of its kind. Alternative schools were sprouting up everywhere, not just in Montreal and Toronto and Vancouver but all over North America. Hotbeds of resistance to what they called the sausage-factory schools of the moral majority, where the command curricula were the root cause of what was becoming known as the generation gap. Everywhere, of course, money was a problem, and by the fall of 1963, *Umbilicus* was not immune. Shabby Shublik gave me the lowdown.

"Sometimes I thought Lennie had read too many encyclopaedias. There were a dozen of us at *Umbilicus*. Cross-hatching was Lennie's term for what we were doing. 'Within the insulated departments of the university,' he said, 'how can you learn anything beyond cubby-holes of data? How can you grasp Newton's intuition of gravity by taking a standard physics course, let alone comprehend how, a little later, he recognized that it was the same force that governed the movement of the stars in the rest of the universe? How can you appreciate the colossal leap of imagination a thing like that was, if you have no idea of the state of knowledge in Newton's time, or of the social and religious conditions he lived under? Without context, how can you grasp the magnitude of Newton's mind or the potential of the human imagination it represents? It's also important to realize what a nasty and vengeful little shit Newton could be ... as a lesson in the practical realities of genius.'

"Some of the teachers we attracted were defectors from university faculties, jaded by their narrow specialities and young enough to hitch a ride on a wild new enterprise. Some were travellers just back from Mexico or Morocco or New York or London or Amsterdam, flush with ideas and hash, and an intimation that something unusual was taking shape. We saw ourselves as pioneers in an as-yet-undefined revolution with the potential for liberating the world from its rusty chains. As a philosopher trained in the scepticism of Descartes and Voltaire, part of me regarded my cohorts as more than a little pie in the sky, but I was still young and couldn't resist their enthusiasm.

"Lennie was the lodestone. Word about *Umbilicus* spread like prairie fire. Before long, the rest of us took small groups in seminars, and we rented a space at an army reserve barracks two hours every week for Lennie's core lectures. The drill hall had a hundred and fifty collapsible chairs and generous standing room. I knew back in Paris that Lennie was a natural born spellbinder, but watching him relieve himself in the pissoirs along the Boulevard Saint Germaine and listening to him sound off in the cafés of Montmartre and the West Bank gave me no inkling of the power of his gift as an orator."

Rachel Carson's *Silent Spring* announced that, for the first time in history, every human being on the planet was being exposed to lethal, man-made chemicals from cradle to grave. I had gone to elementary school in Flin Flon where a green mound from the Hudson's Bay Mining and Smelting Company rose 30 feet high just over the chain-link fence, a stone's throw away from our schoolyard. It was a hill of tailings from the mining process, a mini-mountain of arsenic. Years later, it was the subject of my first investigative report on environmental pollution, and it took me to Flin Flon several times. On a stay-over in Winnipeg on my way back to Toronto, I had an afternoon free. It was Lennie's lecture day in the army barracks on Smith Street.

I turned thirty that year, the same as Lennie. I was probably the oldest person in the audience. There was no advance notice of what the talk would be about. Lennie entered from the back, stopping to talk to people as he made his way to the dais, carrying a cup and a pitcher of what I thought was likely not altogether water. Clearing his throat, his first gesture was to spread his arms wide, as if he were holding a giant globe, and to say in a booming voice with a squinty grin: "Bless you, my children." It was a parody, which clearly everyone had become accustomed to, of a revival meeting. There were titters, and a wave of camaraderie washed through the hall. His standing there, without text or notes, arms akimbo, as if waiting for the muse to descend, put the whole audience on his side before he said another word. He began:

> Wake up Winnipeg! Can't you hear the drums beating over the hill, the rumbling cries of the mob brandishing branches of cannabis and sheaves of poetry? They're coming to break up our cushy nests where 'no dispute can come because of those who sleep'. No more signing up of the young for wars of conquest masterminded by the aging robber barons of the industrial complex. No more listening to sanctimonious proselytising and puerile pontificating from the pulpits of the blessed. No more stunned acceptance of the hidden persuasions concocted by the mind-fuckers of advertising. Time to shake up the silent majority. John Donne called them 'those vulgar heads that rudely stare about'. Wordsworth saw them as industrialized multitudes living in a state of 'almost savage torpor'. It's not World War III that's coming. This time it's Blake's Mental War where the job of every crusader is first to identify and then to expose the enemy, what Blake called effecting a 'the consolidation of error.' Time to storm the Bastille and break off 'the mind-forged manacles' of bourgeois complacency and self-delusion. Our theme today is Pandemonium. You all know this place from the Second Book of *Paradise Lost*.

He spoke of Satan's plunge through chaos and old night for daring to challenge God to do battle. I prepared myself for what I expected to be Blake's view of Milton as a frustrated revolutionary who defended the Puritan God while subconsciously admiring the fiery Satan whom he was obliged to condemn in order to conform to established theology. Lennie fooled me.

> I want to talk about Pan who gave his name to pandemonium, Pan the god of fields and flocks, the god with a human torso and head, but with goat's ears and horns, and goat's legs and cloven hooves. Pan probably derived his name from 'Paon', the Doric word for 'pasturer'. How could it have come to mean 'all', as in pantheism, panegyric, pandemic, or for that matter Pan American Airlines?

Was it because the nature that Pan once stood for was, for the early Greeks, all there was, in other words, everything? And was it this attachment to the natural world that spared them the excesses of superstition that plagued contemporary cultures, and that consequentially in the sixth and fifth centuries B.C. allowed them to invent philosophy? But how did Pan get into the word 'panic'? Could it be because of what Pan, the god of herds, brought about when, in opposition to triumphant rationality, he stampeded his cattle and brought chaos to the town square? Just like the panic at a rock concert that gets out of hand.

Over the next hour and a half, Lennie brought in the trial of Adolph Eichmann, the gentrification of jazz by the Dave Brubeck Quartet, the absurdity of the Berlin Wall, Kennedy's "Ask not what your country can do for you" speech, the attacks on the freedom riders in Alabama, the rise of the Beatles, Pope John XXIII's progressive encyclical, *Mater et Magistra* (he compared Pope John's "forward leap of the kingdom of Jesus" to Mao Tse-Tung's "Great Leap Forward"), and to round things off, the 'panic' of celebrity that destroyed Marilyn Monroe. For the moment, it all made sense. Lennie was mobbed after the lecture, like a faith healer who performed miracles, or was it more like a rock star being beatified by his fans? That afternoon was my only direct exposure to the *Umbilicus* experience. For the rest, I had to rely on Shabby Shublik's account.

"In the fall of 1963, we had over a hundred registered students and God knows how many who couldn't afford the $100 term fee but who came anyway. Of course, it wasn't fees that paid for the school. It was a tangled network of city and provincial grants, including some private endowments which I cobbled together without being able to establish a permanent revenue base. That was one problem, but not the biggest one.

"A student of Lennie's called Billy came from one of Winnipeg's old guard Wasp families. They had what everyone referred to as 'extensive holdings' in the grain exchange, The Hudson's Bay Company, the CPR, real estate, and manufacturing. Billy was a nice boy. He had everything but he didn't want it, and he couldn't stand his family. He was bright, just the sort who would latch on to a charismatic like Lennie. The trouble was that marijuana, practically unknown in Winnipeg a couple of years earlier, suddenly became as big as Johnny Cash and rock and roll. When I got back from France, it was being heavily imported and widely cultivated. Inevitably, it got connected not just with Lennie's classes, but with the whole anti-establishment ethos Lennie stood for (all those pinkos). As my financing sources, even in the public sector, began to dry up, it was a while before I twigged to what was happening.

"Billy's dad learned of Billy's pot-smoking ways which, naturally, he attributed to the influence of the riff-raff at *Umbilicus* and especially to the notorious corrupter of youth, Lennie Boyce. I knew Lennie smoked a lot of pot. Most young teachers did, though not all with the same bravado as Lennie. I didn't smoke any kind of dope, never have, just a lot of cigarettes, unquestionably a worse addiction. Smoking dope seemed to me no more dangerous than driving a car, though I didn't do that either. People I went after for money, even old North Enders who listened to me at first because I had graduated from the Sorbonne, which made them proud to know me, began backing away. It took me a while to wake up. I didn't know one man could turn the entire city against us, until an old rabbi I knew as a kid enlightened me. Billy's father, the rabbi said, had enough shekel power to shut the whole province down if the mood came over him.

"We could pay teachers only a pittance. We held seminars in beer parlours—the Mall, the Marlborough, the St. Regis, the Pembina, mainly the Albert. We thought we had a new vision and we wanted everyone to see it with us. Without our realizing how fast it could happen, *Umbilicus* went down.

"Me, I was damaged but unbroken. I had my Sorbonne degree. To take a tenured university post was a step down from the high-minded standard we had set for *Umbilicus*. But I was getting a little the worse for wear. I wrote letters in search of a haven. It was no shoo-in. I saw no advertisements that read: 'Wanted: qualified philosopher. Must have at least five years' experience philosophising.' But university enrolment was booming and there were jobs to be had by the qualified, so I was OK.

"It was different for Lennie. His credentials were a mess. He wouldn't listen to me about our financial difficulties. Once, he actually turned on me and said: 'It's just money you know. And money is shit.' When he finally got the message that we were washed up, he went into a rage. He brought Billy, who had followed him around like a spaniel for two years, over to my flat and made me explain to him that his father had torpedoed us. When I finished, I expected Lennie to break into a tirade. As ever, he surprised me. He sat staring at Billy for the longest time as Billy did his best to hold back tears. Then all Lennie said was: 'Billy, go back to your family. You're too easily influenced. You're like the baby ostrich that falls in love with the Land Rover that runs over his mother.'

"I'm not sure Billy understood. I'm not sure I did either, but I didn't care. I was fed up with the Billys of the world and their troublesome neuroses. That was in the spring of 1964. I barely saw Lennie over the summer and, when I did, he was morose and incommunicative, except once. We were having steaks, just the two of us, in the Charterhouse, when out of the blue, he said: 'How do you feel about being a Hebe?'

'Good, Lennie,' I said. 'I feel good about it, and you? How do you feel about being a Hunkie?'

'I didn't think you'd ask.'

'This is a problem?'

'The problem is I'm tired of this outfit we're living in. The acquisitiveness every way you look. The greed and triviality, the avarice everywhere. For what? A new lawn mower, aluminium windows, fifty pounds of chrome on the car, a bunch of kids with bawling faces jammed between beach balls in the rear window of a station wagon, the horrific molehills of suburbia. The great chain of buying? Jesus, are we making a sorry civilization or what? The utter cynicism of the corporate circus masters and the sycophants who make up their lies and pump them out to the Aegrum Vulgus, the great credulous unwashed who lap up the lies as if they had no brain of their own, and rush out to grab the next bargain. It's what Ezra Pound said. We are 'a botched civilization, an old bitch gone in the teeth.' I hope I don't sound bitter or ungrateful for my charmed life.'

'So what's this Hebe/Hunkie thing got to do with it?'

'We may have been dog shit in the old country, Shabby, but even dogs had a life.'

'It was paradise under Stalin, I recall my dad saying. Really good too when Kruschev, your Ukrainian, working his way up the ladder under Stalin, reduced an unproductive peasant population by twenty million people give or take.'

'I'd sooner starve under Kruschev than live like a zombie consumer under Lyndon Johnson.'

'He's American, you're Canadian.'

'Same thing.'

'Different history. Take guns for instance. Makes a person stop and think.'

'Don't be such a goddamn philosopher.'

'I can't help it. I am a philosopher.'

'No, you're not. You're a philosophy teacher.'

'Break my heart, you bastard, and you are?'

'I'm a Hunkie from the North End and you're a Jew from the North End and let's not forget it. We come from the debris of humanity.'

"You never knew where Lennie was coming from, but I was shortly to learn what must have been on his mind that day. He was about to marry Katia, a North End girl he had known since they were kids, and they were going to go to the Soviet Union to start a new life. So when he said I wasn't a real philosopher, but only a philosophy teacher, what he was really saying was that I was just another East-European sell-out with a lot of tainted western ideas; whereas he was a true native son, about to reconnect to his ancestral roots, on his way home to the Steppes. It didn't make his put-down any easier to swallow. I was invited to Lennie's and Katia's wedding and two weeks later, they were off to Russia."

Part III
Forests of the Night

Chapter Nineteen

L ennie was no letter writer. The last time I had heard from him by post was in 1959 when he had written from Ibiza on his first honeymoon to tell me about extravagant sex on the Mediterranean and the winds of change blowing in on the Sirocco from Morocco. This honeymoon letter was different.

October 4, 1964

Dear JJ:

You've never met Katia. She's lovely and sexy and you would love her. I've told her about you and she says she thinks you might be okay ... for a Mick. I said you're not a real Mick, you're a fake Mick, a Canadian Mick. You're not even a Catholic. She says she might forgive you for that, too.

I've known Katia since grade school. Guess what? She's Ukrainian. Our first meeting was in the Beacon Theatre on Main between episodes of *The Perils of Pauline* and *Zorro The Whip*. I tweaked her pig-tail when she was sitting in the seat in front of me and she turned around and plastered me in the face with her overshoe. It was love at first sight, although I couldn't see a thing until my head cleared. It's taken twenty years for that to happen.

Katia has been working as a waitress and off and on at Eaton's most of her life, so she has none of that nice little Miss BA quality of the cultured classes. Also she speaks good Ukrainian, far better than mine, thanks to the deracinating influences I have been subjected to. Judging by our many visits to the Russian Consulate, she understands and is understood by Muscovites. As we will be in Moscow any day now, you can appreciate what an inside track that will give us getting situated.

Let me fill you in. I was deeply pissed off by the demise of *Umbilicus*. More than I can say. I had banked heavily on it, and even believed that a free academy could be started on the prairies that would fire a transformation. Jesus, it was great while it lasted. And JJ, I was good. Of course, there was selfhood involved, but only late at night when I was by myself. Around the kids and that motley bunch of hippies and amateur thinkers who came along with me, I forgot about myself and went into orbit. I can't explain it. It was a high like nothing else I've known. And I'm not talking about dope. I never toked before a lecture. Most times, I was so high afterwards from some kind of internal chemistry I had no desire to toke then either. My mind was grabbing in material from all over the place and making sense of it. You know what I mean, that state of excitement when everyday chaos falls into patterns and everything connects. Almost as good as sex, it was. Maybe those highs became more addictive than dope or booze. When they were no longer there, when the organization collapsed and the spirit went out of it, I lost my fix. You could see defeat in everyone's eyes, and all around us nothing but avarice, the despoiling of everything that smacked of quickness and life in the mindless race for money and the cosmetics and gewgaws it buys.

And so I've sailed the seas and come to just outside the holy city of Moscow. I don't think I'll be back, JJ. I've come to realize that just over the wall out there, that's where my spiritual home has always been. How can I explain this to a displaced Celt, this return of mine to the contradictions of the Slavic mind? Are you sure you understand Dostoevsky?

Do you feel at home in the mind of Raskolnikov, murdering an old woman to find out if there is a god or not? Is it possible that kind of speculation is more fully human than sleepwalking with the docile multitude?

I expect I won't see you again this time round, JJ. Katia and I will fade into the landscape when we get where we're going. Memories of Winnipeg and many other things, including when we first met at John Peter's seminar, and the times we had in Toronto with Mark Woodward and Peter Coultry and Mike Nader and the rest of them—they won't be forgotten.

They're at the door for our ride through the wall. I'll post this on the way, in case it's more difficult to get word out from the other side.

Love from Comrade Lennie
(Katia says hello-goodbye).

Life settled in routinely over the winter of 1964-65. Delia and I had a three-year-old boy and a new baby. She worked as part-time nurse and mother. I worked as part-time father and freelance current affairs reporter when I could get the nod from CBC. Ends met. Nothing very surprising happened until one day in early spring the phone rang.

"Hey, JJ, I'm back, me and Katia." He hadn't wanted to contact me until they got established, Lennie said. I walked up Avenue Road hill to a posh apartment they had been given a key to for a month, and greeted them with some nice wine and a 12-year-old Dalwinnie that pretty well bankrupted me. I met Katia for the first time. She made pork chops and pierogies for dinner. Lennie got pissed and fell asleep, and Katia and I talked. There was no awkwardness between us. She said Lennie had often spoken of me and I was just like the person he described, but better looking. With a wonderful laugh, she added, "because (you know Lennie) he told me not to expect much because you looked like a bog Irishman."

"You were a bathing beauty," I told her.

"Who said?"

"I can't tell."

"That big mouth! I can't even swim."

"You don't have to swim to be a bathing beauty."

"No but you have to do a lot of other things."

I fell for Katia, just as Lennie had predicted. And not only because she was a very beautiful woman. She was without pretence. As Lennie slept, she talked to me on into the night.

"What in god's name possessed me when I agreed to marry that big mouth? I knew him from when we were young. Jason, I've got news for you, I think I've known him all my life. From school but before that even, I knew who he was in the neighbourhood. When we got to junior high, kids used to go to Central Bakery and buy donuts, six for five cents, every night fresh. I would see him there buying a couple of dozen and passing them around like a big shot. Later, we went to Argyle School. Girls got crushes on guys and we would hang around his mother's confectionary at the front of the restaurant where a lot of jive talk and giggling went on. Lennie told me he used to notice me but I don't think he did. He was too busy making an impression with his drapes and his Eisenhower jacket and his duck cut and his pointed shoes and his pork pie hat, all that shit those kids did.

"He was a smart-aleck, let me tell you. He talked back to the teachers. When they smacked him–they all smacked kids in those days, and sent them to stand in the cloak room–he laughed at them. When he came back from getting the strap at the principal's office, he would wear this smarty-pants grin and show off his red hands to everybody, as if we were all supposed to goose-step and go Hail Hitler or something.

"I lived only a block away from Sophie's on Main Street between Henry and Logan, and Sophie knew my mom and dad. Everyone knew Sophie. She was a hoochie-coochie, let me tell you. Back of the confectionary was Sophie's Diner and Grill. Her sister, Stella, had a restaurant just down the street, Stella's Steaks and Chops. They used to drink coffee at each other's places, and, when I was older, I would go there too. Just for coffee. Sophie and Stella never touched booze. They sold a lot on the side, and I didn't know what else. They never talked about their business when I was around.

"Sophie loved that son of hers but, do you know what, Jason? He could be a real chump. She asked me once if I would remind him about Mother's Day. I reminded him and, can you believe? He did nothing. Years later, when I was having coffee with Sophie, she showed me a wire Lennie had sent from

Paris. Jesus Christ, you'd think it was announcing that he'd won the Nobel Prize. 'Need $200 fast. Love L.' That's all it said. Two hundred dollars was a fortune. Sophie was tickled pink that Lennie had contacted her. She rushed off to the CPR station to wire the money to Paris.

"When I was growing up, I saw Sophie as a different kind of show girl from the ones who did burlesque at the Beacon Theatre and along Main Street. She was classy, compared to them. She had flaming red hair and dark blue eyebrows. Her lipstick always matched her hair, never a harsh red. She wore rows of necklaces and bracelets and she liked to dress in purple and maroon velvet gowns, with slits up to her tutu. I don't think she knew how to smoke but she carried around a long cigarette holder. She wore a mink stole, even in summer, and she must have had a dozen fur coats for winter. She always had something to say to people, usually a joke, or if someone rubbed her the wrong way, better look out, a dagger to the heart.

"Lennie tracked me like a hunting dog after he got divorced, and there was something about him, even when he was a show-off kid, that attracted me. Oh, he had the gift of the gab all right. He had more gas than a filling station. But that never impressed me as much as he thought it did. He could look right into your eyes as if he could read your mind. Maybe that was it. Maybe it was hypnosis. But, to tell you the truth, I think the idea of going to Russia was part of it, part of the reason for, what the hell, my marrying a lunatic. Who else would say 'Let's get married and go to Russia where we belong'? I'll tell you who else. Nobody else. God only knows who would be numbskull enough to go with him, unless that would be me.

"Following Lennie around Moscow to translate for him, this is what I still hear in my nightmares: 'Why are you here?', the Russian inquisitor said.

'To teach literature,' Lennie would answer. I would have to try to make sense of his bad Ukrainian for them.

'Russian literature?'

'Hemingway and Fitzgerald and Dos Passos and Steinbach, writers very critical of America. And later when my Russian improves, yes, Pushkin and Tolstoy and Dostoevsky.'

'You would make more money teaching in your own country.'

'I don't teach for money.'

'Then for what?'

'For humanity. To help humanity.'

'You work for your government as propagandist?'

'No, I'm Ukrainian. I have come home to rejoin and serve my people.'

"Jason, you can't believe the bullshit. The meetings went on and on, three or four a week, in one ministry after another. And Mr. Know-it-all? He couldn't get it through his head that they weren't going to give him a job. Over and over, they tried to find out why a Canadian professor would come to teach in Russia at one-tenth his Canadian pay. All they could make of it was that he was an undercover agent.

"They thought I was a spy, too. If Lennie was sponsored by the Canadian government to sneak western ideas into Mother Russia, or sneak information about Russia out, then I must be part of the team. I'll tell you the truth, Jason, I had fun at first. I couldn't believe the bullshit they were laying on us. My expectations about returning to the homeland were so different from the stupid way they treated us, at first I took it for a joke.

"The dumbest thing was when they tried to catch me up. This little shit in a shit-brown uniform, wearing coke-bottle glasses on a face like a pig, was going at Lennie full blast when he suddenly turned to me and said: 'And Madame Boyce, what is your opinion of The Great Gatsby?'

"I had read the book off the drug store rack. For me and my girl friends it was a tear-jerking love story, but I had heard it also had a political side. I wasn't going to fall for Porky Pig's trap so I said: 'I don't know any great Gatsby or any little Gatsby or any ordinary Gatsby.'

"None of those baboons who questioned us ever laughed or even smiled. They were like kids I used to take parcels to at the reform school in Winnipeg. They were frozen-fish faces. Lennie had always told me money meant nothing to him and, honest to god, it meant sweet bugger-all to me, Jason. Money was never a thing to fuss about. Here was a guy maybe I could finally love and he said he loved me. So how did we get into the pinch we were in then? Was it marriage that killed what we had before? Or was it because no sooner did we get married than we went off to find the Promised Land in Russia? It may have been stupid of Lennie to go. But it was stupider of me to go with him.

"Suddenly he was invited to sign on for two years at a school of journalism in Moscow. The man from the Canadian Embassy warned us there were all kinds of people like Lennie, guys from *Liberty* and *Time Magazine* and umpteen western journalists who signed up for things like that and got stuck so they couldn't leave when they wanted to. The Embassy man said it was these guys who took up most of his time, begging him to help them get them the Hell out of Russia.

"Lennie asked me what I thought we should do. I said I couldn't stand the place. He said 'They're our people.' I said, 'Not anymore, they aren't.' We argued in the taxi all the way back to the Hotel Berlin. The man from the embassy was waiting in the lobby. He said from what he could gather, we had a very good chance of being arrested as spies. He said he had a 12-o'clock reservation for us. He told us to pack quickly. We had three hours to catch the midnight train to Belgrade."

Chapter Twenty

The summer of 1965 was upon us, making it three years since Delia had seen Lennie. I invited Katia and him for dinner in hope that Delia's hostility to Lennie had subsided. She and Katia got on fine, but her aversion to Lennie remained as lively as ever. She still saw him, she told me later, not only as the sexual predator of the fifteen-year-old child he consorted with years ago in Ibiza, but as an on-going bad influence on ordinary people (for which, read me).

At the expiry of their gratis month in a friend's cushy apartment atop Avenue Road hill, Katia and Lennie moved to a basement flat in the less genteel neighbourhood of Dupont and Davenport. Suddenly they were out of money. Lennie had never talked about his inheritance but now he did–it was gone. I offered him a small loan but he would have none of it. If being broke was a new kind of experience for him, it was as nothing compared to his failure in Mother Russia, and that's what was eating him up.

Katia took work in a refrigerator factory, and Lennie, in a manner of speaking, went job hunting. This entailed not just excavating arts and letters folk at the Pilot Tavern, but staking out a new rendezvous at the Celebrity Club on Jarvis Street, much frequented by CBC workers and a scattering of journalists from the Globe and Mail, the Toronto Star, and the Toronto Telegram. The crowd was predominantly male, as it was in most Toronto drinking holes back then, therefore boozy, bawdy, garrulous, and pugnacious. Lennie moved in like an alpha wolf. Watching dominant males roll over and kick up their legs under his verbal lashings became a popular diversion for those of us who retained spectator status. He still had the smart, fast talk. But it wasn't the Lennie I knew from earlier times, playing the wily buffoon, tempering his derision with humor, urging people to be authentic–listening to people. It was a dark Lennie, witty without gaiety, short on pity. After one altercation with a man twice his size, when it was clear he was inviting a beating, I got him away and home to bed, and then sat listening to Katia as she recounted their flight from the madness of Moscow.

"We got to Bucharest and then to Athens. There was a friend of Lennie's I never knew about. Someone from the time when he had that *Umbilicus* school in Winnipeg. Billy was his name, a runaway from a rich family. He lived on the island of Rhodes with his boyfriend, and somehow, Lennie got hold of him and got us invited there. All Lennie said was that Billy owed him. Jason, as I live and breathe, it was beautiful. After Moscow, it was going to heaven first class. Billy lived at the top of a hill up from that old Knights Templar fortress. He had a big place with marble floors and a view of the sea, and huge fluffy curtains blowing in the breeze. I could have stayed there till they came to get me. Billy's lover was a mute, a very sweet boy. Billy treated Lennie and me like a king and a queen.

"Once, in Billy's car, Lennie and I drove way up the island, as far as the road went. There was a teeny beach there and a little restaurant with a patio over the sea. We swam and we ate and we made love on the sand. I was truly happy, but with the feeling, you know, how will this end?

"We ate out every night at the street restaurants in Rhodes. Tourists were starting to come in and this had a bad effect on Lennie. It was all that world of North America, I guess, that he had tried to escape from. We drank a lot, Billy and his lover and me, but not like Lennie. He would get sozzled every night. I got him into a taxi one night and when we got out, I saw him leave his hand in the door of the taxi on purpose and slam it shut. Jason, it made me sick. He didn't know I saw him, but it was like you would take a gun and shoot yourself in the hand. He broke two fingers.

"Staggering home nights after many Mataxis, he would stop at café tables and bother people. He could pick out Americans even when they looked Greek to me. He would say stupid things like: 'You're a geek, not a Greek'. He would lace into them about things in *Time Magazine*. He would say to someone at a table: 'What are you doing sunning yourself here, man? You should be out killing gooks in Viet Nam instead of sending your blacks to do your dirty work.' Billy was helpless and would disappear like a ghost. I would have to drag Lennie away.

"Lennie never raised a hand to me. I told him, if he ever hit me, I would wait until he went to sleep and then I'd cut his cock off. I don't know, maybe I would have. Anyway, he never did hit me, so I never had to find out whether I meant what I said or not. But one night, he really scared me. We were nearly home, walking by a bar called Popeye's where a lot of Americans hung out. As we passed, he reached up and grabbed the bar's neon sign and pulled it crashing down, and, before I could stop him, he waded into the tables, knocking over bottles and glasses and plates of food. A couple of men got hold of him and beat him up. They did a good job before I could get him out of there and catch up with Billy and his friend. They were terrified. They were at the end of their rope. Well, so was I. Just before we reached the villa, Lennie turned and took hold of me, his face all bloody and his hands cut and bleeding, and he just stared at me. I saw murder in his eyes. I never in my life scared easy, Jason, but he really scared me. I guess I believed, right then and there, nothing would ever be the same for us.

"Thank god, Billy seemed to have an endless supply of money. He got Lennie and me back to London for a bit and then to Toronto and to temporary quarters. I wanted to go all the way back, back to Winnipeg, but Lennie wouldn't have it. He couldn't go home feeling like such a blow-out, I guess, someone who couldn't make it even in Russia, some kind of super-duper world class loser.

"You know, Jason, I never saw Lennie as the big deal other people did. I never lost sleep or gave two hoots about what all his high-falutin' friends and intellectual hotshots thought about me either. Because I got news for you, I was way beyond him. Not in the brain department. He may have been able to quote Blake and Shakespeare and what have you, which meant piss all to me. But all that stuff he knew never helped him know his asshole from his ear hole."

Katia did wonders fixing up the flat on Dupont Street, a dingy place even so. I took over a dozen beers to help with the painting. There was a good-sized basement room and a kitchen, with a staircase going up to a small bedroom on the main floor of the house. At the landing, I sat cutting teeth into a piece of used carpet Katia had bought. I cut slots to fit between the rungs of the staircase. I clipped away and then I lowered the carpet between the rungs. The teeth fell nicely into place. Looking down, I saw Lennie watching. He was nursing a bottle of beer. He threw up his hands and glared up at me. "How in Hell did you make that fit?" he said. It was the episode of my repairing the canoe at Peter Coultry's cabin all over again. I had just accomplished a magic trick. It was as if, in his eyes, I possessed a skill fate had denied him, no matter it was just a carpet-cutting skill. At a time when he badly needed a boost, my simple act of cutting the carpet to fit the staircase rungs seemed to have struck him as a mockery from the gods.

That season, I saw Lennie through a series of frays and skirmishes. They took place at the Pilot Tavern, the old Celebrity Club up on Jarvis, The Embassy Beer Parlor, even sometimes at the celestial roof of The Park Plaza. Lennie partly charmed, partly scared all comers, sometimes it seemed to me doing both at the same time when he got into his cups. He had completed years of study and teaching with nothing solid to boast about, let alone credentials for making a living. He published nothing. With *Umbilicus,* he had created a teaching utopia that failed. He went off to Russia and came back empty-handed. Now all he seemed capable of doing was making trouble. The way he talked to people, it was hard for me to know if he was having them on or if he was tempting them to beat him up.

One day Katia called me, upset. Lennie had disappeared. She was used to him disappearing for a night, even two. But she'd had no word for three nights. Did I have any ideas? I searched his haunts. I asked around. I even checked with the police to be sure he hadn't stumbled or thrown himself into Lake Ontario. Then I thought of Mike Nader. We had lost touch, but I found Mike through the Detroit directory. "Lennie's here, Jason," Mike said. "He wouldn't give me his wife's number and yours is unlisted. He's okay, but thank goodness you called."

Katia stayed in a motel in Windsor and I went through the tunnel to Detroit. With the East European stamps on her passport, she couldn't risk getting stuck at the American border. She would meet us at Canadian Customs on our way back. When I got to Mike's house on Grand River, Lennie was out. He was ready to go home, Mike said, but he was feeling embarrassed about his escapade. He had borrowed some money and gone to a movie. Mike explained:

"Lennie arrived at three in the morning, a wreck. I hadn't seen him since I left Toronto three years ago in 1962. We corresponded for a while. The last I heard he was off to Russia. He said forever. Lennie was one of my best memories of Toronto. He was a good friend and it was a joy to see him again.

But the condition he was in dismayed me. His face was pallid, with a reddish rash across his forehead, and his gestures were exaggerated and jerky. My wife, Grace, took one look at him and went back to bed, I suppose trying to understand who this wraith was and what planet he had dropped in from. I took Lennie downstairs to the rumpus room. My young nephew and niece were staying with us in the spare bedroom upstairs. Remembering Lennie's love of single malt, I broke open a Glenmorangie and made up the roll-away in the rumpus room.

"Lennie said he had bottomed out. 'Seriously imploded' were his words. He had smoked some grass at the Pilot Tavern, bussed his way out to the highway, and gone hitchhiking here and there. There was nowhere he wanted to go, he said, which he recognized as a dangerous state of mind. Then he thought of me. Detroit became his beacon. He got a ride with a trucker. He had a passport stamped by East Bloc countries, a library card, six dollars, and six tokes in his shirt pocket. 'Maybe I wanted to get caught,' he said. It didn't strike me as a particularly impressive piece of self-knowledge. But they breezed through the border, he and his trucker, no questions asked. The trucker let him off downtown in the district east of Woodward. Not a place a nice Canadian boy wants to get lost in at night. He wandered into Paradise Valley and went into Big Daddy's, a haunt I knew well in kinder times when I was going to Wayne University just down the street.

"So, there's Lennie in no-man's-land. At the bar, he told me, the bartender leans in and says: 'You a lima bean in a tar barrel, boy. You best get your sorry white ass outa here.'

'I ain't white,' says Lennie. A clutch of locals gathers round.

'What color you then, ghost boy?' someone says.

'I'm red,' Lennie says.

"There are giggles. Someone says: 'You's pale as a hardboiled egg, daddy. Where's this red?'

"'I'm Russian Red. I'm the first real live fucking Russian Commie you ever seen.' A rumble begins. They decide not to break him to pieces.

'Hey, this man say he a real Commie,' one of the group says.

"Someone says: 'Hey Commie, you wanna live, you gotta pay.' Lennie turns his pockets inside out and leaves them that way. Then he puts the six joints he's been carrying in his shirt pocket on the bar.

'From each according to his means. To each according to his need,' says Lennie. No one is impressed, but one guy reaches out, retrieves a joint, and lights up. He sucks the smoke in, takes a moment gazing at the ceiling, then smiles. Lennie breaks the race barrier."

"You an Elvis humper, Mr. Red?" someone says.

"I hate Elvis," says Lennie.

"Who you like my man?"

"The Temptations, Gladys Knight and the Pips, Smokey Robinson, all those Holland-Dozier-Holland songs that came out with Diana Ross and the Supremes, Stevie Wonder and Aretha Franklin and that great, great song Lennie says, as he sings it and smacks the counter to the beat:

> Sugar Pie Honey Bunch
> You know that I love you
> Sugar Pie Honey Bunch
> Can't help myself
> I love you and nobody else

"But mainly I love BeBop, jazz, Muddy Waters and Sonny Terry and Brownie McGee."

"You could never tell, could you, whether Lennie came naturally to that kind of information or whether he researched it for ammunition? The bar explodes with applause. 'Sing us a song, Mr. Whitey Commie Red.'

"Lennie breaks into the Fats Waller song, singing it, he told me, in his Ivory Joe Hunter voice, the record we used to listen to at your place in Yorkville Towers in Toronto, remember? You can imagine the purity of pitch he was so good at, and his rasping attempt at a baritone.

> Cold empty bed
> Pains in my head
> Feel like old Ned
> Hey what did I do
> To be so black and blue?
> Hey now listen to me
> I am white
> Deep down inside

"Can you imagine? This black pack is listening to this sickly pale Canadian with a rash singing a song about a black man who is not really a bad man because, although he looks black, he is really white inside. And Lennie gets away with it. I've lived in Detroit all my life. It's my city. In better days, I would sometimes be the only white guy in the Wa Ha Room of the Gotham Hotel. I used to go to the hottest spot in town for R and B, a place called 20 Grand. I never got hassled. That was before these times, but even then, I stayed away from Paradise Valley. Ever since the Boblo Island eruption not long after WW II, racial anger has smouldered in Detroit, and Lennie managed to find himself at the epicenter of it and stay alive.

"The men at the bar smoked Lennie's joints and he talked to them. He told them about Moscow and Paris and Athens, and what a life there was out there beyond the Detroit River, what excitement and great fucking there was on the other side of the ghetto. I can imagine the scene. Lennie takes them out of themselves. He gets them thinking of worlds far away where imaginable things are real. He spins them Elysian Fields they rarely dare think about. When the time comes, they put enough money together to get him a cab to my place. Imagine him singing that Fats Waller song to them. The way I see it, it was an attempt at suicide that failed.

"At my house, there's the bedroom where my niece and nephew are, Grace's and my bedroom, the kitchen, the living room, a small study downstairs, and the rumpus room where Lennie was sprawled out. In the morning, Grace looked in and went to work. I was home from my air traffic controller job at the airport on a three-day, so I was able to stand sentinel. The kids kept poking their heads in at this man on the roll-away. Late in the day, I heard him talking to them. Malka is eight, Jebby six.

'So what if you could have what you want?' I heard Lennie say.

'I want a horse,' Malka said.

'Me too,' Lennie said. 'But could you look after a horse?'

'Sure I could.'

'I guess right here in the rumpus room.'

'Hmmmm,' said Malka. 'You mean right here?'

'I want a dog,' said Jebby.

'What kind of dog?' said Lennie.

'A big dog.'

'Big as me?' said Lennie.

'Bigger,' said Jebby, 'but not so snorey.'

"Lenny broke into that phissing, nasal guffaw that I always found so cordial. I stood outside the door smiling and thinking: 'The sneaky bastard. He's gone into teaching mode with the kids.'

"That night Grace confided that she didn't like him. Not only did he seem unbalanced, was I sure he wasn't a pederast? She didn't like the way he came down to the children's level, and the way he kept touching them. She had majored in behavioral psychology, so I had to think about it. I knew more than a bit about how Lennie liked to play mind games about suspected deviants. Hadn't he done something like that to me once? I assured Grace Lennie was not a pederast. I told her Slavic folks and other foreigners hug and touch each other a lot more than we do in Detroit, but that didn't necessarily mean they were sexual perverts.

"It was clear to me Lennie had not turned up on my doorstep by chance. His second night, we had a talk. He told me crazy things. He said he wished he could be a Catholic like me. He rambled on about why it was impossible for him to be a believer. His hatred of authority, he said, was his cloven hoof. If only there was no Pope. How could anyone live with the idea that some old man who worked his way up the bureaucracy and never got laid could achieve infallibility? But no pope, no church universal.

'For western man,' he said, 'only two deaths matter: the death of Socrates, and the death of Jesus.' He said I must think about them only as men like him and me, and that while it's easy to think of Socrates that way, Jesus comes with such an accretion of supernatural baggage that it muddies his footprints. 'What you have to do is take both men straight, a Greek in his real-life historical context and a Jew in his, both men of exceptional intelligence, common sense, and extravagantly high hopes. Socrates didn't have to drink hemlock. What was the charge against him? He was a corruptor of youth. He advocated radical questioning of the status quo. He opposed the tyranny of the state over free thought. Those who condemned him prayed he would recant before they had to kill him, because they knew killing him was against their interests in the long run. It was sowing dragon's teeth. He was offered every chance of escape, not only by followers who loved him, but by his accusers who feared the consequences of his martyrdom. Socrates declined deliverance and eschewed any ceremony or great fuss over his departure. Ready for what he called "that other world", he drank hemlock, got sleepy and, according to the Phaedo, delivered his last words: "Creto, I owe a cock to Asclepius. Will you remember to pay the debt?" Not exactly earthshaking this, requesting his student, Creto, not to forget to make good Socrates' promise to sacrifice a chicken to this new deity from the north called Asclepius. Now that is cool. So what about that other death?'

"Lennie said he understood that for me he wasn't talking about just anybody here, but the Son of God. He asked me to bear with him for a moment and see Jesus as just a man, quite a man for sure, but just a man.

'He's like Socrates in that he can't stand the shit around him, the stupidity and injustice and inhumanity. But he's a young fellow. His insight is intuitive. He doesn't speak like Socrates in the sweetly reasoned dialectic of the wise elder. He speaks in parables. Two kinds of teacher here: the aging sage and the youthful seer. So Socrates dies in a quiet, dignified way, refusing all forms of reprieve. He goes down without protest in the first of the two most iconic deaths of western culture. The other one also rejects all last minute offers of respite. The Gospels make it clear Jesus could have gotten away easily if he wanted to. His last words are not a gentle reminder to honour the debt of a chicken to a god, but a passionate and paradoxical plea to the One God to forgive his executioners. Being only a man, like Socrates, what a thing to say!

'The rest isn't so nice. Take your choice. Lie down and sip a cup of hemlock and go blissfully to sleep. Or watch as they drive nails through your ankles and wrists and leave you to slump and bleed in the sun. It's suffocation that gets you, because you can't stop yourself from sagging onto your lungs. But aside from the pain quotient, does it matter whether you die like Socrates or die like Jesus? When you are given every opportunity to stay alive, why let them kill you? Could it be that, voice of sweet reason or voice of divine inspiration, you arrive at the same wisdom? You've both had it with a fucked up world? You both see that humanity had a chance and blew it.'

"Lennie wore me down more than I knew I was capable of. I concentrated on feeding him and getting him to sleep. After the second day, he settled a bit. He hadn't seen my so-called study. It was off from the furnace room, a 12-by-12 alcove with a basement window, well insulated from where TV and the rest of my family life took place. My books and things are there. Lennie looked around as if he'd entered an enchanted cave. We sat over a pot of tea and he talked about the demeanings of Russia."

Chapter Twenty-One

We got Lennie back into Canada without loss of blood or further indignity. I met him at the Pilot Tavern a week later and barely recognized him. He looked like Tom Wolfe, all spiffed-up in a Haspel seersucker suit I remembered from better days and his elegant Italian shoes that I hadn't seen in years. He must have left them in storage with friends in his rush to plunge into Russia. He had no rash on his forehead and even wore a trace of colour on his cheeks. He plunked himself down, took a swig of the draft I had sitting ready for him, and like a kid who has just made the hockey team, he announced: "I got the call."

It had come from Daniel Warberg in Winnipeg. Head of the English Department, Warberg had seen Lennie perform at *Umbilicus* back in 1962/63 and said he could offer him a job if Lennie could confirm that he was working on his PhD thesis.

The English department at Manitoba was two-thirds old guard from the 40s and 50s, and one-third young Turks. Vince Calley, a Winnipeg original who had done post-graduate work in Toronto under Northrop Frye, was one of them. Two years older than Lennie, Vince was a hard-to-read mixture of the ethereal and the ironic, an academic, part-time poet, painter, actor, and a keen-eyed observer of the passing scene. He told me about his encounter with Lennie upon his arrival at U of M in that fall of 1965.

"I invited him to a faculty party. Among the older members, there were few you could call distinguished scholars. John Peter was certainly one, and a female professor was another. A woman of 50, she was speaking (I felt somewhat self-importantly) about the declining literacy of freshmen, when Lennie leaned over to me and in a not very discreet whisper said: 'Could you raddle that broad if you had to?' I remember swallowing hard and having the distinct sense that a new force had just arrived on campus.

"In my life, and in the life of others on the department who got to know him, Lennie caused a major shake-up. He had an effect on us similar to what the sudden emergence of concern for the environment had on us in the early 60s. He made us rethink everything, re-examine ourselves, not just our professional standing. In what might start out to be a casual conversation with Lennie, you would find yourself going back into things you thought you had left behind. He made you unearth them. I feel my life was just totally changed because of this man. He opened pores, brought out centres of feeling that set me off on all kinds of new directions. I'm supposed to be a merchant of words. But Lennie's effect was so personal and so un-literary, sometimes so raw and so basic, that it shocked me into rethinking my life.

"He offended people continually and yet he fascinated people. There was something elusive about him, something you felt he wasn't giving you, some corner you hadn't turned and something around that corner you couldn't predict, and maybe didn't want to know about. He was never charming. Charm had bad connotations. His word for it was 'smarmy'. The words you needed for him are 'catalytic', 'charismatic', sometimes 'incendiary'. That doesn't mean he was not a supremely moral man in the true sense of that word. When I got to join the cafeteria chat or the talk around the table at the Pembina Beer Parlour (he dubbed it U of M's high table), Lennie retained two ruling passions–Spengler and Blake. Spengler was the grim observer of western civilization's decline. Blake was the engaged visionary out to re-make the world into the heart's desire."

On campuses all over North America, peaceniks were popping up like mushrooms. There were half a million American troops in Viet Nam in 1965 and the blunders of the military were on the rise. Lennie decided that our generation was to blame. We were tainted, and had to learn to identify with the kids, especially the draft dodgers. There were up to forty thousand of them in Canada, many of them in Winnipeg. Founded by escapees of per-secution of all sorts in Europe, Winnipeg took easily to this latest of many waves of conscientious objectors.

Along with new university friends and friends Lennie had grown up and gone to school with, his reach spread out across the city. He was at home in academic circles, at parties of the well-to-do, in downtown beer parlors,

North End pool rooms, and god only knows where else. And of course, there was the growing corps of students and former students who continued to swell the circle around him.

Jackie Steiner was a North Ender of a rare type. On a bend of the Red River opposite Inkster Boulevard, there's a cluster of large brick houses bisected by what was once the ox-cart trail to St Andrew's down the Red River toward Lake Winnipeg. The lots are enormous, some running 200 feet down to the river, remnants of when the river was the fur trade's highway. The modest but stately houses and wide spaces are products of a British enclave that sprang up in the early days around St. John's Anglican cathedral. In later times, the area became populated by Jews who had prospered and elected to stay in the North End instead of flocking south to fashionable River Heights. It was in one of these graceful homes that Jackie Steiner had grown up. She and Lennie were both North Enders therefore, but even had they been contemporaries (they were not, she being a half dozen years younger), it's unlikely they would ever have met across the North Main divide between the posh residents on river side and the working class folk on the west side.

Jackie was petite, cute, and rich. But you would never know she was rich. She may have spent a lot of time worrying about being rich, but she never made a point of talking out loud about it. In the early days, North End Jews and South End Wasps rarely came into contact, except on business, at sporting events, on the crowded sidewalks of Portage Avenue, or shopping at Eaton's and the Bay. After the war, all that changed. Although the university began as a haven for children of the Anglo/Scots establishment, by the 1950s, Jewish kids and other North Enders were swarming in. Had academic merit alone been the criterion for entry, the Faculties of Medicine and Law would quickly have resembled schuls. As it was, opaque entrance prerequisites kept the North End influx at bay for the time being.

Meanwhile, the door to the Faculty of Arts remained wide open to all comers, presumably on the grounds that an Arts degree was no special qualifier for rising above one's place economically, therefore presenting no threat to the social fabric by destabilizing the natural order. What was not so clearly foreseen was the biological thing–rampant sex in hallways and library carrels and in the shrubbery along the Red River, where matters of ethnicity and class, if thought of at all, were reduced to after-thoughts. Much to the alarm of prospering orthodox Jewish parents edging South toward the respectability of the Assiniboine, no less to the embattled Anglo/Scots elite of the old Hudson's Bay Company lands and Wellington Crescent, unbridled mating proliferated and the spectre of intermarriage haunted the land. Lennie's marriage to Angela may have been the precursor of a trend, but it was as nothing compared to the scandal that swept the city the day Heather Symington, only child of one of the great scions of the Grain Exchange, became Mrs. Moise Zaritsky.

Her family one of the prosperous ones who stayed on in the North End in the elite neighbourhood around St. John's cathedral, Jackie Steiner never had to endure such scandal because she married Max Steiner, a young man from just across the street on the humbler side of North Main. Lennie's friendship with them began not because they were all North Enders but because they chanced into a bar one night when he was on a bit of a rampage. Jackie told me what happened:

"Max and I were out drinking at Pierre's Restaurant with friends. Max and I had just married. I had gone to Lennie's lectures at *Umbilicus* a few years before so I knew who he was. He came in to Pierre's pissed to the gills, abusive as all get out, and he immediately stereotyped me as a nouveau riche, Jewish, River Heights Philistine. Max could handle him verbally, but I was devastated. Lennie made me feel guilty about the poor, as if I had created them all on my own. For all I knew I had, or at least my father had, by prospering on the grain exchange without ever having planted a kernel of grain himself, as Lennie loudly pointed out. I didn't know it at the time, but that was just a few days before Lennie married Katia and took off for Russia. He was a wild man, angry and hell bent on rocking the world order.

"When we met again in 1966 he didn't remember his fusillade. I reminded him and he gave me that grand Mongolian smile of his and said: "So who's perfect?" I was happily married with my first child on the way. But something was missing. I started going to Lennie's evening extension class at U of M. The course was called (Lennie's riff on Freud) 'Civilization and its Malcontents.' Before long, everyone in the class knew the West was all washed up. Readings included Kropotkin, Spengler, Ezra Pound, Koestler. Lennie insisted there was nothing unusual in what they were telling us. He said all the best poets and writers had been saying it since the First World War. Western Civilization was terminally ill. And so what were we going to do about it?

"'Back to the Earth' was the movement I got involved in. A colony of young couples and their babies set out to become squatters at a place called Rose Isle. Max and I sort of went. It's a unique ridge of forest and rolling hills a hundred kilometres southwest of Winnipeg that rises unexpectedly above the flat prairie, filled with gullies and trees, the shoreline of pre-historic Lake Agassiz. As it turned out, Max and I didn't stay long. Lennie intended to build an A-frame and spend his summers there but he never got round to it either. Back to the earth didn't seem to work for everybody beyond having theoretical merit.

"Sometimes after class, Lennie would go one-on-one with me and talk about what I wanted to hear. I wanted to hear him lay into the things my mother and father stood for–their materialism, their proprieties, their narrow horizon, their panic if no one came to rake the leaves. I don't think I needed Lennie so much to tell me about the glories of nature at Rose Isle. I needed him to get me started inward. If you looked at me, I'm sure you would never see what was going on inside. I spent a lot of time on my hair and I developed a smile I could turn on and off like TV. I cultivated a detached look. I copied attitudes from fashion magazines. But I was seething inside and Lennie sensed it.

"He made me see myself as a product of *The Ladies Home Journal.* My mother and father told me what a nice young girl is and what nice girls do when they become nice young women, ladies, I mean. I felt imprisoned and I felt contrived and on my way to ... I don't know what. Lennie was an intense listener. He saw through my surface and put into words the anguish I was feeling. It was something he made me see as part of a larger malaise. But it was also personal.

"I wanted to break out, like Nora in Ibsen's *The Doll's House.* But I couldn't dive into experience the way Nora did. I was scared. Lennie knew it and he never pushed too hard. I think he sensed that if he did, I would go over the edge. It's strange how, for a man of such extremes, Lennie kept me on the level. Thanks to him, I came to know that what I was going through was good for me. It was not a spectacular transformation. I wasn't reborn or anything. But it was a big change for me and it lasted.

"Teaching, for Lennie, was bringing you to see how immense the possibilities were, how many things there were to find out about, what satisfactions were on offer. What Lennie revealed to me was nothing less than the possibility of getting human. How had he not just survived but transcended the North End—the stealing and bootlegging, the violence and brutality all around him? It's just so hard for me to bring all that together with the sensibility and intelligence and breadth of mind of the man. I know a lot about the North End, even though I came from a nice street. I know about the North End's much romanticized atmosphere, its ethnic colour, its poly-racial mix, and how it sounds like a great place to grow up in. That's not how I remember it. It wasn't the least like the Muggsy/Glimpy, East Side Kids stuff that glorified New York gangs in the movies. It was cruel, vicious, and real.

"Lennie once let me in on a teen-age strategy of his. He made friends with the biggest, dumbest Ukrainian kid he could find, a kid called Oreste, and he arranged that he would do the talking for both of them. I know this is true. I remember Oreste, a six-foot-two boy even then, always smiling. The Dew Droppers were the dominant North End gang. Lennie had an altercation with two of them. They accused him of using a Dew Dropper pool cue from their reserved rack. He shrugged and walked out of Nordic Billiards. The two Dew Droppers followed, and then Oreste. Then Lennie came back and sat down. A few minutes later, Oreste came in, took the cues the Dew Droppers had been playing with, broke them over his knee, and tossed the pieces out onto the street.

"'I told Oreste to do that,' Lennie said. 'I knew that breaking the cues made life safer for me than just having him beat them up. Pool cues are powerful metaphors.'"

I wondered: could this be Lennie imagining–way back when he was a kid in a pool room–that symbols can be more powerful than fists and guns?

Chapter Twenty-Two

Of all the people in Lennie's Winnipeg orbit, I think Jake Clark became his true soul-mate. Jake was the sardonic performer who sang *Ticky Tacky Boxes* at us at our Honours English graduating party back in 1959. He told Lennie he was caught in a dilemma. He could put food on the table as a popular folk singer or he could paint. But he couldn't do both. "Well, what are you," Lennie had asked him, "a painter or a singer?" "Once he put it blunt like that," Jake told me, "what could I say?"

"Back then, I was playing the taverns and bars and, for a while, I became a fixture at Pierre's, the first real nightclub to emerge from the repeal of the Manitoba blue laws in 1958. Some nights, the audience responded as if I were Billy Graham. I felt less like a singer than an evangelist. I hated it. But that's what Lennie loved most. He wanted to see me change people's lives and he tried to enlist me in the crusade. He would come in late and sit down with groups at tables and just blow them away. He shook them up to the core with his palaver. After he left, they would buy me drinks and say how pointless their lives were and that Lennie had made them feel they didn't have to be that way.

"One guy remembered Lennie from the old North End. When they were teenagers, they worked as salesmen for an aluminium siding outfit one summer. They sold siding to old people who thought it would cut down their heating bills. All the company did was clad aluminium sheets over old clapboard walls. Within a few years the walls would rot and the aluminium sheets would fall off. When Lennie found this out, he had already turned in three contracts. When the boss was out he took them from his desk, went back to the old folks, explained the situation, and tore up the contracts in front of them. He had to make himself scarce for the rest of the summer because the boss wanted to kill him.

"I'm very sentimental about one thing in particular. Lennie and a large group of people were at my closing night at Pierre's. I did my last show and I said 'that's it, I'm free'. Lennie was immediately on his feet applauding, with tears running down his face. I don't know what it was that made him do that. And then everybody got up. Nobody else had tears at first. And then as I looked around, everyone was crying as if their youth had ended. There were faces I had barely noticed before streaked with tears. How did this happen?

"Then there was that pick-up party at my place on Spadina Crescent, the year I spent in Toronto, remember? You were there. Lennie had just got back from Russia. He walked in half-crocked and I went up and put my arms around him and gave him one of those Russian kisses on each cheek. He said: 'For fuck sake, Clark, kiss me on the mouth.' So I did and we fell down on the chesterfield and kissed each other on the mouth, roaring with laughter. There were a lot of people around. I wondered for a moment, are they really into this scene? Am I into it? Is Lennie running some kind of crazy social experiment here or what? Suddenly that was a really big experience. It was a direct challenge to the fear I had been brought up with, along probably with most men in the room, the fear of male affection. I knew Lennie well enough to guess that the kiss was his way of pushing me to the margin to see what I would do. I had started it. Did I have the guts to go through with it? He was using all that Russian stuff, you know, you love someone so you kiss him, or you kiss her. Screw Freud and screw all the Methodist muzzles of the Canadian psyche.

"Lennie was going through some pretty rough stuff in Toronto at that moment, coming back with Katia from Russia with nothing gained. I told him I was going through some strain too, with my then-wife. She was giving up on me, and after two years at the Royal College of Art in London and a summer studying with Kokoshka in Germany, my work was going no place. Maybe Lennie and I shared a mid-life thing. I was selling coffee and donuts at the coffee shop in Union Station in Toronto and eating the butterless cheese sandwich special for lunch at the Sally Anne. Lennie had incredible energy. He was bursting with ideas but he felt worthless. He didn't have a job, couldn't find a thing to do, and that's bound to twist anyone's brain.

Believe me. Then Lennie got his offer from U of M and he and Katia took off for Winnipeg. A while afterward, I followed–short of a wife.

"Barefoot hippies with guitars and disowned kids of patriotic Middle-America were drifting in from East and West as if Winnipeg were some kind of dopester's Mecca. Lennie saw the situation as a creative revolution. He had enormous hopes for it. Overnight he became a force, not just at the university, but all over town.

"I can't nail down the influence he had on me, but I know it was big. He tried to get me to put some of Blake's poems to music. I admired Blake's engravings and I had read his *Songs Of Innocence* and *Songs of Experience*. They reminded me of sitting on a bench in Holland Park when I was at the Royal Academy in London years before. I was feeling down and out in dreary London town when suddenly I had an image of the eruption of spring in far-away Manitoba when the girls emerged from their winter shrouds and broke out in bare flesh again. I told Lennie I didn't feel I could put Blake's poetry to music, but I would try a song in the spirit of Blake's tribute to "Glad Day". I knew that would have special meaning for Lennie, remembering how he had spoken of Peter Coultry, when he got killed, as the lost icon of "Glad Day".

> All those beautiful summer time girls
> Walkin' around, walkin' around
> Make me wish I'm a summer time boy
> Walkin' the town, walkin' the town.
>
> All that beautiful summer time laughin'
> Floatin' on down summer time day
> Sailin' along by the night river shore
> Flyin' along, sailin' away.

"There was an innocence about that song. It was the best I could do to bring Blake to the prairies. When I sang it, Lennie listened as if I were some kind of genius. This guy was blossoming and he was trying to get me to blossom. We spent hours and hours talking on everything from art to psychiatry, and he was absolutely brilliant. And the guy liked me. I was flattered! On so many levels, I felt like an oaf. But he would hear me out. He never passed over what I said. I remember showing him a fish I had drawn, based on a fossil from primeval Lake Agassiz that once covered Manitoba. His face lit up with exactly the kind of joy I wanted peoples' faces to show. He just beamed. "That came from way down, Jake," he said. "From way, way back in the limbic brain some place."

"He couldn't tell me how to draw, but I had total respect for the guy's mind and the way he understood what I was trying to do, even though I couldn't verbalize it myself. He had some kind of weird power, like a water diviner. He could dig into your thoughts like no one I have ever known. And he had a wild face and body language that added a whole new, sometimes comic, dimension to his gushers of words. He acted like a cattle prod on me.

"I know Lennie wasn't happy about analysing everything and trying to explain what was going down. Because of some kind of obsession for clarification he had, I think there was a sacrifice of the artist in him, a loss of what he himself once called 'art's necessary obliquity'. I would sit down and draw and he would say: 'How did you do that?' Sometimes, I would listen to him talk and I would say to myself: 'How does he do that?'

"One day, we were having a toke in my studio and Lennie said: 'Let's write a poem. You write a poem and I'll write a poem.' We both took a pencil and I said, 'what will we write about?' At which point, a bumblebee came in through the window. Lennie said, 'we'll write about the bee.' I wrote a ditty that went:

> Bzzz Bzzz Bzzz
> Goes the bee
> Lands on my desk
> And looks up at me
> You from out West
> I politely inquire
> With your fine yellow vest
> And big round eye?
> What's it you're after
> Stinging or laughter?
> With the wave of a wing
> The bee gave a sigh
> Went Bzzz Bzzz again
> And bumbled on by.

"After five minutes, we compared notes. I read my bee poem. Lennie had written nothing. He shook his head at me. He wasn't surprised that I could write a silly little verse about a bee. What freaked him was that I did it in five minutes.

"I remarried when I settled back in Winnipeg. In the summer of 1967, my new wife, Julia, and I stayed in a cabin at Delta Marsh. Delta Marsh is on the shallow south shore of Lake Manitoba just north of Portage la Prairie. The place is all sky with a tiny rim of water and fields along the bottom of the frame. I did a series of watercolours trying to catch the fields, the low bushes, the duck marshes, the changeable mirror of the lake, and something haunting about the huge sky.

"Lennie came to visit. The south end has to be the shallowest extended body of water in the world. Julia sat reading on a deck chair planted in the sand about a quarter mile off shore in no more than a foot of water. Lennie and I rolled up our pant legs and waded out to take her a glass of wine. On our way we saw a storm gathering in the West, a distant thunderhead that was soon boiling up over the horizon. Lennie later showed me a poem he wrote called "Design at Delta Marsh".

> You looked that day
> On the beach of Lake Manitoba
> As baffled as the children
> Once you tried to teach paint
>
> Standing there with you
> And something to do with the view
> I recalled journeys up Highway Ten
> Passing the long curves of Winnipegosis
> Which promised as oceans do
> Ports and people
> Not just waterscapes
> And silent shallows
> With here and there a marshy point
> No one's ever been to
>
> Daydreams peopled the space
> With apparitions of clam diggers
> On busy low-tide beaches
> In Holland and France

I walked into the water
Searching the horizon for ships
Listening for the hubbub and clatter
Of seamen hoisting sail
Children's chatter along the wharf
And heard no sound but the wind

The only gathering
Was the storm cloud
A dark tower
High as a top hat
That picked up the lake
And shook it inside out
As imagined mariners
Hauled in sail
And spectral mothers huddled in huts
Around candles burning for ships
Floundering under the electric sky

I poked around the beach
For some humanity or derelict
But could not find one bone even
Of a coureur de bois or Indian

Under the sudden pile-up
Of the sky-high thunderhead
A whirring broke the quiet
As millions of mayflies
Swarmed into the rays
Of the last of the sun
Their wings sticking to us
As the first white edge
Of the returning lake
Rolled in over our feet

We turned without speaking
The only sound approaching thunder
And the mayflies churning

> In their demon millions
> Precluding design
> As we hurried back to the cabin
> Making it just in time

"His poem captured the spirit of the inter-lakes better than anything I had ever been able to get down on canvas. He was embarrassed by my praise. He told me not to forget that it was just a work-in-progress.

"When I went visiting with Lennie, doing his rounds all over Winnipeg, there were exceptions, but mainly people were glad to see him. When he was on a roll, he let no one commit what he called 'the sin of inadvertency'. 'Cool' was death for him. It was just trendy, pretentious somnambulism he said. You had to wake up for Lennie. His audience/hosts sometimes became a little more liberal, a little more open-minded, a little more tolerant, but I don't think they knew how far Lennie wanted them to go. The mind-forged manacles he attacked covered the map–religious prattle, ideological fanaticism, political guff, advertising, and above all the sexual taboos of the Victorian inheritance.

"Lennie told me once about a woman he had been with. He never mentioned names. He said: 'I swear to god, Jake, I was sitting in my car about to drop her off and I turned to her and said, "I want to kiss your pussy". 'I was sort of kidding. You know what she did? She stretched herself out in my little car, she pulled down her panties, and she straddled me.'

"He didn't say another word. He just sat there shaking his head in wonder."

Chapter Twenty-Three

Vince Calley, the man who had taken Lennie to his first faculty party when he arrived back in Winnipeg in the fall of 1965, had become his closest ally at the university. He, too, was a Blake/Northrop Frye enthusiast and the two of them hit it off from the start. Himself a painter and poet, he was baffled, he told me, by why Lennie was neither, and how it was that such an intelligent man could sometimes do such dopey things. In the spring of 1967, they took a trip together.

"We drove West to Jasper in the mountains, to an old family place which was practically snowbound. Lennie wanted me to drive through the drifts right up to the cabin so he wouldn't have to walk through the snow. Nature boy. He had bought a camera to record the trip. He said he wanted to take pictures because he wanted to make a book about the mountains. We'd go up trails and he'd stop and take pictures of moss or the bark of a tree, close up with a dioptre lens. We'd have lunch in a pub down in the valley, or else make sandwiches and hike up to the summit and look at mountain clouds. Lennie would see faces in them and click away at everything that caught his eye. Surveying the peaks one afternoon, he quoted from *The Prelude*:

> We also first beheld
> Unveiled the summit of Mont Blanc, and grieved
> To have a soulless image on the eye
> That had usurped upon a living thought-
> That never more could be.

"My god, I thought, he's going to turn us into Coleridge and Wordsworth on their famous hiking trip in the Alps."

'You know why they were grieving?' he said. Without waiting for an answer, he told me. 'Because they were disappointed. The real mountain couldn't live up to their expectation of it, that "living thought" of the mountain before they saw it. Blake would never have said anything like that. He knew a physical mountain is always just a mountain, a big chunk of rock to feed the imagination, and the real mountain, the "living thought", is the one perceived by the mind's eye, with all its mythical associations as the meeting place of man and the gods–Olympus, Sinai, the pyramids, the ziggurats of Sumeria. Maybe that was Wordsworth's and Coleridge's problem, why they ran out of steam. Maybe that's why they spent the last part of their lives lamenting the loss of imaginative vigour, "rolled round in earth's diurnal course/ With rocks and stones and trees", or in Coleridge's case (possibly due to drug withdrawal) choked off from the milk of paradise as in "Rarely, rarely comest thou/ Spirit of delight"; whereas Blake retained his visionary powers right up to his death at seventy.'

"The images in Lennie's camera. I wondered. Were they Blakean or were they Wordsworth's 'soulless images'? Weeks later, it hit me. I hadn't seen any of Lennie's photos. I asked about them. He said he hadn't got round to getting them developed. Then he said when he took the rolls in, they were no good because the film they sold him was stale-dated. That just wasn't credible. There must have been some interesting pictures there. He must have exposed thirty rolls. But I never saw a single frame from that trip.

"Lennie had a streak of unbelievable ingenuousness in him. He didn't tell me he had never used a camera before. He saw me paint, which he couldn't do. He read my poems and saw them getting published, and he said he was working on some stuff himself but it wasn't ready. I don't think he had any problem believing he was brighter than any of us. So what should he be doing? He must have thought, for a moment, that a camera might be the answer. With no idea of F-stops or film stock or grain or resolution or lighting or framing or composition, he must have believed, for a moment, he could become a photographic artist. I suspect when he got his pictures back he couldn't believe how bad they were–out-of-focus flora, meaningless clouds, landscapes more clichéd than post cards, maybe even worse than the soulless images that so depressed Wordsworth. I'm pretty sure he was humiliated because he never once brought up the subject of photography with me again."

At the opposite end of the Winnipeg social register, as distant from Vince Calley's River Heights as Bukovina from Berkshire, Dmitri Wenchenko became another member of Lennie's enclave. Dimmy got as far as grade ten when he discovered a facility for cartooning. He quit school to work as sign painter, then a silk screener and founder of an art co-op. Soon known as 'The Coop', it occupied the ground floor of a onetime office/storage building on Princess Street where, on the upper storey, Jake Clark had his studio, and just above Jake's studio, Lennie later occupied a flat. The Coop became a rallying point for like-minded radical artists and activists. Dimmy's specialty was posters. Unlike Jake, Dimmy found a buoyant market with the arrival of the poster craze, and was eventually able to open his own gallery to deal exclusively with prairie artists, in retaliation, he declared, to the elitist closed shops of the self-proclaimed centre of Canadian art in Toronto.

You could easily be fooled into thinking Lennie and Dimitri didn't like each other, that their common Ukrainian roots, far from acting as a bond, were a source of hostility. I saw it that way at first until Dimmy explained.

"Lennie was a good chess player, more than good. I was good, but not that good. Pretty soon, we had this 'I'm a Uke, you're a Uke' type thing going. That's what got him started calling me 'Dimmy', as if I was some kind of dim bulb because I wasn't a big time intellectual. I got back by calling him 'Dummy'. And I wasn't just pulling that out of a bag. He could really do dumb things sometimes. I was always amazed what a hotshot people thought he was. I thought of him more as ordinary, only with a weird streak. Oh, he had the smarts all right, but he wasn't wise. I used to tell him he was just another dumb Hunkie with a bag full of tricks. I watched him a hundred times being a sweetheart with people, when really he was having them on. They never seemed to twig. Maybe it was some kind of Ukrainian thing, a way of revenge for being shit on as a DP when he was a kid. See, I'm ten years younger. When I was growing up, being Slavic wasn't something you were ashamed of any more. There were Hunkie millionaires and judges by then, even a Hunkie mayor. I was proud to be Ukrainian. It wasn't that way when Lennie was a boy.

"At a party at the Coop, Lennie came in falling-down drunk. I gave him hell. I said he was giving us the bad name everyone thought we deserved. He wanted to fight. He was egging me on, yakking and grinning at me, trying to get me pissed off. He kept saying, 'let's go outside.' It was like he wanted to get hurt. He wasn't about to suck me into that kind of bullshit. I outweighed him by fifty pounds.

"Then there was the time I took him home to meet my mom and Lennie lit up right in front of her. 'Imagine!' my mom said, 'a professor rolling his own.' She asked him, was he a dentist doctor or a doctor doctor? He said neither, more sort of a philosophy doctor, which really impressed my mom.

"But she's no babe in the woods. She dug what he was smoking. If she'd caught me smoking pot, she'd have called the cops and then tried to figure out a way of getting me out of jail so she could beat me on the head. For Lennie, it was different. He was a Professor Doctor. But here's what kills me. What did Lennie think? Didn't he know enough to draw a line between our wild hippie ways and a babushka from the old country?

"I gave Lennie hell about it. The next thing I knew, I was getting a lecture. He told me we'd got to quit sneaking around like a bunch of kids chewing Sen-Sen so our mothers wouldn't smell tobacco on our breath. We'd got to be honest and open and let people know that pot is harmless and fun and probably healthy and all the rest of the guff I've heard a hundred times over. But Lennie could sure drive a point home. By the time he got through with me, I was frazzled, goddamn near ready to march on parliament to get pot legalized ... as long as I was able to do it without my mother finding out.

"As far as I ever learned, Lennie's adventures with forbidden substances never went beyond what he considered the mind-enhancing variety–pot and hash, and experimental mushrooms and flowers and acid now and then. Nose candy had still not made it big into the social register, horse was disparaged, and the more elite pharmaceuticals hadn't yet been invented."

Chapter Twenty-Four

In 1968, Lennie was invited to do off-the-cuff movie reviews on CBC radio. One I heard was on *Bonnie and Clyde,* assailing the greedy banking system that forced sharecroppers off the land and made them criminals. It brought him to the attention of the singer Ben Gibson, who headed up *Country Time* out of CBC Winnipeg. With his thundering twelve-string Gibson Guitar and his resounding baritone, Ben had nothing in common with the Canadian country luminaries of the time like Tommy Hunter. He was more like Johnny Cash, raw-looking with the same craggy face, big hair, guttural voice, and slowpoke manner. He was about the same size, too, six feet two and an ox.

Thirty miles east of Winnipeg, at Bird's Hill, Ben had a *real* ranch. He had *real* stables and horses, even *wild* horses, mustangs that could still be found in the foothills of the Rockies. He brought a few back to his ranch every year and broke them in himself. For Lennie, no less for me, this was a man of mythic significance, a survivor from a world we imagined once existed, now long gone.

And Ben could sing! He did junkets all over North Dakota and Montana and the bad lands of the Canadian prairies, in part because his TV show out of Winnipeg was never secure. He was too erratic for CBC and CBC was cutting regional shows to save money. So what attracted Lennie to Ben? Was it the hurly-burly of the roadhouses Ben talked about? Did Ben's rural life remind Lennie of his first western movies in the long-gone movie houses of Main Street? More curiously still, what did Ben see in Lennie that made him like him? Ben explained:

"We had a nodding acquaintance at The Riviera where a lot of us at CBC used to go to juice it up and rehash the week. At first, I found the chip on

Lennie's shoulder, all that Hunkie-North End bullshit, a pain in the ass. I wasn't interested in it and when he got into that bag, well it wasn't something I let him get away with. But I liked watching him talk to people. He laid certain things on them, nothing you'd call plain nasty, but for sure something that checked out their capacities.

"In conversations, people would sometimes say 'I don't want to go there'. That was like cat-nip to Lennie. Wherever 'there' was, that was exactly where he wanted to go, to dig into, to get out into the open. He reminded me of those flimsy five-legged starfish switching legs against the single muscle of a clam. The clam would eventually just have to open up.

"My ranch ... well it meant a lot to him when Irene and the kids were there. He would sit down at Bird's Hill and try to work out how, after all the waves of immigration and the god-awful slums of Winnipeg in the early years, there might be some way of living humanly. He told me once that he loved me. He said my voice was pure West without the hokey, pseudo-religious bunkum of a lot of country singing. That made me some kind of icon for him. I could get off the pavement, put my hat on, ride my horses, and breathe the country air. He didn't know how to do that. He wanted to go on a canoe trip. He wanted to build a log cabin in the wilderness. He wanted to learn the tricks of nature. When he got off the concrete and onto the grass at Bird's Hill, it transformed him. He became very introspective, very quiet.

"We'd get songs going, with Jake Clark playing on his rusty guitar and singing along, and toke up, and get into discussions in the kitchen with our elbows on the table. We would talk about my three kids, and Lennie would talk with them when they came in. They loved him. He would always have a little go-round with each of them. Even today, they tell me about things he talked to them about that stayed with them.

"Still, there were things Lennie and I would talk about when the kids were around that I didn't like, certain things he would say that were true enough, but not to my taste at the time. If there was a good argument for censoring what children hear, I would have gone along with it, based on some of those nights, because things they heard had no context. The life I led as a travelling man ... it was a blank in terms of their life experience ... and it drew a blank from them. How could they understand what I was doing? Don't blame dad, right? Blame influences, the outsiders. But here's the miracle. By making me talk straight with the kids, even when it hurt them, they one day understood that Lennie was a good man, even though they had no idea at the time how he was setting them up to be honest with themselves. And you know what? It was because he made no concessions to them, never spoke down to them, gave it to them eye to eye, about the vagabondage of the road ('emphasis on the bondage part', Lennie used to say), the drinking and wild living that went with me on the road, and then how the road would inevitably cost me my home and my wife. Goodnight Irene! Sometimes I wanted to croak Lennie, but then I would realize it was the truth he was telling. He made us all face the music. And that's why we didn't end up living some kind of awful bullshit as a family, pretending things were the way they weren't.

"There was an old Manitoba Maple stand out in the pasture, nothing grand, trees the Indians used to collect a coarse maple syrup from. I named the place 'Meadow Chapel'. One sunny day when the light came streaming through, I sat with Lennie and we did some grass. I had a big tame old mare the kids used to ride when they were small. I got Lennie up on her bareback, and she walked him around the woods like a Shetland pony. I have never seen those squinty eyes of his open so wide. I couldn't get him off the horse. When I did, he said the horse felt to him like a creature from another planet. I had an old hat I gave him. 'Holy Shit!' he said when he put it on. 'I'm John fucking Wayne.' He really dug that hat. He kept it hanging above the French doors in his apartment the way a cowboy would hang up a trophy he'd won at a rodeo.

"My life went into a tailspin. My wife, my children, my ranch, my horses, my voice, everything came crashing down around me. It sounds corny but it was Lennie who got me into a higher order I can't explain. Call it spirit or whatever, an energy that goes way beyond any individual. It comes into the world sometimes through nature, even through animals, once in a while through humans, and I believe Lennie was a generator of that energy. Look at us with our penchant for going around in circles and chasing our tails, getting caught up in our own egos and competitions, and what Lennie used to call our 'blabberinths'. In spite of his own inner ruckus, that son of a gun–he coaxed me out of the pit."

Chapter Twenty-Five

B y the fall of 1968 marijuana wasn't the only thing arriving with the falling snow. A new politics descended with it. Trudeau's multicultural-ism was on everyone's lips and ignited the young everywhere, as Canada's transformation began from outpost of the British Empire into a multi-ethnic conglomerate. Coast to coast, kids sewed the flag to their packs and headed for Europe or the Far East and, when they came back, hitch-hiked the Trans-Canada Highway, camping in Winnipeg, the half-way house. Everywhere in Winnipeg a non-stop bash was going on, with booze flowing freely and pot from local gardens and hydroponic emporia as easy to come by as Players Light. Kids were returning from Mexico with mushrooms and Peyote and Mescalin, and LSD was coming in like Tootsie Rolls with the draft dodgers and flower children from the States.

In the spirit of the multi-cultural times, CBC Television in Toronto launched a series of so-called "bear-pits", featuring guests from a mix of backgrounds. One episode imported Lennie as representative of North End Winnipeg. The set resembled not so much a bear pit as a circus ring. The audience sat on bleachers surrounding the host, who played ringmaster. Invited participants from across the country occupied pre-arranged spots throughout the studio audience. The format was known as 'live-to-tape', which meant that it had the look of coming to you as it happened. The host, a prominent TV personality, performed adroitly, singling out (as if by instinct) a finely balanced representation of ethnic types from the bleachers— an Azorian construction worker, a Pakistani restaurateur, a Chinese nurse, a Jamaican storekeeper, a Mexican bus driver, and a token Slav, Professor Leonard Boyce. It may have been the bogus atmosphere in the studio or the supercilious manner of the host that prompted Lennie's response when his turn came. Or it may have been something Lennie just had to do.

"Professor Boyce," the host asked, "your background, I believe, is Ukrainian?"

"That's right," Lennie said.

"Can you tell us, Professor, how is it that a Ukrainian has a name like Boyce? Surely that's a Scandinavian or an English name."

"Well, it's like this," Lennie said. "We mid-European immigrants changed our names all the time when we came over, so we would become more easily accepted here in the New World. Resansoffs became Ransoms, Billichucks became Billies, Goldbergs became Golds. I even knew one family, the Finkelsteins, who changed their name to Fink. Perhaps they were unaware of Pinkerton's mercenaries, the thugs hired by Rockefeller to beat up workers, thereby giving modern English the pejorative word 'Fink'. It was very hard on the Fink kids growing up in North End Winnipeg. Gloria Fink had a terrible time. Her brother, Harvey, stayed more or less in hiding for years. I had it easier. My name was Boychuck. My mother changed it to Boyce for professional reasons. You see, she ran a brothel and she thought it would make guys like you feel more comfortable if you thought she operated a Wasp establishment when you came over to her place to get laid."

Pandemonium! They called for the ultimate censor: "Stop tape!" The celebrated host fled the studio like a boy scout who'd just stepped on a hornet's nest. Lennie was ushered onto Jarvis Street by security. Back in Winnipeg, it became known as Lennie's Toronto Triumph. Everyone was proud of him. It was a decisive victory in the war between East and West. Of course, I knew Sophie had done her share of bootlegging, and Lennie had told me about the poker games that went on in the back of her restaurant. But until then, it never registered that she might also have run a bordello. I thought at first it possible that Lennie was just pulling one of his bad boy ploys and couldn't resist deflating the TV host. But as it turned out, what he said was true.

A new sub-culture was emerging in Winnipeg's River and Osborne area. Funky restaurants sprang up, introducing such radical new ideas as 'eating out'. Music pubs and poetry clubs took spaces in old buildings in the warehouse district. Retailers of transparent vinyl dresses, panty hose, mini- skirts, pant suits, Nehru jackets, and granny glasses displaced flower shops, beauty parlours, and dry cleaners. A kitchen supply store on Osborne became a meeting place where you could buy Scottish smoked salmon, canned truffles, chocolate-coated locusts, off-beat utensils like lemon zesters, cherry-pitters, exotic food processors, specialized pots, or, if you were a trusted customer, just plain pot.

The chief purveyor of such goodies for Lennie's crowd (and rumor had it, for most of the rest of the city's dope fiends) was a nineteen-year-old called Zebediah who lived in a cube van with a logo on the side that read: "Zebediah Exterminators–We Make Mouse Calls". Inside the van, Zebby had what he claimed to be the best hi-fi system in Winnipeg, which he powered in shopping mall parking lots from the A/C outlets provided free for the block heaters of shoppers' cars to keep their engines from freezing in winter while shopping. Always on the move from lot to lot, taking advantage of the free electricity, not only for his hi-fi but for his fridge, stove and space heater, he boasted about never having to pay a hydro bill. While in appearance an Ur hippie, with ragged beard and bulging eyes, it turned out that Zebby had graduated from a two-year extension accounting course and was quietly salting away a fortune by clever investing. He was the first pusher in my experience to offer home delivery. Everyone knew when a stash had come from Zebbie (except, apparently, the law) because each bag, however large or small, contained a complimentary package of Chiclets chewing gum.

In 1968, Winnipeg became my base camp once again. I was in the middle of researching a current affairs story I'd been tracking for a year, the diversion of the Churchill River into the Nelson River and the creation of giant new hydroelectric plants on the Nelson River. Lennie, I found, was staying at motels and sleeping around at friends' houses. Katia had moved into Place Louis Riel just off Portage Avenue, next door to Eaton's where she had gone back to work. Lennie said it wasn't necessarily a permanent separation. More like a breather.

Marital matters aside, the way his fortunes had shifted into high gear since his failure in Russia and his bottoming out in Toronto astonished me. Here in Winnipeg, he was the teacher hip kids told each other they had to sign up for. He was in hot demand by the non-stop pot party that was set in motion by what he called "The Found Generation". His extemporaneous movie reviews, using films as evidence of the decline of the West as the war in Viet Nam was descending more and more into absurdity, cemented his standing among the young as a herald of the counter culture. He spoke at gallery openings, New Left rallies, student protests, peppering his language with denunciations of 'corporate corpses', 'parliamentary paralytics', and 'geriatric zombie elites'. He championed Aldous Huxley and Timothy Leary and their adventures with conscious-expanding drugs. Herbert Marcuse was regularly on his lips: "What does it mean to live a normal life in a sick society?" Nietzsche, as always, kept popping up: "Bourgeois society seeks the order of inertia .... We pursue energy, the joy of the life force." At one demonstration I attended, breaking through loud cheers, Lennie shouted: "Which will it be? Eros or Thanatos?" The crowd came back with a chorus loud enough to make a hockey team proud: "Eros ... Eros ... Eros!" Lennie was in his element. I enjoyed the revelry, but I couldn't help reminding myself of what happened to the infamous Children's Crusade of 1212 A.D. when the children were exterminated before they reached the battleground.

"'Okay, JJ, I'll admit it," he said. "A lot of these kids have become instant activists and they have a problem. They're children of privilege and that gives them an 'illegitimacy complex'. It leads them to concentrate more on out-raging their parents than joining the cause. They parade around campuses in black Che Guevera berets with Fidel and Mao pins, wearing beads and sandals and wanting to join the demonstrations in Washington, or else donning backpacks and heading for Toronto's Yorkville and the pharmaceu-tical lure of Rochdale College, a whole range of gestures aimed at eradicating class softness and establishing something like revolutionary authenticity. A few go so far as to join one or other of the ultra-radical groups in the US like the Black Panthers and the Weathermen, flirting with ideas of insurrection and guerrilla warfare as if they were just ideas. It seems never to occur to them there could be blood on the flowers even in the hot house. Sure, I stood in front of the crowd shouting "Eros or Thanatos". Maybe I'm getting too old for such shenanigans, but I'm treated as the real thing because there's nothing I have to prove. I rose magically, don't you see, from the proletarian welter of the North End, and that gives me near-absolute legitimacy as a revolutionary.

"There is a kind of re-evaluation of values going on but not a trans-valua-tion of values. What is a true trans-valuation of values? It's not some piddling parental truce that lets the children march in protest and come home for supper. I want a true commitment. That's what demonizes me in the eyes of the old guard. They see me as a barbarian. And not just the old guard. To some of the more reticent young academics, I'm an irresponsible subversive who gives the rest of them a bad name and threatens their pension. One of them told me that he sees me and my bunch as the fulfilment of Matthew Arnold's prophesy over a century ago of creating a world where, 'Swept with confused alarms of struggle and flight ... ignorant armies clash by night.' Good old Matthew Arnold. He loved sweetness and light. He just couldn't get over the idea that the French Revolution might spread to Britain and undercut the happy life of the comfortably educated, genteel children of the privileged classes known as Victorians, many of whom, truth be told, possessed little sweetness and precious little light.

"Do you realize, JJ, what amazing changes have taken place in the decade since you and I first met? Just take the world of sexual taboos after the coming of pills and pot that brought easy contraception and chemical whoopee. Not only is promiscuity no longer a sin, it's a badge of hip. At a party in a mansion on Wellington Crescent, where ten years before bare-foot guests would have been turfed out, I went to find a toilet. On my way, I stepped over first one couple, then just around the corner on the next landing another, both couples in coitus. My passing showed no sign of causing interruptus. I tried to remain blasé. But really I couldn't. The recklessness, the spontaneity, the naturalness of the scene I have to confess–I found it marvellous."

I broke in. "So when you come right down to it, Lennie, it's all about Eros after all, just as it was back in those halcyon days in Ibiza."

"Don't be a smartass, JJ. You semi-reformed Methodists make the mistake of thinking that it's just about sexual freedom versus repression. You might as well say it's all potheads versus square heads. Or it's all youth versus age, or haves versus have-nots. Sex is huge, alright. But there's more to it than just a sea of pumping asses. There's a bubbling surge of energy, a revolt against life-denying restraints that stifle and sicken the human animal. Blake said it a century before Freud: "He who desires and acts not breeds pestilence." That doesn't mean there's no price to pay. There's exhilaration but also relationships that blow away like tents in a storm. Katia and I are in that limbo called separation. I sway between trying to mend fences and knocking what remains of them down. I get up, up as hell when I'm on the move, and I get deep down in the pit when I stop. The shrinks no doubt have a name for it, schizoid or bipolar, or something with a new name the amateur pshychoanalysts are poised to foist on the world."

Chapter Twenty-Six

In the fall of 1968 it was a busy time at the big table in the Albert. Surrounded by a gaggle of moochers, idealists, cowboys, rock and rollers, shills, and regulars, Lennie was on the rampage. He was dying to join what was happening in Chicago at the Democratic Convention, but with a passport stamped with Eastern Bloc registrations, he could not risk a border crossing. He would never get back.

All he could do was quote from the press: "Abbie Hoffman, Jerry Rubin, and others descended on Mayor Daley's city today with their war cries: 'Bring sleeping bags, extra food, bottles of fireflies, cold cream, lots of handkerchiefs and canteens to deal with pig spray, love beads, electric toothbrushes, see-through blouses, manifestoes, magazines, and tenacity.' Jerry Rubin brought along a pig and nominated it for President as 'Pigasus the Immortal'. Hoffman promised a demonstration of public fornication that he called a 'fuck-in'. The press was forewarned: 'Psychedelic long-haired mutant-jissomed peace leftists will consort with known dope fiends ... to get the pants off the daughters and wives and kept women of the convention delegates.' A formal statement from the newly-minted Yippies proclaimed: 'The life of the American spirit is being torn asunder by the forces of violence, decay, and the napalm-cancer fiend. We demand the politics of Ecstasy. We are the delicate spores of the new fierceness that will change America.'

As Lennie went on to acclaim the courage and audacity of the Chicago Seven, the chatter around the table died down. I had seen it happen before, but I never understood it. It was as if a wand had been waved over the table as heads turned toward Lennie.

"Chicago's just the beginning, folks. Sure, the Age of Aquarius has arrived with unisex clothing and gold chains and necklaces and wild excursions into astrology. Speaking with one voice, the Neo-American Church, the Church of the Awakening, the Native American Church, and the League for Spiritual Discovery have announced that '... psychedelic substances are sacraments, that is, divine substances, no matter who uses them, in whatever spirit, with whatever intentions.' LSD has moved out of the closet into, as it were, the main stream. Meanwhile, the Aswan Dam was formally opened, thereby re-arranging forever the flow of the Nile and the nutrient balance of the Mediterranean. In the encyclical Humanae Vitae, despite world-wide over-population and the Canadian Bishops' near apostasy in the notorious 'Winnipeg Statement', Pope Paul VI dug in his heels and reaffirmed the ban on condoms. In Southeast Asia, a small contingent of American military advisors has become a half-a-million strong. Some fifteen thousand of them are dead so far. We all know Che Guevera has been tracked down with CIA assistance and assassinated in Bolivia. Martin Luther King was shot and killed; a little later in a hotel kitchen in California, Robert Kennedy, too. Chairman Mao built a bold new society in China in which adolescent Red Guards are instructed to slaughter their teachers. Russian submarines able to launch nuclear warheads hover off the east coast of America. Imprinted on us by Sydney Lumet's *Fail Safe* and Stanley Kubrick's *Dr. Strangelove*, the unspeakable but plausible absurdity of a nuclear error haunts our imagination. Masters and Johnson have revealed what copulation is really like for both men and women, right down to measuring orgasmic intensity with neuro-sensors. All through the spring and into the summer, student demonstrations have erupted on campuses in Berlin, Paris, Madrid, Mexico City, Tokyo, even in Warsaw and Prague. It begins to look like repression of legitimate student protest by the ruling powers is pretty much as viral in the West as in the East. Whether we are in the throes of a cosmic transformation or merely experiencing a strange psychotic convulsion, it looks like it's going to be, if not the eve of destruction, certainly a hard day's night. Let's all sing that old Negro Spiritual: 'God gave Noah the rainbow sign/No more water, the fire next time.'

"I have nightmares about those poor brain-washed teeny-bopper pilots napalming Vietnamese peasants from 2,000 feet up, laughing all the way back to base like schoolboys who've just quaffed the communion wine. It's not their fault. No one's wakened up their imagination. They can't picture the burning flesh they've left behind. We've got to hope some bozo in Colorado with his finger on the nuclear button doesn't suffer from the same mental deficiency. Now, here's a case for you where imagination really counts. An ignoramus in the Pentagon simply can't imagine the consequences, just like the teen-age pilots doing the napalming. Suddenly, for no reason other than the lack of imagination of a cretin, the button gets pushed and everything's kaput."

As the decibels rose with the beer consumption, Max Steiner, Jackie Steiner's lawyer husband, drew me aside. On earlier occasions when I had met him, he came across as a reserved, ruminative, quiet sort. But I had been told he was very sharp, a classically sardonic North End boy who carried a verbal shiv which he used without mercy when provoked–a good lawyer. I knew his wife, Jackie, had been an enthusiast of *Umbilicus*, and later on taken Lennie's extension course on "Civilization and its Malcontents", which led to Max and her becoming part of Lennie's growing band of sans-culottes.

"You're a journalist," Max said. "What are you looking for here?"

"An environment story, I think," I said.

"And a Lennie story?"

"Well, yes. Maybe that, too. Have you known him long?"

"I remember him," Max began, "from when I was a kid and later at university. Then, I didn't see him for years, until one when I went to pick up Jackie after a night class she was taking with him. After that, we would meet around town for a beer and a chat. I got to know him better through the Coop, located in the old Ryan building I manage for a group of investors, which is how I got interested in silk screening. It's a harmless hobby Dimitri Wenchenko and the others at the Coop indulge me in. Not without irony, they say it is a great release for my frustrated creativity. But they have to be careful. Hell, I can foreclose on them before their paint dries, can't I?

"Lennie was there at the Coop a lot. He had things to say that appealed to me. I'm no revolutionary, but I could never trust authority at face value and Lennie couldn't either. I felt a bond there. He could tell a story a hundred times better than I could. I can argue a case in court and I almost always win. That's how my mind works. But I've never wowed a crowd the way Lennie can. Look at him. Has he got this mob prattling all around us energized or what?

"Lennie is a very smart guy, a magnetic guy. In a curious way, Jackie and I have been a magnet for him. Our house is one of his regular stopovers. After his split with Katia, he turns up and camps for a few days in our rumpus room. We might hardly see or hear him down there. Unless he comes upstairs, we leave him alone. He is always very quiet with me when we are one on one, just small talk, nothing about issues. I get the sense Jackie and I are an island of tranquillity in his life which he seems to have little natural talent for, and yet badly needs once in a while. And you know how it is around this town. It's pretty much a badge of honour to be to be considered up close with Lennie Boyce.

"As kids, Lennie and I were poor until things got better with the war. We didn't know anything else and we didn't expect anything other than living hand-to-mouth. I was born in 1932 and my father didn't get a steady job until 1941. When I say Lennie and I made small talk that's the kind of thing it was about. We didn't discuss ontology or eschatology on any kind of a regular basis. I would tell him how I used to go to the store and buy a stick of gum for one cent and split it three ways because I had a brother and a sister. He said when he bought gum, he chewed up the whole stick by himself because he was an only child except for a half-brother he didn't like. He was making it up, of course, because his mother had a confectionary and I'm sure he helped himself to plenty of gum. I made things up too and it would get us exaggerating. Remember, this was long before Monty Python's 'Oh you think you were poor?' When I saw that skit years later on TV, I felt like suing them for breach of copyright.

"I would say to Lennie that I used to go to Kildonnan Park where a crazy old lady threw breadcrumbs to the pigeons. As soon as she left, I would chase the pigeons away and have my lunch. He would say he used to go up the CPR tracks north of Higgins Avenue with a little wagon and a gunny sack to bring home coal chips that had fallen off the coal cars so he could keep him and his mother from freezing to death.

"Lennie lived near us in a shack at first, and then later, when his mother prospered, he moved in above her restaurant on Main. I imagine that, when he got up in the morning, he had breakfast in the restaurant. When he came home from school, he had supper in the restaurant. That was a big difference between us. Never mind his freewheeling kid's life. Never mind he never had Chanukkah or Seder. I think the thing he missed having, without knowing it, was a family sitting around a table the way mine did.

"There are times when I've seen him as super Wasp, and times when I've seen him as super Slav, times when he was super rational, and times when he sounded like he was possessed. He does nothing by halves. It has to be maximum forward thrust whatever phase he's in. Maybe he's a closet schizophrenic. When he's down, he's really down, and when he's up, he's in the stratosphere. But labelling him is no help in understanding what makes him tick. And it's certainly no help in explaining his effect on people.

"He discovered that on the utility floor above Jake's studio, past an ancient elevator mechanism and an old hot water cistern, there are living quarters that must once have been occupied by the building's caretaker, a place long vacant and gone to seed. Lennie was insistent. I caved in and let him have the place. He was ecstatic. He planted a big kiss publicly on my mouth and moved in. In the initial stages when he was actually doing things by himself, cleaning and hammering and painting, it looked like he was becoming a new man. He wasn't the clumsy klutz he thought he was. He soon brought in professionals, but I never saw him happier than when he was giving them advice on his colour scheme or installing a paper towel rack above the sink all on his own.

"He invited me over when it was done up. It's very comfortable, a big main room, a bathroom, two good-sized bedrooms, and one small room turned into a workable kitchen. The big room was cluttered with cushions and books. All the walls are bright yellow, except for one blank white wall. That was open for any of his painter friends to leave their mark on, Lennie said, so long as they painted their piece in fresco using any combination of the brilliant primary colours he claimed Blake had used. No brown, he said. Blake hated brown, what he called the smudges of Rembrandt and Van Dyke. Before long, the wall looked to me like a reasonable representation of chaos. There are no obstructions from the west facing windows, and the view takes you out past the city toward Portage la Prairie. The main room faces east, leading through a pair of French doors to a thirty-foot stretch of flat roof covered with crushed rock over tar and bounded by a two-foot parapet along the ledge, all the makings of a roof garden. It looked to me as if Lennie had finally found a perch he could nest in."

Chapter Twenty-Seven

It's hard to know what to do when a couple splits and you like them both. It seems to be expected that you take sides. I suppose I was expected to side with Lennie. But I couldn't do that anymore than I could side with Katia against Lennie. It was as it had been from the beginning with Lennie, impossible to stay clear of the fray. On one of my many trips to Winnipeg in 1968, working on various items about the North, I met Katia for steaks and drinks at the Charter House.

"I got to know Lennie's mother when I was six or seven. All the kids went to her store to buy jawbreakers and Cracker Jack. She was very splashy in our eyes, a real voroshka. One day when I was with her, she told me she never wore panties. We laughed and laughed about that. I didn't know what she meant by telling me. I don't know to this day what made me laugh with her about it. She could always get you going. I saw a lot of her, not much of Lennie because he was always off do I know where? Maybe reform school. Later on I got to know the layout of her place. It was a three-story brick box that faced Main Street and ran a long way back to the alley. At the front, off Main Street, were the soda bar stools and the confectionary where the kids would go. Further back were diner booths along both walls. Behind them, was the kitchen and behind that, through heavy curtains and a crooked hallway, was where men played cards and drank Goreelka made from wheat and potatoes. You couldn't get to the second floor except from an entrance in the back alley, but when she invited you, you could go straight up to the third floor from the confectionary. It was a huge place to my eyes, running the full length of the building. Sophie's bedroom looked out onto Main Street at the front, and there was a hallway and a bathroom and Lennie's room and a kitchen at the back. Between Sophie's bedroom and the back, the big central room was like Arabian Nights, draperies everywhere, carpets on the floor and walls, big stuffed chairs and sofas, lace doilies, knick-knacks and doodads wherever you looked, and two big shiny copper spittoons at front and back.

"When Sophie invited one or two of us school girls up for milk and cookies, it was a special treat just to walk through that room and gaze around. It was like another world. We always went through to the kitchen where we sat at the table, listening to Sophie speaking Ukrainian, telling us how beautiful life was in a place called Bukovena, then half in tears, telling us how people went hungry there, got beaten up, and sometimes just disappeared.

"By the time I was ten, although I had never been on Sophie's second floor, I knew women stayed there and that men would go up the back alley entrance to meet them. But, honest to God, Jason, I never thought much about it. I was used to seeing drunks squabbling and pushing each other around outside the beer parlours on Main Street. I took things as they came. Did I know what prostitution was? Well, not exactly. It was something grown-ups did. I didn't know a lot about what grown-ups did, but I was never much surprised when I found out.

"One day, I made my way up the back fire escape to the third floor with some movie magazines Sophie had sent me out for. Red Yuri—you've heard Lennie talk about him—was in town, sleeping in Sophie's bedroom up front. I stopped in the hallway behind the kitchen when I heard a stranger's voice with an Irish accent:

'Come on, Soph,' the voice said. 'Give a man a run at it, won't you?'

'Eddie, you just don't measure up,' Sophie said.

'Jesus, Soph,' he said. 'Look what I got here for you. It's got a mind of its own and it's dyin' for salvation.'

"There was a whoop of laughter from Sophie, and then she shouted at the top of her voice: 'Yuri, Yuri, get the hell over here.' There was a stirring from the front of the house and then the sound of Red Yuri shuffling down the hall into the kitchen. 'Yuri, show Eddie here what I'm talking about. Go on show him!' From what I could tell Yuri must have shown him, because the next thing I heard was Eddie whining like a dog. 'Jeez Sophie, you sure know how to break a man's heart. Why'd you have to bring that goddam freak into this?'

"I'm not saying I heard stuff like that every day, Jason. But I heard a lot. So it made me into a coarse Hunkie broad, right? What can I say? So The North End wasn't refined. But I never stayed up nights wringing my hands because life wasn't like the movies. I cried at *Mrs. Miniver* and *How Green Was My Valley*, same as everyone else. I cried for days after *A Tree Grows In Brooklyn*. That didn't mean I was a softy. When I got older, I was no goody-goody myself, but I was no pushover either. My mom and dad never learned to speak English beyond the hello-goodbye variety. But they were strict about my staying out late and traipsing around with horny baboons. My home was just your normal, everyday Ukrainian madhouse.

"Lennie's was completely cuckoo. Living at Sophie's day by day must have had a pretty big effect on him. So I've known him most of my life, and later slept with him and married him and had my daughter by him and the rest of it. That's why I think I know him better than anyone. Except sometimes when I get to recalling things, I wonder if maybe I knew my thirty-second cousin better than I've ever known Lennie.

"Crazy things happened in 1968. I remember clearly because it was when I got pregnant with Katrina. Lennie had always longed for a kid. After three years of regular sex and another year of on-again off-again, it looked like we weren't getting any place. Lennie never treated me like one of those Henry the Eighth wives. He got it into his head that he was sterile, that he was the one to blame, not me, and that was that. The crazy bastard even told me once that not being able to have kids was a doom the gods laid on him because he had defied them.

"After our fiasco in Russia, then Greece, I knew in my heart the end was coming. When Lennie got taken on at U of M, I imagined for a while we might be able to pull it off together. But by 1968, with us living apart mostly, our marriage was close to kaput. At the university, a lot of people believe he is some kind of Mahatma Gandhi. Who am I to say he isn't? He has a whole army of followers around him–university types, artist types, CBC types, taxi drivers, bartenders, bouncers, young friends, old friends, friends from River Heights, friends from St. Boniface, Mormon friends from Steinbeck, freaks from the circus, do I know? Count them. I went along with him at first when we went visiting, but I didn't feel good. It wasn't because they talked about things I wasn't interested in, or even because I got the feeling that Lennie had screwed half the women in the room and they pitied me. By then, Jason, I don't think I gave a hoot who he was screwing. I just got to the point where I didn't feel like being around all that mess and confusion.

"It was a strange thing. In Lennie's gang, women got to know each other not from contacts in their own lives, but through their husbands or boyfriends. That way, I suppose, I got to be as much a friend of Jake Jasper's wife, Julia, as of any of the other wives and girlfriends, although it was a different kind of friendship than I had with my old crowd in the North End. I was always comfortable with them in a way I never could be around the wives and girl friends of Lennie's friends.

"I began to notice a change in Julia. She stopped being a bystander like me and began joining conversations and getting as heated up as the men about this or that notion. I had seen it happen before and I recognized what it was. She had fallen under Lennie's spell and he was going to turn her, nurse or no nurse, into a goddamn philosopher.

"Poor Julia,' I thought. 'She's jumped on the roller coaster to god only knows where.' But I'll be honest with you, Jason. I envied her, too. It might have been easier for me if I'd tried to go along for the ride. But I never could. Was it because I didn't have the guts? Or the brains? Or just that I was pretty sure I could see where it would end up? Whatever. Julia jumped on board. I couldn't. We stayed on friendly terms, and then there was an event."

Chapter Twenty-Eight

When I first met Julia, she was the subdued, withdrawn woman Katia described. With the growing frequency of my trips to Winnipeg researching the Churchill River Diversion story, I saw a lot of her and I was witness to her transformation. Years later, she told me no one was more astonished than she was at the change that came over her in so short a time.

"Even before nurse's training, I was intrigued by psychology, thinking in my naivety that it was a way of getting to know what makes people tick. My nursing teachers advised me not to trouble my head with such matters, and to get on with physiology and nutrition and bed-making techniques. All I found time to read outside course work were a few paperbacks, one by Freud, I remember, about dreams, and another by Jung about the male and female sides of people. When Jake first introduced me to Katia and Lennie, I liked her but I was awed by him. He bombarded me with questions I couldn't answer and teased me for accepting the stereotype that nurses aren't expected to have ideas. It wasn't until I met Lennie that I realized there was nothing to stop me from going ahead and learning about psychology if I really wanted to. It was a lightning bolt.

"I don't know if you can understand, Jason, how Jake's and Lennie's world changed me from the way I was brought up. My life got complicated beyond anything I had ever imagined. What I was taught to expect was, I would fall in love on a moonlit night, preferably in a gondola in Venice. I would then move into a nice house on a tree-lined street in suburbia and have kids. In our retirement, after a marvellous life together, my husband and I would stroll along a quiet beach hand-in-hand and watch the sun go down before going home to have dinner with our grandchildren. Was that a cigarette ad? Guess what? That's not what happened.

"My first shocks came from all the gritty things you learn in nursing about bodily functions, from shitting and pissing to sex. I'll never forget what Lennie told me about that once. It was the first time I realized that poetry could mean something. He quoted me that line from William Butler Yeats: "And love has pitched its mansion in the place of excrement". After three years of nurse's training and then practical experience, there were few mysteries about what goes on in the mansion. It gives a girl a very different perspective on the male body than the one cheerleaders jump up and down about at football games. But all that was kindergarten before I took up with Jake. I'm not talking just sex here. The disarray of an artist's life, the hand-to-mouth existence, the indifference about clothes and what other people think, a whole new order of friends than the ones I'd been used to, their passionate talk about everything under the sun, their sublime carelessness. What a difference! Jake excited me about a world of art and ideas I had no inkling of before I met him. I don't know if he noticed how astonishing it was to me. There was certainly no Pygmalion thing going on. If there was, Lennie, not Jake, was Henry Higgins.

"Lennie got me to look at movies in a new way, so I no longer sat there stupefied, just letting the story cast its spell. I watched for how the movie worked to make me respond one way or another, and I tried to figure out what it was saying beneath the surface, about society, about life. Far from spoiling movies for me, it made them immensely more interesting. At the Garrick with groups of friends on Saturday afternoons, like kids at a Fun Club, we must have seen *2001* a dozen times, enveloping the second floor balcony in clouds of marijuana while we tripped our way through Kubrick's psychedelic effects and speculated about that mysterious slab of cosmic chocolate bar that floated out in space, and the baby in the cosmic sac.

"At first, I was terribly unsure of myself. Lennie taught at the university and he was the centre of the table when artists and academics and journalists and that lot got together in the boozers or at the Coop or up at Jake's studio. But I got over it. Lennie treated me no differently from anyone else. When he realized my interest in psychology was real, he took special interest in me. He advised me on things to look up in the library, and answered my questions about what I was reading. He spent time with Jake and me talking about how psychiatry got started and what a powerful force it had become.

Jake rarely joined in. But he listened with curiosity (sometimes, I thought, with a certain amusement) at Lennie's wilder utterances."

Chapter Twenty-Nine

During Lennie's on-again off-again cohabitation with Katia at the Place Louis Riel, Julia and Jake invited them for dinner. Julia said it was her idea because she thought it might help get Lennie and Katia back together. Katia told me her version of the evening, which, with Julia's version later on, ended up giving me two witnesses to the same event who don't know what the other witness said. Katia first:

"Jake cooked local-caught frogs' legs and local wild rice and after dinner, we listened to the Iron Butterfly and an old Flamenco guitar record by Peppi of Ibiza. Jake rolled joints and they all smoked. I was still no good at smoking. I drank a lot of wine instead. I didn't mind them getting mellow. Something in me was there with them. But something wasn't. Once I sensed where the evening was heading, I was tempted. I never had trouble enjoying sex, Jason, I'll be honest, and with Lennie pretty much off it those days, at least as far as I was concerned, I thought what the hell? Sometime long after midnight, Jake walked me home. He came to the Place Louis Riel and we went in and sat down. I heated up some left-over fried chicken and a few holopchies, and poured him Scotch from a bottle Lennie had left one night when I kicked him out. Jake reached out and put his arm around my neck. He gave me a kiss on the forehead, then on my lips. Then he started to laugh. I started to laugh, too. I thought we would hurt ourselves laughing and falling around like a couple of kids. Between you and me, Jason, that was not the sexiest moment of my life.

"Don't ask me what went on between Lennie and Julia. I wondered about it, but I knew as well as I'm sure you did in those days, that he was screwing around all over the place, so what did it matter if he was also screwing Julia? As long as he wasn't living with me, I just accepted that was the way it was going to be. I can tell you for certain, Jason, God is a woman. I never met a man who would make a rule like 'thou shalt not commit adultery'. What I think now is how silly we must have looked, a bunch of grown-ups running around like teenagers trying to bed each other as if there would be no come-uppance. Thank god for Jake's laughter and the warmed-up chicken and holopchies. We sat and ate together. I felt at home with Jake that night and have ever since. And I never worried about not feeling sexy. I could still feel sexy when it mattered.

"It wasn't long after that I told Lennie I was expecting in the spring. I thought he would go loony, he was so happy. He took me to dinner at Dubrovnik, the swankiest restaurant in Winnipeg–"High Class Hunkie," he called it. He came back afterwards to sleep with me and he vowed he would change his ways and settle down. La-la-la. For three weeks, he never smoked anything or drank a drop.

"Then, one night, he came in plastered. Remember how he could sit there silent and then start singing in that cracked, high-pitched voice of his? Ben Gibson's wife's name was Irene. Remember her? She adored Ben and his music but she couldn't put up with him when he came home wild off the road. She finally left him. I'd heard Ben and Lennie sing that Leadbelly song together the way the Weavers used to sing it back in the 50s. Lennie made it sound a bit like Leadbelly, mournful and bluesy:

> Last Saturday night we got married
> Me and my wife settled down
> Now me and my wife are parted
> Gonna take another stroll downtown
>
> Sometimes I live in the country
> Sometimes I live in town
> Sometimes I take a great notion
> To jump into the river and drown
>
> Irene goodnight Irene
> Irene good night

"Jesus, Jason, it broke my heart. It was just a dumb country song I had heard a hundred times before. But he sang it with such feeling. What that man could have done if he wanted to!"

"I used to wonder if he was chasing around so much because he thought there was a chance he might have a kid with someone else. That was before I got pregnant. As I sat listening to him sing, it dawned on me what was bugging him. Way back he had convinced himself that he was sterile. So it had to be Jake who had knocked me up the night of the frogs' legs dinner. Lennie never said it to me in so many words so I brought it out in the open. I told him he was nuts, that Jake and I had just laughed a lot and eaten holopchies. I told him nobody I ever heard of got pregnant from holopchies. I told him to ask Jake if he didn't believe me. Nothing doing. It got into Lennie's head that I was carrying Jake's baby and he wouldn't listen. In a way that's way beyond me, I swear to you Jason, I got the feeling that even though it spooked him, he took some kind of kinky satisfaction in the stupid idea that Jake was the father.

"When she was born in May 1969 I wanted to call her Natasha, but Lennie called her Katrina, and that was the name that stuck. You were the one who told me that William Blake's wife's name was Catherine. There was also Catherine the Great, and of course me, Katia. You said that was probably all in the back of his mind when he called her Katrina, and that Catherine meant 'pure' in Greek.

"At first, the gossips thought Katrina was Jake's baby, too. Lennie was no blabbermouth, but nothing much went on in his crowd without everyone being in on it. You know babies. At first you can't tell who the hell they look like. By the time she's a year old, she looks so much like Lennie–same forehead and nose, jutting jaw, rusty hair, and eerie green eyes, though without the squinty eyebrows–that even he can't deny he's the father. But it's too late for us. Lennie is spinning off somewhere I can't understand and I don't like at all. I have a kid to bring up, and not just to bring up, but to shelter from the jumble and muddle spreading all around. It's a mess that, as far as I can see, Lennie is up to his keister in."

Chapter Thirty

Julia's version of the night of the frog's legs dinner came later. "Remember," she said, "How sexual experimentation was pretty much a moral obligation in 1968. Not just for twenty-five-year olds like me, but for over-thirties like you guys too, married or not. People who shied away from crossing sexual frontiers wound up feeling guilty, or worse–left out to dry. I don't mean everyone. I'm talking about the artists and intellectuals and the pot-smoking tribe, not the everyday population or the nurses I worked with. And I don't mean pot was the cause either. There was an excitement you could feel like a twang in the air. It never left me even when I was on duty in the palliative care ward. Maybe I felt it even more there with death all around.

"As we savoured the frogs' legs, the talk after-dinner got racier and racier. Nothing was said directly and there was no specific signal. At one point, Jake and Katia just got up and left. Lennie and I shared another toke and didn't say a word. The atmosphere pulsated. The next thing, we were on the carpet together beside the hi-fi, and that's as far as we got for the next little while.

"I had found Lennie sexy from the beginning. He was no Marlon Brando but he had an intensity you couldn't miss, something that broke right into you. Still, without the circumstances of that night, I'm sure we would never have become lovers. I don't even want to call us that. Jake was my lover and he continued to be. You couldn't call Lennie's and my relationship an honest-to-god love affair. It was more like adultery by mutual consent, a kind of social thing. It was exciting, but not in the old way, not exciting because forbidden. It was exciting because it was not forbidden, would be more like it.

"But here's the peculiar thing. Jake and I never talked about that night. During our assignations, Lennie and I never talked about what we were doing either, or mentioned Jake or Katia. And afterward, when the sex ended, we never again referred to our times together. It was like going into space and not talking about it when you got back to earth. Earth is earth, space is different. Maybe you go out there for a while and come back. But you're not likely to go out there again.

"I didn't know, and I don't know to this day, what went on between Jake and Katia. Did they have sex? Did they talk about Lennie and me? Katia and I barely saw each other anymore, not because we avoided each other, but because she was expecting and she steered clear of the downtown crowd altogether. Here's a peculiar thing. Jake and I had always been open, not hiding anything. But Jake never asked me about Lennie and I never brought up the subject. I can't speak for Jake and Lennie. They continued to spend as much time together as ever, if not more. Did they talk about Katia and me? I don't know what men say about women when they get together, probably horrible things. But in this case, I don't think they talked about us at all, or even referred to that night. I think they were both too old-fashioned underneath, too squeamish, not hip enough. I think, no matter how close they were to each other, it would have embarrassed them to compare notes about humping each other's wives.

"One thing nagged me. I was reading one of Freud's biographers: 'Each of Freud's relationships with a man in the early period of psychoanalysis is mediated by a woman. In this triangle, Freud's possible homoerotic feelings for the man may have been aroused and sublimated.'

"I had no resentment about Jake's and Lennie's friendship. It gave them both pleasure, and it radiated warmth and fellow-feeling to everyone around them. But could it be that, inadvertently, I was in some kind of weird erotic triangle? It wasn't that I felt there was anything particularly unhealthy about it. I didn't honestly give a damn about such things. But even if they didn't treat me that way, I felt vaguely ... demeaned. I stopped meeting secretly with Lennie. He never made a fuss about it. Life soon got back to normal, if that's the right word for it."

Chapter Thirty-One

With a layover in Winnipeg in early 1969 I headed over to the Coop to see what was doing. The place was empty. The back and front doors were open, as the doors of an easy-going small-town newspaper office might have been a hundred years ago. A spring breeze fluttered papers on tables and the trimmings overhanging drafting boards and silkscreen beds. I walked through to the antique freight elevator at the back and got in. The wood-framed elevator squeaked and groaned. At the top, I pulled back the springy wooden slats and stepped out behind Kelly's studio on the seventh floor. I heard Lennie talking and went in.

The studio was jammed. Lennie arched out his arms and said: "Abracadabra! Jason Faraday has come to join the cause." He motioned me to a cushion, and carried on. I gave a tiny wave hello. Lennie was saying that *Newsweek* reported 500 underground newspapers in the US carrying the New Left and counter-culture message to two million readers. Every university city had a protest organ, not just in the States, but in Montreal, Toronto, and Vancouver. The *Winnipeg Free Press* (Lennie called it the *Winnipeg Slave Press*), and the *Winnipeg Tribune* (the *Winnipeg Fibune*) were toadies of the old entrenchment who treated Manitoba like a fiefdom. There were big issues—the political timidity of the university and its connection with gouging corporations, the money lust of the onyx-eyed Philistines, the sex-fright of the moral majority, the grim rectitude of the nuclear family, the fascism of the police. But the real Goliath, Lennie said, was the here-and-now assault on nature represented by the Churchill Water Diversion Project and the sinister gnomes of a multi-national consortium called Churchill Forest Industries. They were about to plunder Manitoba's rivers and forests, Lennie said, with the leverage of Manitoba's own tax dollars, and then sit back smacking their lips at the way they were able to play the rubes in Manitoba's government for suckers, without spending a Swiss franc.

It had been a while since I had seen Lennie so fired up. The regulars were there–Jake and Julia Clark (painter and nurse), Vince Calley (poet/academic), Dimitri Wenchencho (artist/cartoonist), Ben Gibson (cowboy/Orpheus), and Jackie and Max Steiner (self-professed bourgeois radicals). Seated on too few cushions, the tally included latter-day Jansenist autodidacts from St. Boniface, disenchanted Mennonites from Steinbach, Luddites from across the ethnic spectrum, young idealists recently released from high school in River Heights or the North End. Prominently, though off in a corner, was Zebbie the Toke of Zebediah Exterminators Inc. He gave me a finger wave and a smile of greeting. Zebbie knew a client base when he saw one.

Lennie was in the midst of announcing that what they were there for was to make their own newspaper. It would be called *The Gadfly*. With a felt pen, he scrawled the mission statement on a piece of plasterboard left over from his renovations:

> *The Gadfly* will be the enemy of privilege, elitism, environ-
> mental degradation, and tyranny over the individual in all
> its disguises–whether political, economic, generational,
> sexual, or religious. *The Gadfly* will give no quarter to the
> forces that stunt and smother life, to institutional powers
> that cripple individual expression and creativity, to the
> mills of industry run by crony capitalists, to the hubris of
> technology, the lethal virus of advertising, and all forms of
> mental sclerosis.

No one called for revisions, or even asked why *The Gadfly*. This moment was as close as I ever came to attending a gathering of Holy Rollers. Lennie was so compelling that if he had suddenly asked a special act of someone, barring an assassination (but I wouldn't count that out), I believe that person would have tried to do it. After declarations of solidarity and choruses of commitment all round, everyone old enough to drink and some who weren't, gravitated to the Albert beer parlor and plunged into noisy strategies. At closing time, a few of us went back to Lennie's and talked some more before the last of the stragglers but me drifted off.

By then it was early in the morning. Lennie made coffee. The two of us sat watching the light come up from the East through the French doors of his rooftop aerie. He wanted to know what was up with me. I told him I was in the middle of research on a big story.

"Have you heard of something called NAWAPA?," I said.

"Meaning?"

"North American Water and Power Alliance. It sounds lunatic but it's real and it's been around at least since the 1940s. Parsons, a huge engineering conglomerate seriously proposed it to the US senate in 1964. Since then, its promoters, openly or covertly, include bankers and oil moguls and every multinational corps you care to name, as well as several US presidents. Its premise is simple. Canada has twenty times more fresh water per citizen than America. The western US, more particularly California, with a population larger than Canada's, has already sucked up rivers so that they virtually peter out before they reach the sea. The ancient aquifers east of the Rockies in Colorado and Arizona are drying up faster than earth scientists can track what's happening. Californians are having to stop watering their lawns, for pity's sake. Golf courses are going dry. Look at it this way: when they get really thirsty down there, three hundred million Americans won't let thirty million Canadians hog the continent's fresh water."

"So what's their plan?" Lennie asked.

"How about a seven hundred kilometer trench ten kilometers wide down the belly of the continent?"

"That's crazy."

"The Fraser, Yukon, Peace, and Athabasca will be reversed into the NAWAPA trench. North flowing rivers, even the mammoth Mackenzie and Nelson, will be redirected south. All the James Bay rivers will be turned south as well, by the Faustian engineering feat of damming the mouth of the Bay."

"Jesus, JJ, if they're not stopped, this new breed of Wall Street water rat will turn the entire continent into a wasteland before anyone opens their eyes from their long winter's sleep."

Since the appearance in 1962 of Rachel Carson's *Silent Spring,* we all imagined ourselves environmentalists. For Lennie, what he now dubbed "The Water Conspiracy", took instant precedence in his register of social ills. In view of the water diversion plans afoot in Manitoba, it also gave him fresh fodder for *The Gadfly.*

Chapter Thirty-Two

The three key people Lennie brought in to share the masthead had complementary skills. Vince Calley, the academic, had some rudimentary experience in publishing scholarly stuff and knew about galleys and proofing. Jake Clark, the painter, had been doing covers gratis for small literary magazines ever since university and could draw and do paste-ups and layouts. Max Steiner did a regular column called "Justice on Trial", and he was a whiz at editing everybody's words to keep them simple, and making up smart captions, and headlines and last-minute fillers. And then there was Lennie, with more elusive qualifications. There was to be no regular editor. The idea was that each principal would take responsibility for one whole issue on a rotating basis. That meant each of them had two months to assemble the edition he was responsible for.

The others took on tangential roles. Ben Gibson became a pretty good photographer for a musician, and even wrote a few angry pieces about scams in the music industry. Jackie Steiner wrote an on-again-off-again column about the exploitation of women in the business world called "Matri Money". Dimitri Wenchenko drew cartoons. Nurse Julia helped with accounting, circulation, and proofing when she had time. Who but Zebby The Toke looked after distribution? He had the advantage of coming onboard with some already well-established territories.

Lennie insisted that if there were to be an editorial policy, it would have had just two criteria: first, subjects had to be local or else global happenings that had a direct bearing on local issues. Secondly, the paper would give voice to what Lennie saw as the bottled-up rage of the young who were being brushed aside by the mainstream media while, to his mind, the young were bursting with fresh ideas and creative gusto.

The top third of the front page of the first issue of *The Gadfly* in February 1969 featured a pen sketch of a midden littered with the skulls and rib cages of Indians and wildlife, overseen by a huge leering rat. Jake Clark's creation for sure, revisiting the style of a series of ink drawings from his England days featuring huddled, grinning skulls in the London Underground.

William Blake got two sidebars. On one side: "To create a little flower is the labour of ages." On the other side: " … if we but knew what we do/ When we delve or hew/Hack and rack the growing green!" The policy statement Lennie had scribbled on plasterboard in his apartment the day of the paper's inception made up the rest of the front page in bold typeface.

Lennie's maiden editorial, with input from Vince Calley, came on page two, superimposed over a pen sketch of a rotting, life-sized Lake Winnipeg Goldeye:

> We brought to North America all that was wicked and ugly from Europe and little that was good. We brought racial hatred and religious strife. We brought a love of money and a fear of sex that has made us strangers to the land and to each other. Yet there are things in Manitoba we *feel*, even if we don't have the words to talk about them—a sense that this land has a radiance, a power, a personality all its own.
>
> Once we had an opportunity, as newcomers, to inhabit the space of the prairies imaginatively, to learn about aboriginal people, their music, poetry, mythology and art, and so to become a part of a civilization long attuned to and at peace with its environment. That opportunity is gone. Now we disrespect not only the people who were here first, we despoil the world around us as we grow to hate ourselves.
>
> *Commerce, Prudence and Industry*—that's the official motto of Manitoba. Who imposed this pernicious shibboleth on us? Could something be missing in our lives? Why is it there's no fun anymore going down to Portage Avenue on a Saturday afternoon and walking with the crowds? Are Salisbury Nips, Simon's corned beef, and Kelekis's hot dogs on North Main the only homegrown pleasures left that

haven't been displaced by corporate hamburgers? Why have so many lovely old buildings of the downtown core been converted into parking lots? Is there no life in Winnipeg without a brand new sod lawn, an asphalt driveway, and a two-car garage? Where have all our children gone? Why have they grown up and moved away?

As Southern Indian Lake is flooded, will my hydro rates go down by a penny or two? Is that the reason for the apathy of our populace in the face of the massive inundation of the northern wilderness? Should I stay here with such people or go away? Can life be less stupid elsewhere?

I don't think so. It's a global thing. We can't escape it so we might as well stay home and fight. We are performers and painters and writers and musicians and intellectuals. We have theatre. We have ballet and a symphony orchestra. We have libraries and universities. We have more than the HBC or the CPR or the Grain Exchange ever imagined. We have marshes and farmlands and fast flowing streams and rivers and wild creatures and forests and spaces that 99% of the world can only dream of. This is it, the end of the rainbow. Our America is here or nowhere.

All occasions unite to inform us of one indisputable fact. Our generation is dying. Our children smell our corruption and reject us. This is the real cause of the generation gap and student revolt. That we take clubs to them and imprison them because they choose life is the most reliable and accurate symptom of our decay. We use Hitler's technique of the Big Lie to console ourselves. We accuse our youth of violence when we are the most violent generation the earth has ever spawned. We never scruple to napalm children in our fight against Communism. For the sake of democracy, we foment coups all over the world in countries we have no understanding of.

With all haste, we must awaken our minds and our sympathies. This world can tolerate no more sleep-walking. We can no longer sit stoned in front of our television sets while a handful of magnates conspire to manufacture our future. We Manitobans, here at the heart of the continent, we can turn ourselves around. We can slay the dragon. We can show the world that systems are made by humans and that humans are not made to conform to systems.

It may have been no *Gettysburg Address,* but there was no "Cuba si, Yankee no" or "Hippies of the world unite" stuff either. Knowing Lennie's allergy to pen and paper, I was relieved. What I read even managed to catch some of the flare of his oratory. The first issue was unlike anything to be found in the established press. Overnight, it became the talk of the town. Environment looked to be the big topic, but there were other issues. While Lennie meant the paper to concentrate on Manitoba, he also aimed to take it beyond parochial concerns. Under the heading, *Pensées and Polemics,* squibs appeared from time to time that were undoubtedly Lennie's doing:

From the moment of birth, when the Stone Age baby confronts the Twentieth Century mother, the baby is subjected to forces of violence, called love, as its mother and father, and their parents and their parents before them, have been. These forces are mainly concerned with destroying most of its potentialities, and on the whole this enterprise is successful. By the time the new human being is fifteen or so, we are left with a being like ourselves, a half-crazed creature more or less adjusted to a mad world. This is normality.

R. D. Laing

They fuck you up, your mom and dad. They may not mean to, but they do.

Philip Larkin

In 1673 the British military commander in North America, Sir Jeffrey Amherst, became the first modern practitioner of germ warfare when he authorized the distribution of blankets contaminated with smallpox to American Indians who were making life difficult for European settlers in Pennsylvania.

Encyclopedia Britannica

The new modes of aggression destroy without getting one's hands dirty, one's body soiled, one's mind incriminated. The killer remains clean, physically as well as mentally. The purity of his deadly work obtains added sanction if it is directed against the national enemy in the national interest .... If Freud's theory is correct ... we may indeed speak of a suicidal tendency on a truly social scale, and the national and international play with total destruction may well have found a firm basis in the instinctual structure of individuals.

Herbert Marcuse

So God help me, I can perceive nothing but a conspiracy of rich men procuring their own commodities under the name and title of a Commonwealth.

Thomas More

One edition of *The Gadfly* was given over to the subject of Law and Order. The captions jumped off the page at you in the non-linear, non-sequential manner of a McLuhan *essai concrète*. Graffiti-like letters dripping paint (or maybe it was blood?) read:

HERE COME DA COPS
HERE COME DA JUDGE
LOOK OUT! HERE COME DA GUMMINT

A short piece under Lennie's name, attacking the Winnipeg police for repressing campus protest and for raiding private homes in search of drugs, began with a quotation:

> The streets of our country are in turmoil. The universities are filled with students rebelling and rioting. Communists are seeking to destroy our country. Russia is threatening us with her might ... yes danger from within and without. We need law and order. Elect us and we shall restore law and order. Those who fear that law and order is under threat today please keep a level head." The lines above are quoted verbatim from a speech by Adolph Hitler delivered at Hamburg in 1932. That was some years after the time when he couldn't get beyond the rank of corporal in the Austrian army because, as his superiors said, he lacked leadership ability.

An entire page was filled with a macabre ink drawing of Jake's where we looked over the shoulder of a semi-naked hippie facing a bevy of priests, preachers and police. Beyond them in the courtyard, visible through two barred and arched windows of what could be a medieval cathedral of the inquisition, or a prison, was on one side, a gallows under construction and on the other side, a TV crew setting up to grab the action. The text was Blake again:

> Prisons are built with stones of law
> Brothels with bricks of religion

By chance or coercion, Gallery One One One at the University of Manitoba's School of Art hosted an exhibition of Blake's engravings of Dante, Milton and the *Book of Job*. *The Gadfly* managed to reproduce, on newsprint, quite recognizable reproductions of four plates from *Job* along with a review attributed to Vince Calley and Lennie:

> Blake thought that Dante, like Milton, was a true visionary, only impeded by fetters of moral law forged by the ratiocinative bias of the Renaissance. Like Milton, Dante was imaginatively more at home among Devils and the Damned than among Angels and Saints. It takes some hard thinking

to grasp what Blake meant when he wrote: "Moral virtue is righteousness according to the law, not the spirit". He knew that the imagination is re-creative energy, not outward prison bars of law and order. He knew intuitively that artists must be revolutionaries and mutineers. They seek life which is dynamic and self-renewing, not acquiescence, conformity, and stagnation—just other words for death.

This is what the story of Job means. It may be Blake's final utterance on the necessity for man to free himself from "mind forged manacles", the restrictive commandments of "Thou Shalt Not", that nullify love and make of human relationships a code of precepts and punitive rules. This is not authentic morality but footling moralism. This is true of art also. By following the letter of the law instead of the spirit of the law, the imagination, like Job, is in danger of falling victim to the ego or selfhood, what Blake calls in this context "The Accuser".

We first meet Job as an establishment figure who is just and virtuous for one reason only—for his adherence to law and order as commanded from without—not from any inner impulse. Satan, the Accuser, is the self-righteousness within Job's mind. Because Job conceives of God as a bestower of wealth he loses his wealth. Because he fears he must eradicate bodily desire he is afflicted with boils. Because he sees his children as no more than extensions of himself, he loses them. His friends believe Job is being made to suffer for sins he has concealed from the world. They are members of "the Elect" who hold the naive and illiterate belief that all suffering is a form of divine retribution. The more they accuse him of sin the more he protests his innocence.

Out of the whirlwind the young and fiery Elihu shows Job that God is no remote Accuser with the Book of the Law in his arms, but a forgiving and loving humanity. The Behemoth and Leviathan of war and the inhuman inflictions of man onto man, are not from afar, but from the self-righteous, muscle-bound, and unexamined moral code that Job himself so unthinkingly accepted. Finally, understanding the inanity of his early certainties, Job sees the light. Satan is cast into the fires of annihilation. Job is re-united with his children. Together they play musical instruments and sing, making art, the purest form of prayer.

With my remembrance of Lennie once calling his old roommate, Mike Nader, the best editor he had ever come across, I asked Vince what it was like to co-author with Lennie. "I did the same with his inaugural editorial for *The Gadfly*, you know," Vince said. "But don't get me wrong. In both pieces, all I did is work on the structure and some re-phrasing. The ideas were all Lennie's."

It was never expected by the founding fathers of *The Gadfly* that Jake Clark (no intellectual like the others as he protested to the end) would do more than the layout and artwork and oversee his obligatory edition every two months. The article he wrote came as a surprise (not least, he later told me, to himself). He titled it *Confessions Of A 35 Year Old Drug Addict*. From his relentless foraging through obscure records and journals, Lennie came up with a neat counterpoint to lead into Jake's article. It was by one Harry Anslinger, Commissioner of the US Bureau of Narcotics in 1932.

Marijuana is only and always a scourge which undermines its victims and degrades them mentally, morally and physically. In the earliest stages of intoxication, the willpower is destroyed and inhibitions and restraints are released, the moral barricades are broken down and often debauchery and sexuality result. An egoist will enjoy delusions of grandeur, the timid individual will suffer anxiety, and the aggressive one will often resort to acts of violence and crime. Dormant tendencies are released. Constant use produces an incapacity for work and disorientation often leading to insanity.

Jake's piece took it from there:

In the Fifties when I was a university student, I remember being at a party where one of the discussions was about marijuana. None of us knew anything about it but we had read things about the California coast. We read the beatniks–Kerouac, Ginsberg, Corso, Ferlinghetti, and their mentors, Henry Miller and William Burroughs. And there was Norman Mailer in *Advertisements For Myself* to explain to us the difference between beat and hip. Statements like, "I don't need drugs to show me where it's at", were bandied about, but there was a feeling underneath of being left out, for me as a musician, especially of being left in the outback of the painting scene.

A couple of years later, I was in Europe and had my first smoke of grass. My eyes got a strange tingling behind them and everything I looked at had a sharpness and clarity that I had not experienced before. Music seemed to walk off the record player and parade around the room. It was so unfamiliar I felt anxious. Then I thought, "So that's what all those musicians are up to." The word "cool" got big, and I began to think I knew what it meant. With women communication became a thing of touch only or maybe a smile. The music and the grass brought us together, and made words tedious and largely meaningless.

I was not really of the generation of the hippies and the drug culture. I was a few years too old. But I knew what they were about. They were not just a flash in the pan. They had become a very large social fact and it was clear they wouldn't just go away. I was stunned by the fear and hatred older people seemed to have for the young.

Eventually, in my world, grass became an integral part of a social evening. There would be some booze and some wine and in an hour or two we would all be mellow–relaxed and enjoying each other's company. It was a kind of decompression from the world of rush, a communal thing. When a toke passed you could take it or leave it. No pressure. People dropped out and in as they felt like it. There was always deep involvement in the act of eating. Eating took on a mythic quality as in Buddhism and Hinduism and I suppose at The Last Supper. The Eucharist thing though was a bit of a stretch, where you ate the lord like a cannibal. Weird.

At a party we were having some smoke. The police arrived and we were all arrested. Until we got out of jail, Winnipeg was short a couple of professors, a mechanic, an insurance salesman, two musicians, a lawyer, a nurse and her friend, a waiter, a journalist, a politician and a poet. Imagine the threat we posed to law and order before we were apprehended. With us in custody, imagine how the incidence of robbery, rape and homicide must have plunged, and how secure the folks in suburbia must have felt.

I am certainly addicted to cigarettes and to coffee and when I go on a booze bender I know I have a hard time stopping. By myself in my studio I also become a slave to Leonardo's sketches and to listening to Glenn Gould's *Goldberg Variations*. I don't need smoke for those things. But smoke doesn't hurt. When friends come round and talk into the night we get high together and do some traveling through each others' heads, usually with joy and laughter. And with an intimacy way beyond what goes on at big splash parties.

I've been to those parties where everyone seems interested in telling you how happy or successful or rich they are while they're looking over your shoulder for a piece of tail. A quiet toke reminds me how much I don't feel at home there. It reminds me of that Emily Dickenson poem: "The soul selects its own society/Then shuts the door./On her divine majority/Obtrude no more." I like that idea. A little toke can do a lot for that kind of thinking. I can't figure out what something as sweet and personal as grass can get the straight world so all tied up in knots about.

Another issue of *The Gadfly* focused on education, peppered throughout the pages in horizontal and vertical side-bars with apothegms clearly from Lennie's grab-bag.

School is a ritual of initiation that introduces the neophyte to the sacred race of progressive consumption.

Anonymous

Any attempt to reform the university without attending to the system of which it is an integral part is like trying to do urban renewal in New York City from the twelfth storey up.

Ivan Illych

These days there is no such thing as amateur psychoanalysis.

Roberta Dales

Nothing in education is so astonishing as the amount of ignorance it accumulates in the form of inert facts.

Henry Adams

To this (as calling myself a scholar), I am obliged by the duty of my condition: I make not therefore my head a grave, but a treasure of knowledge; I intend no Monopoly, but a community in learning; I study not for my own sake only, but for theirs that study not for themselves. I envy no man that knows more than myself, but pity them that know less. I instruct no man as an exercise of my knowledge, or with an intent rather to nourish and keep it alive in mine own head than beget and propagate it in his.

Sir Thomas Browne

An open mind, to be sure, should be open at both ends, like the food pipe, and have a capacity for excretion as well as intake.

Northrop Frye

It is a miracle that curiosity survives formal education.

Einstein

Chapter Thirty-Three

One of Dimmy's cartoons suggested by Lennie showed two plump pigs in a pigpen, with a factory in the background bearing the sign *Sausage City*. Two piglets were making off through the bars of the pen, heading into the bush. Seeing them sneak away, one plump elder said to the other: "That's all the younger generation seems to care about nowadays. Escape from reality." The other plump elder, watching the piglets escape, concurred, adding "They're all useless."

Another picture, not a cartoon but a photograph, displayed two perfect breasts (by Ben Gibson, the singer become amateur photographer). He told me a nursing mother who was a friend of his agreed to pose for the photograph because she had heard about the danger of DDT and she detested Nestle's propaganda about the advantages of early bottle-feeding. The caption under one breast read: "Milk in such containers may be unfit for human consumption." Under the other it read: "Keep out of reach of children."

Jake set up two centre pages to be pulled out and used as posters. The first, called *The Churchill River Water Diversion Plan*, showed two Indians fishing, above them an immense dam about to burst. The second had the title: *Churchill Forest Industries Park*. It pictured a highway lined with advertising billboards showing swimming beaches and fishing camps and summer cottages. In gaps between the billboards were vistas of tree stumps and desolation.

With two mega-projects—the Churchill River Diversion and Churchill Forest Industries—poised to assault Manitoba's northland "'Ecology'", a new word in the popular lexicon, became a clarion call. The Manitoba Lennie came back to from Russia was for him a land of pristine forests and waterways that, however distant from his personal experience, ignited his imagination.

This land was under siege by the world-wasters, and Lennie was out to take them on.

In 1966 Duff Roblin's Conservatives had declared *Churchill Forest Industries* a bonanza for the North. By spring of 1969, under Ed Shreyer's newly elected (supposedly environmentally sensitive) New Democrats, allegations were being made that Churchill Forest Industries, a nebulous consortium of Zurich financiers, was acquiring timber rights to one-seventh of Manitoba with the help of a forty million dollar loan, and a further sixty million dollar loan promise, from the Manitoba Development Corporation, an instrument of the provincial government. Winnipeg's financial leaders, along with New Democrat Environmental Minister Sidney Green, were overjoyed at the promise of new investment, new jobs, and fat ripple revenues. On the other side of the ledger, where Lennie and his bunch stood, the story was that the Swiss consortium was buying rights to exploit a huge spread of northern wilderness with negligible environmental impact studies, with the prospect of huge profits, and to round off the deal by financing it largely with Manitoba's own tax dollars.

The Gadfly achieved city-wide notoriety by 1969, but for Lennie, it had not got through to the young the way it should have. Posters had become all the rage in the counter culture of the West, just as so-called "big character posters" had become the main propaganda device in Mao's China, and radio and the megaphone for Hitler. For Lennie, that was it. They would supplement *The Gadfly* with poster back-ups and he would out-speechify Hitler. Next to a photograph of former premier Duff Roblin shaking hands with a grinning Oskar Reiser, president of Churchill Forest Industries, the *Gadfly* poster read:

FROM ZURICH TO THE PAS
THE $100 MILLION BARGAIN OF A LIFETIME

Manitoba 100th Anniversary Sale
250,000 Square Miles
Immediate Delivery
Virgin Air, Streams,
Lakes, and Forests
Waiting To Be Exploited

Foreign Investors Welcome (Small Business need not apply)
Come to Manitoba – No Risk Involved
The last Frontier of Free Enterprise

But hurry. 34,000 square miles have already gone!

Lennie engaged a brilliant young economics student to research the financial structure of the deal and his report in *The Gadfly* caught the attention of the national press. It concluded with a list of unanswered questions.

1. Who are the real owners of CFI?

2. How much have they received from Manitoba and how much more do we owe them?

3. What is the ratio of Manitoba government investment to the CFI consortium's investment? In cash not paper.

4. What is the track record of CFI and why is it so hard to uncover its past?

5. What is the truth about CFI's involvement in the Catania pulp mill in Sicily that resulted in a $70,000,000 loss to the local company?

6. Who are Technopulp of New Jersey, Monoco AG of Switzerland, MP Industrial Mills of West Germany, James Bertram and Sons of Edinburgh, and Pack River Company of Spokane Washington?

7. How long is Manitoba committed? The contract offers harvest options for sixty years, the same time it takes a pulp tree in the North to reach exploitable size.

For its upcoming 100th Anniversary Manitoba adopted the slogan: *Growing to Beat '70*. Lennie organized a conference. Jake made a poster to promote it showing a highway jammed with an endless convoy of logging trucks and the smokestack of a paper mill pouring smoke into the sky. The title of the conference was "Manitoba: Colony within a colony within a colony within a .... " Keynote speakers were all young, smart, vocal, informed, and left.

Late in the day of the conference, a xeroxed drawing circulated. The calligraphy was so intricate you had to look carefully before the image came through. It was of a glowering, hunched-over figure with dead eyes and broken teeth, wearing a silk top hat. In his hand he held the trunk of a tree he had just torn up by the roots, the roots dripping blood. Below, in small print, the caption read: "Last Will and Testament of a Corporate Visionary":

> I live upwind from the smokestack, upstream from
> the slag dumped in the river. By the time the air is
> fouled, the river is poisoned, and all the trees are
> gone I'll be dead. So what the fuck do I care?

Chapter Thirty-Four

Sex, drugs and rock and roll continued apace, universities became, in more ways than one, a hot bed. Sex between tutor and tutored may have been common from the Greek symposia to the British public school, but with the rise of co-education, it took on a more heterosexual character. There was nothing merely personal about it as far as Lennie was concerned. The joy of sex was foundational to all humanity's hopes for freedom and self-fulfilment.

Passing through Winnipeg on a scouting trip for a story I was working on about the depletion of the Lake Winnipeg Goldeye, I sat with Lennie at the Albert and we got talking about teaching. We were in a bantering mood.

"You're not a journalist," Lennie said. "You're a preacher."

"You're not a teacher," I said. "You're a lecher." I quoted a poem I liked by W.D. Snodgrass called *April Inventory*:

> The blossoms snow down in my hair;
> The trees and I will soon be bare.
> The trees have more than I to spare.
> The sleek, expensive girls I teach,
> Younger and pinker every year,
> Bloom gradually out of reach.

"It's my downfall, JJ, growing old amid the young. What is the attitude of women students toward professors, especially English professors? It's a horny situation. One reason is that there are so many English professors, and a lot of them are young and spry. But there's another reason. English professors bring an element of exoticism into the mundane world of family and high school that young women are fleeing from in droves. This new breed of stud, a dozen or so years their senior, speaks eloquently and my god, reads books!

Unlike the everyday variety of college boyfriend the girls' age, these guys are groovy. If a girl digs Blake's 'Better murder an infant in its cradle than nurse unacted desires' and thereafter thinks that repressing desire amounts to an act of anti-life, how can she resist life?

"I know this is bad news, not to say flagrant injustice for faculty wives. Their expanding waistlines and dilating stretch marks are no match for the taut bellies and peach-fuzz flesh of willing and lubricious co-eds. Without question, a wayward thirty-five-year-old in lustful pursuit of a twenty-one-year-old nymphet makes a ludicrous spectacle, although you have to wonder—is the male alone the villain of the piece, as a growing chorus of female activists claim? After all, without acquiescing females over the age of consent (and therefore responsible for their actions?), male professors would be obliged to remain true to their marriage vows however hot, wily and wild their extra-curricular fantasies."

It was typical of Lennie that he would ridicule the "ludicrous spectacle" of January pursuing May, and then turn round and become what he ridiculed. At 22, Laura Gunn was a rarity. Black-haired and golden-eyed, she had been freshie queen, a cheerleader and a party girl until she chanced into Lennie's second year course. His reputation as a pied piper was well established by then. Jolted by the piper into an unexpected interest in poetry, the next year she rushed to sign up for his course on Romantic poetry. It turned out to be a life-altering experience for her. I found Laura and interviewed her in the mid-70s not long after her release from a Chilean prison. Her candour surprised me. She could be as blunt as Lennie when it came to matters of the heart.

"My boyfriend Grant and I had been going steady and we were talking marriage. His family was one of the old dynasties of Winnipeg. Mine wasn't old but they were rich. Both of us had our own digs not far from River and Osborne and we spent a lot of time together. His family knew we slept together. As pillars of propriety, they also knew how to wear blinkers when it became apparent there was little they could do about it. Grant had his own money. By then, to a modest extent, so did I, inherited from my grand-mother when I reached the age of consent. But that didn't keep my parents at bay. They did everything they could to keep me away from Grant, pressing me to find a nice Jewish boy.

"Grant and I took Lennie's course on Romantic Poetry not because we were particularly interested in the period but because Lennie had been so brilliant the year before on Spenser and especially on Milton, whom he obviously disliked yet seemed drawn to like a moth to a candle. I'll never forget his opening words: 'In philosophy, they start you off with some arguments about why God exists and then they give you some other arguments about why he doesn't. That's metaphysics. In *Paradise Lost*, Milton says he's going to justify the ways of God to man. That's theology. Well, despite Milton's propensity for discursive speculation, I'm going to have as little to say as possible about metaphysics and theology. This is a course on poetry. Get ready for it. We'll be talking about myth and metaphor here, not about abstract thought boxes.'

"The 1968/69 syllabus for Romantic Poetry listed Blake, Coleridge, Wordsworth, Keats, Byron and Shelley. We spent the first eight weeks before Christmas on Blake, the last two weeks on Coleridge and Wordsworth. Lennie's Thursdays became the best time of the week. We did some Keats, Byron and Shelley in January, then returned to Blake until spring, with forays into W.B. Yeats who wasn't even on the curriculum. I don't remember a single student saying, 'But sir, what about exams?' I have talked off and on to classmates from that year and they have told me it was the high point of university for them. I wonder if that year wasn't the high point for Lennie, too.

"Maybe what the class became was a kind of group therapy. That was fine. I think that's what we wanted. We hated the impersonality of the university. What Lennie offered wasn't suety, thumb-sucking stuff. He wasn't laying his own neuroses on us or bringing in cushions so we could sit in a circle on the floor and blabber aimlessly at each other in the manner that got so popular with young professors at the end of the '60s. It was always the text first for him. What the poet had to say, his words. It was amazing the way he could lead you into the heart of a metaphor. You might have seen it in a misty way. Then he would shine a light that would clear the mist away, relate it to other elements in the poem, and make the image glow. And not just illuminate it, connect it to our lives.

"When he quoted Blake's 'Prisons are built with stones of Law, Brothels with bricks of Religion,' Lennie brought in the penitentiary at Headingly where two-thirds of the inmates were Indians, and the street corners of

North Main where runaway fourteen-year-old Indian girls, who had been brought up by nuns in residential schools, were working as prostitutes. He would not let us take poetry as something back in the past or out there in distant lands. It was right in front of us, alive. He was not just a virtuoso or some kind of sorcerer with words. He meant what he said. He had absolute conviction. He could be comic, like when he impersonated Kafka walking into a Manitoba spring and rubbing his eyes in disbelief at the simplicity and purity of the landscape. He said Kafka may have been a great genius, but he was too drenched in mid-European gloom for our tender Canadian ears. Kafka's character, Gregor Samsa, who 'awoke one morning from uneasy dreams to find himself transformed into a cockroach,', now how could such a man, Lennie asked, enjoy a Manitoba spring?

"Lennie connected Blake's fiery prophet, Rintrah, who raged against injustice, with the trial of the Chicago Seven. He saw Chicago as the epitome of the chasm between old and young as the old sent their young off to war to protect their accumulation of commodities. It was no longer just Columbia and Berkeley, but big international hot spots that were seething with student rage throughout Europe and beyond.

"Grant and I must have seemed to our classmates the perfect couple. He was tall and blonde and blue-eyed of the Wellington Crescent Ultra-Wasp genus. I was dark-haired 'with a tawny front' in the tradition of Cleopatra, as Lennie liked to say, 'if Cleopatra was indeed a Jew'.

"By my time, cross-ethnic mating in Winnipeg was less of a calamity than it had been a generation earlier. Grant's and my real problem wasn't just his fiercely Anglophone family and my fiercely Jewish orthodox parents. It was sexual. No matter what we did, Grant could barely get started making love before he had to stop. We read about it. Premature ejaculation and all that. Grant went to a shrink. We talked about it. I kept assuring him that it didn't matter, that I was okay with the situation. Then Grant came up with an idea. Mate-swapping was on the rise, much discussed in books and movies and the New Yorker, not to mention gab sessions late at night smoking pot. Grant told me that Blake's line, 'The lust of the goat is the bounty of God', got him thinking. He said he wanted me to have sex with Lennie.

"Grant's place was bizarre, a habitat available only to a millionaire or a millionaire's son. He had it built to his own design on a vacant lot on the Assiniboine, the site of a demolished native residential school. It was a huge one-room structure, circular on the model of a railway roundhouse, forty feet in diameter, twenty feet high at the centre, with a gallery-like balcony running round the circumference. The lower part of the walls, as in a teepee, provided storage for birds' nests of old bicycles, bales of straw, antique ploughs and scythes and ox harnesses from the early sod-breaking days, the body and disassembled parts of a Ford model T, the rusting skeleton of an old river boat engine, antiquated Evinrude outboards with manual whipcords, shelves of National Geographic, Popular Science, *The Beaver* going back to 1912, and, hanging everywhere, every kind of animal trap from leg-hold to several speculative models of Grant's with patents pending. A lot of Grant's family money had been made in the fur trade. He believed in fur but he also believed in Animal Rights. The conflict was one of his lesser frustrations.

"There was a kitchen on one side of the mega-igloo, and a Spartan dining area and music centre on the far side. Otherwise, there was nothing but a custom made bed, twelve feet square, at the centre of the circle, sprawling there, ready for a helicopter to land. Grant invited me and Lennie over for dinner. He coached me on what I was to do. The whole idea terrified me, but I don't deny it excited me too. I played the game, mostly with my eyes, and Lennie picked up on it. If he had been the one to initiate the event, not me, he would have fooled nobody. He looked strained. Grant, of course, paid no heed and did the talking. Then suddenly, he announced that he had to run up to West Meadows, his family's game preserve, to check out a new animal trap they were developing. He got up and put on his goose-hunting jacket. "You guys finish your coffee," he said, and was out the door. Minutes later, Lennie and I landed on the giant bed.

"Grant called the next afternoon and came over. He looked awful, still wearing the duck-hunting jacket. When I made tea, I sat down ready to talk, but before I could start, he began to cry. 'Don't say anything,' he said. 'I didn't go to West Meadows. I parked a block away and came in through the back up to the balcony. I saw it all.'"

"Whatever he had expected to gain from the experiment (was it also an effort to be faithful to the spirit of the times?), whatever I had expected by going along with it, didn't come to pass. In time, there was neither guilt nor regret, just confusion. The saddest thing was that Grant quit Lennie's class and Grant and I avoided each other. From that time on, once, sometimes twice a week, I spent the night with Lennie. He had his own place by then and wasn't living with Katia so I didn't have to feel like a marriage marauder.

"I was with him one day at the Bay shopping for a book for his daughter. The children's section was right next to the philosophy section. With the clerk looking on, I said, picking up Bertram Russell's *History of Philosophy*: "Oh Daddy. Get me this one!" We laughed all the way down Portage Avenue but we both knew change was coming.

"*The Gadfly* was receiving fewer and fewer submissions from students. Luis Humerus, a Communist from Chile, was an exception, reporting regularly on the progress of the Chilean bid for power by Salvador Allende. I began seeing more and more of him over the winter. My parents were hell-bent on my summering in Israel to discover my heritage. Instead, come graduation, I took off with Luis for Chile to join the campaign to make Allende the first Communist president in South America. I recommend my action to all young radicals in search of a cause, on one condition, that they have parents standing by prepared to spend a lot of effort and money when the time comes to get them out of prison."

Chapter Thirty-Five

An editorial in *The Gadfly* in the summer of '70 summed it up. Under the heading: "For those of you still reading the snoozepapers." It read like a requiem:

> Maybe we were naive, maybe we started the paper at the wrong time, maybe it is our continuing problem with distribution (the Hudson's Bay Company book store wasn't the only one to kick us out), maybe it is that our format intimidates people. Whatever the reason, we have not been receiving your copy. Until we do begin receiving your contributions and stories and news leads, we are replacing our typesetting equipment with a second-hand electric typewriter, a stapler, and a photo-copier. Not nearly as nice but a hell of a lot cheaper.

One bright spot for Lennie was Katrina. By Christmas she was a year-and-a-half. If Lennie arrived at Katia's apartment drunk or high or in one of his states, which she said she could detect by his voice even on the lobby phone, she wouldn't let him in. Otherwise, he visited when he felt like it. He came with baby clothes three times too big, and a box of chocolates or a mix-master or oven mitts for Katia. Once he brought a tricycle because he said riding a bike was important to a kid and he wanted Katrina to learn to ride as soon as possible. To Katia's alarm, he brought a cocker spaniel one day because he said every kid should have a dog in order to appreciate that there was more to the world than human beings. There were creatures that had flesh and blood like humans but didn't act the way humans do. Place Louis Riel didn't allow dogs.

"Don't tell them," Lennie said.

"Dogs shit," Katia said. "You have to take them out."

At that, Katia told me, he just stood there staring at her, then shrugged his shoulders and went out the door, leaving her with a spaniel she had to take to the pound. Lennie behaved like a choir boy when he visited, Katia said, romping for hours with Katrina, getting into her playpen with her, sometimes just sitting watching while she slept. But Katia began turning him away because he started arriving either half drunk or half high, and even half became too much for her anymore.

Student rebellion was being suppressed around the world. In Montreal, the hearings on the Computer Riot at Sir George Williams University were over, but the racial issue smouldered on. After being sentenced in the Chicago Conspiracy Trial by Judge Julius Hoffman, Jerry Rubin gifted the judge with his book called *Do It!* Inscribed inside were the words, "Julius, you radicalized more young people than we ever could. You're the country's top Yippie." Billy Graham declared that "A hurricane of cataclysmic proportions is about to break on the world," a surprising statement for a visionary who didn't realize it already had. Jimi Hendrix and Janis Joplin died. Anne Koedt's book, *The Myth of the Vaginal Orgasm,* came out, and feminists were meeting with mirrors to share their appreciation of the beauty of their vaginas. In May, the National Guard opened fire at Kent State, killing four students. Geographically removed, dilatory as always, but relentless when it came to connecting with the Zeitgeist, student protest in Winnipeg broke out in marches and sit-ins. Not only did students boycott classes, faculty dissenters prepared to go on strike.

It wasn't hard to see Lennie's quandary. He had been recruited without the requisite credentials by a courageous department head in the mid '60's during an unprecedented shortage of PhD's in the Humanities. With the baby boomers coming of age, the Beatles still singing "All You Need Is Love", Timothy Leary urging the young to tune in, turn on and drop out (from society, not from learning), and soothsayers like Ivan Illych advocating radical educational reforms, arts enrolment had skyrocketed throughout Canada and the US and the system needed teachers. Just as abruptly, by the end of the decade, retrenchment set in. Nixon became President. In Canada, Trudeau brought in The Official Languages Act. No one could predict that, within a year, he would follow it up with The War Measures Act in Quebec.

The student enrolment boom was going bust. All across the country, universities were tightening up on the academic credentials needed for tenure and no tenure meant no job.

In Winnipeg, a new regime took power with a new university president, a no-nonsense administrator when it came to student unrest, with a background in the wartime military, and a dedication to rigorous academic standards. Many said it was what the university needed to save it from anarchy. There sat Lennie, egregious ringleader of protest, expected by radical students and staff to spearhead resistance to cut-backs, rising tuition, curriculum stagnation, military/scientific complicity in the war, and a whole grab bag of discontents, not excluding opposition to the more conventional members of the science and engineering faculties who supported the Churchill River Diversion project. In the old days in academe, seniority (not always accompanied by competence) led willy-nilly to a lifelong professorial appointment. No more. All across the country, but especially at U of M, it was not just 'publish or perish', but get your Doctorate union card (as years before, Marshall McLuhan had counselled Lennie to do) or go packing.

I continued to visit The Coop, the Albert, Jake's studio, and Lennie's flat. New Hippie (and now Yuppie) outposts sprouting up around River and Osborne kept up the rampageous pace of the '60s, as a flywheel keeps spinning after the engine has stopped. Lennie called me in Toronto one night. He was high, but not incapacitated. He talked about his despondency at the state of *The Gadfly*: "So there I was, charging over the hill with the bullets whizzing by, and when I looked back, there was no one behind me." I knew it wasn't true. His friends had kept things going longer than made sense, often with little real input from him. I asked him if that was why he had called, to cry on my shoulder, because if it was, he should hang up and I would call him back so I could cry on *his* shoulder. I said he sounded like the Scots flag bearer marching into the fray beside the battalion's piper who was supposed to scare the shit out of the enemy with his bagpipes. But it didn't work. The battalion was mowed down. Only the flag bearer and the bagpiper remained standing. "For Christ's sake, Angus," the young flag bearer said to the piper, "play them something they like." "Can't you play them something they like?", I asked Lennie. That sort of goofing around always got a rise out of him. Not this time. He was silent and then he said, no, he wasn't calling to seek my consolation. He was calling for camping advice.

He had never forgotten our fishing trip that was spoiled by the bear carcass hanging in the trees. But especially, he said, he remembered watching me fix the canoe at Peter Coultry's place because now he needed my expertise. He was planning a major wilderness outing and he wanted me to send him a list of what he needed. I said I was a bit out of touch on these matters but I would think about it and get back to him. I ended by suggesting he have a nice toke and a nice sleep, and I never thought about his canoe trip again until sometime later when Jackie Steiner brought it up.

"That's what he was going to do as soon as spring came, that canoe trip. You have to understand Lennie out in nature. One summer, he and Jake Clark came out to our place on Falcon Lake with Max and me and some others. It was a magnificent weekend, absolutely glorious, one of those fine Manitoba fall times with the sun beating down and the crackle of falling leaves and the smell of clean air.

"Lennie and Jake sat inside our screened porch, adoring the sight of the lake and the Technicolor of the dying leaves, barely moving from the porch all weekend while drinking in the splendour of the season along with a pail of vodka. The rest of us were down at the dock, swimming and water-skiing and jiving about. Every time I went into the cabin, the two of them were talking about nature as if William Blake had invented it. Apparently, Blake loved nature but also saw it as a prison unless you approached it the right way, and Lennie made the right way, whatever it was, sound very complicated. At the end of the afternoon, Max asked them how many mosquito bites they had. They knew what he meant, laughed with him, and looked a bit hang-dog, a bit pissed and apologetic, because they didn't have any at all. Cripes, if Lennie went canoeing, he would need you to paddle the canoe, Jake to cook the shore lunch, and Max to work out the legal aspects of the trip.

When Jake Clark talked to me about Lennie's plans for his forthcoming wilderness adventure, he said he thought Lennie was nuts. "That canoe trip radically bothered me because it was not ... LENNIE. Anyone who knew him knew that the last thing he could do was survive in the bush with a canoe and a Swiss army knife. You know where he got that canoe trip? He got it from a TV show about an Indian building a birch-bark canoe. It's an old NFB film. This old guy makes a canoe for his grandson. He does everything Lennie wanted to do. He's a craftsman who understands how you use nature to make something that takes you through nature, and this old guy has it all in his head. When Lennie saw that program, for weeks he was obsessed with it. Then he came up with this brainy notion that he's going to get a canoe. Zebby the Toke is going to drive him out to The White Shell and drop him off in the bleeding wilderness. Get it?

"The first couple of times he talked about it, I didn't pay attention. Then I argued with him. I said 'You can't do that. You don't know how to do that. There are certain things you need to know,' I kept saying, but he wouldn't listen. Shit, Lennie out there alone would have gone nuts in a day. I mean, who was he going to talk to? When he was cool, his mind was a fountain, when he was hot, it was a volcano, shooting ideas up by the metric ton. But he had to have something to bounce them off besides the great goddamn blue beyond of the White Shell wilderness.

"Lennie worried me, man. Something was coming apart, not just in him either. Out there too, out in the world. Was it that goddamn Viet Nam War? Were we getting too old? And bad dreams! I had them and so did Lennie, and we talked about them, and here's a weird thing–they overlapped. I kept dreaming about a mountain, about my being a mountain with lava underneath ready to erupt. He had a dream about a mountain at the same time. He told me it must have come from his reading Malcolm Lowry's *Under The Volcano*. Well, I never read that book. But in my dream, the mountain exploded, dumping magma down its side and shooting clouds of ash into the air and turning everyone into stone, like at Pompeii or Herculaneum. In Lennie's dream, he'd be waiting for that kind of eruption, but what happened instead was a bunch of letters of the alphabet shot out like old time ticker-tape, an explosion of letraset, and it didn't stop coming until it covered the whole landscape and everyone was inundated in a Noah's flood of printed paper.

"There was a huge rally that spring. It wasn't at the university but at Market Square, just back of Portage and Main, what was left of the old city centre. And it wasn't just students who came, but a lot of people who didn't like the politicos who were running the show–the old Conservatives and the New Democrats. It didn't make any difference. Both parties fell into line as the Churchill River Diversion project went ahead. One banner the protestors carried read:

GREED AND IGNORANCE
Manitoba's Toxic Cocktail
Bottoms up Folks

"I guess there were two thousand people gathered on that frozen night. In the cold, the huge audio speakers on either side of the outdoor stage made the voices of the speakers ring like hammers on iron. The speakers ranged from those who opposed the flooding of Southern Indian Lake on ecological or aesthetic or humanitarian grounds, to those who opposed it because property they owned on Lake Winnipeg would be threatened by flooding and that would devalue their real estate.

"I was sitting beside him when his turn came to speak. 'We have here the spectrum of mankind from the niggardly self-interested to the lunatic romantics,' he whispered to me, and then he got up and went to the podium. He said a lot of things I remembered from the first editorial he wrote for *The Gadfly*, about Manitoba being a gift from the gods, and the water and trees not being commodities to be bought and sold on the market, but living things to be understood as the circulation system and lungs of the body of nature. The ruckus of the audience died away and Lennie's voice crackled through the frigid air, a blacksmith's hammer at the forge. He said:

William Blake foresaw two hundred years ago what is happening today
in our city, how our downtown is abandoned except for the Hell's Kitchen
of Main Street where down-and-outs gather and self-destruct, like the
farmers who left their farms during the Industrial Revolution in England,
seeking the riches of the factories of Manchester and Sheffield where they
and their children quickly became slaves. As I walk Portage Avenue and
North Main where I grew up and see the streets abandoned by all but confused groups of Indians drawn in from the North by television images of big
city glamour, I see Winnipeg the way William Blake saw London in 1810:

I wander thro' each charter'd street
Near where the charter'd Thames does flow
And mark in every face I meet
Marks of weakness, marks of woe

In every cry of every man
In every infant's cry of fear

> In every voice, in every ban
> The mind-forg'd manacles I hear

"Jason, I have seen Lennie perform before, at my place and yours, around the table at the Albert, at the Pembina beer parlour, in the classroom and at public rallies, but I have never seen anything like what I saw that night. I mean, how do you quote Blake, a complex, apocalyptic poet, to two thousand people from the voters list who've never heard of Blake and yet manage to keep them listening? Maybe it was the speaker system. Maybe it was the chill air that froze their attention. It was more than rhetoric or histrionics. His words rang out with utter conviction.

> How the Chimney-sweepers cry
> Every black'ning Church appals
> And the hapless soldier's sigh
> Runs in blood down Palace walls

> But most thro' midnight streets I hear
> How the youthful Harlot's curse
> Blasts the new born Infant's tear
> And blights with plagues the Marriage hearse

"I swear to you, Jason, when Lennie finished, the audience may have forgotten about Southern Indian Lake and the Churchill River Diversion altogether, but they heard and responded to something like a universal lament for mankind. It was a bloody miracle."

Chapter Thirty-Six

On a chilly morning at the end of the 1970 spring term I met Lennie on the Fort Garry campus for breakfast. We picked up bad Danish pastries and bad coffee and went to his office. He looked worse than when I had seen him last: hands shaky, cheeks pale, a sweaty red rash on his forehead reminiscent of exam time in days gone by. His office was in the new wing of the Arts Building, skimpily modern, not like the cut-stone solidity, marble floors, and spacious ceilings of the old Arts Building where we first met. Without books, his office would have been as antiseptic as an emergency ward. But there were books everywhere, not just on the shelves but piled high on a long nun's table and leaning in tottering stacks all over the floor. The effect was to fill the room with such welter and disarray that its box-like austerity was almost redeemed.

Lennie didn't touch his coffee. He sat staring out the window, saying nothing, took a bite of his Danish, began chewing it, spit it into his waste basket, then dropped the rest of it in.

"So what do you think?" he said.

"About?"

"About your coverage of the Churchill River Diversion fiasco?"

"I think there are fewer and fewer surprises."

"The bastards. The NDP prove as bad as the rest of them. It drives me nuts to think about that wilderness going under water, those Indian bones floating up from old burial places as the water rises. And Manitoba Hydro selling the proceeds to Minnesota!"

"So, stand up. Do a scathing editorial for *The Gadfly*."

Lennie gave me a long, searching look before he spoke. "Don't mock me, JJ. Don't leave me thinking *et tu Brute*."

"What are you talking about?"

"You don't know? Last week *The Gadfly* went belly up."

I didn't know. But I wasn't surprised.

"I'll tell you the story sometime." Right now I've got enough to think about." He got up and walked around the room, picking up a book and moving it somewhere else, picking up another book and setting it back down where he got it.

I tried a joke. "Quite a filing system you've got there." It used to work.

"Everything's mathematic form today, JJ–tidy, regimented, modular, dehumanized. Look at this building. An architectural filing cabinet. Anyway, not to worry. I'm getting the boot. The word's out. The new president's going for my jugular, not just because he doesn't like me. It's for symbolic reasons. He figures that, by ridding the university of trouble-makers like me, he can show everyone he means business. And he knows he can nail me because I don't have the letters after my name. 'Finish your thesis' I hear you say. Why not? You know goddamn well why not. It's my twin curse–verbal diarrhoea and compositional constipation. I'm a doomed dyscriptic. If there isn't such a word, there should be. Tell you what, I'll give you three grand to ghostwrite my PhD thesis."

"You're joking!"

Lennie was off and running: "Same old Mr. Clean. Okay, let's look at the ethical question. I'm being kicked out, not because I'm incompetent, but because the establishment doesn't like my politics or my life-style or maybe just my body odour. That's dishonest. Why can't I play the same game? I don't believe in the system, never have. Learning and scholarship are not things you can package in little boxes and deliver like fast food. Not long ago, there was no such thing as a professional English scholar in today's sense. It's a modern perversion. It's about as important to life as toothpaste and sleeping pills. Look what it's produced–umpteen English 'scholars' in North America alone. I went to a Modern Language Association conference in New York years ago, so I know. The gifted scholars are fine, and they would be fine without the system. The rest (fill in your own percentage) are boring little gnomes and pundits with areas of expertise so encapsulated they're like a showroom of goldfish mouthing at each other from separate bowls. If I can do the job, if I can teach my students to get excited about ideas and hold my own with my peers, why should I be excluded from a livelihood in the groves of academe? Just because I don't comply with the system's insistence on modular mediocrity and a chain of published sausages? What did Socrates ever write down? Or Jesus Christ for that matter? All we know about them is what someone else had to say about their teaching."

"Whoa Lennie," I broke in. "This is treacherous territory. Never mind the ethics. I think they call it suicide. It makes Dr. Faust look like a lightweight."

"You're a hard man, JJ. Of course you're right. Having a thesis ghost-written makes me a plagiarist and a fraud, no better than a kid cheating on exams or a professor publishing his grad students' ideas under his own name. And oh yeah, as for Dr. Faust. He wasn't trying to get a doctorate when he gave in to the temptations of Mephistopheles. Why would he? He already had a doctorate."

Did Lennie really mean it? I knew him too well by now to express outrage. As likely as not, he would laugh and say: "Just kidding, Just checking you out." But this was big. He could be serious. The trouble was, I couldn't gauge how serious. I let it hang in the air as he resumed his pacing among his pillars of books. I tried an evasive tactic. I asked him how his plans were coming along for his camping trip.

"Good", he said, and momentarily perked up. He pulled a binder from his desk. He must have forgotten his drunken phone call asking me for camping advice, because he didn't chide me for not responding.

"I got Max Steiner to sit down and fill me in on the stuff I need," he said. "He and Jackie have made a half dozen trips down the Oiseau River in the White Shell and they know all about it." As I read the list Max had made, it looked definitive, a little too bulky for the Boy Scout survival kit of my youth, but nothing you couldn't squeeze into a cube van. I was completely out of touch with the latest in wilderness survival gear, but I approved the catalogue like a loyal campfire boy.

Sitting at his desk fingering the rash on his forehead, Lennie suddenly leaned forward and said: "I can't do the seminar today."

"What? Revenge on the institution?"

"Nothing to do with that."

"You can't just leave the kids sitting there. Last seminar of the year and all."

He got up and started to pace again. "I can't do it anymore. Last week, half-way through, I started to wonder what the hell I was talking about. I began to babble. The kids looked at me strangely. I had to stop. I told them I was on medication and would have to go lie down. I just walked out of the room."

"Were you?"

"What?"

"On medication?"

"No. I was on nothing. A few tokes the night before. Since when did that matter?"

"No uppers or downers."

"Nothing. I don't do that shit anymore."

"Then what?"

"I don't know JJ. I just lost it. Too much ... disruption."

"Well look, you can't just abandon your class."

"I'm not going in. I can't face them. I can't stand there and expostulate." He looked sallow and itchy. He reminded me of Paul Newman in *The Hustler* after he'd had his fingers broken for being too clever at snooker. The seminar was at three o'clock in the afternoon. It was just ten in the morning. I suggested a walk.

Lennie led the way past the agricultural barns by the Red River. One after another, the kids we passed greeted him. They were farm boys working on their Agricultural Diploma. They were called "Aggie Dips", the butt of jokes by their intellectual superiors in Arts and Science. The worst job in the English Department was to get stuck teaching the one English course these boys were obliged to take to help their reading and writing skills. Lennie had requested the course. No one cared what he taught. He got them to read passages from Plato's *Republic*, Castiglione's *The Courtier*, Machiavelli's *The Prince*, More's *Utopia*, Milton's *Areopagitica*, Newman's *The Idea of a University*, Carroll's *Alice In Wonderland*, Freud's *Civilization And Its Discontents*, Huxley's *Brave New World*, Orwell's *Animal Farm,* and Mailer's *Why We Are in Vietnam*. The questions he got from the farm boys, Lennie said, were almost always better than the ones he got from his honours English students. One boy came up to him after class, worried about Nietzsche's concept of historical recurrence. If every effort to change the world ended in a new reign of terror, the boy wanted to know, what was the point of trying to change anything? "I choked," Lennie said. "I didn't have an answer."

What was clear to me was that the boys in the agriculture compound loved their English professor. At first I wondered if Lennie took me there to impress me with the breadth of his sway. Then one of the boys told me about the goats. He said it was an old-time belief of farmers like his father, as yet unproven by agricultural science, that goat smell prevents disease among cows. Then he winked at me and said: "It also kills pot smell."

I walked with Lennie past the experimental farm and we sat by the Red River. I told him I had come back to reading Blake, not so much for edification, more for entertainment, and I was finding new things all the time. Gradually, he came out of himself, and we played. He quoted Blake on Swedenborg: "'There can be no *Good* Will. Will is always Evil. It is persecution to others or selfishness.' Old Billy could really cut through the shit couldn't he? Before Nietzsche or Adler, and long before the power freaks of today, parents who can't let their children be themselves, lovers who fight for domination, little Caesars, all that lot–Blake saw it pure and clear."

I came back with: "What about what he meant when he said: 'Active Evil is better than Passive Good'? I always thought that could be dangerous if you weren't very careful."

"He's being ironic," said Lennie. "What the comfortable call Satan is life's energy. What the comfortable call angelic is entropy. Distinguish the wheat from the chaff, clarify the line between real Good and real Evil, between forgiveness and accusation. It means using your intelligence to see what is really going on. It's central in Shakespeare, distinguishing reality from appearance. 'I know not seems,' says Hamlet. When Lear chooses Goneril and Regan instead of Cordelia, he falls for their appearance over her reality. Distinguishing between them is first of all what Blake sees as an exercise in articulation. He calls it the 'consolidation of error'. He might have said: 'how can you fight it if you don't know what it looks like'? Context is all. 'I come not to bring peace but the sword.' Every half-wit since the crusades has taken that as a call for mass slaughter in the name of Jesus Christ. Jesus was a poet for crying out loud. He spoke in parables and homilies. Whether you believe in him or not, he stood for peace and forgiveness, not for random slaughter. The peace he opposed was moral complacency, Blake's 'little moony night where no dispute can come because of those who sleep.' The sword is the wake-up call.

"Fighting evil isn't defending some fatuous code of conduct like chastity. 'Let pale religious lechery no longer call that virginity which wishes and acts not, for everything that lives is holy.' For Blake, fighting evil is fighting on the side of an active, creative, life-affirming exhilaration. Good is not the purity of a heart frozen in passivity–that state of inertia of the lost souls in Dante's Inferno who never used their human potential to do or create anything, and so cannot be said ever to have actually existed. In this context, how can being active be evil? A person has just to use his head a little and not run off like some simple-minded fundamentalist with a set of beliefs as literal as a grocery list that was planted in his psyche when he was too young to think for himself."

Lennie was warming. He smoked a joint. I took a cocktail to be sociable. I never had to argue my reticence about smoke with him. Since the day he introduced me to pot in the back alley behind the Pilot Tavern ten years before, he never pressed me. We joked about it. I said what it did to me was make me so cool I went into cold storage. He agreed it made me sleepy and stupid and very poor company.

I said Blake's idea of sexual liberty could have a down side. "When Blake wrote: 'The true method of knowledge is experiment,' and people applied it to sex as so many have done recently, he was asking for trouble, or at least setting us up for it."

"Context again," Lennie said. "'Those who restrain desire do so because theirs is weak enough to be restrained' and 'Prudence is a rich ugly old maid courted by incapacity.'"

"Finally we agree. Blake said it: 'What is it men in women do require? The lineaments of gratified desire. What is it women do in men require? The lineaments of gratified desire.' Simple, eh?"

I thought I could trump him with: 'Children of a future Age, reading this indignant page/Know that in a former time, Love! Sweet Love! Was thought a crime.'

Then, he came up with a line I had never come across before: 'When a Man has Married a Wife he finds out whether Her Knees & Elbows are only glued together.' The sheer silliness of the line expressed so ingenuously by Blake and pulled so unexpectedly from Lennie's hat left me stymied.

By eleven o'clock, we were having a merry time and Lennie was much improved. "Here's the deal," I said. "I'll go in first and give the students an angle on Blake. I'll do the warm-up. As in a rock concert. Then you come in with the big show. What do you say?"

Lennie was lying back on the grass looking at the sky. "JJ," he said. "You are definitely a devious son-of-a-bitch."

"Well?"

"OK. Let's do it."

We grabbed a sandwich and went back to his office. Back in my teaching days, I had lectured on *The Songs of Experience* and I decided I would use what I could remember as a lead in. I asked him what he would talk about. "Well ... the rest of it," he said. We sat for the next two hours without talking. I flagged a few pages of an anthology with the usual Blake selections. He rifled through *The Collected Works* and Frye's *Fearful Symmetry*, but took no notes. The 2:50 PM bell sounded.

"Ten minutes to show time." I said. I was churning inside from apprehension but I couldn't let on.

"You're not just devious, you're brutal," Lennie said.

Chapter Thirty-Seven

L ennie stood in front of the class and smoothed down his hair. The puffy cheeks and splotchy forehead of the morning were nearly gone. "Have you ever heard this?" he said. "It's from an 1808 notebook of William Blake addressed to God. It reads: 'If you have form'd a Circle to go into/Go into it yourself & see how you would do.' Now that's no way to talk to God is it? But then as Blake said, any god that would confine you to a circle, make you a gerbil on a tread mill, a prisoner with no exit, trapped like the hands of the clock, can't possibly be a god you could like much, can he? Blake called that version of God 'Nobodaddy'. Let's start from there."

There were twenty students in the room. Lennie said I was a friend he had invited to say a few words about Blake. He said we had studied Blake together as graduate students under Northrop Frye, and although I had gone into broadcast journalism, that didn't mean I had become altogether debased and beyond redemption. Then he took me by the arm and ushered me to the front with exaggerated solicitude as if he were a rabbi at my bar mitzvah. He got the laugh that was needed. What could have been a frosty reception to an outsider like me melted instantly, and the rush of stage fright I felt after so long a time since last I had stood in front of a class vanished. I talked about *The Sick Rose, Ah! Sun-Flower, London,* and even *The Tyger.* I knew them all by heart so, although I had the text in hand, I never looked at it when I spoke the lines. This was partly to show off. But it was also the way I had been taught as a youngster. Learn by rote. Never mind what the words mean. Trust them. Get the rhythm and sound in your head. Meaning can wait. I never understood what people thought was wrong about learning poetry by rote. Once you get the words down, you can let the chords of the great poems roll through your mind at any time, no matter where you are–at a dreary party, at thirty-thousand feet with nothing to look at but boring blue, if need be, sitting in jail.

Having poems by heart also meant you never had to look away from your audience, and that made them pay attention. With Lennie's students, I adopted a quasi-Socratic mode. Is the sunflower like a man, aging shoulders bending toward sunset in the same way the flower tracks the sun across the sky? Or is it a flower which, when looked at closely, seems to have a human face inside it, a kind of throwback to a pagan world when people anthropomorphized the forms of nature? In *The Sick Rose,* phallic and vaginal imagery aside, I asked what the relation was between the rose as time-honoured symbol of love and the worm's 'dark secret love' that invades it? What's the difference between being imprisoned in real iron chains in a dungeon and the mind-forg'd manacles of *London?* In *The Tyger,* who is the blacksmith and what is he forging? Why is every sentence in *The Tyger* interrogative, like this one? The class got into a free-for-all and all I had to do was play moderator. I was winning. The half-time buzzer sounded and my shift was over before I knew it.

Lennie sat slouched in his chair, head down, legs straggling forward. For a moment, he didn't move. Then, mimicking the nasal whine of James Cagney, he said, "You dirty rat!" There was a moment of silence, and then the kids broke out laughing. They recognized that Lennie and I were competitors of sorts, that I had acquitted myself with honour, and that now the onus was on him to perform. I sat down and flipped on my recorder as he walked to the front. He moved the podium I had used and set *Blake's Collected Works* and Frye's *Fearful Symmetry* on it, returning to them from time to time to read passages he had flagged. He began slowly, with long pauses as he paced the dais, looked down at the floor, rubbed his jaw, and then looked up to scan the room, squinty-eyed. I half expected him to stop and balance over a chairback as Northrop Frye had done so precariously in our classes with him years ago, but Lennie had his own style. He came down from the dais and walked up and down past the desks as he spoke.

"When I first looked into Blake he seemed a bit crazy to me. I had read that he saw visions of angels and kings and queens, and even a vision of the soul of a flea, which he drew. He said his superbly drawn flea, a terrifying portrait of imbecility, was the reincarnation of bloodthirsty man who, if he didn't come back as a tiny biting insect, but say as a creature as big as a horse, would depopulate the earth.

"Walking with Holman Hunt in the rural Soho of 1800, with market gardens and wild bushes a short distance away, Blake paused and bowed in the street. His friend Holman Hunt asked him why. He said he was paying his respects to St. Paul who had just passed by. Maybe Blake was not the sort of friend you want to go out drinking with on Saturday night.

"Another picture I get of Blake is with his life-long wife, Catherine. She signed their wedding certificate with an X, and yet in later life she exchanged ideas with him and helped him with his frescos and engravings. In the picture in my mind (and this is factual), the two of them are cavorting about naked in their garden at Lambeth reading *Paradise Lost* to each other as if they were Adam and Eve before the Fall.

"So how did this odd man come to write some of the most incendiary poetry in the language and, after a hundred and fifty years of neglect, gradually attract many of the sanest literary minds of our time to the job of instating him in the central canon of English literature–along with Chaucer, Spenser, Shakespeare, Milton, Wordsworth, Keats and Shelley, and (after Blake), Yeats and Eliot and maybe Auden and Thomas? It's been quite an enterprise.

"Helping to unravel the golden thread of Blake's vision, one of the earliest and still best books on the subject is Northrop Frye's *Fearful Symmetry* (1949). Personally, I can think of no other book I can reread every few years and still be left sitting on the edge of my chair, page after page, the single exception being some of the works of Blake himself, the ones I think I understand. Without Frye, I would never have begun to make headway with Blake. Let me recommend Fry's advice. He once impolitely wrote: 'Read Blake or go to Hell.'

"According to Blake we all have at least one thing in common: 'All of us on earth are united in thought, for it is impossible to think without images of somewhat on earth.' That's fundamental. We have concepts and ideas but they are abstractions, fossils of ancient images that have lost their force, just as the word "understanding" no longer conveys the picture of a person standing under something or holding something up. Original images fade into abstractions–truth, beauty, love, god. Call the abstractions concepts. Concepts are units of reason. Reason, no doubt one thing that distinguishes us from the beasts and all that (okay, maybe our flexible thumbs too) processes these units of reason by what we call *ratiocination*, meaning, etymologically, reflecting on *the ratio* of one thing to another, establishing a common denominator, not an individual thing at all. Take the so-called public, or the taxpayer, or the voter, for example. What is it? Is it a number? Something you can hold in your hand? A handful of marshmallows? It has no identity. It's like a statistic about fatal car accidents. It has existential meaning only if you are the one killed, or if you knew the one killed. Only an individual has identity. This horse, this tree, this rose. This person killed. The concrete object is the *real* thing, and as the word *image* indicates, it is the unit of that other faculty we call imagination. Reason works with generalities. Imagination works with what Blake calls 'minute particulars'. And images are what else but sights immediately in front of our eyes, or pictures in memory, or maybe a third thing larger and more potent than present or past images which Blake called Vision.

> Every Eye sees differently.
> As the Eye, Such the Object....
> The Sun's light when he unfolds it
> Depends on the Organ that beholds it.

"Is this true? Blake distinguishes three ways of seeing. The image of the rose we have in memory is the least distinct, its unique lineaments blurred into the ratio of a rose. As family, genus, and species, it is part of the taxonomy used by botanists. Then there's the rose while we are in the act of seeing it. But do we see it *with* our eye, or *through* our eye? To catch on to what Blake's getting at, we have to know what he means by Corporeal Understanding as distinct from Imagination. 'Mental Things are alone Real; what is call'd Corporeal, Nobody Knows of its Dwelling Place .... Where is Existence Out of Mind or Thought?' The eye as mere receptacle of impressions from the outside world is a blind eye, what Blake calls an instrument of 'single vision and Newton's sleep.' What it sees is not a specific bird, only a feathery thing with wings. But 'How do you know but ev'ry bird that cuts the airy way/Is an immense world of delight, clos'd by your senses five?'

"What this means for poetry, the language of images, is that there are two kinds of allegory. The first Blake calls allegory of the corporeal understanding; in other words, the allegory of A equals B. Pilgrim in *Pilgrim's Progress* equals

Everyman. Pigs in *Animal Farm* equal the Politburo and its apparatchik. The second kind of allegory, what Dante and Spenser knew as the anagogical level of meaning, and what we sometimes call symbol or archetype today, Blake calls 'allegory addressed to the intellectual powers.' Translate the term 'intellectual powers' as imagination. For Blake, they're the same thing.

> Allegory addressed to the Intellectual Powers, while it is altogether hidden by the Corporeal Understanding, is My Definition of The Most Sublime Poetry.

"But there is a third way of seeing. The great tragedy of humanity for Blake (virtually the fall from paradise) is that we have gone to sleep and allowed our senses to shrivel and stagnate.

> If the doors of perception were cleansed every-
> thing would appear to man as it is, infinite.
> For man has closed himself up, till he sees all
> things thro' narrow chinks of his cavern....

> What is now proven was once only imagined ....

> Everything possible to be believed is an image of truth.

"This third way of seeing is the way Blake sees, not by way of fading memories or by way of receiving sense impressions, but by the human imagination seeing not *with* but *through* the eye. This he calls Vision.

> All that we See is Vision, from Generated Organs gone as soon as come, Permanent in The Imagination, Consider'd as Nothing by the Natural Man.

For Blake the world exists as we impose our mind upon it, which is the same thing as saying that we create it by seeing, hearing, and feeling it. There is nothing but absurdity in the way most people envisage space. How can a child, worse still a grown-up, watch an astronaut in space on TV and still keep in his head the idea that heaven is just around the corner from him up there in the blue yonder where, if you are righteous and submissive, you will end up? To do what? Flap your wings? Play a harp in a cloud? Bow to Jehovah? Seduce lubricious virgins forever? In terms of speculation about the firmament, Pascal sounded the alarm: 'Le silence éternale des éspaces infinies m'affraie.' Blake saw nothing but non-entity out there too. 'Where man is not, Nature is barren.'

"This is usually where Blake gets accused of being a mystic. If that means he sees beyond the 'Mundane Shell' (his word for the cosmic egg inside which mere natural man lives his merely natural life), then mystic he is. But the word 'mystic' normally means something quite different–a person in touch with inscrutable wisdom and powers beyond the mental scope of ordinary mortals, what Yeats, who *was* a mystic, called 'images from beyond the mind.' Blake not only rejects such superstitious notions, he brands them pernicious, a word he reserves for all things inimical to human values. This does not mean he is saying something as simple-minded as 'everything is ultimately knowable'. Of course, there are things beyond our powers of comprehension, like how a dog's mind works. What Blake deplores is manufactured mysteries. The enforcement of such mysteries is tyranny's most effective weapon. It's the weapon used by priests and tyrants to intimidate and bamboozle the uninitiated, enslave the masses, and make wars. These are history's great bogymen, 'terrific forms of torture and woe' (Behemoth, Leviathan, the Great Whore of the Apocalypse) who, once they are confronted with clear eyes, dissolve into illusions, like dragons in mythology and nightmares when you wake up.

"Blake asked, where is the way beyond the world of endless days and nights, the perennial recurrence of seasons, incessant birth, maturation, and death? Where is the shape of time that is not a circle but a spiral, ascending? Time is a swaddling cloth wrapped round the newborn that soon becomes a winding sheet preparing the corpse for burial. Yet we know in our hearts that 'the bounded is loathed by its possessor.' We know, Blake reminds us, that 'the same dull round, even of a universe, would soon become a mill with complicated wheels' like the factories of the industrial revolution. Blake envisions industrial England's machines aping the cosmic mechanism of the great clockmaker god of Newton and Locke, the Deist's prime mover, the loveless demiurge of blind time ... and that takes us back once again to Nobadaddy.

"Blake's antagonism to the mindset of the Deism of the Enlightenment, his insistence on a contrary, human-centred world view, sounds naive, even a bit loony. The reason it is neither is that he organizes the forms of what the heart desires. He doesn't drift in a haze of wish-fulfilment or delusion, or in the random hallucinations of drug-induced consciousness expansion.

He articulates a final purpose in history outside time's ostensibly fated recurrences. He humanizes time and space. He does it from the inside of the mind out, not from any distant god's perspective from the outside in. He sees it as a child might see:

Each grain of Sand
Every Stone of the Land
Each rock & each hill
Each fountain & rill
Each herb and each tree
Mountain, hill, earth & sea
Cloud, Meteor and Star
Are Men seen Afar.

"From his earliest utterances until his death at seventy years of age ('my garden fruitful seventy-fold' he called it), Blake saw reality as the world we create by means of our imagination. He never ceased believing that we could turn fallen nature into the land of our heart's desire–not a return to the lost garden of Eden, but an advance forward into the grown-up, city of justice he called Jerusalem."

I sat as a student, like the rest, watching Lennie navigate the room. I have always respected what I had heard of his teaching. How could I not? From the first day I met him in John Peter's class long ago and listened to him strike sparks about John Donne, I knew he could inspire. Then there was graduate school, when he shone so brightly among the gentlemen scholars of U of T's *ancien regime* of letters. And I had not forgotten standing anonymously at the back of the drill hall in Winnipeg in the first flush of the '60s, when he seemed as much a performance artist as an intellectual, and spellbound an audience like a pop star.

Watching him now, I wondered why I had never been the kind of teacher he was. Did we once compete in earnest? I supposed so. Maybe that was why I moved off laterally. I was a good teacher in my time, but not like him. As he roved the aisles, hesitating, contemplating the floor, then looking up as if to each person individually, his words seemed to be coming red-hot from the forge, as if he truly were a son of Los, Blake's sweat-soaked blacksmith in his dungeon, stoking the fiery hearth, pounding his hammer on the anvil, twisting the sinews of the tiger's heart with his chain and callipers, black-smith, wordsmith, blasting forth the new formed shapes of his imagination.

I saw that what was happening as Lennie spoke was not something he could help from happening any more than he could make it happen on demand. "Sing heavenly Muse" was the way Milton put it. Now Lennie's muse was singing to him. Yes, he may have asked more of his audience than they could handle. But wasn't that what teaching was about? Wasn't that how learners learned? He didn't conduct a seminar. He didn't query as Plato's Socrates did. In a way he was closer to Aristotle, the peripatetic, because he never stopped pacing while he spoke. Otherwise, I have no doubt his technique bore little resemblance to Aristotle's austere syllogisms. I wondered if perhaps Jesus might have walked and talked this way too.

I looked at my watch. There was still time before the five o'clock buzzer and no sign of questions from the class. They were transfixed and so was I. This was not the beat-out Lennie I drank bitter coffee with that morning. This was Lennie as angelic messenger.

Chapter Thirty-Eight

Consciously or not, Lennie pulled off a manoeuvre that was pure Northrop Frye. Without saying a word, he stood scanning the room, making it clear that questions would be welcomed, at the same time looking as if he didn't really expect any. As Frye had done, he let a full thirty seconds go by. What was it for? To let things sink in? Was it for dramatic effect? I couldn't tell with Lennie any more than I had been able to tell with Frye. But the result was the same– a collective hope that someone would speak up to make the class respectable, to confirm that they had been listening and were smart enough to have something to say. No one spoke up and Lennie resumed.

"Let me tell you a sort of fairy tale. It's very simple. Once, before space and time, there was a man called Albion. Up close, he appeared to be a multitude. Farther away, he looked like many nations. From a great distance, he was one man, an antediluvian man-god colossus. Genesis and other biblical fragments about creation are ambiguous. Some say God created the world out of nothingness, some say that's impossible and there must first have been something. Then came the six days of creation, culminating in Adam and Eve, and followed shortly afterward by the apple episode. No one agrees on what came first, God or nothingness, or what exactly the tree of good and evil means. Can knowledge be considered evil? Surely, only by the stupid. Blake came up with a great idea. There was not first a Creation and then a Fall. Creation and The Fall are the same event. Original sin that brought about the fall wasn't pride or disobedience or (heaven and Milton forbid), uxoriousness. It was inertia, a descent into passivity. In a manner of speaking, Albion fell asleep and the fallen world of history became his dream, a kind of Finnegan's Wake where Finnegan lies comatose in his coffin as history drifts on in its cycles of atrocity. Nature (trees, streams, flowers, animals) is nowhere a paradise, as some would have us think, for instance, Wordsworth. On the contrary, nature is an abattoir, an endless circle of life and death based on the principle of mutual consumption where one creature survives by eating another. Tennyson, a late romantic, must have felt deeply conflicted if not schizophrenic in having to come to terms with Wordsworth and Darwin at the same time. He could not abandon the nostalgia in which 'splendour falls on castle walls', but still had to face the reality of 'Nature red in tooth and claw.'

"According to Blake, I think, although Albion lost consciousness, he didn't dissolve into non-entity. History and the physical world are the basement of the fall, with a role to play in human redemption. That's another thing Blake means when he says: 'Eternity is in love with the productions of time.' Nature supplies the striving, incarcerated imagination with the mental fodder, the images, for recreating not Adam's and Eve's prelapsarian garden, but a new place, a golden city of fully awake human consciousness and love, where to be is to perceive and to perceive is to create the real world of the heart's desire.

"How are we to imagine Albion's fall? How are we to envisage a divine human form, existing in eternity, who collapses in upon him/herself through a lapse of imagination, and becomes inundated and set awash in a sea of clock time and indeterminate space? How does this human/god form, a mental construction after all, shrivel into the material world that came to encircle it as if it were inside an egg, an embryo not yet born, imprisoned and encased in Blake's Mundane Shell? Humpty Dumpty sat on a wall. Humpty Dumpty had a great fall."

Lennie walked over to the podium, looked up at the ceiling as if calling down lightning from the gods, picked up Frye's *Fearful Symmetry*, and began reading in a quiet voice that was almost like a song:

> What we see in nature is our own body turned inside out. From our natural perspective we cannot see this for the same reason that a fly crawling on a fresco cannot see the picture: we are too small, too close, too unintelligent, and have naturally the wrong kind of eye. But the imagination sees that the labyrinthine intricacies of the movements of heavenly bodies reflect the labyrinth of our brains. It sees

that lakes and pools reflect the passive mirror of the eye. It sees that the revolving and warming sun is the beating and flaming heart of the fallen Albion and it is reproduced in the "Globe of Blood" within our own bodies, our heart. It sees that the tide flows and ebbs in the rhythm of Albion's fallen lungs. It sees that the ridges of mountains across the world are Albion's fractured spine. It sees that the natural circulation of water is a human circulation of blood. It sees that nature is the fossilized form of a God-Man who has, unlike other fossils, the power to come to life again. It sees that what vibration-frequencies are to colour, what a prosodic analysis is to a poem, what an anatomized cadaver is to a body, so the physical world is to the mental one, the seamy side of its reality. And it sees all this because it realizes that when we see ourselves as imprisoned in a huge concave vault of sky we are seeing from the point of view of a head that is imprisoned in a concave vault of bone.

Lennie set *Fearful Symmetry* down and returned to centre stage, surveying the room, again without speaking. Who would break the silence? Lennie had done it in John Peter's class years ago. This time, it was a girl. Her face was almost lost in loops of curly black hair. She wore tiny round John Lennon glasses that made her look not so much hip as ominously intelligent.

"You called that a fairy tale," she said. "Does that mean it's just fanciful? Like the Humpty Dumpty stuff?"

"Well, fairy tales have a certain truth, don't you think?" Lennie said.

"But what I mean is, are you saying they are really deep down true, fairy tales and such, like the story about Albion you just told us?" Her manner wasn't at all aggressive. Intense rather, agitated.

"Do you mean factually true or true as metaphor?" Lennie said.

"I just mean *true*. I mean not just fairy tales. Blake's whole picture of things, which I find hard to follow because of all the dizzy names he gives his characters ... Tharmos, Enitharmon, the Four Zoas ... is it true? Sections of *Milton* and *Jerusalem* make a lot of sense to me. Then I lose it. It won't stick together. So I want to know what you think. Does Blake's world make sense to you? Do *you* personally believe it's true?"

"You are asking a bottomless question," Lennie said "It's like asking whether I believe in God or whether I believe in love. First of all, no two people I know mean the same thing by God and love, and secondly there's no agreement on what people mean by belief."

The girl chewed her finger as she stared at him. She re-arranged her body, ran her hand through her hair without disturbing a curl, removed, then re-perched her glasses, and went on. "Blake seems to be saying that metaphor is not so much a faded image like the shadows of Plato's cave, or a tangible or visible manifestation of the numinous world of pure mind that the German transcendentalists are always going on about, but rather the real truth of the matter. That would make metaphor not just a figure of speech. It would make metaphor reality. Isn't that right?"

This girl (and I knew Lennie saw it as clearly as I did) was what we had always claimed we wanted in a student—a thinker, a challenger, an original. I wondered if Lennie could handle her. I was sure I couldn't.

"There's a line," Lennie said, "in a letter Keats wrote to his friend Benjamin Bailey: 'The Imagination may be compared to Adam's dream. Adam awoke and found it truth'. Do you mean reality in that sense?"

"Okay, sir," the girl said, "my question was off-kilter. Let me put it this way. What is the reality status of your fairy tale about Albion and how the world came about?"

"My fairy tale is a metaphor. Metaphor means 'to transfer, to carry across'. It suggests a border or a crossroad or an interface between two dimensions."

"So there must be two places, one here and one somewhere else. Otherwise, there would be no place to carry anything across to. A crossover between what and what?"

"Here's something Shelley said: 'I always seek in what I see the manifestation of something beyond the present and tangible object.' Does that tell you anything?"

"Jesus, sir!"

"Schopenhauer said: 'What the visionary sees is not the correspondence of the object world with something beyond, but coherence among correspondences.' Get what he means?"

"I wonder if you realize it, sir. You are answering my questions with questions. What I really want to know is, do you believe in Blake?"

Lennie came to a halt. I could tell he loved the spunk of this girl, her sincerity and her intelligence, and he was running dry. He backed away. "If you want to know what I believe or don't believe because you think it will help you decide what you believe or don't believe, I think you may be falling into a trap. We're dealing with imaginative literature here, not final causes. What if I don't believe anything Blake says? What if I'm a closet Zoroastrian? Will you turn away from Blake and become a Zoroastrian just because I'm a Zoroastrian?"

It was as if she didn't hear him: "Blake thinks time and space are illusions," she said, "and that history will end in apocalypse when time and space disappear. Your Humpty Dumpty or Albion or whatever, presumably with the help of all the king's horses and all the king's men, will put Humpty together again and Albion will resurrect into some sort of divine humanity. So when does the apocalypse happen?"

The end-of-period buzzer sounded as if on cue. Lennie walked over to the podium, put his books under his arm and, his sense of relief apparent to me, turned to the girl as he made his way to the door. "For you, my dear," he said, "it wouldn't come to me as a great surprise to learn that the apocalypse has already begun."

Part IV
Caverns of the Grave

Chapter Thirty-Nine

A few days later, a kind of apocalypse *did* take place for Lennie's friends and lovers. I was in Toronto. It was 6:00 in the morning, May 26, 1971. Jake Clark was on the phone: "Lennie is dead."

The gathering at the Albert when I arrived in Winnipeg was like the aftermath of a tornado. Women were crying, and so were a few men. The old guard of *The Gadfly* were in shock. No one was talking.

Jake and I helped Katia get Lennie quietly buried in West Kildonan Cemetery next to his mother. Max and Jackie Steiner organized a memorial at Kildonan Park on the bank of the Red River, letting it be known that the idea was to honour Lennie's well-known aversion to the solemnity of conventional funerals in preference for the celebratory spirit of an Irish wake. Two hundred people gathered, the most diverse group I had ever seen in one place before in Winnipeg. There was no ceremony, only impromptu testaments as Max invited people to the microphone. As the more demure mourners departed–university colleagues, politicians, business people, patricians–the wake atmosphere prevailed. By midnight, it was pandemonium. Amid surges of a dozen guitars, singing, and shrieking, the law arrived and broke up the crowd, making a bonanza of arrests for possession, as if in a final gesture to Lennie's memory. It was clear something more than Lennie had died.

Under the headline, *Magistrate Calls For Investigation Of Profs And Drugs*, the press opened fire, quoting from judge Pulack's judicial inquiry into Lennie's death:

> Perhaps it can be a lesson or a warning to society that an
> individual such as the late Professor Boyce was in very close
> association with what can be termed the drug culture in the

city of Winnipeg, as is evidenced by the drugs found in his suite.

One Morris Dutton, a student of Lennie's wrote:

> *The Tribune's* gratuitous insult to the dead may not be actionable, but it displays a disturbing insensitivity and ignorance. University professors are far more likely to learn the joys of pot from their students than vice versa. Leonard Boyce was one of the best teachers the University of Manitoba ever had.

This set off a furore of retaliation from the moral majority. The Regional Commissioner of the Boy Scouts of Canada carried out his obligation as Akayla by writing:

> In extolling the fine qualities of Professor Boyce, Morris Dutton states that 'Lennie Boyce was one of the comparatively small number of people in Winnipeg who actually tried to help young people to enrich their lives and awaken them to a sense of value.' I say Rubbish! I don't waste my time with the argument that marijuana is not addictive. I'm too busy helping young people 'to enrich their lives and awaken them to a sense of value'.

Churchmen and politicians beat their breasts in paroxysms of sanctimony about degenerate professors corrupting the young. If Lennie had failed to breach the Pharisee fortress in life, his emanation continued to fight a rear guard action in death. Young Mr. Dutton was one of the pro-Lennie commentators who made it regularly into *The Tribune* and *The Free Press,* undoubtedly because the contest between hippie kid and Eagle Scout couldn't help but sell papers. Young Mr. Dutton retaliated:

> It is sad that our present age still abounds with self-righteously indignant anachronisms such as those presented by the rulers of the boy scouts. The idea of young people in silly hats and neckbands, keen to earn camp cook and knot-tying badges to put on their sleeves, is over. Get it? It's gone. We don't trust daddy Eagle Scout no more.

Some academics joined the counterattack and got into the popular press. University people who had never openly shared his radical notions began speaking out. The man who had the courage to invite Lennie back to U of M from the East in the mid-60s, his first boss, joined the chorus.

> No amount of analysis will sum up the complex humanity of this rarely gifted, rarely tormented friend, colleague, and teacher. We all remember his commitment to his profession and to his fellow beings, his honesty, his sensitivity, his eager quest for freedom, and alas for his abiding desolation in his failure to reconcile these things with the misery, hypocrisy, and servitude he found everywhere about him. People sometimes said he was a cynic and faultfinder. He was. Nothing but paradise, the fulfilment of our highest hopes, would do for him.

Vince Calley, Lennie's closest friend in the English Department and co-founder of *The Gadfly* wrote:

> I remember basking in the light of his intelligence: an uncannily vivid person, a visionary, an idealist, a reformer with the soul of a poet-priest who gave fully of himself to the world. Few would deny he was also the walking contradiction Kris Kristofferson sang about, and yes he was certainly a silver-tongued devil, partly truth and partly fiction. Lennie must have died as he lived, strangely driven, reaching for, celebrating the hope he was always sure he saw beneath the mire. He loved to quote Yeats' lines about the contradiction of the human predicament: 'I must lie down where all the ladders start/In the foul rag and bone shop of the heart.'

Time passed. The uproar in the press died down. As the '70s came on, the '60s started to look irrelevant. But aftershock among those who had surrounded Lennie didn't fade so fast. Returning to talk to them five years after his death, I found many still distressed, as if their feelings had been in cold storage and when I turned on my tape recorder, a thaw set in. There was grief, bafflement, even anger, as if Lennie had in some way betrayed them. And there was guilt too, a sense of something they had failed to do. Some people couldn't hold back tears even after so long. I found it hard to tell whether their regret was for the death of Lennie only, or equally for the passing of an extraordinary era. Ben Gibson was not well. His performing days had ended and his family, once so revered by Lennie, had broken up.

"When I was told Lennie was dead, I was torn right up. What I think now, what it did to me personally, was jar me right down to the bone. The last discussion we had, I didn't really listen to him. I think he was trying to tell me something, looking for some response from me I didn't give. I don't feel anything like guilt about it. One thing Lennie and I always agreed about was that guilt is bullshit. If you did something, well, you did it. No point whining about it. I would just like to have been more perceptive and have read the signs better, and been able to put my arms around him and give him a hug. But it didn't happen. You don't see. A guy takes you to the edge and points you at it and you don't see.

"Lennie was a watering hole. You could go to him and he would refresh you. You could be out there with your shield up and everybody beating on you and there was Lennie who would listen to you and get you into a perspective on yourself. Let me put it this way: if Jesus Christ was a man of outstanding humanity and he belonged to a group of people who shared his outlook, Lennie would be one of that gang."

Jackie Steiner told me, at first, she just didn't want to talk about Lennie. I explained that I was trying to find out if his influence on people had lasted. She gave in.

"Lennie's death was just a catastrophe in our world. I ask myself, what happened after he left? Well, the world became a hell of a flatter place, and a sadder place. At the time of his death, I would have said we'll go on and take what we learned from him and understand things better. But I don't think we can keep our hold on those things, except maybe in some secret part of ourselves. I don't know if the world can carry on without its Lennies to keep us awake, to snap us out of this terrible daze that creeps in as we grow older. Well sure, you have to mature, slow down and become sensible, I know. But I miss the fireworks, the wild sessions at *The Gadfly*, the fights we had, the night-long debates about politics, life and love. And the things he taught me about myself.

"It was a time of such potential. It was like what Wordsworth said at the beginning of the French Revolution: 'Bliss was it in that dawn to be alive/But to be young was very Heaven.' When he was young Wordsworth opposed the West Indian slave trade. When he got older, to register his disapproval of slavery, he used honey in his tea instead of sugar made from sugar-cane. Shit, Jason, is that what it comes down to? I don't feel blissful about things any more. No, I don't. Is that what Wordsworth meant when he saw it all slipping away: 'Where is it now, the glory and the gleam?' Well, where the hell is it?"

"Vince Calley told me Lennie had once talked to him about his aversion to the way western culture responds to death, and he could never forget Lennie's words: 'Take some guy surrounded by rottenness and it really bugs this guy out. What does he do? He's had it with it all. So he jumps out a window. And what do they do with him? They scrape him up, put him in a box, and the poor bugger, they put a smile on what's left of his face so his family and friends can look at his cadaver and see how happy he was.'"

As I loaded talks I had with friends into my Lennie file, I had to ask myself again what was it that had drawn us so close together? He was pretty much the brightest guy I had ever known and I felt privileged to be one of his circle. But I knew there was more to it than that. It had begun in university. In different ways, we came from backgrounds that would have given us little chance to be there in an earlier era. We saw this at our first meeting and a bond was formed. As time went on, I began to recognize a certain reserve in myself in contrast to Lennie's extravagance. I saw myself as basically a man of order and he a man of energy. Apollo and Dionysius. Too much order and you atrophy. Too much energy and you fly apart. Yet without both in a dynamic relationship, there is no life. When Lennie was around, we had life. We surely had what, in one of its many forms, is called 'love'.

Chapter Forty

However forthcoming friends were in their recollections, the particulars of Lennie's death remained a mystery. Where had he gone that last day? Who had he seen? Was there anyone who noticed anything peculiar about him? The trail began at the Steiners, as Max explained:

"He drove up in his Toyota and we invited him in for coffee and bagels. We were used to his unexpected visits. I hoped this one was not going to turn into one of his brooding retreats, because that always put pressure on the family, just knowing he was camping downstairs, just thinking about him, whether we saw anything of him or not.

"Nothing to fear. He was not only cheerful, he wore his Cheshire grin. After coffee, he took us to the front window and pointed outside. He had just returned from The Happy Adventurer and there, on his roof rack, was a brand new, bright yellow, 13-foot fibre glass canoe. Jackie and I congratulated him, and went out to help take the canoe down and store it beside our garage. We all had a shot of brandy to celebrate the first step of his wilderness adventure.

Dimitri Wenchenko saw him next. "It was just after lunch. I was finishing up a silk-screen poster at the Coop when he walked in and challenged me to a game of chess. It was a regular thing for us. I was good, but not that good. I knew he liked me, but naturally that doesn't count in chess. I could beat him only when he didn't care, or when his head was out in space somewhere. He could concentrate like a weasel. He could whip me twenty games. Then I would win one game and say: 'What's the matter, Hunkie-boy? You lost the touch?' He liked that.

"When he walked through the door that afternoon, he had a strange air about him, kind of wild, kind of cockeyed. When he set up the board I told him I didn't feel like playing and he called me chicken shit. I said all right, but I'm going to ream your Hunkie ass today. We played a couple of quickies to warm up and I came close to winning one. Then, a bell rang in my head. I was playing hot as a poker. I was into endgame and I had him. Two moves, that would be it. Lennie must have seen it too, because he suddenly hunched over the board for a good five minutes before he touched his last knight. I moved as planned, he moved again; then, out of nowhere, he said, 'checkmate.' I looked down and there it was.

"He walked over to Jake at the silkscreen bed and said: 'I've just played the best game I've ever played in my life.' I knew his moods inside out and I can tell you for sure he hadn't been drinking or smoking or speeding or doing any kind of shit that afternoon. He was au naturel. He was just incredibly intense. He had that look about him as if you could wave your hand in front of his face and he wouldn't bat an eye. I had to push off and I remember saying next time we'd play for the Hunkie championship of the world."

Lennie's next stop, unless there were way-stations in between I never found out about, was at Katia's apartment at the Place Louis Riel.

"Lennie turned up around noon. It took me by surprise. He knew enough to phone ahead if he wanted to see Katrina. Instead, I got a call from the lobby. He had a birthday present. Katrina was going to be two years old in a week. I said are you crazy or sane right now? He promised he was sane, and he sounded okay, so I rang him in. He had a shopping bag full of books he'd gotten at some second-hand store. I don't know how many volumes, maybe a dozen, a Children's Encyclopaedia. They were full of old drawings like the Charge of the Light Brigade. I said, you crazy son of a bitch she's only two. But she's talking, he said. Sure, I said, Momma, Dada, caca, she's a genius. He said Freud was reading Shakespeare at age eight and John Stuart Mill's father was teaching him Latin at age four. I said, why didn't he bring her a dress or something? He said, 'clothes you grow out of, books you grow into.' I reminded him that he was not John Stuart Mill's father and maybe Katrina had inherited fewer brains from her father than John Stuart Mill had inherited from his father. I said, given that Lennie was her father, we were goddamned lucky Katrina had inherited any brains at all, and thanks to me, some clothes to wear.

"We carried on like that until Katrina started to cry and I put her to bed with her bottle. Lennie went in and sat there, watching her go to sleep.

When the baby sitter came, he left with me. We walked the block together up to my job at Eaton's on Portage. I remember us talking about how we all used to steal jawbreakers at Sophie's Confectionary when we were kids, as if she didn't know, and we had a good laugh. When I turned into Eaton's to start my shift, he leaned down and gave me a big smack right on the lips. All afternoon at my notion's counter, while I demonstrated eye shadow and lipstick and all that shit, I kept thinking what a schmuck he was, and smiling to myself about those goddamn books he brought for Katrina, and what a big smack on the lips he had given me. When I got home I noticed a piece of paper stuck on Katrina's crib that read:

Proxy For Katrina

Summer's fields lie fallow
Gardens turn to vacant lots
Trees rot at the marrow
Flowers wilt in window pots

Then the river catches fire
And fiercely burns away
Fish fry in the flaming mire
Immolation, judgement day

Snow falls, nothing to enfold
But poisoned grass and weeds
Nothing saved from killing cold
But here and there some seeds

Darling daughter freshets spring
And yearly wake the world from sleep
This is my green offering
That you sow joy and so joy reap

After leaving Katia, Lennie must have carried on the next two blocks to the Albert where he met Jake for a beer. "I wish I could remember better what we talked about. There was this strange feeling that he was there, but he wasn't there. He didn't seem to know what to do next. Hell, I thought, maybe he was just being normal, just in one of his regular anxiety moods. Looking back, it's easy to make things up. But I sensed something spaced-out about him. I suggested a boilermaker to perk him up but he didn't want one. He said, 'Have you got any dope?' and I said, no, but I thought Zebby the Toke had some. It was too early for the crops but Zebby grew his own, hydroponically, known as Number One Northern. I had literally seen people pass out on that stuff. It was just superb. But you had to learn how to handle it. You had to smoke a joint and wait, not rush into a second. In other words, use your head, don't use *up* your head. Lennie knew that as well as I did. We left around five o'clock. He said he had to meet somebody and I pretended that I had work to do on a new piece.

"A little after nine, he passed by overhead on his way to his flat. I remember the time because I was getting ready to go pick up Julia at the hospital when her shift ended at ten. I was on the phone when I heard him walk directly overhead from where my desk was. I knew his walk. I heard him laugh, one of those high phissing laughs of his, and then give that little cough. I thought maybe he had someone with him and they were making jokes or making out. Once, I thought I heard footsteps coming back down stairs, but they were way off on the edge of my mind as I finished my business on the phone. I still had half an hour to kill before going for Julia and I thought, well, I'll go up and shoot the breeze with Lennie until it's time to go. I went up the stairs and down the hall to his flat and looked in the living room. Nobody there. I went to the kitchen and there was nobody there either. I thought maybe he was with a chick in the bedroom, so I began to tiptoe back down the hall.

"Suddenly, the Red Army came roaring up the stairs. The door burst open and I was surrounded by cops. Before I knew it, they had cuffed me, and then they ignored me as they went about searching the flat. There was a full dime-bag right in the middle of the kitchen table and two ice-cold hash pipes. Lennie had scored after he left me at the Albert, is all I thought, but it looked as if he hadn't used any, just left it on the table. I knew it was Zebby the Toke's stuff because the complimentary box of Chiclets was sitting beside the bag. I heard one of the cops say Lennie had been found in an alley. What flashed through my mind was that it must have been him I thought I heard going back downstairs when I was on the phone. But that hardly gave him enough time to go and get beat up in the alley. No, I thought, there's something else going on here. Without telling me anything, the cops took me to the station on North Main. I was getting really worked up and finally

I went over to the desk and asked, 'What the hell's going on here, what's with Professor Boyce?' At precisely that instant, this big cop walked past carrying Lennie's bloody jacket. 'Well, right now, buddy,' the desk cop said, 'your Professor Boyce is dead.'

"The shock was so great, I was completely cool. I phoned Julia at the hospital. I told her to pick up a bottle of scotch or two because I was going to need them. I didn't get home until the next day. The stupid bastards held me on suspicion of murder. Sure, I pushed Lennie off the roof, then I sat down and didn't bother to hide the grass bag while I waited for the cops to come."

Katia didn't get word right away. As the reality of what happened sank in, Jake tried to call her but the police wouldn't let him. Katia told me how she heard:

"Katrina was asleep. I was watching Johnny Carson just after 11:00 when there was a knock on the door. It was the police. I always thought Lennie would get in a car accident. He was a lousy driver. I said, 'Was my husband in a car accident?' They said yes. I said, 'Was anyone with him?' And they said no. I said, 'Is he dead?', and they said yes. And I went berserk. I screamed and I ran at the cops. They said I'd have to come and identify the body and I said no, I wouldn't do it. Jason, I can't tell you. I went nuts. Then my sister came over and a whole bunch of friends, and I went to the police station and then to the morgue. Jesus, what a mess. They said he landed on his feet. I don't have to tell you. I knew something like this was going to happen, something violent, ever since that crazy time we spent in Greece, maybe ever since I knew him as a kid. We had been apart for a while and I had made a home for Katrina and me and I knew there was no way Lennie and I were ever going to get together again. But it still knocked me cuckoo. I want to cry right now but I won't cry. I won't cry because it's not worth it.

"There's one thing I can tell you. When Katrina was born and he came to see me in hospital, he said thank you to me for the most precious thing in his life. He always wanted a girl and I always wanted a boy. He got his wish. Now, that ought to tell you something. How could he kill himself when he had his daughter to think about? He may have been nuts but he wasn't completely crazy. Jason, Lennie did not commit suicide."

A so-called New Fatalities Act had just passed in Manitoba, taking inquests out of the hands of coroners and placing them under the jurisdiction of the courts. This put the investigation of Lennie's death into the hands of a Judge Pulack who wrote: "I cannot determine in all honesty and fairness as to whether this in fact was a suicide or an accident, or caused by some person or persons unknown. We know what the deceased died of and how he came to his death. But only the deceased and perhaps some divine power know the full truth. Therefore it will have to be ruled an accidental death."

Did he commit suicide? Was it an accident? Was he murdered? Who would decide? Katia never ceased to believe Lennie had tripped and fallen. Everyone agreed publicly with Judge Pulack's finding of accidental death. There was speculation that the judge, himself Ukrainian, may have been ethnically influenced. The judgement meant Katia could collect Lennie's university insurance and use it to help bring up her daughter. Of course, he went along with it, but Jake didn't see it that way:

"Remembering Lennie's laughter on the stairway, I never had a shred of doubt that the guy had walked out the French doors onto the roof and straight over the side. Maybe he thought it was his canoe trip and he was on his way to the unspoiled wilderness. Was he on something? That last afternoon the guy was in the grip of something bigger than all the dope in the world. If there was dope involved, I guarantee all it did was make him smile on the way down."

Chapter Forty-One

What I couldn't account for was Lennie's movements from the time he left Jake around five o'clock at the Albert until the time Jake heard him go up the stairs to his apartment at about ten. The answer came in a letter from nowhere.

May 21, 1976

Dear Jason Faraday:

It's five years to the day since I last saw your friend, Lennie Boyce, whom I understand you are digging around about. Never mind who I am. And please, do not make an effort to find out. The chance of your succeeding is remote. And the chance of your causing big trouble for me and for yourself is very high. Believe me on this. Just call me... Molly Bloom, as Lennie did, and leave it at that.

I first met Lennie at a social function in Winnipeg, nothing to do with the university. The Winter Club, you may speculate, or maybe at a gallery opening, or the symphony, or the Winnipeg Playhouse. People were milling around and we bumped into each other, literally. He looked at me and right out of the blue he said: 'You are indescribably beautiful.' 'Piss off,' I said. Jesus, had I had enough of two-bit Lotharios sniffing at me.

Maybe a year later, my husband and I were at a Winnipeg gala, one of those places. Everyone was there–the sports elite, media moguls, the ballet and symphony and theatre and university people, and all the old and parvenu money of the town. It was Winnipeg's annual ritual designed to convince artists that a little patronage did not mean selling their souls, and to persuade the money magnates that a little contribution to the arts (tax deductible) would not only not hurt their bottom line, but help elevate Winnipeg into cultural significance.

"Remember me?" Lennie said, bumping into me again, this time not by accident.

"No," I said, though I did.

"I have to tell you," he said. "Forgive my bluntness. I have never yet met a woman I seriously wanted to make love to as much as I seriously want to make love to you."

I had never heard such brass. I thought of myself as pretty unflappable. But for a moment I was completely stunned. Then I said what I always imagined something too hateful to say. I said: "Do you realize I could have you beaten up or arrested or both?"

He smiled at me, a taunting smile. "Oh that you would arrest me! Caress me! Embrace me! Disgrace me!" Then suddenly his look turned sober. He took me by the elbow and said: "I've got to have you, you know. You are the most exquisite woman I have ever seen."

I pulled myself away. I could think of nothing to say. I was furious. This was a scene you wouldn't find even in a Harlequin Romance. But I didn't forget him. Months later when I saw him again, it was at a garden party in one of the grand old mansions on Wellington Crescent. I was surprised to see him there. It was a very exclusive crowd. I was standing by myself in the semi-darkness of the terrace overlooking the Assiniboine. Behind me the music played and people were dancing as if they were still in Strauss's Vienna. Lennie came up beside me and whispered in my ear: "The grave's a fine and private place, but none I think do there embrace."

He leaned on the balustrade facing the ballroom over my shoulder. There was no moon, only the light coming through the French doors. I could just make out his face. I stayed facing the river and said nothing. He reached down and touched me through my skirt and I didn't move. Without pausing, he came up under my skirt and held me. I clenched my teeth so as not to make a noise. He turned to face the river away from the light and I turned to face into it. I unzipped him and took him in my hand, without a word. The strangeness and danger of it was like a drug. Anyone watching from inside the French doors might have wondered what we were talking about so intently.

We went out through the garden to the parking lot and got into his car. We writhed and gasped as we struggled in the back seat, like teenagers at a drive-in. Lennie helped me get myself back to together and then drove off. It was a chore, let me tell you, going back to join the charade.

I was not *out* of love with my husband. We even enjoyed intimacy from time to time. He spoiled me. I admired his energy and ambition in the tough world of power and money. I suppose you could say I lived a charmed life with him until Lennie came along. I was 35. Lennie was what? 38? We ravished each other.

After that first night, there was no argument about the absolute necessity of keeping our relationship secret. We would never go to his place or to mine, and never appear in public together, never even get into the same car together. The reason, I told him, was that my husband was not only rich, but a possessive and a ruthless man when provoked, quite capable having Lennie killed if word ever got out about us. Lennie knew who he was up against and made no protest. If he had other lovers, we agreed, they would never be a subject of discussion between us. Same for me. And he was never to interfere or even ask about my relations with my husband.

Until the end we honoured that pact. I don't quite know why I break the silence now. It's not to set the record straight or anything noble like telling the truth. I expect it's just that a hermetically clandestine relationship like ours, a fierce passion in a vacuum, once it's over, eventually feels as if it never happened, unless another human being knows about it. Like it or not I guess that's your role, Mr. Jason (was it JJ he called you?), even so long after the liaison.

Men had always made me feel beautiful. I had pretty much accepted myself to be what my husband once referred to as a piece of finely glazed porcelain. I liked the look of myself naked. I found talk and love-making in front of a mirror more exciting than silent churning in the dark ... until Lennie came along. Talking and visual play were just a beginning, he told me, like teenage necking. But they could also be distracting. Real Eros went beyond words and the visible world. Of course, being Lennie, he needed words to make me understand. Ultimately, he said, Eros is an all engrossing, all-encompassing thing, a soundless, sightless re-alignment in the body with the drumming pulse of the universe. I came to believe him.

As he opened that world to me, drugs came into play of course. I wasn't exactly a novice. Pot was a regular part of my husband's crowd in the discreet, recreational fashion of the rich. But I had never touched the major hallucinogens. I knew Lennie had tried everything on earth. I was able to get my hands on two tabs of LSD so Lennie and I could have a go at it together. Late in the afternoon (it was that last afternoon on his last day), we were in a highway motel and I brought out the acid.

His alarm surprised me. It was the only time, as I was never one of his students, that I heard him deliver a lecture. Never go beyond a little pot or hash, he told me. Never touch the heavy stuff unless you're Aldous Huxley. He launched into a litany of case histories of drug deaths from Lenny Breau, the genius guitarist who was a friend of his, to Lenny Bruce and Janis Joplin and Jimi Hendrix. He scared the hell out of me. I gave him my capsules and he flushed them down the toilet.

When he came back into the room, he said he had a surprise for me that was better than drugs. He had brought along a boom box and he turned on Ravel's *Bolero*. For the next eternity, we made love to the gradually rising volume and quickening tempo, in sync with the music right to the climax.

As we dressed to leave, I made a remark. I don't know where it came from. It was one of those idle bits of information that lodge in your mind. I said: "Did you know Ravel was a homosexual?"

Lennie stopped dressing and stood looking at me with an expression of bewilderment on his face. "What's that supposed to mean?" he said.

"Nothing," I said. "Nothing at all. It's just something I read some place." A few minutes later we parted in our separate cars. It was the last time I saw him.

So now you know what no one else does, Mr. JJ. You know about the secret love of Lennie Boyce and ...

Call me Molly Bloom.

Finally, five years after his death, the letter filled in the time lapse between Lennie's departure from having a beer with Jake at the Albert and his return home when Jake heard him going up the stairs to his flat. After that the trail ends.

Part V
A Garden Fruitful

Chapter Forty-Two

Passing through Winnipeg later in 1975, I took Katia to dinner at Dubrovnik. I was told it was the best restaurant in town with a Slavic flavour, and where if you liked you could drink a gallon of vodka and no one would think the worse of you. I remember a huge bill, but mainly a warm feeling, as always when I was with Katia. Not a sexual feeling. Or if it was, I stifled it out of respect for my dead friend. Katia sent me a note later on.

Dear Jason:

Lennie's boxes got waterlogged when the water main bust. There was nothing much in them because Lennie didn't write much and what he did write he usually threw away. Anyway, when I was house cleaning the other day I found a few papers that survived Noah's flood. You can have them if you want.

Thanks for dinner at Dubrovnik.
Which I do not remember.

Always
Katia

I went over to her place next trip. Katia ordered in Chinese and offered me the remainder of a bottle of scotch I'd left there during my previous visit. She handed me a brown envelope. Two poems bore the same postscript in Lennie's hand: "to be revised". They were dated May, 1971, the month Lennie died.

Free Fall

Hell bent on freedom
It was our golden age
As if we had till kingdom come
Upon a gilded stage

That's when everything was new
And nothing barred the way
All sensation our purview
Performed as in a play

Now as golden leaves turn dun
Prodigal debts come due
Failing to do what we could have done
We did what we can't undo

The next poem had only two scribbled revisions, as if it too had been set down pretty much all of a piece.

Falling

The shadow of the falcon
Falls across the garden
Then with a rush
Of swooshing wings

Bird and shadow meet
And the skewered vole
Rising skyward
Gets new vision

Like Adam in Eve's
Last embrace
Before the fall
The vole beholds it all
The vanishing tree
The fading garden

Seen from on high
With a falcon's eye
A momentary flash
Sub specie Alternates

The dropped vole
Skitters from the sky
Earth whirling
Air whistling by

Then the thump
With no echo
When the vole
Hits the ground

As I read these lines, Katia watched me closely. "I know," she said. "It sounds like he was thinking about jumping, doesn't it? But just because he was thinking about it? That's bullshit, Jason. That crazy bastard thought about everything. Answer me this. If everyone who thought about committing suicide went ahead and committed suicide we wouldn't have this goddamn population explosion, would we? Take me, for one. I sure as hell wouldn't be here to take up room. So, the inquest said he landed on his feet and people who trip by accident usually don't land the way he did. So, what if he tripped and stayed upright? That would be just Lennie's luck. You know his co-ordination was always piss-poor. Jesus, do you think I want Katrina to grow up having to think her father killed himself?"

I tried to get the image in my head of Lennie entering his flat, grinning until his eyes were all but shut, walking through the French doors, utterly convinced he could fly, and taking the leap. In the motel with Molly Bloom, even if drug-free as a baby, had he somehow generated a chemical of his own that had convinced him it was just a step into the western night to land him in the place at the end of the canoe trip–the place that would end all torment? Or had he possibly not flushed Molly Bloom's LSD down the drain?

I thumbed through Katia's packet of photographs of early Ukrainian settlers. They were a miserable looking lot–stoic, hard-bitten, unforgiving.

"Did you ever think he might have been pushed?" Katia asked me.

"Who would push him?" I said. Mentioning Molly Bloom and her forbidding husband would serve no purpose this late in the day.

"Was there a woman?" she asked.

"With Lennie, there was always a woman somewhere," I said.

Katia was no ostrich. She knew about Lennie's escapades. We sat in silence while I rifled through clippings and fragments of lecture notes. I paused on Judge Pulack's legalese about the possibility of "a person or persons unknown". I remembered Jake's words: "Once, I thought I heard footsteps coming back downstairs," then Molly Bloom's words about her husband: "a possessive and a ruthless man who, if provoked, could quickly have you killed." Had Lennie been murdered for the most clichéd of reasons–a jealous husband?

The last item in the envelope was a letter on the back of a piece of lined foolscap. It looked like one-finger typing on an antique Smith-Corona.

May 9, 1971

Dear Leonnard,

Well just a few lines to say hi 1 guess, you could say that any way. Well I sure hope you don't mind me writing to you. I just had no one else to write to. I sure hope you know what I mean. Well you see what I mean, I'm so use of writing to someone I have to or I don't feel right for the rest of the day.

Eileen Courchene is in here right now and she was the one that put me up to writing you, you understand. I sure hope so anyway. So much for that gossip; besides I have more to say. I been in the Manitoba home for girls for two bloody weeks now and pretty sick of it already, of course who wouldn't be. I was picked up at my grandmas at about 7 in the morning. I'm going to Marymount home in the near future.

I talk about you all the time, I hope you don't mind and if you do please tell me that if you answer this letter which I hope you do answer. But if you don't wasn't me writing to you don't answer it.

Have you seen Norma around lately? I wrote to her but never got no answer, I don't really blame my family turning against me, It is my own fault bitch around will I. The maids here or house mothers are really nice. At least they try to be. Some of them bug the ass right off of me.

I wonder as I lay in my bed at night if I will ever see you again. I hope so anyway. Maybe you never want to see me again, but I want to see you, Norma told me a lot about you. Oh Leonnard I think the world of you, oh it hurts just to think that I'm falling in love with a stranger.

Would you please answer this letter if you at least care for me. Leonnard I love you. Well would you please write back. I have to go now.

Love

Lucille Lapine

"It's a child, isn't it?" Katia said.

"Lapine is an old Métis name," I said. "There was a Lapine who died fighting with Gabriel Dumont at Batoche in 1885. Sounds like she's in a detention centre."

"Sure, and for what?"

"Shoplifting?"

"Jason don't give me bullshit. She was hooking. Don't tell me that asshole Lennie was so hard up he had to score a little Indian whore."

"That's not how I see it, Katia. Lennie probably sat up all night and listened to the girl's story. He was probably the first person in her life who ever paid any attention to her. The sad thing is she would never have heard back from him. Within a week of her mailing the letter, he was dead. I wonder if she ever read about it in the newspapers? Or if she just felt jilted by another person who talked nice to her but didn't really care?"

"Did he have to know every deadbeat in town?" Katia said. "I feel sorry for the little girl same as you do. But I save up some sympathy to feel sorry for myself sometimes too."

"That poem," I said, "The one Lennie called *Free Fall*. It sounds like it was about him and you. The date on it. It sounds like he was thinking about you right at the end."

"You mean all that about 'we did what we can't undo' stuff?" Katia walked over to where there was a row of framed photographs on the mantelpiece, one of her and Lennie and Katrina as a baby in happier times, another of Katrina about nine years old with a mass of curly red hair and a smile featuring a mouthful of braces. Before I knew it, she reached out and sent the pictures clattering across the floor. She burst out shouting and stamping her feet. Not a Katia I had seen before.

"You sons of bitches and your words. You thought all you had to do was put things into words and everything would be hunky-fucking-dory. You thought you could run around screwing everything in sight, boiling your brains with booze and dope, just so long as you had a big-time experience. Then you could go away and put it into words, isn't that it? You had your university ideas and your big words and your goddamn William Blake. Blake, schmake! You know what Lennie said to me once? He said Blake said, 'The cut worm forgives the plough'. He told me to think about it! I said, 'I don't have to think about it you Mr. know-it-all fancy pants! Do you take me for a complete dodo? You might think you're some kind of big man plow, and I'm nothing but a worm waiting to be cut to pieces for fertilizer Well I'm not! Did it ever occur to you you're the dodo, not me?"

"It's okay, Katia," I said. I tried to calm her down. "He really loved you, you know. He really did."

"You goddam eggheads! Like a gang of yappie kids you were. I wasn't stupid. I just kept my mouth shut. Yak, yak, yak you'd go on into the night. Like crickets rubbing their legs together to make a noise. Drinking all the time. Doing all that dope. Running around humping your students and each other's wives. I knew. All I ever wanted was a sensible life, a nice house and some kids. I would have been happy with a stupid picket fence. Goddam you all, Jason! All I ever wanted was a life. Just a regular life. What's so wrong about that?"

I sank in my chair. This was a Katia I wasn't ready for. I felt like a stand-in for Lennie, for all the waste and shame and disappointment Lennie had brought her. It wasn't rational, but I felt a terrible complicity in the pain he had given her.

"So I have a daughter," Katia said. "Blow the roof off. The fuss Lennie made over her when she was born! Well, I know he loved her, but in what way? Sometimes I think what she meant to him was no more than proof that he wasn't sterile after all. Do you know what Vince Calley, that toffy university genius, told me once? He said Lennie was convinced the reason I didn't get pregnant for so long was that he hadn't smoked enough marijuana. Now what kind of nitwit could come up with a hair-brained notion like that? Jesus, Jason! Jesus! You bastards!"

She broke into great heaving sobs and covered her face in her hands. I got up and held her in my arms as she stood shaking. It lasted a minute or two. Then she straightened up. She dabbed her eyes and began to pick up the pictures and pieces of glass from the floor. She gave me a teary smile. "Cripes," she said, "if you didn't know better, you'd think I was in love with that honiak."

We ate the Chinese food. Afterwards, we sat in the semi-darkness in front of the pretend fireplace. Katia drank green tea. I had finished the heel of scotch left from my previous visit and was working my way into the bottle I had brought with me. Katia was first to break the silence.

"There are things you don't know, Jason." Her voice was soft but intense and it made me sit up. She spoke as much into the fake flames in the fireplace as to me. "It wasn't Sophie who pushed Yuri off the balcony."

"Then who?" I could feel the truth coming. I had always wondered.

"Sophie doted on Lennie. When she knew she was dying of cancer, she fooled them all and took the rap for Yuri's death. She was no dummy, let me tell you, Jason. Lennie toppled Yuri off the fire escape and Sophie knew it. Lennie hated Yuri because, when he was a kid, he had to watch him punch Sophie around. But there was more to it than that. Smacking a woman was no big deal in those days. What Lennie hated most about Yuri was that he stood for everything that people thought about Ukrainians as dumb bohunks.

"Lennie was home from Toronto for Christmas. Sophie was asleep. Yuri was out back on the fire escape, puking into the alley. Lennie threw on Sophie's housecoat and followed him out. Yuri was a big man. But he was leaning a long way over the railing. Lennie took him by the heels and hoiked him over. That's the word Lennie used when he told me. He said he 'hoiked' him over. I guess you could say like father like son. Yuri landed on his head when he hit the pavement and Lennie landed on his feet, but it didn't make a whole lot of difference in the long run, did it? What a hell of a family!"

I was still processing the idea of Lennie as possibly a victim of a homicide himself so I wasn't ready for what came next. "Yuri was Lennie's father, you know."

"No," I said. "Lennie's father was Mike Feschuck, the man who was shot or else shot himself on the CPR tracks above the Higgins Avenue underpass, back in 1934, three years after Lennie was born. It was in the papers. I dug out the story in the library. I've got the clippings."

"That was Lennie's wishful thinking," Katia said. "Did you ever meet his so-called cousin? Boris was Sophie's son by Feschuck, not Lennie."

"Boris the undertaker? Boris, the best man at Lennie's and Angela's wedding?"

"That's him. He's a lawyer now. He's Mike Feschuck's son by Sophie. He's Lennie's half-brother, though Lennie would never say so because he couldn't stand Boris, even when they were kids. Boris lived with Sophie's sister as if he was her son. He grew up ashamed of Sophie. That's the way it was in those days. Did Lennie really believe Feschuck was his father? He wanted to believe it, I know. Feschuck was respected. He was some kind of North End underworld hero connected to the Bronfmans and the liquor trade. He made headlines because his death was a big mystery. Well too bad! Yuri was Lennie's real dad, not Feschuk."

"How do you know all this?"

"Sophie told me. But she didn't have to. Yuri had the same squinty eyes, the same Roman nose and cheek creases when he laughed, the same kinky hair. Lennie's was rusty, not red, that's all. Yuri's features were wider, thicker, not as clean-cut as Lennie's. But the resemblance was there like a bad copy of a picture."

I tried to imagine what Lennie might have thought if he hadn't known Yuri was his father, and how different it would have been for him if he had known. This suddenly became a huge question. I asked Katia:"Did Lennie know who Yuri was before he "hoiked" him off the fire escape?"

"You tell me," she said. "Sure, he knew in some way. How could he look in a mirror and not know? I never let on I knew and he never told me he knew. Maybe, in one of his screwball ways of thinking, he never really told himself. What if Sophie had not been dying? For sure, she knew Lennie pushed Yuri over the railing. Would she have pleaded guilty all the same? Knowing her, I think she would have, to protect Lennie. What I really wonder is, would Lennie have let her take the rap? That would have said a lot, wouldn't it, about what kind of person Lennie really was? But Sophie died and that ended it."

The scotch was getting to me. I could feel myself slipping out of a tragic into a tragi-comic mode. It was making me see Lennie as a partially picaresque figure, somewhere between Tom Jones and Raskalnikov. A line from a play came to mind: "... it was a bitter life he led me till I did up a Tuesday and halve his skull." This was Christy speaking in Synge's *Playboy of the Western World*, boasting about how he had split open his father's skull in a bid for independence. It was received by the locals as an act of self-realization that made Christy a hero throughout the West of Ireland, elevating him into a legend who would "go romancing through a romping lifetime from this hour to the dawning of the judgement day." And then I thought of Katia and Christy's last love, Pegeen Mike, after she had let Christy go: "Oh my grief, I've lost him surely. I've lost the only Playboy of the Western World."

I saw that Katia's instinct was more than half-right about our bunch. Our literary education had a way of diverting us from the pain of experience by solacing us with words. We had words for every occasion, if not our own words then someone else's. Maybe words became too important. Maybe we went chasing what we called experience, not so much for itself as for raw material to be transmuted into language. Maybe it wasn't just Lennie but the lot of us who were never quite sure of an experience until we could talk about it. But there was a difference. There was something none of the rest of us could do and Lennie could. When he spoke, and the situation called for it, like Christy in *Playboy of the Western World*, he could make words sing, for himself and for everyone within range.

Chapter Forty-Three

Incredible, I thought, that I have spent twice as many years on earth as Lennie did, yet even though he's been gone so long, memories of him and his time remain overpowering. On a fallow afternoon on a visit to Toronto from my new home on the west coast, a notice in the paper caught my attention. Glendon College was hosting a conference on Northrop Frye. The definitive edition of his works was near completion at U of T Press, and volumes of diaries and letters and notebooks were tumbling out. Canada's once pre-eminent literary critic, after a time out in the cold, looked to be in for a revival. The line-up at Glendon College looked awesomely scholarly. My interest was not. Casually nostalgic, you might call it. It was either Frye or a movie, and nothing good was playing.

I took a seat a long way back so I could see the speakers and the questioners without being expected to participate. Part way through the session, a woman caught my attention. I had trouble keeping my eyes off her–the wide forehead and high cheekbones, the swirl of copper hair, the Mongolian eyes, something even about the tilt of her head. Who was this beauty? She turned to catch me staring and I looked away. She caught me again just before the break. As I filled my coffee cup in the hall outside the conference room, she walked directly up to me: "Do I know you?" Close up and face on, I was certain it was her, and yes her age was right. "Katrina Boyce?"

"Yes. I'm sorry but I ...."

"Jason Faraday."

She gave me a quizzical look, then a sunburst of a smile: "Omygod! Jason Faraday. My dad's old friend."

"We were at university together," I said. "I wasn't far away when you were born."

She let out a breathy laugh. "I expect I've changed a bit." The way she switched so swiftly from earnestness to jest was just like Lennie.

"I recall meeting you at eight or nine," I said, "with, you know, a mouth full of metal. But it's not just that. It's your hair. I've seen it before. It's the unusual colour of Lennie's mother's hair." The unexpectedness of our meeting, the striking beauty of Katrina, must have left me gaping.

She smiled. "I know what you're thinking. You're thinking I look like Lennie. I've heard it before."

"I see you read minds like him too," I said. It was more than a resemblance and yet no single feature stood out as in Lennie's craggy face. All was proportion and harmony in Katrina. And the eyes were different, not Lennie's narrow, disappearing eyes. They were wide pumpkinseed eyes like her mother's, with Lennie's faintly oriental edges. Her smile put me at ease. "You look like Lennie all right. But explain to me. How can that be since he was not beautiful?"

"Mom told me about guys like you. 'Beware the sweet talking devils', she said."

"I haven't seen Katia since ...? Is she ... well?"

"Alive? Yes, and well. She gambles. She lives in our old house in the North End with my Aunt Stella. They go to the races and the casino together. Big stakes. Two dollar bets on the horses and twenty-five cent trips to the slots. She assures me she's ahead of the game. It could be she's telling the truth. Also I hear she has a boyfriend, a retired railway conductor with a Cadillac. She thinks she's keeping it a secret from me."

"God! Katia! I thought the world of Katia. The gambling doesn't surprise me. There was a lot of gambling back then, not just for money." The next session on Frye was about to convene and people were drifting back toward the conference room.

"We must talk," said Katrina. "Are you anxious to return?" I assured her that my grasp of Frye's *Anatomy of Criticism* had by now (and not for the first time) approached its limit, and I would welcome a recess. We moved off to an alcove and sat overlooking the forest of maple and aspen that dips down into the Glendon College ravine with such colour in the fall. It was Keats' season of mists and mellow fruitfulness, a pointillist painting of flaming reds and yellows.

"The slow, smokeless burning of decay," I muttered as we sat down, barely aware I had spoken.

"Robert Frost," she said.

"Ahh, the tradition lives on."

"Tradition?"

"We see these dying leaves. But it's not just a colourful picture. It's oxidation, Frost's 'slow, smokeless burning of decay'. You know what he means. I know what he means. Autumn is a kind of furnace. So now we've got communication between a young woman, an old man, and a dead poet. Lennie would have called that the secret power of metaphor. Thus 'the tradition lives on'."

"What a lovely idea. I thought you might think I was being a show-off by identifying Frost's lines ."

"Well, you were. So were we all show-offs when we had the words and got the chance. That's part of the tradition, too."

As the chatter in the foyer receded, we sat sipping our coffee until Katrina spoke: "When I was growing up, I kept running into people who told me about Lennie, how well-known he was, what a great teacher he was, what an influence he had on their lives, but never anything specific. Even my mother never said much but generalities, and she was an expert at changing the subject when I asked. By the time I was a teenager, right into my university years, I didn't much care. Isn't that universal among the young–so busy trying to break with their parents and to figure out where they stand with their friends they can't be bothered with the past?"

"I'm pretty sure I remember feeling that way."

"It was strange when I went to University because there were still professors who had known Lennie. Some, when they realized who I was, looked away and hurried by. And then there was Vince Calley. I took his class on Milton. I've seen pictures of you and Lennie and him together."

"Vince was an excellent fellow. He was, I believe, a great hero of Lennie's but at heart he was a moderate."

"That was bad?"

"In some ways, for Lennie, it was Canada's curse."

"Vince was a godsend to me. I think he saw me as a special responsibility. I went to him for help with my work and even with personal problems. Yet despite his fatherly ministrations, whenever the subject of Lennie came up, he was as evasive as the others. I had a notion why. Although it was never the official verdict, the general view on campus among those who went back that far was that Lennie had committed suicide. How do you treat the daughter of a suicide? It must have been awkward for Lennie's contemporaries."

"Everyone had their own idea about what happened. There was a lot of grief and anger and confusion and for some there still is. Yes, I suppose people would be awkward with you."

"It didn't stop me from taking a fourth year course on Blake and the Romantics, the course I was told Lennie once taught and ...well ... here I am. By the time I became genuinely curious and wanted to know more about my father, it was too late. What surprises me is that there are almost no records. Lennie published nothing I know of, besides a few pieces in that underground newspaper, *Gadfly*. What else? A trunk full of costume jewellery and knick-knacks belonging to his mother (Sophie with the hair like mine) whom I never knew, a box of old photographs of immigrant looking people without identity, a yellow canoe still hanging in Katia's garage when last I was there, a cowboy hat she leaves hanging in the upstairs hall. Not a lot to go on."

"In the early 60s," I told Katrina, "I secretly decided to aim for a job in journalism. My group of budding hothouse intellectuals was becoming conscious that we were living in a special era that brought all the old values under fire to an extent the world had never seen before. It was not just our fractious little group but a tide that was sweeping McLuhan's Global Village. For me, Lennie had mythical underpinnings. He was, I recognized early on, not just a child of the times but one of its dynamos. I set up a file on him, my idea being that sometime in the future, I might be able, if not to tell the story of the period by tracing his footsteps, at the very least help myself resolve whether we were all crazy or dangerously sane."

"You have a file?" Katrina was excited.

"I used it once to make my pitch to a CBC radio boss in Toronto for a program I called *Who Killed the Sixties?* He turned livid when he realized Lennie was the centrepiece of my story. 'That goddamn barbarian!' he roared. What had happened back when the producer was working his way up the ladder in Winnipeg, was that he had invited Lennie, as a luminary at *Umbilicus* Free School, to add spice to a panel on higher education. It was live television. The subject was *So Little for the Mind*, by the educational reformer Hilda Neatby. The grand lady was there in person. Her complaint was that the increasing permissiveness of the educational system was creating a generation of ignoramuses. The other two panellists were high school principals, staunch upholders of the conventional classroom and the rigid curriculum. They agreed fulsomely with Hilda, saying only that she didn't go far enough in clamping down on so-called 'progressive education'.

"A half-hour into the program, Lennie had contributed not a word. The producer was beginning to regret having invited him when Lennie rose and made his way toward the back of the studio. Anticipating something enlivening, the producer directed a camera to track him, until he realized what was happening and called franticly to switch back to a close-up on Hilda. 'That crazy bastard,' the producer barked at me years later from behind his desk in Toronto, still in a rage as though it were yesterday, 'he walked right up to camera two and pissed on the pedestal, live coast to coast, before I could cut away! I goddamn nearly got canned.' That, needless to say, sounded the death knell for my proposed radio documentary called: *Who Killed The Sixties?*"

"What was he doing?" Katrina covered her mouth and broke out laughing.

"He was doing Lennie," was all I could say.

"And your file?"

"I had a box of tapes and notes. I put the box away and pretty much forgot about it."

"You still have it?" said Katrina.

What had I let myself in for? Should she be allowed to see it? There was plenty in it to hurt her, no doubt much her mother would prefer forgotten, and would perhaps never forgive me for exposing her daughter to. Might it inflict serious damage on this lovely, intelligent young woman, unlike her father, so seemingly at one with herself? What good would it do her? What would Lennie have wanted?

Why of course, he would have wanted Katrina to have the box. That was always paramount—to get past the delusions people try to live by, to go for the hard truth, however painful—that's what made the whole enterprise worthwhile. If she truly were her father's daughter, that's what Katrina would want, too.

"Any chance I might do some snooping?" She had suddenly become serious.

"I'm going to take a look for it when I get home," I told her. I was playing it safe. I could still say I couldn't find it and weasel out of it if I wanted to.

"What brings you to a seminar on Frye anyway?" I asked.

She eyed me askance. No question she twigged my evasion. She heaved her shoulders and sighed. "I've a new book. It's called (forgive me) *The Poetics of Vision: Milton, Blake, and Yeats.*"

My god, I thought, is it possible this is the book Lennie never wrote? As I looked out on the ravine, a burst of late sun set the trees on fire. I felt disembodied, I suppose, dizzied by the sudden blaze of colour and my failing eyesight. Katrina stared at me, waiting. I said, "You understand that if I am able to find the box and give it to you, I can't guarantee it will make you happy."

For a full minute she sat looking at me. Then: "You show me yours," she said, "I'll show you mine." Her sudden, impish smile was pure Lennie. We laughed as if we had known each other for ages.

As we sat pondering the splendour of the ravine, Katrina broke the silence: "'The force that through the green fuse drives the flower/ Drives my green age.'"

I had no choice but to fill in the next line: 'That blasts the roots of trees/ Is my destroyer.' I felt I was drowning in the richness outside the window, adrift in the dense language of Dylan Thomas, dazzled by Katrina's graceful bearing and lovely face. For the first time in a long time, I remembered what it felt like when I was first in love.

Again, she spoke first. "Lennie certainly never left much behind, did he?" It wasn't a question, more like a sigh. The sadness in her voice forced me to say it:

"He left *you*."

"Still the silver-tongued devil, eh?"

"Not as silver-tongued as Lennie was. Remember Blake's line? 'Eternity is in love with the productions of time'. It was a favourite of Lennie's and of mine too."

"Still it's strange, isn't it? What were my dad's productions? No music, no painting, no books."

"Nothing you'll find in galleries or libraries."

"Then what?"

"What about those productions of another kind—acts of concern that increase the world's stock of good will, feats of articulation that wake up sleeping minds, arouse people into richer life, but leave no monuments behind except in the lives of others? I guess I'm thinking of those rare few, the teachers who really teach? What if eternity loves their productions too, however ephemeral they may seem?"

"Wouldn't it be a great thing if it did?"

"It would be a wonderful thing for Lennie," I said. "The eternal 'what if?'"

"Wouldn't it be a wonderful thing for everyone?" Katrina said.

Postscript

Horncy Island, BC
General Delivery

Dear Katrina:

Our meeting in Toronto had a strange effect on me. It took me back to a time before I met Lennie, to a basketball game I played with the University of Manitoba Bisons. We were losing. I was facing a jump ball with the six-foot-eight centre of the opposing team. The match-up was so absurd, the crowd was laughing as we crouched, waiting for the referee to throw up the ball. A sudden impulse came over me. When the moment came, I didn't jump. Instead I grabbed the big centre's shorts and he jumped out of them. The crowd roared with glee. With his shorts between his knees, the centre chased me all over the court in a rage until the referee intervened and ejected me from the game. As I sat alone in the locker room, I grinned to myself. As I reflect on the episode tonight, it suddenly strikes me as a very Lennie thing to do.

I know I was born with an impish urge to irritate, to knock things out of kilter, sometimes more than that, with a genuinely devilish impulse that could have damaging consequences. I know I shared this impulse with Lennie and he knew I shared it. I resisted it all my life. He rarely did. Was that the reason I never pushed myself to the limit because he did it for me? It was Lennie who never gave up seeking ways to break the mould, to rattle the bars of our ordinary lives, to execute some unexpected swerve that would shatter the bonds of complacency. Maybe that was why I never lost sight of the rise and fall of his star, why he had such a hold over me when he was alive, and continues to have over me to this day.

My encounter with you, Katrina, brought memories of the '60s tumbling back and I did something quite absurd. On my way back west after our meeting in Toronto, I made a stopover in Winnipeg and booked into an airport hotel with the intention of revisiting old friends. It had been years. I knew Vince Calley had disappeared into Papua, New Guinea. I'd heard that Laura Gunn, Lennie's erstwhile student lover, rescued from prison in Chile, had emigrated to Israel. But still in town and alive were Jackie and Max Steiner, Jake and Julia Clark, Ben Gibson, Dimmy Wenchenko, and Katia. It was late in the evening. I listed their phone numbers on the hotel stationery, poured a scotch, and lay down to decide who to call first the next day. The last thing I remember thinking is how easy it is to return to a place, but how futile it is to recapture a time. First thing in the morning, I boarded the shuttle bus to the airport and caught the next plane home.

Your book on the visionary poets arrived. I won't plunge into it until tomorrow because there's an NBA triple-header on. I've tried enjoying classical ballet but I prefer the 'gymnastic ballet of basketball' as Lennie called it. My habit is to cheer for the loser. Then if the loser wins, I am able to tell myself I was really rooting for the winner all along.

It reminded me of Lennie and his love of *The Hustler*. The idea there that some people are born winners and some people are born losers haunted him. He often spoke about it. Which one was he in the long run? For 'long run', read 'eternity'. *Sub specie aeternitatis* again, by which Lennie meant something like: "Don't put second things first", or even: "Keep your eye on the big picture or trivia and inconsequence will bury you alive". I suppose the flip side of that notion is again: "Eternity is in love with the productions of time."

The Lennie 'box' went to you by courier today. I fear you may be distressed by some of its contents, but censorship was a sin for Lennie, the worst kind of mind manacle, and anyway if I tried to play that game I wouldn't know where to begin.

Give my love to Katia. I leave it to you to decide whether you want her to know about this stuff or not. And also I send my love to you, my dear young lady.

Jason Faraday

PS: Reading Blake the other day, I came across this passage and wondered if you were familiar with it:

Permanent, & not lost not lost or vanish'd & every little act,
Word, work & wish, that has existed, all remaining still ....
Shadowy to those who dwell not in them, mere possibilities
But to those who enter into them they seem the only
substances

CPSIA information can be obtained at www.ICGtesting.com
Printed in the USA
LVOW06s0707131215

466462LV00002B/79/P